ROGUE ROYALTY

IMDALIND ACADEMY, BOOK TWO

REBECCA ETHINGTON

Ebook ISBN - 978-1-949725-35-3
Print ISBN - 978-1-949725-34-6
Printed in USA
This Edition, July 2019

CONTENTS

For My Kids

Never Give Up

THE COMPLETE IMDALIND SERIES

BOOK ONE: *Kiss of Fire*
BOOK TWO: *Eyes of Ember*
BOOK THREE: *Scorched Treachery*
BOOK FOUR: *Soul of Flame*
BOOK FIVE: *Burnt Devotion*
BOOK SIX: *Brand of Betrayal*
BOOK SEVEN: *Dawn of Ash*
BOOK EIGHT: *Crown of Cinders*
BOOK NINE: *Spark of Vengeance*
BOOK TEN: *Flare of Villainy*

THE ACADEMY BOOKS
The Gauntlet
Rogue Royalty
Broken Renegade
Reluctant Seer

Find me online in my Facebook street team! We have monthly giveaways, sneak peeks, competitions and more!

INTRODUCING THE IMDALIND RUBY COLLECTION

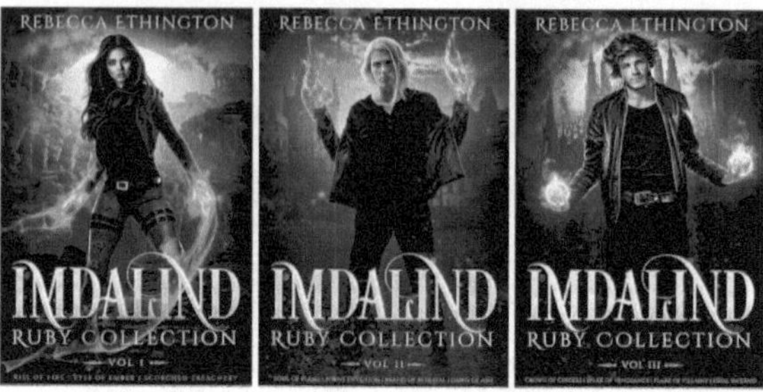

The entire Imdalind Series, in chronological order, with over 100k in new content and point of views. Extended Editions aren't just for Hobbits. <3

GRAB YOUR COPIES NOW.

1

———

GEMMA

"We are in the right place to end everything."

I repeated the words I had said to my best friend Ed a few hours ago, before the sun had set and the call to bed had rang through the long halls of the dorms. Before the crickets had started their incessant chirping and everything from the last few days had finally hit against me in a dark, cold, weight.

I had blown up the royal families precious Gauntlet days ago, and somehow they had let me live. Not only lived, but forced me to enroll in the school that I had tried so hard to turn to rubble with one well-placed blast from my broken, illegal, magic.

I had expected to be dead.

I had boarded that bus never expecting to make it back.

Instead, I was at the same school I had tried to destroy; magic fixed, if not restrained by a devilish looking blonde woman, Mira.

She didn't look much older than me and had a smile that would burn the shade of a demon. I shuddered just thinking about it.

I rolled over on the blankets I had pulled to the floor, the hard, musty carpet better than the overly soft bed they had provided me.

After a lifetime sleeping in sewer tunnels and the occasional holey hammock, I had no plans on sleeping in one of those puffy elevated body snatchers anytime soon. The floor was the only thing that reminded me of home as of yet. And, as a special bonus, it wasn't going to swallow me like the marshmallow stuff they had served for dinner.

The fluffy clouds of marshmallow was by far the weirdest thing they had served us. Everything else had been mostly normal, with piles of meats, cheeses and colorful cakes coated with sugars and a million other things I had to ask the name of. All of them delicious, foreign delicacies to everyone at home. Well, unless I was blowing up groceries stores, and I wasn't there to do that anymore. It was all a reminder of exactly why I had blown up that Gauntlet. Why I had agreed to come here at all.

Of what I was going to do, and who I was planning to kill.

If I could at all.

If I was supposed to anymore.

"End everything," I whispered to myself, the words musing in the dark.

I had blown up the Gauntlet, I had faced the queen, all with one desire. To overthrow the monarchy. Then I had come face to face with the queen, the queen with wicked dark eyes and a skill that sent shivers down my spine. I swear I could still feel that deep black weight of her magic press against mine, the endless well of power tugging at my own, as though it was trying to devour it.

I would never forget the weight of that power, the way her and the King's eyes had widened, the weird glance they had given each other when they had realized what I was saying. When I had realized they hadn't known.

Thousands of people slaughtered. They hadn't known.

I turned over again, my body restless as the crickets sang, as the moon continued to travel over the musty carpet, counting down the minutes until the first day and the question that was pressing against my heart, against that Štít that controlled my magic.

The deal I had made with the queen.

To work with her, while I secretly plotted to end her.

It was only in the hollow darkness of the still night that the deal began feeling like a deadweight.

Perhaps even an impossibility.

A hollow knock echoed through the darkness, the sound sending me bolting up, hands flared toward the door that I was sure the noise had come from. Of course, with how soft it was it could have come from some squirrel falling off the sill outside of the window.

A piece of paper slipped underneath the door, sliding across the wooden threshold to come to a stop against the carpet. The grind of paper was loud in the dark, my muscles and magic tensing as I waited for the sound of footsteps, for the door to be blown off its hinges, for the CCC to barge their way in, or any number of horrors I had come to expect.

Nothing. Nothing but silence and a piece of paper.

They were still there.

Bolting to the door, I jumped over the squishy armchair and nearly slipped on the wood as I threw the door open, magic buzzing in preparation to attack.

I half expected Sia to be standing there, smug smile in place as she threatened me, throwing fire or stones at me. But the hallway was empty, the fire bearing sconces flickering against the dark stone between the doors that lined the hallway.

"Hello?" I said louder than I probably should have given that it was well after midnight. Who cares if I woke anyone up? I mean, someone had clearly meant to wake me up.

Wake me up and bail.

Lame.

Glaring to the silence, I slid the door shut with a bang, hoping that it would disturb my favorite next door neighbor, Sia's, beauty sleep.

No noise, no yells, no clicks of doors. Just me and the crickets as I stood in the darkened room, staring at the piece of paper on the floor.

The paper was unmarked, the heavy sheet frayed along one side, like someone had torn it out of a book. The paper was thick enough for that too.

I've battled the CCC, faced the queen, blown up a Gauntlet, and this lame piece of paper slid under my door in the middle of the night was the thing that was going to turn my nerves to pools of fear.

Great.

Holding my breath, I unfolded the page, my not so hot reading skills slowly making its way through the loopy writing.

'Gemma,

Everything changes tomorrow, I wish you luck in your classes and hope you will find yourself on the right path.

Do not be scared of your past, do not let yourself be blinded by the future.

Let me know if you need anything. We'll be in touch.

-Joclyn'

"Joclyn?" I said aloud, my brow furrowing. Joclyn, like the queen Joclyn? Like the one who rules over us and sees into the future and bound my magic and expects me to still be working with her.

Damn. Didn't know we were on a first name basis.

Didn't know I had gotten myself in so over my head that I was now getting letters from the Queen, letters that were vague and threatening and somehow supportive all at once.

Letters that were offering me help.

"What rat shit have I mixed myself up in now?" I sighed, crumpling the letter in my fist and trudging back to my nest of blankets, the soft squishy things feeling as cold and hard as the floor now.

I needed to end this. I had planned to end this. But I had also been forced to help the Queen.

"End everything..." I whispered, uncurling the paper and lifting it over my head, staring at the first few words. "Everything changes tomorrow."

Changes.

Ends.

It was as though she knew. Seeing as she could see into the future, she probably could.

A twisted smile spread over my lips as I thought of the days ahead, my magic buzzing and building as I lay in the blue moonlight I had coaxed in to mimic the light that would stream in from the grate back home.

The queen may be offering me help, but she was only one tendril of a web I needed to weave to complete my plan. One spire of the royal family I was surrounded by.

Prince Rowan was handsome, sure, but the second he had stepped out of his carriage with that bitch Sia on his arm he could have been some god damned Greek God with iron pecks or some shit and I wouldn't have cared for him.

The second she had kissed him, that he had kissed her back, it was near enough to sign his own death warrant.

Well, not death per se, but I was certainly going to make use of him.

Rowan was nothing more than another little web in my plan. Hopefully, my ticket into the diamond-studded halls his family called home.

Get close to Rowan, and I'm closer to ending this.

"We are in the right place to end everything," I hesitated. "We are in the right place to change everything."

I liked that better.

"We are in the right place to change everything."

The powerful declaration filled the empty dark of my room like a banner, the hollow promise clinging to the dark walls and the sliver of moonlight. It dripped from the lavish furniture and spread over the floor.

I boomed until it became a living thing, a promise.

"I'm going to change everything."

Those royal idiots had done more than enroll me in Imdalind Academy.

They had enrolled me with their prince.

They had triggered the end.

2

ROWAN

Of all the endless, sleepless nights I had experienced in the last few years, the night before the first day of my forced enrollment in Imdalind Academy was the worst.

Back home in the caves of Prague the long hours had become normal. I had gotten used to not sleeping, to keeping myself occupied, to running into my father in the kitchen in the wee hours of the morning, to late-night chess matches when Dramin visited. I even found solace in the long lonely hours when no one in my home was awake.

It was all comforting in their own way. Familiar.

In this damned school, all of that was gone. Swept away in my massive suite my cousin Cail had assigned me, the far too large space full of furniture that was brushed with gold and opulence that wasn't me, bed piled high with blankets I would rarely use thanks to my unfortunate inheritance.

My mother, in her all-seeing wisdom, had sent over a few things ahead of me. Drawing supplies, piles of books, and a few broken relics from when she was a child that I enjoyed tinkering with. VCRs and DVD players, things with letters instead of actual names.

They had been all wrapped up with family photos and a letter from both her and dad. One labeled. 'For Now,' and the other 'For Later'. I only opened the one, I didn't want to know what the other one had to say.

'Row -

I know attending the school was not what you wanted, but I am proud of you for facing a world with the hope of making it better. It will be, in so many ways...'

I almost skipped forward; I wasn't in the mood for the brooding Drak predictions that boiled my blood.

'Circumstances may have gotten worse in the last few days, but we wanted you to know that we are proud of you.

You have always had a heart big enough to swallow the world. You get that from your dad, I think. Be brave. Be strong. Follow your heart, it won't fail you. Of this, I can promise.

-Mom'

Dad's was even shorter.

'Rowan -

You inspire me every day. I love you.

-Dad'

Sometimes I was sure he secretly wrote greeting cards with the way he talked. If only it had been enough to stop me from wanting to fall through the floor.

Nothing but getting out of this place could solve that.

Even after unpacking my trunk, hiding the mug in one of the many drawers that littered the room, and throwing a few shirts on the floor, I couldn't get comfortable. I had spent the dark night hours wandering between the rooms in my suite, looking out the windows that were such an oddity in the caves of Imdalind that they made me nervous that someone would see in. That someone could sneak in. Like Sia, who had stalked me all the way to my door before I had slammed it in her face, a last-minute promise to see her tomorrow hissed through the wood.

If she snuck through my window I would be sure to throw her right back out of it.

Letting my pencil drag over the paper I had been drawing monsters and dogs on all night, I turned up my stereo, letting Dave Grohl's ancient voice sing over the long, yellow rays of sun that had begun to stretch over the floor, igniting the air into fireworks of their own kind.

Specks of white caught the light, shimmering and moving in a sunrise that painted the stars in streaks of orange and yellow, swallowing them whole. A dance, a beautiful dance that ignited against my fingers as they twirled and snatched at the light.

It was so different above ground, watching the sun peak over the mountains, and stream through the massive pine trees that I had been told on more than one occasion had been burned to stubble by my Aunt Wyn in one of the final battles of the war.

Living amongst it made it feel even more like a fairy tale than it had when I was a kid.

"One last thing before I quit. I never wanted any more than I could fit into my head." I sang along as the sun filled the room, a red-breasted bird announcing the day that I had dreaded for the past six years.

"Please don't let this be a shit show," I said with a sigh, leaning back in my chair and pulling the class schedule I had been doodling on closer.

Period One: History of Imdalind with Professor Analine Krul

Well, that sounded boring, and embarrassing. Learning about my own family history from my cousin who Dramin and I used to tease was adopted. How someone so stern was born to the two weirdest people I knew I still couldn't figure out.

Period Two: Wind Based Powers and Control with Professor Lexia Stone

Lunch

Period Three: Royal Dispatch - Headmasters Office

Period Four: Healing and Defense with Professor Etma Diarius

Okay, I changed my mind. It all sounded boring. And Royal Dispatch? What kind of nonsense was that? I closed my eyes, pinching the bridge of my nose as warmth and magic pooled in my neck. At least I had the added benefit that I would be sleeping through half the year.

I had already sat there for an hour longer than I should have in the hopes of missing breakfast and my Uncle's speech. Much longer and I would cause a scene walking into the main hall in the middle of it. Might as well get this over with.

I didn't even bother to smooth the wrinkles in the shirt I had worn all night, I grabbed the starched jacket and threw it over my shoulder, only grabbing my prepacked satchel of books when I realized I should probably look like I was as new to magic as the rest of them.

Thankfully, the hall was empty, Cail having placed me in one of the largest dorms in the school, in a hall normally reserved for teachers. It would have been nondescript if it wasn't for a plaque with our family name overhead. 'R. Krul' He should have hired one of the Chosen to keep a giant neon sign above me at all times.

'Make way, the king's third son, Rowan Krul, brooding Eternal and your last chance to mate into the Royals coming through.'

I could feel the darn thing blinking above me as I moved toward the excited voices, toward the shuffling of feet and catcalls as everyone prepared for the first day of a school they had dreamed about their whole lives.

Everything grew quiet the moment I stepped into the main hall. Tables of fruit, muffins, oatmeal, and piles of cereal were left forgotten as every single head turned toward me, hundreds of identical expressions peering right at me.

Oh damn. I kept my head high and wandered in. All of the

propriety training Father had forced us into was good for something.

"That's him isn't it?"

"Oh, he's as handsome as his brother."

"Oh my god, look at his hair. He's so cool."

Voices followed me as I weaved my way toward the last remaining empty stretch of a table, watching the wooden bench fill up as dozens of Golden's realized where I was headed and changed their seats to match.

I was about to grab some toast and seek shelter in my cousin Analine's classroom when a shriek broke through the banter. The sound pulled everyone to silence, the irritating resonance slicing down my spine like a knife.

"Rowy! Rowy, over here."

Rowy? No one called me that. Possibly, because it was the stupidest nickname I had ever heard. Well, except to the girl who was now frantically waving to me from where she sat at a table on the other side of the room, surrounded by a dozen brand new Chosen. I recognized them at once. They were the children of many of the elected Chosen leaders who had breezed in and out of the royal families offices for much of my life.

I tried not to groan, really I did, but it seeped out as I forced a smile her way, giving her the tiniest of waves. It was enough. She shrieked and raced across the room, pushing an Undermortal out of her way. I could feel her magic prod against me the closer she came, the wave of her perfume assaulting me.

Oh god, that smell from the carriage yesterday wasn't an accident.

"Rowy!" She continued with the damn nickname as if I liked it, it was all I could do to keep the smile plastered on my face. "I was so worried you would miss breakfast. I saved you a seat and some toast, just in case."

I would say the gesture was nice if she didn't wave to half a dozen people as she weaved her arm through mine, practically dragging me after her. Taking the long way, of course.

I wasn't sure if I was on parade, or she was.

"Guys. This is Rowan," She spoke at full voice the second we were in earshot of her friends. If earshot counted for yelling distance. More heads turned, more eyes swooned, more hopefuls smiled before their faces fell in shock.

I forced myself to smile and wave. Although, not to the snot-nosed Goldens she was trying to introduce me to, but to the few girls at the table we were walking by. And the guys who were staring two tables over, and to a pretty blond Undermortal who blushed so deeply even her hair went pink.

That made me smile more, it was cute... oh god, I sounded like Talon. I needed to back this truck right up. That was not a trip to douche-bag lane I was hoping to take.

"Rowan is King Ilyan and Queen Joclyn's son." Geeze thanks for pointing out the obvious. "He will be eating with us." Sia continued through a tick in her jaw as I continued to smile and wave at everyone. She had obviously seen and not approved of my momentary lapse in royal judgment. "Rowan and I are together."

I collapsed onto the wooden bench she had been settling into with a thud, her arm wound around mine so tight that I almost dragged her down in my near collapse. Her high-pitched giggle resonated in my ear as she fell into me, forcing the irritating sounds even though she fixed me with a scorned expression. I guess she thought she didn't have to put on a show now that she had kissed me in front of everyone.

Yeah, time to put a stop to that.

"I am showing her around Imdalind Academy for the first little bit," I corrected her. Saying it out loud made the whole thing seem more ridiculous. We were both new here, how was I supposed to show her around someplace I had only been twice before?

She didn't seem to care about semantics, her long-nailed fingers pressed into my forearm, her magic flaring in a murky rage that was pressing against me in what I am sure she thought was a warning. I had the good sense to smother myself in a shield before she touched me, there was no way I was letting her magic mix with mine again any time soon.

"What he means," she said with an elongated warning, her fingers pressing into me, "is that daddy was worried I would be scared after everything that happened, so the King agreed to have Rowan escort me."

Her magic was boiling now, the same heat burning through the murky brown of her eyes as she peered into me. Even though she was smiling, laughing, the warning was screaming against me like nails pounding into the back of my skull. Every muscle in my back tensed.

"I think we hit it off in the carriage yesterday, don't you?"

Her fingers pressed harder against my forearms, a bit of magic trying to break through. Stronger shield up!

"Are you going to introduce me to your friends?" I asked desperate for a change of subject.

"Ah yes," she instantly brightened, thankfully shifting away from whatever tongue swapping she had been hoping for. "This is Tasha." She gestured to the girl with long ruddy hair and enough constellations on her face she could be her own solar system. "Melinda, Carly, Em, Joseph." She gestured to the four others who were all staring at me with different arrays of wonder. "And Miko."

"We've met," he grinned, extending his hand.

"Yes, a few times if I recall."

Miko was broad shouldered, a mess of dark hair falling over deep green-blue eyes. He smiled with all the smug arrogance I had come to expect of the Goldens, and my brother. He reminded me so much of Talon it was making me uncomfortable. He shook my hand with what he had hoped was some kind of cool magic trick. All that happened, however, was that his palm warmed, a little white spark fizzling from the tip of his thumb.

I chose to ignore it and his face fell.

"Nice to meet you all," I said, scooting away from Sia in an attempt to find some breathing room. She countered it, scooting even closer and giving me what I am sure she thought were lovesick eyes. Thankfully my cousin had chosen that moment to stand from the ornate staff table at the top of the hall and turn to face us, a wide smile stretching over his face.

"Welcome!" He announced, his voice magically enhanced and pulling the focus of every formerly chattering student. "Another year in Imdalind Academy has begun. What a wonderful year it will be! With more new students than ever before, powerful new friends, and a whole new generation of Chosen born into our family. Welcome all to this, our seventieth year!"

Cail raised his hands high, smiling over everyone as they all cheered and stomped their feet until the old wooden rafter rattled.

"Imdalind Academy has trained and created Chosen from all walks of life, as they learn and grow. As they find their place among their peers and among the four branches of magic holders that walk this world. The Skříteks: The powerful magic of love and light, the guards of our world."

Before he had even finished speaking, the room had exploded, the groups of older students who had tested closest to the Skřítek magic line erupting in pride.

"The Trpaslíks: Breakers of rock and manipulators of fire. The Builders." More screams, more whoops and hollers as they pounded feet against floor and knives against tables. Cail's' face spread into a wide smile. As one of the few true Trpaslíks left, he had every right to be proud.

"The Vilỳ: Power of air and water, the peacemakers. The artists and those who guide the world in every way." Unsurprisingly, every Golden around me moved into a cheer. New magic users always wanted to be like the Vilỳ. Not that I blamed them, on paper they were so strong, so power hungry. In person, Rinax was irritating.

"The Drak." Cail gave no explanation, which was fine. The room had gone eerily silent, not one of the Chosen calling out in support of the deranged power. Although I could have sworn more than a few heads turned my way given my parentage.

Or rather, my mother.

"Each magic is a pillar in our world. Their gifts and contribution to this school and to our community is a tradition we are proud of," he continued after a moment, "and one that we will continue to cultivate as we bring so many people together and unite our people."

I swallowed, willing my back to stay straight. It was clear my father had written this portion of the speech. It wasn't going to work nearly as well as they hoped it would.

"We hope that all of our new students, no matter where they come from or what their journeys to these halls may be, will seek to strengthen themselves and find friends in places there once were enemies as we all work together to bring our people together."

He paused, but instead of applause there were only hushed whispers from the other side of the hall. The sounds filled the cavernous room like a sack of bees. I lifted my head, peering over hundreds of heads to where one tickling laugh had broken through. The sound calloused, if not a little beautiful. They were all clustered together, fake smiles plastered to their faces as they looked up to Cail. Even with the uniform, the Undermortals stuck out. Colored hair, piercings, tattoos painted over their skin.

Cail shifted, straightening his jacket before he leaned over the podium and boomed in a voice that was too full of scorn for him.

"Here is to a great year, and to a great first day! Here is to a powerful future."

Dad hadn't written that.

I stared at him, Sia knocking against me as she hissed about getting to class. I didn't even flinch as she planted a kiss against my cheek and took off. I sat staring at my cousin. Magic burned against the back of my neck as he smiled at me, his last words burning against my heart just as violently.

Yes, the speech was clearly written by my dad, but not all of it.

Keeping my eyes on my cousin, I stood with my bag in my hand and jacket over my shoulder and left the hall trying not to drag my feet too much as I made my way to class.

The whispers and turned heads followed me through each dark stone hall, many of the goldens even going so far as stopping in place to watch me pass. Judging by the strength and control of the magic that surrounded me it was clear that more than one of my rubberneckers weren't first-years either. Magic pressed into me at every angle, assaulting me as they tried to sense my power. To connect with me.

I could already tell that my shield was not going to come down anytime soon. Thank god Ryland had taught me how to shield my magic completely, I didn't need any curious onlooker getting any hint about the dangers that were brewing inside of me.

The halls may still be full of students, but every desk in my classroom, save two were full, eager faces turned up to me the second I entered. Did everyone know my schedule? The only saving grace was that Sia's wide toothy grin wasn't staring up at me, or plastered to my side. Didn't make any of the eager eyes any less traumatic.

"Good morning, Rowan," my cousin Analine said with a grin that was far too knowing. "Glad you could join us. Your seat will be your seat for the semester. So, choose wisely."

She gave me a wink, god maybe she was as much trouble as her mother. She knew exactly what she was doing.

Every eye followed me as I stepped through the desks, moving closer to the two chairs that were placed side by side. Which will it be? The chair surrounded by brunettes, or the chair surrounded by blondes. What was this class, made up of a million girls and me? Oh wait, the boys had occupied the seats around the edge, looking at me like I had already stolen their spoils of the hormone war.

Trust me, dudes, they are all yours.

I had no sooner sunk into the seat on the left, giving all of the collective blondes around me a sigh of relief when the door to the classroom slammed open, banging against the opposite wall and sending a few cracks through the old plaster. Everyone around me jumped, but I was frozen in place, jaw locked as she walked in.

Fishnet stockings, combat boots, bubble gum pink hair that fell in graceful ringlets over her bright violet eyes. She hadn't even bothered to cover the tattoos on her arms, or neck. The dark lines danced over her skin in a million stories that I wanted to trace. Wanted to understand.

"Whoops. Sorry to interrupt. I didn't mean to be late, first day and all." She didn't sound sorry. Analine wasn't buying it. She stared at her, fuming as she clopped through the silent classroom in those massive boots, clearly making as much sound as she could as she weaved her way to the last open seat in the class. The one right next to me.

The blondes looked pissed.

"Nice tie, your majesty," she said, giving me a wink and a pop of her gum before she threw her shit-stained boots onto the desk, crossing her ankles and sitting back in her chair like something I had seen in a TV show Aunt Wyn had shown me once.

I had forgotten about my tie. It was still untied around my neck, the top two buttons of my shirt were open, my jacket was thrown over the chair. In fact, we were the only two in the classroom that weren't in perfectly pressed uniforms. Even the Undermortals at the back had worn the full ensemble.

"I'm ready, Teach. Educate me about your glittering perfect history." She leaned forward, peering at Analine over her boots. "I want to know about all the damn lies."

Everyone around us gasped, appalled as she popped her gum again, the Undermortals in the back of the room snickering.

I sat, staring at her as she threw me another wink, the simple action sending my magic into overdrive.

I was having trouble controlling it. It had been hard enough keeping myself in check after she had ripped the Gauntlet to shreds. Then she had been shackled and escorted by my parents to gods knows where. But now, she was right there.

I had spent years dreaming of the girl who was now inches from me, the tangle wood scent of the shampoo she had used drifting over to me and testing my control even further.

Her spunky winks faded when she caught me staring.

"Didn't your fucking parents teach you any manners?" Her eyes darkened as she hissed, just as Analine started the class, introducing herself as Professor Krul and spouting off facts about herself that I had either known or witnessed through my entire life.

The rest of the class was a blur, a blur of dizzying magic and terrifying buzzing that jumped between my fingers as I tried to control myself. I felt like I did when I was a child and accidentally blew up the bathroom for the third time. Like I was about to explode.

She was more than a girl who had haunted my dreams for years.

She was a goddamned fuse.

I burst out of my seat and down the hallway the second class was dismissed, desperate to get away from the smell of her, the magic of her. I left a string of pouty girls behind me. I needed air, or at least the chance to get some of this energy out that was trying to take control. I still had one more class before my class with Cail, which if I was lucky would be nothing more than a daily chess match.

I was surely going to explode long before then, seeing as Gemma cut me off, hand on the frame of the door I was about to duck through.

"Let me see that," she said, popping a bubble that matched her hair as she took my schedule from my hand, eyes widening as she scanned it, keeping a finger with a big ugly burn on it away from the paper. "Looks like someone has a death wish."

She winked again, handed me back my schedule and left me standing, jaw agape as she smiled, chuckling. I must have looked like I had been punched.

"Nice monsters," she said as she dodged me and skipped into my next class. Our next class.

If I had to guess, she was going to be in nearly all of them.

3

———

GEMMA

I HAD NEVER DONE ANYTHING SO MIND-NUMBINGLY BORING AS attend school. Sitting in classes, being lectured at about how to produce sparks, shields, fire, and a million other things that I already knew how to do was testing my patience in ways I would have assumed impossible. Except now, thanks to the nasty dust that Mira had implanted in my heart, I had to relearn them. I had to figure out how to do them the 'right way', two words I was actively rebelling against.

I was only three days into my mind-numbing four-year education at Imdalind Academy and I was already sure I was slowly melting from the inside out.

If they could make a Prince go through with it, it was clear there was no way I could talk myself out of it. I did, however, have the solace that he looked as bored as I did. Which made messing with him even more entertaining.

If I had to make nice with the guy in order to get my powers back, and perhaps get closer to the royal family, I was going to do it.

"He's looking at you again," Eddy whispered in my ear,

cutting through my buzz of thought as the chatter of the lunchroom increased in volume.

"Good," I whispered, refusing to look back at the prince and instead scooped more fruit onto my plate. "That's the whole point, Ed. Tease him, befriend him, use him."

At least I had been able to accomplish something in between the mind-melting numbness of class.

"No, I mean, he's really looking at you. Did you flash him or something? Because this is a stalker level stare you are getting." Eddy leaned over to where I was picking at the overcooked peas on my plate and hissed in my ear. I batted him away like he was a fly and took another bite of the fruit that I had recently become obsessed with.

This whole place was made of food. Not only were the expensive ice chests in each dorm room loaded with delicacies, but piles of anything and everything lined the massive tables in the cafeteria three times a day. Much of it was left uneaten and forgotten when students got up and left, leaving the Undermortals to pocket as much of it as they could before leaving to their next class, or their dorms, or any number of places.

I was already trying to devise a plan on getting all the leftovers I had stored out of here and back home on the weekends. Perhaps I could even track down the kitchens and figure out what they did with what was left on the tables. So much food, gone to waste.

I popped another cube of the delectable watermelon in my mouth, peeking behind my pink curls to the boy who sat three tables over, Sia Demarco slung around him like a scarf.

"Maybe he's obsessed with the idea of wearing women as clothing and has confused me with a mink coat."

Eddy spit out the orange juice he had been drinking, spraying the vibrant color over the Undermortals on the other side of the table from us. They all laughed and threw tiny bits of food at him. No one dared spare more than that.

Kara and Geo were two Undermortals from my community back home. I didn't think anyone else had made it here, but seeing those two on Monday morning was like some kind of serendipity. It was going to make it a helluva lot easier to organize everyone with more than Eddy and me on our side.

"Don't waste the goods, Ed!" Kara shrieked, throwing a mostly eaten bit of celery at him.

"Well, if Gem would stop talking about skinning people--"

"Skinning people!" I shrieked a mouthful of watermelon dripping over my chin. "Who said anything about skinning people?"

They all looked at me, smiles tugging at the lips as they tried to hold in laughs.

"At least we aren't eating them. God, Gem, you look horrifying." Eddy smiled, the others' laughter breaking into a shriek as he wiped the red juice from my chin with a napkin so white it was nearly blinding.

"I didn't know it was so juicy!" Everyone was laughing again, including me, including Rowan who was once again staring at me from the other side of the hall.

The laughter faded immediately.

"Geeze, what is it with this guy?" I snarled, leaning down enough that Geo's back would hide me from view. I had clearly gone overboard with teasing the guy. I mean, ya, it was fun, because he was clearly scared of me and was always shaking when I came too close, but this look was different. Deeper.

Like something had changed.

I restrained the sudden need to throw a fireball at his head.

"Stop looking like such a beautiful pink coat, Gem," Eddy teased, ruffling my hair. I batted him away, giving him a warning zap that didn't have nearly enough of an effect thanks to Mira's handiwork.

"Mink, Ed. *Mink* coat."

"I know." He winked and I pushed him away with the palm of my hand, stealing another piece of fruit before going back to doodling monsters on the paper I had found in my bag. I had never drawn before; it was kind of fun.

An eye, a beard, a million features that I had either seen or imagined when I stared down the dark tunnel as a child. Or when I wandered down the cold stone tunnels where we had found the Vilỳ that had bitten me in hopes of asking the creature to kill me. To show me where the Tarn armies had taken my parents.

I cringed and scribbled out the monster I had been drawing, stealing a bland piece of bread instead of the fruit that time.

I only got one bite in before the bell rang, announcing the end of lunch, and the return to the monotony that was school.

"Is everything in place for tomorrow?" I asked as we all shoved papers, books, and food into our respective bags.

"Everyone I've talked to is all in," Kara said, putting a second apple in her satchel before throwing it over her shoulder.

"Me too." Geo gave a nod.

"Perfect. Keep them in your room until Ed and I come for you." They all nodded, faces grim, smiles pulled into a straight line as the joy of a minute ago was drowned by our real purpose for being here.

"Yes, ma'am," Kara and Geo said together, knocking their heels as Adrian had trained them all to do nearly a year ago.

"Great!" I said brightly, raising my voice as a few Goldens moved closer. "Have so much fun guys! I'm so excited to go visit him this weekend."

The two didn't even flinch, they just beamed, nodded and

turned away, prattling about their next class as though I had released them from some spell.

"Stay in their rooms?" Eddy hissed in my ear as the two ducked out the door, us following not far behind. "Are we conducting espionage now?"

"Weren't we always?" I gave him a smile and took another bite of my bread, wishing I hadn't forsaken the fruit for this bland monstrosity. "Besides, we have to stay one step ahead of someone who can stay three steps ahead of us. I only know one way to do that."

"Like a rat trap, draw them away and then gorge on their flesh."

"Ed. That sounds so much worse than me skinning goldens." I meant it as a joke, but two of the glittering brats had overheard, the poor dears yelping and scuttling away before I could say anything. "How bad do you think it will be if word gets out that I am a cannibal?"

Eddy laughed, "See you in Defense class, Gem." He waved behind him as he turned down his own hall, leaving me to trudge toward Professor Georgio Gregario's mind-numbing lecture on basic spells.

Students whipped past me. Blazers and god-awful plaid skirts turning into a blur as everyone tried to make it to class on time. I, however, slowed my pace, taking bite after bite of my bread as I continued my trek of drudgery. I had no plans to ever be to one of my classes on time, seeing the appalled look on the teacher's face when I blasted my way in ten minutes after the bell was probably never going to get old.

Bread may not be as sweet as fruit, but this fluffy warm stuff they served us was definitely growing on me, maybe next time I would slather some of the yellow butter on it.

I walked into my Basic Skills class after Professor Gregario had already given his daily intro and sighed an exaggerated apology that sent all of my people at the back tittering.

"I didn't mean to be late," I muttered as I approached the seat Sia had chosen for herself, the girl's green eyes narrowed at me as she flipped her hair behind her. "That prince dude stopped me in the hall and I lost track of time."

This class happened to be the only class I had without Rowan; the boy locked away with the headmaster on something called 'royal dispatch'. It was unfortunate, or would have been if this wasn't one of the only classes I had with Sia.

All I had to do was mention the word prince and she was sent into a sighing, humphing, hair flipping disaster.

"Find your seat," Professor Gregario snapped behind me. I picked up my pace, giving Sia a smile as I sunk into my seat. The girl snapped to face forward as though I had slapped her.

"Please take out your books and turn to page two hundred and two," Gregario went on, ignoring Sia's latent sighs, "there you will find instructions for four spells. One for each branch of magic. Skřítek, Trpaslík, Vilỳ, and Drak. We will be working towards the attempt and hopeful completion of these spells for the next nine months..."

"Nine months?" One of the Undermortals to my left shrieked, cutting the old man off and earning himself a glare.

As if anyone needed a reminder of how long we were to be locked in this endless prison.

"Yes, these four spells are some of the most important you will learn while in my class. At the end of your second year you will be tested on these four spells. The one which you can perform with the greatest proficiency will be your focus for the remainder of your time at Imdalind Academy."

Everyone started buzzing then, Professor Gregario turning and scratching the names of magic into the board as people pointed out the different spells and chattered about which they wanted to be most aligned with. Weirdos, the lot of them.

I leaned back in my chair, threw my feet on my desk and tried to ignore the list of magic and spells that would be tested. I wanted to blow things up, not 'fire a ward through a true shield' whatever that was.

"In order to be placed as a Skříteks," Gregario went on, chalk squeaking obnoxiously against the board. "You will need to be versed in shields and defenses, which is why a completed shield and a ward is listed as the skill."

He turned around then, eyes glazing over the class before he smiled, the man looking crazed before I felt his magic buzz and he vanished from sight. My feet fell off the desk, eyes wide as I stared at the place he had been. I couldn't even feel the gentle buzz of his magic from before. It was as though he had vanished.

"What the fuck?" The girl next to me shrieked, everyone around me gasping in awe. The Goldens in front of us, however, looked about as bored as if they had been all knocked unconscious, one even yawned.

Blubbering, I tried to keep my shock contained but totally failed when a blast of light ripped from the back of the class, slamming against the blackboard in a million sparks.

I might have shrieked, not that anyone noticed. Everyone else yelled too. A few Goldens even jumped at the impact, everyone shrieking when Professor Gregario reemerged with little more than a pop. The guy standing right on top of the desk to my left. He was lucky I didn't attack him.

I had never seen anything like that.

"All branches of magic can perform shields, but it is the usage of shields in relation to the attack that Skříteks do exceptionally well."

"Remind me never to get in a fight with them," I said, a few people nodding in agreement. "Well, until I learn to do it better."

The laughter died down, Gregario fuming as he tapped his toe, the action enough to regain control of the class.

"Trpaslíks," he continued, back to scratching chalk against the blackboard. "Can manipulate rock, and in some rare cases fire. They are the builders and their destructive power can be quite intense."

Gregario smiled, flicking his finger as a giant rock on the table under the window cracked into two solid pieces.

"The spell is much more impressive when done by a true Trpaslík, trust me." He gained a few snickers from the Goldens, as if they knew what he was talking about, but I couldn't look away from the stone, from the perfect line that ran right down the middle. Just like Wynifred's attack when Adrian had tried to attack her in Last Pyre.

A perfectly managed explosion, hardly any damage. Yet Adrian had been thrown across the massive cave and into a wall. There had even been fire. Much more impressive, and a tad bit freaky. I shifted in my seat. Starting to realize where this was going.

"The Vilỳ are traditionally peacemakers. Not many possess these powers despite all of you bearing the bite of the tiny creature." Gregorio wasn't writing on the board anymore, he extended his hand, palm down over the desk as a wind ran through the room, the invisible force lifting and spinning different items in turn. "The power of wind, of water. All of you will possess this in its lowest form, but to possess the power of a Vilỳ, is to fly."

"Dude. If Vilỳ's are the ones that get to fly, count me in," one of the Undermortals said, even earning themselves a few nods from the Goldens.

"I can guarantee you, it is a skill that many are jealous of," Gregario said with a smile. Clearly, he had hoped for that skill once upon a time as well. Guess we weren't getting a demonstration. "Years ago, the skill of flight was possessed by all magic wielders, before the mad king brutalized the poor things and all pure Vilỳ's were removed from our world. Without the bite from a true Vilỳ, or being born with the pure magic of a Trpaslík or Skřítek, flight is now only available to those blessed with the magic of a Vilỳ in their bite."

Everyone looked disappointed, the sighs and longing in their faces clear.

I was struggling to stay in my chair.

This douche canoe was lying between the gleaming white teeth of his smile.

The true Vilỳ's, the ones that weren't turned into snarling brown monsters by the mad king weren't removed from this world. There was one left.

Rinax.

He had bitten Eddy less than three weeks ago.

My spine straightened as a pain radiated through my chest, iron barbs spreading through my chest from where Mira had put the Štít.

"Ouch," I hissed, slamming a fist into my chest like she had when she placed the thing, right after she explained how we could never tell anyone exactly which Vilỳ had been the one to give Eddy his mark.

Okay, okay. Point taken.

"The Drak," Gregario said, everyone shifting forward, eagerness dripping from eyes and tongues as the air grew heavier. "Drak's are the rarest of them all, as you know there is only one living Drak. Only five that can perform the Stutter that is used to test for the power. All of which are in the royal family."

Smiles and whispers rumbled through the room, the sound echoing in my head as the Queen's words buzzed against my skull. I could have sworn I felt that same dark pressure of the Queen's magic seeping in from under the door.

"I know you are hopeful of testing correctly in this skill, but in my seventy years of teaching, not one student has mastered the stutter required."

"A stutter?" someone cut in, this time a Golden. Oddly, they looked as confused as we did.

"Yes, the movement between time and space. Imagine being in Imdalind Academy one moment, and then back at home the next, with nothing more than a thought. That is the power of a stutter. That is the power of the Drak."

Everyone was back to whispering, but I was rigid in my chair, staring straight forward, even as my mind was pulling me right back to the room after the Gauntlet. Right to the hollow voice of the Queen.

"Come now, Professor," Sia said from the middle of the room, the shrill tone of her voice pulling me away from the memory. "That is not the only power of the Drak. They also possess sight."

"Ah yes," Gregario mused, turning back to his board and scraping the chalk over the surface, drawing what looked like a bumpy mug on the surface.

"Draks' power comes from the Black Water which they can conjure from a single mug, formed from the mud around the pools they use to harness their power. They can see into the future, and into the past with this water. Some say that to touch the water gives the Drak access to your soul, to everything that lies before you." I nearly jumped, my heart was pounding on the outside of my body with how loud it was pulsing, with how much it was banging against my bones. "Black Water is the source of all magic. Some say the scar on the King's hand comes from the powerful stuff, and that it is that water in his veins that has made his power so much stronger than his brother's."

"In his veins? You mean it's still there? It never goes away?" I asked without thinking, my fist clenched into a tight little ball.

"Well, no one knows for sure. This is all rumor, of course, no one outside of the royal family has seen the Queen give sight in over a century. No one has even seen Black Water in as long. Both the queen and the source of her power is as secretive as it is dangerous."

A buzz of noise exploded around me, the hive of questions blending with the hollow echo of the Queen's sight, with the images of me in the water she had held in her palm, or the burn that now graced my finger, right where I had touched the water.

Where that water, that super-powered magic water had burned me.

This time I didn't need the radiating pain over my chest to remind me to keep my mouth shut. I didn't want word of that getting out. Because I didn't want anyone else to know what I had seen.

What I had done.

And what I was going to do.

4

SIA

"I swear, if I see Gemma sidle up to Rowan between classes one more time with that ass hanging out of her tiny jeans, I am going to lose it." My snarl ripped through the small sitting room of my dorm, but Miko and Tasha didn't even look up from where they sat in the overstuffed armchairs, tapping and giggling at their phones, elbowing each other as they shared who knows what.

"Hello? I said Gemma is a whore and I'm going to rip her heart out." I stared at them, waiting. Still nothing. "Look at me when I am talking to you!"

I slapped the palm of my hand against the coffee table, the impact sloshing the amber liquid that Miko had brought out of the glass tumblers, leaving it to spread over the mahogany surface in slow snaking lines. The two jumped, dropping their phones to their laps as they glared at me.

"Holy hell, Sia," Miko rumbled with that low tenor of his. "What the fuck is wrong with you?"

"You aren't listening to me," I snarled grabbing one of the overfilled glasses and letting the liquid burn my throat as I chugged it. "I'm talking to you about something important."

"Which important thing is it now, Sia?" Tasha asked with a sigh, already going back to her phone. "Is it that the Drain girl looked at Rowan? That she talked to Rowan? That Rowan talked to her? That Rowan didn't kiss you fifty times today. Or, my personal favorite--"

"Her ass is hanging out of her jeans." The two spoke together and I almost lost it.

My temper had boiled deeper with each of her snotty responses, my fingers clenching against the glass I still held, magic and fury boiling until the tumbler cracked in a web.

"We've heard it all, Sia. It hasn't even been a week since school began, and we've heard it all," Tasha snapped, Miko chuckling as they both went back to their phones.

Fecking whores!

"No, you haven't." I snapped the thing out of her hand. I would have crushed it, maybe I still would. I was in the mood for a fight,

"Hey!" She yelled, jumping to grab the phone back from where I was holding it above my head. She looked like a cat with a string.

"This is important, Tasha, sit your ass back down or I'll snap the thing in two." I narrowed my eyes at her, lifting my finger and letting two carefully constructed sparks lift from the tip.

Tasha sat, sinking into one of the deep green armchairs.

"Good."

They had awoken with their magic nearly a full week before I had. A full week of playing with the power and feeling it rumble in their veins and a few of my sparks scared them. I expected more from two Golden children, they were born and bred by Chosen, raised to hold magic. Maybe they didn't know what was coming

"I said, that Drain is bringing down the whole school. Yes, her ass is hanging out of her jean shorts, and yes she is getting too close to my boyfriend." They gave each other a look, but I plowed on. It was wasting my time having to constantly remind them how they were supposed to treat me, especially now that I was dating the prince. "I would hate for her to get too comfortable here. I would hate for her to start to think she can get away with stuff like that. You know what my mother always says; 'you let the bad behavior grow and it will spread like a disease'. Her disease is spreading."

I had both of their attention now, Miko's phone was back in his hands, his eyes sparkling as the corner of his mouth pulled up in a smile that I had thought was handsome once.

Well, before Rowan.

"What are you suggesting?" Tasha smiled, nails tapping against her forearm as she crossed one arm over the other. "Or rather, what do your parents want you to do?"

Miko snickered and I looked between the two of them, my lip curling. "I take it you know, then? Did your parents call?"

"No," Miko said, his shaggy blonde hair shifting as he shook his head, grabbing his own glass and draining it halfway. "But we know that look in your eyes, Sia. My parents were very specific when they asked me to assist you with anything you need. Besides, I have sat around enough dinner tables hearing about the Great Samantha and Giovani Demarco and all the good they are doing in our world. I suppose that good is continuing..."

He was fishing for information. Poorly. He might as well have been throwing livers to bears with how obvious he was being. Not that I wouldn't tell him, but my parent's actual involvement in everything that was going on wasn't exactly something they wanted getting out, especially to the girl that I was supposed to kill. The girl that had serendipitously been placed right next door to me, not that I thought she was smart enough to press her ear to the wall.

"Well, they aren't feeding me information on some

underground movement," I sighed, pouring myself more of the biting alcohol. "But I am sure they are doing more than blowing up cathedrals."

The two looked at each other with a smirk, Miko refilling his own glass as he looked at me, his eyes unwavering.

"I like that. I never understood that guy's obsession with churches anyway," Miko laughed at his own joke. Glasses forgotten, he leaned closer, perched on the edge of his chair as our voices dropped, the air growing heavy with conspiracy.

I tried to snap a shield around us, letting my magic stretch into a bubble like my defense instructor had been teaching us all week, but I wasn't sure that it worked. Well, more than making everything around us look wobbly. It would have to do.

I knew what I needed to work on next. It would be needed, especially with meetings and neighbors and wondrous plans taking form.

"You know, Sia," Tasha said, grabbing her phone back from me. This time she pocketed it. "I was starting to think that you and Rowan were going to have all the fun and you were never going to ask Miko and I to join in."

"Never!" I feigned shock and took a sip. "I had to wait for the right time is all. Besides, it's not like Rowan is ready to do more than smile and wave. I'm starting to realize why he was kept under lock and key for so long. I've never met someone so awkward. So... Stupid and bumbling! He hasn't kissed me once. I sure as hell ain't any closer to getting our magic to link. I can't feel anything from him, not even when I kiss him. I'm starting to think that maybe he doesn't have magic. Useless twat."

I threw my hair over my shoulder, nose in the air. They chuckled, but I couldn't find it in me to join them. Truthfully, magic or not, there was something about Rowan that was drawing me into him. Even if he didn't have the balls to kiss me.

"Well, we are here now," Miko said, refilling the glasses again. "I'll forgive you for dragging your feet."

"It's been less than a week, Miko. I wasn't going to send out invitations to participate in a murder on the first day."

A murder. The words boiled and braced against my ribs, fear pulsing with the eagerness at the task that was before me. Kill the girl? Yes, I was still eagerly planning that delicious end. It was everything that went through it that I was still struggling to accept. The dethroning of the royal family. After so many years striving for a place with them, of getting so close to Rowan, I wasn't about to give that up yet.

I wasn't going to share the second part of that plan with them, not until I convinced Rowan to bind himself to me. Having their parents leave them in the dark might have been a bit of a blessing. Killing the girl was easy compared to the forced revolution my parents were leading.

"Murder?" Miko asked, his tongue darting out to lick his lips as though he was hungry for it. "Is it who I think?"

He knocked his head toward the thin wall to our left and the laughter that was echoing through it, the damn Drains that were visiting the bitch were so loud I could nearly make them out word for word. I let my smile stretch and gave him a single nod, both of their eyes lighting up.

"Perfect," Tasha said, "I never understood why she was let in here anyway. We might as well blow up half the school and see if it gets us an audience with the Queen."

"She had an audience with the Queen?" I nearly jumped out of my chair, even Miko was looking at Tasha as though she had tried to serve him spoiled milk and not the fiery drink she was sipping on. The laughter that bled through the wall was a cruel accent to what she had said.

"Yeah," Tasha said, waving her hand to the side as though she wasn't dropping one of the biggest news bombs of the day. "I was one of the last through The Gauntlet. They had been about to give me my mark when she blew the thing to shit. While you were flat on your back, screaming bloody murder, I saw them catch her. I saw Talon punch the shit out of her, saw Rowan and his mom show up out of fucking nowhere and they all dragged her off to a room. The queen was in there with her, for a long time..."

Her eyes spread with each word, as though she was telling the most dangerous tale of the girl who blew up the Gauntlet. As if she is being in the aftermath was more important than the fact that the bitch's explosion had broken my back. I would have to remind her of that later, we had bigger problems now.

"So, she was alone with the queen--"

"And the king, and Ryland, and Mira... Didn't your mom tell you?" Tasha said, her awe drifting to a haughty smugness. I pursed my lips. "I told my parents and they said they would pass on the information."

"They didn't. At least it didn't make it to me," I growled through the tick in my jaw, the anger of what I could only identify as betrayal winding up my back.

My parents hadn't told me. They wanted me to dispatch the Drain to hell but hadn't given me more than a thread of information on what I was going into. The failure at my 'honorary' acceptance to Imdalind Academy was running deeper than I had expected. It was going to take more than one murder to build myself back into their trust.

Much more.

I didn't want to think about what that meant, or what me being paired with Rowan was leading to. Once I finished this job, I could ask more of them.

"You don't think that the Queen did anything to her do you?" I was suddenly nervous, the vile feeling refusing to move as I waited for Tasha to respond. "Like what Gregario said in Basics today, about the water."

"The Queen is stupider than we thought if she used the water to give her more power," Miko laughed, shaking his head. "Besides, that's all rumor. It's clear the Eternals aren't telling us everything. Didn't you say Rowan told you something about Wynifred in the carriage ride over here?"

"Yeah, he said she killed an entire race of people before she defected to fight with Ilyan."

"So, the King's sister-in-law is a murderer. Figures," Miko said with a dark laugh. "I bet she killed the Draks, that's why there aren't any. I bet Ilyan even had her kill them. Kill all the Draks but Joclyn, so the queen can be the only one."

"You're probably right, would make sense seeing as it's not in the history books. All those say is that Wynifred Krul fought valiantly for centuries. But if she massacred an entire race of people on Ilyan's orders they clearly aren't as good as they make it out to be. That's quite the cover-up. Wonder what other secrets they are keeping."

I swallowed, peering between them. Only Miko was meeting my gaze head-on. A shout and more laughter broke through the wall, it sounded as if they broke something. No one moved.

"I don't want that kind of people leading us. Do you, Sia?" Miko's eyes were wide, shaking.

"How much do you know?" My question was a low whisper, barely heard over the noise that was serving as a shield on its own.

"Enough." Miko smiled, leaning closer, the hungry look taking over his eyes again. "I have a bad habit of listening in doorways, and my parents have a bad habit of leaving doors open."

"Tasha?"

"You think I trained for that Gauntlet for years so I could go to school?" She laughed at herself and leaned back in the chair, pulling out her phone and tapping on the screen again. Although this time I had a feeling that it was for a different reason than silly photographs. "I've been waiting to play the game with everyone else."

"Perfect." The nerves were gone, swallowed by an eager buzzing as the two sat back, lifting glasses and smiles in my direction.

"Okay, so what do we want to do first?" Miko asked after we all took a drink, the laughter growing into a dull roar that bled through the walls. We all turned to it.

"I want to find a way to end her in defense class. A powerful spell, sent the wrong direction," I said to the wall, to the laughter that would be silenced by the end of the month if I had my way. "It has to appear to be an accident, but I have no intention of making this an easy death, especially with how she thinks she can be friends with my boyfriend. She needs to hurt."

"So, we need to find an attack that will kill her slowly," Tasha said, tapping her phone again before she put it down.

"I think I know just the one," Miko whispered, smiling at his glass before he drained it. "What do you say we try it out first?"

5

ROWAN

It was getting harder to keep my eyes open. I had contemplated sleeping at about two that morning, my body finally ready to drift away into what I was sure was going to be a haunted slumber. This close to the end of the first week, I knew I could make it one more day. My plan had always been to sleep through most weekends so as to not call attention to my weird sleep schedules. We hadn't told most of the teachers what was going on, for security reasons.

Which meant I had to make it a few more hours.

A few more hours of monotony and forced smiles and then sleep.

It was the perfect excuse for what was really dragging me through the halls, and the girl I wanted to see.

Gemma.

It was dumb. With this pathetic and vile role I was being forced to play with Sia, possibly dangerous. Last I heard the Chosen's' protests had become increasingly violent; this pathetic chess match might be the only thing that kept us from drifting to a full war.

I kept telling myself it wouldn't be much longer, but even I was no longer believing the lie.

"You're gonna let me cheat off you, right?" Gemma hissed half way through class, when Analine was going over a world map with some students at the back.

If I hadn't been so focused on her I might not have heard her at all.

"Excuse me?" Damn, my voice was totally shaking.

"Your family lived this shit, didn't they? I mean, this is like the sweet story of how your parents met and fell in love and got married and had lots of sex and babies."

"Ew." My jaw clamped and I tried to turn away, but she plowed on.

"Don't they regale you with stories of the good ol' days when you're sitting around the spit roasting pigs? I mean, you have to be bored out of your mind."

I blinked, "That's the most ridiculous thing I've ever heard. We don't roast pigs."

"Fine, rats then. You're still bored. I can tell." She smiled and nodded to the paper on my desk, the one covered in my signature doodles, monsters and dogs that were poking their heads around questions like "What happened in San Antonio, Texas that triggered the fall of Imdalind?" and "Tell how Ryland's role in Spain tipped the scales."

Yes, I knew the answers to both. I had heard the stories far too many times. I wasn't sure what part of the stories were public knowledge or which parts were Mira and Ryland trying to battle out who had the highest body count or longest scar.

Two hundred years after the war and they still bickered about it. You would think Ry would have given in by now.

"We don't eat rats either." Even thinking about it made my stomach twist. Not because I had been vegan for my entire life, but because I had more than my fair share of dreams of Gemma catching and skinning the beasts. Or going hungry when there were none.

"Well, you're missing out," she said with a grin and a wink. "Maybe I'll invite you to dinner and we can eat ourselves some rat. Yum, yum."

She added that last part when my face soured, I must have been going green or something with how loud she laughed.

"Head down, Miss," Analine snarled sweeping up behind her and slamming her hand into the back of Gemma's head as she pushed her toward the untouched paper on her desk.

I nearly jumped out of my chair, ready to throw my cousin off her. I didn't know what had gotten into Analine, it was like she had a vendetta against all the Undermortals in the class. I curled my fingers around the edge of my desk, trying to keep my magic restrained even though it was boiling.

"We do our own work in this class." Analine jerked Gemma's head down once more before she swaggered away, giving me a warning look.

She had warned me not to challenge her authority in class, but I was starting to think that was a request I couldn't follow. She had always been kind of a bitch at home, but this was taking it to new levels. There was no way Cail would agree with her.

"Dude, your cousin's a douche," Gemma hissed, rubbing the back of her head while she stared daggers at Analine who was now talking to a student near the front.

"Dramin and I have been saying the same thing for years," I mumbled staring at my paper and trying to ignore the heat that was buzzing against the base of my neck. My magic spread over my skin like a blush, something that I was sure was getting worse with how she looked at me.

Paper. Keep my focus on the paper.

"Dramin? Your brother?" she asked, I nodded, not trusting

myself to look at her. Staying awake this long was clearly taking its toll.

"Well, at least I know there are two Eternals that aren't total douchebags."

"You including me in that?" I asked, sparing her a glance, she was back to lounging in her chair, feet on her desk as she grinned.

"I thought that was obvious," she gave me a wink and my magic flared, the power sparking thanks to the gleam in those lavender eyes. "Well, except for your taste in women. Sia Demarco knocks you down a good sixty percent."

"So, a half-douche then?"

"Definitely a half-douche." She gave me that smug, saucy grin before darting back to her paper, starting up doodles of her own as Analine sauntered by, warning clear in her eyes.

"Don't worry," Gemma said, not looking at me. "There's hope for you yet, Princey."

It was hard to ignore the way my stomach flip-flopped at that.

By the time I had dragged myself through Professor Stone drawling on about wind magic, lived through Sia hanging on me at lunch, and failed in a chess match with Cail, I was struggling so bad that my swagger was more of a stumble. It was with a yawn that I walked into the large sunken theatre where our Healing and Defense class was meeting.

The room was huge, with no seats, no desks. Instead, it was made up of large stone steps that rose around the main stage. The whole thing was covered in pockmarks and smoke stains from decades of battles gone wrong.

Both my brothers had been forced to take this class, even though we had been trained by both Ryland and Mira in both fighting and healing. Which would be why they were never given partners and instead waited around to be used for demonstrations. It was a waste of my time, which was fine as chances were high I was going to fall asleep on the top most stair, as far from the stage as possible.

All of the windows had been thrown open to hopefully coax a breeze into the stifling classroom and prod the magical smoke that was about to clog the air back out. It wouldn't be the best seat in a few minutes, but right now it felt divine to sink to the floor and lean against the wall, close my eyes and feel the breeze dance over my face, pulling at the long dark strands of my hair.

I was settling in for a five-day nap when the shriek that was becoming unfortunately familiar broke through the buzz of the other first-years.

"Rowy!" How, in my exhaustion, had I forgotten that this was the one and only class I had with Sia? A blessing in disguise seeing as I was supposed to be her glue-stick boyfriend for the foreseeable future. The downside was that it made her super clingy and more irritating than I had thought possible.

She was already heading right for me, taking the massive raised steps two at a time, as she batted her eyelashes at me in signature hummingbird impersonation. Well, it wasn't the best option for me to fall asleep in class anyway.

"Hi Sia, How's your day?" I stifled a yawn, speaking as politely as possible as she tried to lean in, sparkly lips already puckered. I turned my head at the last minute, letting her mark up my cheek instead.

"Fine," she pouted, setting her bag on top of mine and sitting as close to me as she could. Everything from shoulder to knee was plastered against me. "Better now. I hate that we don't have any classes together, Rowy." I really needed to get her to stop using that name, and kissing me, and sitting so close she might as well be on my lap. Which I was sure was her ultimate hope. "Are you sure you can't talk to your cousin about changing your classes to match mine?"

Her voice had lifted an octave, the use of Cail's family title a bit too familiar. I turned my head to see Gemma and two of her friends sit a short distance away. Sia always put on a show when there was an audience. This was a gold mine for her.

"I'm sure," I spoke low, giving her a look. She smiled, batting her eyelashes and shifting herself closer. This must be what being wrapped up in cellophane felt like. I shimmied away, leaning closer to the window in a desperate want of air.

"Good afternoon class," began Professor Diarius, or 'Etty' as she had been trying to get us to call her, as if that made her cooler. "As you know, this week we have been focused on shields to help us prepare for this course. Beginning next week, we will begin to work in pairs so that we can master these and other skills. Today, I will be assigning you your sparring partner for the rest of the year. You and your partner will work together so as to perfect your skills and prepare you for the defensive magic and healing portions of your exam at the end of the year. I invite you to get to know your partner. Understand each other's strengths and weaknesses so that when we begin on Monday you will be able to more accurately defeat them."

The class instantly broke into a buzz of sound, the rumble breaking over the whisper of wind that was tickling over my nose. I let my eyes drift closed.

"Rowy! We could be partners!" I jumped, nearly smacking my head on the window frame as she yelled in my ear. "Do you think if I ask she will team us up?"

Sia was prattling on like the rest of them, the noise pulling into angry roars in my exhausted mind. I didn't even have the energy to tell her that there was no way in hell we would be partners. She would find out soon enough.

Professor Diarius began calling out names, handing out packets to each pair as everyone shuffled to their partners. Some were shocked, some pleased. Most looked beyond disgusted. It didn't take long for everyone to figure out what she was doing.

"She's matching Goldens with Drains," Sia snarled under her breath, the word on her tongue twisting in my stomach.

"She's matching people," I corrected her, forgetting to keep my voice down as I leaned back again. God, I really should have skipped this class. I wasn't going to make it.

"Sia Demarco and Madeline."

"Sorry, baby," Sia whispered in my ear, like I cared. I didn't even open my eyes, I gave her a wave and sunk into the wall more. What I wouldn't give for a pillow.

"Pater Smyth and Alfonz."

The breeze felt so nice, I wonder if anyone would notice if I took off out the window and soared back to my dorm.

"Rowan Krul and Gemma."

So much for being half asleep. I was officially full awake. This time I did hit my head on the window frame as I jerked straight upright, eyes wide as I turned to Gemma who was full on laughing as she jumped up and strutted down to collect our packet from the professor, waving and blowing a kiss to Sia.

Shit. Sia was already fuming, there was going to be some backlash for this.

"Please begin working on your packet together," Professor Diarius continued as Gemma made her way back up the steps to me. "Once you have finished your packet, please turn it in and I will give you some small practice attacks you can begin with today."

She stepped out of the center of the sunken stage, moving to the first pair and sending the room back into its buzz of energy. Sia's glower was already burning a hole in the side of my head.

"Someone really has it out for you, don't they, Princey?" Gemma waved the papers in front of me, she didn't so much as flinch when I snapped them out of her hand.

"Don't call me that." That came out much harsher than I had intended, not that she cared. She was chuckling to herself, sinking onto the stone step as she pulled a pencil out from behind her ear.

"Then what would you like me to call you? Snookems? Honey ass?"

"Honey ass?" The words choked on a laugh on their way out.

"You know... Sweet cheeks." She gave me a wink. "I know that's what your girlfriend calls you."

"Not my girlfriend." My eyes flicked to the girl in question, the tiny glance a huge mistake. She was looking at us so intently that I was sure she was trying to use her magic to make Gemma explode.

"Trying to gain back that sixty percent?"

"No!" I jerked, Sia's scowl deepening.

"Well aren't you just the King of Defiance today," Gemma laughed, thankfully pulling my focus from Sia and her laser eyes.

"Not the king." I couldn't help the smile that time, my magic boiling under my skin as I leaned closer to her.

"Oh, excuse me, the Prince of Defiance, then." She adopted a baby voice and tried to pinch my cheek. I dodged before she made contact.

As much as I wanted to feel her touch, feel her magic, I wasn't ready to put my shields to that big of a test.

Thankfully she didn't try again and instead adopted her own window seat, fingers interlaced behind her head.

"My name is Rowan." I sat back again, the wind choosing that moment to drift through the window and tug the longer strands of my hair over my face. She snickered, I was sure I looked like something you would see in one of those movies, 'My Evening with the Prince' or some nonsense. Although thankfully most of the characters that saved the poor peasant girl were based on Talon, it was still an association I wasn't interested in making.

"I would move those out of the way," she nodded to the hair, "but not only are you a big strong man and can lift your hand all on your own, but I don't want Bitchy McBitch back there to punch my face in."

My hair and clothes were blowing around in a rage. A growing torrent of wind, no longer a breeze. Odd, seeing as Gemma was sitting untouched. I gave Sia a look and the wind died down.

"Sorry, not Bitchy McBitch. Your girlfriend."

"Again. Not my girlfriend." I shoved the hair out of my face with as much grace as an elephant.

"Well, you could have fooled me. Is it something you Eternals do then? Let spoiled Chosen's kiss you and rub your legs and call you weird pet names. I mean, I banged one of my guards once because I needed him to stay focused on the job. That was too far for me. I couldn't get the guy off me. The ones who want something out of you are always the clingiest."

I couldn't even form words. I sat there, staring at her, trying to follow what she had said.

"Your guards?" I choked on the words when they finally emerged.

"Yeah, you know, the guy that watches my back while I blow up your shit. Banks. Grocery stores. Clothing stores. Don't you have one of those?"

"Someone who blows up shit?"

"No, Princey," she smirked, "a guard."

I shook my head. "We can generally take care of ourselves. That and we don't usually blow up buildings."

"Well, you are missing out on all the fun." She rolled her eyes and went back to glaring at Sia.

"Don't you have any remorse?"

"I could ask the same of you. But no, I have no remorse because I have nothing to be remorseful for. I fed, clothed, and kept my people safe. I did my job."

"Your people?" I asked. Her face spread into a wide grin.

"You aren't the only royal brat in this club." She gave me a wink and leaned against the wall, kicking her feet up to lay across the wide stair beside mine.

My heart skipped a beat, the warmth that was pooling in my stomach and pumping through my veins turning into an inferno. I was fine with this; I think part of me had been waiting forever for this. Sia however was not, her eyes were shining red as she turned. Gemma was already blowing her a kiss and wagging her fingers at her in a way that only spelled trouble.

"Do you think if I shrunk her head to the size of a turnip anyone would notice?" She was peering through her thumb and forefinger at Sia, pinching her fingertips together as she smashed her head.

I had to cover my mouth to stop from laughing.

"I'm sure everyone would notice, Gemma," I was beginning to think that every time I said her name was going to lead to some form of heart palpitations. I really needed a change in subject. "So, how does your childhood affect your day to day choices?"

"Excuse me?" she asked, whipping around to face me. I waved the packet of papers in her face.

"The assignment. It's all questions for us to get to know each other." I flipped through the pages, scanning the questions and realizing that my quick deterrent had turned into a minefield.

"Well, I'm not answering that until you do. How has your childhood affected your life, Rowan?"

I think my heart stopped beating when she said my name.

"Pass. What is your least favorite attribute?" I said, determined to ignore her and reading the first question my eyes fell on. That was worse. "Who is your favorite relative and why? Who the hell wrote this?"

"You're really good at this, Princey. My turn." She snatched the papers out of my hands, giving me a papercut that I quickly healed. "When was the last time you cried?"

"I'm not answering that." Especially considering it was last night, when I had felt her magic alongside mine. Before that was last month, when I had woken from an especially traumatizing dream featuring the girl right in front of me and the moment she had lost her father.

"Fine then. Why are your eyes green when everyone else in your family has blue eyes?"

My stomach flipped. Not because it was something that bugged me, but because she had noticed.

"That question isn't on there," I said through clenched teeth. She shrugged.

"How about this one: why are you here if you clearly already know how to use your magic?"

"I could ask the same of you."

"That's easy." She flipped her hand to the side. "Your mother seems to think she can teach me remorse. Or maybe she thinks that's your job."

All I could do was stare at her, trying to figure out how to respond when thankfully Professor Diarius swept her way over to us, looking us in the eye from where she stood, one step down.

"How is it going over here?"

"Fine," Gemma said the same time that I said, "I think there has been some kind of mistake"

Both Gemma and Etty's eyes flashed to me, the teachers smile fading.

"A mistake?"

"Yes, me and my siblings. I'm not supposed to be assigned a

sparring partner." I kept my voice low, trying my best to use the tone that so many in my family used to get their way.

I regretted the tone and the request immediately. It wasn't as though I had no reason, but seeing the shock on her face still hurt. It wasn't that I didn't want to be partners with her, it was that sparring in public with her was going to open up quite a few problems that I would rather keep locked away.

"Oh, I see," Professor Diarius began, her usual smile still trying to find its way back onto her face. "I know you already have an extensive magical training, Prince Rowan." Damn it. She said Prince. I may have gone too far with the diplomatic urgency. "But so does Gemma, although hers is informal, she possesses a skill that would be dangerous to pair with any other student. It's lucky you are here really." She laughed then, Gemma forcing a weird tinkling sound alongside, the false sound only adding to the glare she was giving me.

"See, no mistake, Princey." Gemma said, eyes glinting.

"I would be prepared, however," the Professor continued, giving the two of us a look. "With your skills being so advanced it is likely that you will be sparring partners for the duration of your education."

"Shit on a rat ball. You've got to be fucking kidding me." So much for prodding me, Gemma was obviously none too happy about this set up either. Several heads turned at her outburst, some of the Undermortals chuckling, including that guy that she went everywhere with.

Edward, I think.

Maybe that was the guard she was talking about. I wonder if she liked him.

Oh god, these thoughts should not be in my head.

"Well, work on that packet so you can begin your training. I am sure there is much you can learn from each other." Professor Diarius smiled and hustled away, giving Gemma a look that made it clear that even she was scared of the girl. I would be too with the look she was now giving me.

Great. I now had two girls glaring daggers at me. Never thought I'd say this, but I would actually like to go back to the swoony blondes.

"Don't you dare ask me any of those shit questions. Make up some sob story and call it good. I'm not answering those. I can tell you aren't either." She popped her gum and leaned back against the wall.

I stared at her, my heart aching at the question before me. Knowing I could answer each and every one, for the both of us. Too many years of dreams, of piercing realities that I was only barely beginning to understand.

I might know her better than I thought.

6

GEMMA

THE DOOR SHUT FOR THE SECOND TIME, THE SNAP A HOLLOW ECHO as twenty more Undermortals snuck into the couch filled portion of my dorm, eyes wary as they looked through the dim lights at everyone else. It was clear that most of them didn't know each other. Hell, I didn't know most of them. Ed, Kara, and Geo had done a good job.

This was more than the first years who had pulled their way through the Gauntlet ahead of the Goldens. This was also the smattering of our people who had been brave enough to run in the three years prior. You could see years of ridicule and defeat swallowing the color from their eyes, a tiny bit of hope trying to pull its way through.

Let's see if we could put some of that back.

"Is this everyone?" I asked a yawning Eddy who approached with two paper cups full of the coffee stuff that he had discovered on one of our raids and quickly become obsessed with, the guy had danced, literally danced, when he found it in my cabinets yesterday. He was trying to push his obsession on me, but the stuff was bitter and biting.

This morning it might be just what I needed, though.

Last night Sia and her friends had been laughing, at full voice mind you, about some string of attacks. About emptying the drains of the "Vile Scourge", or whatever it was she had nicknamed us today. I wanted it to be wrong, for her to be padding her own ego, but that dark light in her eyes, the way she looked at me...

I wasn't about to take any chances.

If the Chosen were increasing their attacks against us, fighting back for taking their precious spots in the academy, then we needed to get ourselves doing the same.

Hopefully without any freaky prying eyes getting wind of it.

In hopes of escaping the queen, I had decided that three in the morning was the appropriate time for our meeting and had pulled everyone out of bed before the sun had even thought about peeking over the mountains.

Now, it was just a sliver of light in a sapphire sky.

"Pretty sure this is it for today," Ed said after draining coffee cup number two. "I'm sure it will grow. One week isn't enough to grow an entire underground rebellion inside of the king's school." He gave me a grin and grabbed another coffee, sighing in delight.

"Well, you guys did great either way," I nodded to Geo and Kara, the two chatting to some very angry Undermortals who both had the tattoo of the ghost on their neck.

A burning ghost.

The mark was from a community dangerously close to the burned-out slave camps near the Med, The Wastelands. I had only ever heard rumors about the Ghostlanders, about the feuds and bloodlust that ruled the place. I had thought it was all a story. But if it wasn't, no wonder they looked so pissed. There wasn't much in that part of the world but death, there was a reason most Undermortal communities sprouted up beneath the major cities.

"Good morning everyone!" I said as loud as I dared, Eddy taking two steps to the side, grateful to blend into the crowd and melt into his coffee. "Thanks for getting up at this awful hour to sneak away. We have some food in the back, Ed made some coffee stuff, and feel free to lounge anywhere as long as you keep your eyes open."

There was a smattering of laughter, the nervous chuckles coming from the back a bit different than what I was used to. It was like at the beginning, when I had first gained enough control of my powers to blow stuff up that would do us good and not lead to collapsed tunnels. It had taken time to convince Last Pyre that rebellion and attack were worth it, too.

"I'm Gemma. If you don't know anything about me, know this: I was bitten by a Vilỳ when scavenging for food ten years ago. I was eight and almost died. My community, Last Pyre, hid me from the Tarns and the CCC for years." I pulled my shirt back, revealing the burning wand tattoo above my breast that signified Last Pyre. Eddy, Kara, and Geo did the same, turning to everyone as they stood with me.

"I grew up in Last Pyre," I continued, letting my shirt fall back into place. "It's my home. But we all know that our underground safe havens aren't always that way. That's why, starting last year I began leading the people of Last Pyre, my people, in the reclamation of our world. We have destroyed over a hundred of the Chosen's buildings. Reclaimed what should have been ours in the falling brick and burning roofs of banks, grocery stores, clothing stores. We have fed more than five communities, clothed as many people as we could, and even stole a few books in the hopes of teaching the kids to read. We are still working on that one though."

More laughter. The joy mixed with awe as everyone looked between them. The ones from the communities that had been impacted by Last Pyre turning to those who may have never heard of us in whispered affirmations.

"We have done it all under our goal of reclaiming a life for ourselves, of ending the class system the Eternals have put in place, and dethroning the family that created this hell." I hesitated, the expressions on those same damn royals after I had burned their Gauntlet to hell flashing through me.

The shock.

Their promise that they wanted the same thing we did.

I still wasn't sure I believed them, or if I ever would. None of that mattered now. I straightened my back and looked over the crowded room, pushing the guilt and the questions away.

"All the glitters were never gold," I said with a nod, my heart swelling as more than half of the Undermortals repeated the words at full voice. "It's our mantra, it's our promise. It's the words I spoke when I destroyed the Gauntlet last month."

I had saved that part for last, unsure of how they would react. I had no way of knowing if I had injured any of our people after all. Instead of outrage, the room broke out into whispers. Questions, shock, and joy wiggled through everyone as they came alive.

"You were responsible for that?" Someone asked near the front, a girl with a dragon tattoo circling her arm, the winged lizard stretching as she flexed her muscle.

"I heard about that, but the Goldens were saying they killed the culprit..."

"I heard the same."

"My sister saw the attack; she saw them take the girl away..." One of the third or fourth-year students near the back whispered everyone turning to her "She said it was a girl with a pink mohawk."

She was looking at me like I had sprouted wings and turned into one of those damn Eternals.

"They made me trim it down. I guess hair can't be cool here."
I snickered, but no one responded passed staring at me in
shock.

"How are you here?" That same girl with the dragon tattoo
asked. "Why didn't they throw you in The Wastelands? If you
blew up the Gauntlet why would they send you here and not to
the death camps."

Her question garnered another round of mumbles and
questions, everyone suddenly looking skeptical again. I glanced
at Eddy. We had talked about this; we had expected this. I also
didn't expect any of these guys to believe me if I told them that
the Eternals didn't run those death camps.

If you believed them.

Which I didn't.

"I didn't come through unscathed," I began, speaking slowly
as I jumped on the weird low table in the hopes of pulling their
focus back. Gratefully the tiny thing held my weight. "Those
damn royals got a few good hits in," I rubbed my jaw, ignoring
Ed's raised brow at the partial truth. "They threatened to kill my
family," it was a lie but it was doing the job every eye was on me
now, "They sent me to the CCC," that lie got a gasp or two, "They
shackled me," partial truth, "they locked me up until they
decided what to do with me," more lie than truth, I doubt you
could call the fancy hotel they put me and Ed up in a dungeon.
"They restricted the magic I have," unfortunate truth, "and I'm
not allowed to leave the campus until further notice."

The mumbling continued, anger mixing with confusion. Too
many people realized that I hadn't quite answered their
questions.

Shit.

"Look," I said loudly, pulling their focus. The two from the
Ghostlanders looking especially perturbed. "It wasn't a slap on
the wrist. Their damn Queen gave me a choice, let her bind my

magic and stick me in this prison, or remove my magic completely. But I can't very well continue a revolution with no magic."

That got the Ghostlanders attention, it was nothing more than a side glance at one another, but I saw it.

"A revolution?" One of them scoffed, glancing behind him at the faces that were quickly becoming eager. "You can't be serious. So, you've knocked over a few stores. Congratulations. We've done that, too. Even without magic," he nodded to his companion, "all it led to was more of the CCC raiding our tunnels. More of our people murdered and dragged off to The Wastelands. More pain. When those vans showed up we knew we had a chance to change our lives, so we took it. We feel bad for those we left behind, but we can't fix everything."

"That's where you are wrong. We can change everything. You would be stupid not to see that." I was walking on dangerous ground, the two were glancing at each other with even deeper distaste. His fingers had suddenly begun smoking.

It hadn't occurred to me how dangerous this was, pooling so many Undermortals with brand new magic into one room. I already knew I wouldn't be able to stop anything that happened. I wasn't sure what the older students skills were in that area.

Damage control before my dorm room was damaged.

"I know it seems impossible," I spoke calmly, letting my voice carry as I rotated on the table. Every eye turned to me as the wood below my feet began to crack. "It was when we were living in tunnels underground. When we were nothing but a whole bunch of Drains," a few near the front flinching as though I had spat acid on them. "But we aren't Drains anymore, we never were. Its time they know that. When they gave us magic, they gave us power." More and more people where nodding, so I plowed on before the Ghostlanders could steal them away again. "Last Pyre was one community, with one person with a bit of drippy illegal magic. Every time I exploded a building I would pass out for days, too tired to do more than swear and demand food."

"She did too!" Eddy piped up, a few scattered laughs echoing from the back.

"I couldn't fight." I continued, giving Ed a brief smile of thanks. "I couldn't do much more than steal tampons and soda in the beginning. But we found a way."

I paused, waiting for the nods of approval, of eager anticipation. It hadn't taken this much to convince Last Pyre to fight with me the last time. But I guess it wouldn't take much when you were presenting a platter of food to a starving village. They were already surrounded by food, beds, and every luxury you could think of.

They had already forgotten the ones left behind.

"Yes, they fought back. I can't tell you how many times the CCC raided us. How many times my people hid me and guarded me in the hopes of keeping our tiny little revolution going. In the hopes of blowing up one more building. We lost people." I paused, my throat closing up as hundreds of faces flashed before me. It still ached. It always would, but letting myself get bogged down over that shit was not going to convince any of them to stand with me. "We were going to lose people anyway. We lost people from the moment I was born. We lost people the day I was bitten and in the years before I learned how to control this," I flared my fingers then, the lights flickering as I sucked the electricity from them, pulling it into me and around them in a spark of light that looked much more impressive now that my magic was in working order. Even with the bind the queen had on me.

A wave of awe moved over everyone, even the more skilled Undermortals near the back smiled with a tiny bit of hope.

"Those dratted Eternals made one huge mistake. They put

over a hundred Undermortals into this Academy this year, they brought us together. Us," I gestured to them widely, everyone looking around as the dozens of others that had crammed into this room. "All of us, people from more than a dozen Undermortal communities in the world. Communities I have only ever heard whisperings about," I nodded to the Ghostlanders, "And communities that have joined me in raids," Another nod to the lone Fire Fate that sat on the floor that led to my bedroom.

"We are here, a spiders web of people that can carry the revolution into every tunnel, every crack, every drain. We can flood the Chosen out of what should be ours. We can change the world."

"How do you suggest we start that?" a voice said from somewhere in the crowd. "It's not like we can afford visits on the weekends. No one back home can read or write so I can get them a letter."

"Food." Eddy provided from behind me, thankfully not joining me on the tiny table, I wasn't sure the thing could support both of us.

"Food?" The same voice returned, the owner lost in the crowd.

"Yes. I'm sure you've noticed there is no end to food in this place," Eddy chuckled, patting his belly and making it clear he had been hoarding more than coffee. "So much so that they have to throw it out. But if we take it back to our communities on the weekends we can start spreading the news, spreading plans. We can start organizing our fight against them."

The Ghostlanders shifted, eyes darting from them to us, before the taller of the two laughed.

"You think the Eternals--"

"I'm convincing the Eternals to give us the fuel to their own demise. They will be the ones that bring about their own end, that feed the armies that fight against them. That spread the plans and organize a force that they have underestimated for too long."

I got a few nods that time. These guys were a tough audience. I had to be very careful about what I said. I wasn't about to tell them that the chatterbox of an Eternal had already promised to take food to Last Pyre, but who knew if that included any other communities.

They had messed up this far, they couldn't be trusted to do things the right way.

"How do you plan on convincing them to let us take the food back, or even get there? We are as trapped in here as you are. We may be allowed to leave, but we have no way to get there." More murmurs and head nods followed the red-headed girls' question. Not that I blamed them, the girl had a point.

I didn't like the answer any more than they were going to.

"After I blew up their damned Gauntlet, I struck a deal with the queen." The outrage broke out immediately. The glimmers of hope in their eyes heading to that of betrayal. I gave Eddy a told you so side glance, but he just stood there smiling and bouncing on his heels.

"So that is why you are still alive? You already sold yourself out, and you expect to keep leading us like some kind of pet project?" One of the Ghostlanders said, his lip sneering as though I was some kind of poison come to infect the air. "You can't defeat someone if you've crawled into bed with them."

His statement was only causing the rumble of disappointment to take control, the anger and frustration coating the air like a virus.

"Haven't you ever heard of a double agent you dip shit?" I said, finally snapping, silence fell over the room. "I made the deal not for them to pad their ego. Not to work with the bitch, but to save us all. Let us eat their scraps, so we can leave them all to rot."

That shut them right up, the narrowed eyes and mumbled frustrations bleeding into the wave of smiles, of determination, or exhilarations that I was used to.

Knew we'd get there in the end.

"All the glitters were never gold," I said, letting my magic spark above my head like fireworks, the banner of the revolution coloring the room in glimmering shades of orange.

This time everyone responded, and my stomach knotted to my toes.

7

———

SIA

"BY LOCKING OUT ALL THOUGHT YOU SHOULD BE ABLE TO REMAIN focused on your magic, find that tight warmth in your chest, the hollow in your soul where your magic lives. Understand where it dwells and how it moves within you..."

Professor Etma Diarius was a madwoman. When I signed up for The Gauntlet, and Imdalind Academy, I hadn't realized that part of my magical education would involve me laying on my back in the middle of the classroom, with my eyes closed, listening to some weird flute music while Professor Diarius spoke in a voice that belonged in one of the seedy bars in the low district. Not in a classroom, and certainly not in a classroom with twenty-six students who were supposed to be 'acquainting themselves with their magic.'

Well, twenty-five students. For the second day in a row, Rowan was a no show. In fact, he had been missing for the past four days. I had tried to track him down all weekend, even pounding on his door at one point, but no answer. The plans I had made for us had gone to waste. I had spent days alone instead.

Days locked in my room, spying on Gemma. Practicing

magic. Wouldn't have been so irritating if she hadn't woken me up in the middle of the night, dozens of voices bleeding through the wall.

Luckily for her, I was too tired to care or I might have blasted a hole in the fecking wall.

"Breathe in and bring your magic into that warm spot in your heart where it likes to hide, breathe out and press it out, let it spread over you and press against your skin..."

I shifted my weight against the hard floor, the magic that was supposed to be calm and controlled raging and boiling instead. This was a giant waste of time. We were supposed to be learning how to defend and heal, not how to let our magic breathe through us like some living thing. I was supposed to control it, not the other way around.

Someone snickered to the left of me. I wasn't the only person who saw this exercise for what it was. Stupid. My partner, the dirty Drain that I had been paired with for the entire year, seemed to actually be trying to accomplish the task. Either that or she was snoring.

"Focus on the power against your skin, on the weight of it. Imagine it becoming a wall, a firm base that nothing can press through. Build your magic into a protective blanket that wraps around you..."

Someone else snickered and I lost it, hair shimmering down my back as I sat bolt upright and turned to Professor Diarius. The madwoman was still wandering through the students, her own eyes closed as more than half the class snickered and smiled, a pair of Goldens one step up from me were even arm wrestling.

"I'm sorry, professor." I spoke in the sweetest voice I could muster, putting on innocent curiosity as Professor Diarius, and everyone else, turned to me. Madeline jerked as if she had been slapped. Guess she was sleeping then. "But is there a point to this? I know I'm not the only one struggling to stay focused or even stay awake for that matter. I had hoped we would be sparring today. I know I am not the only one."

Several of the Golden's around me smiled, nodding in agreement while most of the Drain's shifted away from us. The sparring matches on Monday hadn't gone well and I was eager to kick Madeline's ass again. Even if we were only testing the basic effects of sparks against skin.

"Mastering our shields and acquainting ourselves with our magic is vital to be able to spar and defend and even heal," Etma said with a snap, her eyes narrowing at me as she made her way over, the sharp tap of her leather shoes a hollow countdown in the massive space. I hadn't even noticed that the flute music had stopped. "If you expect to be able to accomplish any of these skills, then I would hope you take this class seriously."

"Oh, I am taking it seriously," I said, batting my lashes. Etma didn't seem phased at all by my charms. She huffed and pinched the bridge of her nose like she was irritated. Great. Clearly, she wasn't as supportive as Professor Analine. I would have to see if I could fix that. "I'm not feeling stretched. I feel as if I've already mastered my shield and am ready for something more complex. Many of those born to Chosen families feel the same."

Professor Diarius smiled in that slow lazy way that I had come to expect from the teachers, as though they had spent too long being underwhelmed by worthless Drains and Goldens that had failed to impress them. I already knew I would be the one to change that. Not because I had spent my entire life working towards this, but because no one in the room could match the strength of my magic.

"Maybe it's because I slept so long after my bite," I continued with an exaggerated sigh, looking from Professor Diarius to all of the wide eyes around me. Well, all but Gemma, the girl was still lying flat on her back in the high corner she usually sat in with Rowan, tracing shapes on the ceiling. "The queen said my magic was stronger than any other, I must be mastering things faster than everyone else."

"Care to test that?" Professor Diarius asked, more of the previously sleeping students around her popping up like daisies, looking between me and the teacher with wide eager eyes.

"I would be honored to." I jumped to my feet, smoothing my hair and skirt with extra flare, confident in my abilities after spending the weekend working on it.

I had to do something after my boyfriend went MIA. Shields and secret attacks had won out, perhaps I would get lucky and be able to try that out as well.

Bringing my magic up to the tight wall around me, I faced the teacher, ready for her to attack, ready to splinter her magic and show everyone in this room exactly what they were facing. I would have preferred to do it on a day that Rowan was there, but I was sure he would hear all about it.

"Gemma," Etma Diarius called, peering over my shoulder.

"Yo." The answer echoed from the back of the classroom. I was about to turn, sure the girl was being told to pay attention.

"If you would--" Professor Diarius' request was cut short when a flash of white exploded from Gemma's hand and something hard and warm and awful slammed against my side. Whatever shield I had pressed against me shattering as my magic retreated back into me, flooding bones and veins as it tried to heal whatever I had been hit with.

Biting back a scream, I dropped to my knees. I tried to snap the shield back into place, but it wouldn't come. I couldn't even find where the power had gone, Diarius's ramble about hearts and hollows had vanished in the pain.

"Well, that wasn't what I had in mind..." Diarius sighed from above me, her worried face cutting in and out of focus.

"You're supposed to breathe your power out, Sia," Gemma

said as she and a few others chuckled. "Let it press against your skin and flower like a tree in the wind."

More laughter, even Diarius was smiling as she hovered above me, hands on my face as she checked for injuries.

"That's enough everyone," she said as the last of the pain eased away and I finally found my magic. "Let's take this opportunity to--"

I jerked to sitting before she could finish her sentence, letting my magic boil in the same way it had all weekend. The attack I had worked so hard to perfect flew right to Gemma and her ugly smug grin, to her stupid pink curls and purple eyes. Who the hell had purple eyes anyway?

Yellow sparks streamed right to her. Her smile never faltered, even as my attack shattered into nothing an inch before it crashed and burned on her nose. The sparks fell harmlessly to the ground, leaving black smears against the stone.

"What the hell?" I shrieked, fists pounding against my thighs before I caught myself, quickly rearranging my features from fury to shock.

"Press your power against your skin, Sia," Gemma said, stretching her arms wide. "I'm a mother fucking stone wall."

The class broke out into howls of laughter as I jumped to my feet. I was ready to send another attack her way, even though my bones were screaming in agony from whatever she had hit me with.

First, she thinks she can get away with talking to my boyfriend. Now she humiliates me in front of everyone?

Screw making it look like an accident.

"Enough," Diarius said from behind me, her magic snapping in a visible well between us as Gemma sank down to the floor, laying back down and tracing shapes in the air like the last few minutes hadn't happened. Well, except for that smug grin that needed to be wiped off her face.

"Bitch," I hissed, sinking down to the stone step that was still steaming with Gemma's residual magic.

"As you can see, shields are a vital part of our learning, as is the control of our tempers. We cannot spar effectively until we have mastered a basic shield. Or if we are prone to outbursts. I cannot teach you more complex attacks until then." She looked around at everyone, the last few students to wake up looking around the class in groggy confusion. "Each week our shields grow stronger and we will add more skills to this foundation. First, we must master the foundations. We can never guarantee that we will be evenly matched in a spar and we must be prepared to face magic stronger than our own."

"Stronger?" I hissed to myself, turning from the teacher to Gemma, who had sat up to give me a grin. The bell buzzed over the hollow amphitheater and people gathered their bags, heading back to their dorms, or yards, or whatever they did at the end of the day.

"Thank you, everyone! Please work on your breathing before bed tonight, we will continue this lesson tomorrow," Professor Diarius yelled over the bustle of everyone bolting for the door. She was already making her way back to the cluttered desk in the corner. The weird flute music had already made a return.

"Professor Diarius," I said before she could move too far away, trying to keep my voice sweet even though my back was aching. I grabbed my bag and limped after her, my left knee screaming with every step. What the hell had that girl hit me with? "There must be some mistake, professor. Gemma... I mean... she can't be stronger than me. I slept longer than anyone in this school. The King was certain that the power--"

"Your shield was strong, Sia, but not strong enough," Diarius said with a finger in the air. She was still plowing toward her desk, leaving me to continue hobbling after her. I doubt she noticed. "Especially when faced with unregulated magic like

Gemma's. Because of her history with her magic, she is in fact, stronger than you. Perhaps you will catch up to her before the end of the year, for as you must learn control, so must she. She may have stronger magic now, but you have the potential to master skills faster as you will build with a base of rules and understanding. Working from the correct places is easier than working backward, trust me."

"So, if I keep breathing and imagining my magic as walls, I can beat her?" I asked, leaving Diarius to sigh and look up before going back to shuffling papers on her desk.

"There is no 'beating' anyone here, Sia," Diarius said, sinking into her frayed chair and looking up at me with that same disappointment from before. It only made my blood boil more. "We practice our skills this way as it is one of the best ways to master power. There is no beating because there is no fighting. There is only practice, work, and perfection."

I nearly laughed, I actually had to bite my lips to stop from doing so. Practice, work, and perfection was the mantra my parents had pushed into me from a young age. It clearly did not have the same meaning. Here those words were surrounded by flowers, at home they were written in blood.

8

ROWAN

Six days. I had slept for six days.

Unsurprisingly, it had taken me longer than expected to fall asleep after my class with Gemma. But after tossing, turning, and more than a few shouted swears to the ceiling I had fallen asleep, and slept for six days. It was my longest stretch yet. Hopefully, it was just because I was extraordinarily tired and a bit emotionally drained after my first week at Imdalind Academy.

Not just because my Drak magic was becoming louder.

The dreams that had plagued me weren't really promising of it being some issue with exhaustion. I had woken up crying after watching hundreds of men storm through what looked like an old subway tunnel, the tubes lined with graffiti and splashed with blood as the wall of muscled men took hundreds of Undermortals down with swords.

Swords. Like some archaic murder scene.

Blood had splashed over everything as children screamed, as boots pounded, as people begged to be allowed to live, to be taken to The Wastelands, wherever that was.

I had no way to tell when the massacre had taken place with

how fast the scene kept changing, different tunnels flashing in my mind's eye as the horrors grew. It wasn't until the screaming rebel in the middle of all of that blood appeared that I could even guess what I was looking at. Gemma stood, the lone protector between her people and those who had come to slaughter them, magic swirling all around her.

Healed, centered, perfectly strong magic.

It was her, alone, against hundreds. She didn't even flinch.

I very rarely dreamed of the future, my vision of the Gauntlet being one of two. Three now. Not that it sat any better against my chest. The dream had ended with Gemma, standing before my brother Talon. The massive guy was on his knees, yelling something I couldn't hear before she put her hand around his neck and...

The memory was freezing and I pulled my race toward the class I was already late for to a stop, forcing myself to catch my breath and push the entire thing from my mind. Impossible. There are some things you don't forget. Watching your brother's head get lobbed off was going on that list.

He may be a jerk, but that... that...

I swallowed, straightened my jacket and pushed open the door to my second-period class, which had to have been the loudest thing known to man. Every head turned, Professor Stone's demonstration of wind-powered levitation and localization ending with a bang of wood against stone as the log she had been lifting fell to the ground.

Professor Lexia Stone was a Chosen, bitten during the war and bonded to one of the Skřítek guards that had fought alongside my father for generations. She had been one of the first to marry an Eternal. Well, after Aunt Mira. But that story was weird.

Lexia had been around my whole life, which was why she looked more irritated than awed at my late arrival. The frizzy brown bun atop her head was bobbing as she narrowed her equally as dark eyes at me.

"Sorry," I began, running my hand through my hair. "I..." I stuttered to a stop.

What the hell do I say? I overslept? I am harboring gifts from another race of magic that does weird things to my body? I'm bored out of my mind and can't be bothered with these lessons?

I clearly should have given more effort to working out an excuse for my weird sleep cycles, or found out if the teachers had been warned. Doubtful considering how much we were trying to conceal it. Instead, I stood at the front of the room with my mouth hanging open, a wave of hushed laughter rolling through the class that was all completely focused on me.

Great, guess I should have paid a little bit more attention to the class starting times, I could have skipped this one altogether. Thankfully, Professor Stone came to my rescue, waving me off.

"It's no worries, Rowan, I am glad you could join us."

I bowed to her as I would to my father when he decided not to punish me, gaining myself more giggles as I turned toward the sea of students, all sitting before desks covered with logs of their own. Maybe I would get lucky and find a seat toward the back. Disappear in the crowd like the Undermortals did. Like Gemma did.

Thinking of her name pulled my focus right to her, perched on a rickety chair as she stared, her dark eyes and quirked eyebrow raised to me in confusion. My heart seized in my chest, the thing pounding so loud that I was sure everyone could hear. Which is probably why they were all staring at me like I lost it.

"To continue," Lexia Stone bellowed over the class as I nearly fell into my seat. "The control of your magic and of wind is vital in order to master any of these skills. If you are lacking control, then you will never advance past this level one course, I can guarantee you. The minute lifting and manipulation of objects using only wind power is our first step. This is why we will focus on the lifting, spinning, and dancing of these objects for the next three months..."

She gestured toward the side of her desk where three boxes lay open, ready for everyone to gather their supplies.

A top, a playing card, and a feather.

Everyone else was excited, chatter waving through the thirty or so others. I nearly slammed my head into the desk just to make sure I hadn't accidently been sent to hell. I had done this when I was five. I even taught Angie how to do it last year. Could they at least have started me in the fourth and final year instead of making me go through all of this? No wonder Talon was such a womanizer, he had to find something to do in this mess.

"Look!" Someone hissed to my left and I jerked as I watched the top from Professor Stone's desk begin to spin and lift itself from the desktop. I didn't feel so much of a whisper of wind. Perfect control.

Ms. Stone looked at me with a furious expression, I shook my head, mouthing 'this isn't me' to her.

"I have a question," Gemma yelled from the back of the class, the loud clomp of her boots echoing over the squeal of chairs and desks as everyone turned to watch her saunter between rows to a now fuming Professor Stone, finger pointing to the top as tiny sparks flew from beneath her nail. "What if you already know how to do this? Do you want those of us who might be bored out of our god damned minds to knit you a blanket instead? We can make it in your favorite colors."

"There will be alternate tasks once you have mastered this skill," Lexia said through clenched teeth as the bell rang. No one moved, they sat frozen to their desks. Heads ping-ponged between Lexia, who was fuming, and Gemma who rolled up her jacket sleeves and put her hands on her hips like she was preparing for a duel. The normally marked wrists of the Chosen visible and bare.

Another sign that she wasn't like the rest of us. A revolutionary. A fighter.

A killer.

I didn't know what to think of her anymore. What to believe, my magic was as confused as my heart, both raging and flooding and screaming inside of me.

"Does it include levitating you, because I could get behind that." More than a few students laughed, then gasped, as a blast of wind moved between the isles, rushing right toward the teacher with clear intent.

My chair ground against stone as I stood, sending the old metal thing to the ground as I waved my hand and banished her wind, the magic fading into nothing. Papers, hair and everything else that the foolish gust had picked up falling to the ground like lead weights as I stood there, facing Gemma and her smug smile.

The same smile as in my dream. When she faced the army. When she beheaded my brother. The memory of the images grew stronger as my head spun, tiny hairs on the back of my neck picked up with the warmth.

"I won't let you do that," I growled, unsure of which Gemma I was talking to, and what exactly I was going to stop.

The girl of now.

The girl of later.

Her smile faded as my scowl deepened, leaving the two of us in a stand-off, our magic buzzing through the air. I had felt her magic before, felt the strength of it, the way it warmed the air and danced playfully against my own, both of them humming with the power of the earth. Before, my magic had rejoiced at that touch, fire moving through my veins.

Now it felt tarnished, dead, against me. Everything felt dead.

Dead and warm and... My head spun and I clamped my eyes shut slamming myself back into my seat in what I was sure she would register as defeat.

Right then, there were worse things than losing a pathetic stand-off with her.

"You are dismissed!" Lexia bellowed when other students began to show up, eyes wide in confusion as to what they had walked in on.

"Poor Princey," Gemma scoffed in her usual taunt as she turned on her heel and went back to her desk.

I was the first one out the door, bolting towards my defense class, wishing it would feature Uncle Ryland and a place to blow off steam. Maybe I could convince Professor Diarius to let me demonstrate something.

Like blowing something up.

"Rowy?" That shriek was the last thing I needed right now, it ran through my spine, straightening every bone and snapping every muscle together in preparation for the onslaught.

It came before I was ready for it, the tiny body and spindly arms of Sia Demarco wrapping around me from the back, her fingers pecking at the buttons on my blazer like a hungry bird. She would starve before I let her continue that.

"Hi, Sia," I sighed, removing her from my back and moving around to face her, which was ultimately more dangerous, as she immediately went for a kiss. I held her down, large hands on her smaller ones as I held her in place. Thank god she didn't fight me that time.

"Is everything alright?" She asked in a voice that was too reaching, even for her. "I was getting so worried! I had our whole weekend planned, I even got us tickets to a show in town, 'My Prince, The Hero'." It took everything to keep the smile on my face. "But then after class on Friday, I couldn't find you. Did you go back to Imdalind? To see your family? I would have liked to see them again. Next time make sure you take me, you are supposed to be escorting me, you know."

Sia, in Imdalind, at a family dinner. There was no chance in a million burning apocalypses that I would let that happen. If only to protect Angie from her ego.

"It's nothing like that," I said, continuing on our trek toward class, cringing as she wrapped her hand around mine, her skin was clammy, like she had been licking her palm.

"Then where were you, I was so worried?" So, fucking nosey.

I was actually surprised that she hadn't shown up at my room and dragged me out to the show dinner, or whatever it was she had planned. Then again, she probably tried. It usually took one of my siblings jumping in my bed or ripping my door off its hinges to wake me up most days. Which, now that I was thinking about it might be why I slept so long. Having no one there to wake me up equals long uninterrupted hours of sleep. This whole Academy thing actually might be better than I thought. If I could work out an excuse to where I vanished to for days at a time.

"Rowy?" She prodded, tugging on my arm and pulling me out of my thoughts. "Where were you?"

"Sleeping," I spoke without thinking, so much for coming up with some epic excuse. I guess convincing her the Eternals were actually part of some spy network was out. Of course, I highly doubted that lie would help smooth things over with the Chosen.

"Sleeping?" I wasn't sure if she was curious or disgusted. Time to get this back on track.

"Yeah, that or throwing up. I wasn't feeling well." I had never seen Sia move so fast, especially when it involved stepping away from me.

"Ew," she gasped, her face tangling into disgust as she wiped her palms on her plaid uniform skirt. Man, if that got her to move that fast then I needed to pretend to be sick more often.

I had found my excuse. Everyone had been spreading rumors I was chronically ill for years, time to embrace the horrible, vomit-filled reality.

"Yeah, it was awful," I sighed dramatically and forced a cough as she took another step back. "It's gotten worse since I came here too. My body had to acclimate to living above ground or something." It was bullshit, but she was still looking at me like I was going to hurl all over her. It was a beautiful sight. "I'm still not feeling the best, but I didn't want to miss any more school."

I forced another cough, wishing there was a way to make myself turn a natural green color. Didn't matter, I had clearly already taken it far enough.

"You poor baby," she crooned the words, wrapping her hand around mine, although she still kept a solid foot between us. "Let me know next time, I can have someone bring you soup or something."

I bit back my laugh. The extent of Sia's caring for someone was sending a maid to deliver soup. Heartwarming.

"Yeah, I will." Another cough escaped as we reached the door to the courtyard for our Defense and Healing class, the massive wood door swinging open and giving Sia a quick escape route from me and my germs. She blew me a kiss as she skipped off to her sparring partner. I had a feeling that she wasn't going to be coming any closer for a while.

Professor Diarius was already lecturing about the different shield types, but paid no attention to either my or Sia's late arrival. She prattled on as I climbed the long steps toward what had become my usual spot and the girl who was enchanting spitballs to slam into the side of Sia's head.

It should have been funny. I should have smiled, but I

couldn't. It was the same as before, when she had stood up to Lexia. All I could see was that dream.

All I could see was her ripping my brothers head off as she laughed.

All I could see was her spitting at my father's feet as they put her in shackles after the Gauntlet.

All I could hear was my brother's voice naming her as the enemy in that blood-soaked hall. As he claimed she wanted to kill us all.

She turned to me, smiling with something I couldn't place, the grin sending my magic into overdrive, even as my heart froze. As I froze.

Her smile faded as I stood there, staring, everything pulling me in two directions.

I said nothing before I turned and walked out of the classroom, leaving the lecture, and the girl behind me, sure the grin had been just a shadow of the dream, and praying that she didn't want to kill me, too.

9

———

GEMMA

"Get up you turd," I snarled under my breath, elbowing Eddy in the side. He was inches away from collapsing onto the pile of books in front of him, the drool that was dripping from his mouth already pooling on the old leather cover.

He didn't move. He grunted and shifted down, more drool dripping onto the lake he was slowly building. Professor Analine, or Anal-line as I had started calling her, was facing the blackboard, a map labeled "Spain" pulled in front of it. Wherever that was. I didn't care about most of this stuff, anyway. I did care about Eddy not getting in trouble. We had survived a month in this torturous hell, I was determined to make it two. I still hadn't figured out what detention was, but I was sure it would be hard to continue the revolution from it.

Anal-line was still facing the map, but was due to spin around with some punctuation about the battle she was talking about any second.

"There were an estimated four hundred thousand Trpaslíks who stood with Edmund, facing only seven of our men. We were clearly outnumbered, even more so seeing as the Queen's brother Dramin was only months away from death and unable to fight..."

Death. Destruction. Epic battles. Professor Analine was drawling on like she was half dead herself. No wonder he fell asleep.

"Hey, ass-hat," I snarled right in his ear. "Wake up!" I prodded him again, sending a slight spark of magic into his rib cage. This time it had the desired effect.

"Catch the rat!" He jerked himself awake, arms jerking forward and sending the books on his desk right into the head of the Golden brat that was sitting in front of us.

The girl howled in pain as a corner of a book rammed into her neck, everyone around us turning with varying looks of horror on their faces. Eddy blinked himself awake, still mumbling about the rat stew that used to be his favorite.

Okay, so that hadn't gone the way I thought at all.

"Excuse me, Mr. ... Mr. Edward," Professor Krul began, hands folded over her chest in such a way that you really couldn't look anywhere but at her long blood-red nails as they tapped against her floral print shirt. Blood and flowers. It was a slightly horrifying image.

Eddy flung around at the sound of the dumb name everyone still thought was his, eyes blinking furiously as everything came into focus. The shock on his face faded to horror as Professor Krul stepped closer to the back of the room where I and my people had segregated ourselves.

I had originally been sitting in the middle of the pretty sparkling golden brats for this class, but after Prince Rowan had turned into a giant royal dick, I had moved myself to the back. Something that the Krul didn't fight over even though these were supposed to be assigned seats for the year.

It was safer back where the air didn't feel like some kind of black weight was pressing against me.

I could still feel it. It just wasn't as bad when he sat five rows away, staring at me with giant purple bags under his eyes. Looks like he needed to do another of his week-long disappearing acts soon.

Rowan's inability to act like a human was not the problem. The raging bitch that was storming through the aisles toward us, was.

"Shit," I groaned, resisting the urge to send her across the room before she got much closer. She had murder in her eyes, a look I sent right back as I leaned over the weird U-shaped desk. Yes, there was nothing more than a sliver of wood between us, and yes, she could nail me to the wall in two blinks, but I wasn't about to let her touch any one of my people.

She ignored me completely, moving right to Eddy who had now sunk into the tiny desk like the thing could hide him. It couldn't.

"It appears you have something to say," Professor Analine drawled in that same condescending tone she had used on that very first day. "I am sure the sprawling knowledge that you received in your underground home school has taught you much about this Abby and its historical significance. Care to share with the class?"

She gestured around her, but not to us, just to the Goldens behind her. They all broke into rolling giggles, the mocking sound echoing against the walls from everyone. Well, everyone but the Prince who was still staring with an expression that made me wonder if he had been punched rather than just forgotten how to sleep.

"Well?"

God, did she have to make it harder for me to restrain myself?

I was officially fuming, my fingers curled around the edge of the desk as the smell of burning wood drifted through the air. It was probably good my magic was restrained, or I would have exploded the desk in her face by now.

"Professor," one of the goldens near the front of the class said, raising her hand like she was trying to get her attention. "I believe that Drains don't have school. They come uneducated. Which is why they are all assigned basic Reading and Arithmetic classes upon enrolling."

"Oh, I know." Their tones made it clear that they both knew.

We all knew. We were the ones that had to sit through that damn class every day. Yes, our math and reading might be lacking, but we weren't children. The teacher, Toper Smythe, was still 'teaching' us to count.

It made me want to punch something.

Like Analine who was smiling at me like her grin could cut her face in half.

"Which is why I'm surprised Mr. Edward here has such sprawling knowledge to share," Professor Analine continued, looking down her nose at us. "Unless, of course, he was simply sharing a recipe for rat stew."

More laughter rattled around the classroom, the Goldens giving each other high fives, like they had won some great argument. The Undermortals around me, however, were looking as furious as I felt. Rage darkened their features, tension and magic swirling through the air as everything threatened to explode.

"Seeing as you know so very much. Why don't you tell us the history of Rioseco?" She smiled. Her grin, matched with that nose, was making her look like one of the monsters I used to think hunted the subway tunnels at night after all the children were tucked into their beds. She was as evil as that, anyway.

This room was about to explode and she didn't even care.

Someone needed to get this under control. Seeing as she wasn't about to act like the adult in this situation...

"Rioseco is an ancient abbey located in the middle of," I checked the map again just to make sure, "Spa-in." I sounded out and a few people chuckled. I ignored them, plowing on. "It was where one of the largest battles in the Great War was fought. It was also where our king and queen were married... eh, bonded," I gave Rowan a pouty look as I forced a tear to fall over my cheek and looked toward the sky like a love-sick teenager. I even added a sigh to my montage, surely that was appropriate. Rowan glared and turned away from me, the muscles in his back pulling through his white shirt. Jerk.

"It's where the school is located now," I continued, ignoring the still flexing muscles in Rowan's back. "It's all relovited--"

"Renovated," someone hissed behind me and I quickly amended myself. But it was too late, the Goldens were back to their giggling. Screw them. I gave Analine a bigger grin.

"Did I miss anything?"

"Yes." She sounded like she was turning into a snake.

"Yes? Like that someone died here or something?"

"Like the fact that I had directed the question to your friend here." I think I got spit in my face with how she was leaning over me, snarling at spluttering like she was.

"Oh, whoops," I said, as innocently as I could. I even batted my eyes a few times. "I didn't know. I mean, I've never been to school and all."

This time it was the Undermortals turn to laugh, and Analine's turn to fume and storm away. The stomps of her ugly black heels drowned out by the bell that announced the end of class.

It didn't escape my notice that Rowan was the first one to get up and rush out, like always.

"Two pages on the history of Rioseco. Due Monday!" She roared as everyone gathered their stuff, the groans of the class multiplying as several people shot me a dirty look. Like the essay was my doing? Idiots. Anal-line got the name for a reason, she would have assigned it anyway.

I did the only thing I could think of. I smiled, waved, and blew a kiss to one especially glowering Golden. The smoke flowing out of her ears was not a good look.

"Please tell me you have worked out how to get the food out of here," Eddy hissed under his breath as he shoved his drool covered book in his bag. "I think it would make this a whole lot easier if we were actually doing something to stand up to these bastards."

"Not yet," I grumbled, face falling as the last of the Goldens rushed out, leaving me with no one to antagonize.

"Well get on it. I know one person you can ask." He gave one quick look to the side, toward the woman who was seated behind her desk, sipping tea and glowering at papers like most of the Golden's did.

Seemed like a pretty bleak future if that's what was waiting for us. Scowls and paperwork.

"You can't be serious." I was going to be sick.

"You know how important this is, Gem, and your friendly neighborhood prince officially has a stick up his ass. Unless you want to call up your BFF the Queen, it's time to change tactics." I had a feeling Eddy's statement was more warning than I was used to from him.

I waited until he turned his back to let out an exhale.

It wasn't exactly like I had been dragging my feet, but he was right. The douchebag prince I had been hoping to ask had suddenly stopped staring at me, talking to me. Even started avoiding me. In defense class yesterday he gave me one-word answers and kept enough space between us to let a flood of rats through.

So much for getting on his good side and weaseling my way closer to where I needed to be.

Maybe it had something to do with the fact that he was sick all the time. He missed more classes than he was in them. Or maybe it was the fact that his girlfriend and I had turned into arch-nemesis and in a rage of jealousy she demanded he stay away from me. That one was more likely.

He was a prince. Correction, he was a douche who did not deserve a second thought, or my worry. I shoved the last book in my bag with a bit too much force and made my way to the front of the classroom.

Oh god, this was going to hurt.

"Excuse me, Professor," I put on the tiniest, meekest, voice I could, trying to tap into my inner Golden, which was much harder than it should be. I only ended up feeling like I was made up of lies and vomit.

Okay, maybe I was doing it right.

Professor Analine looked up, a smile on her face. Well, until she saw it was me. Then she went right back to organizing whatever it was she was working on.

"What do you want?"

I was actually surprised she didn't call me a Drain. It took every bit of muscle not to roll my eyes at the tone in her voice, though my lip might have curled into a sneer. Thank god she was looking at her papers again.

"I was actually wondering if you might tell me how I can get an audience with the Queen?" I was barely able to get the question out before she laughed with a loud mocking sound that echoed off the stone walls of the empty classroom, pulling the focus of a few students who were passing by the door.

"The Queen?" She was laughing so hard now that her question was more of a shriek. I really needed to find a way to vent my frustrations that wasn't violence. Otherwise, this ladies face was going to be mince by graduation. "You think you can see the queen? You think the queen will want to see you?"

"Well, I have already seen the Queen." I began, physically forcing my snark down my throat as if it was that vile leaf stew they kept serving us. "We had a nice conversation about the weather, bombs, and the future. It was quite lovely. She said that if I needed anything to ask, as Rowan isn't talking to me anymore--"

"Rowan was talking to you?" She was on her feet in a flash, hands flat against the surface of the table as she stared into me.

She seemed genuinely concerned. Disgusted even. I mean, it wasn't surprising. She hated me and keeping me and my kind away from her precious prince was clearly a priority. I still took a step back on principle. You couldn't just show up at some fancy school and leave behind the war zone you were raised in, everything about her screamed 'warning'. Plus, I had a better angle to flip the desk in her face if the conversation went that way. I wasn't ruling anything out.

"Yes, and other students, and the teachers, and his na-- girlfriend," I quickly amended, she was still a nasty ass, but Analine looked ragey so best to keep it simple.

That calmed her down and she settled back down in her seat, going through papers and banging drawers open and closed in an orchestra of frustration.

"Anyway," I was hesitant, something was up with her. I mean she was always kind of the head of the bitches, but I had clearly struck a nerve. "Seeing as The Prince," I made a special effort to emphasize the title, "isn't talking to me, and the Queen offered to help. I was wondering if you could help me get her a message."

Analine continued shuffling the papers, clearly ignoring me now. She was dumber than rocks if she thought she could get rid of me that easily. I stood there, absolutely still, absolutely silent.

I could stay like this all day if I needed to. It was a skill any Undermortal needed to master at a young age. When the Tarns and the CCC were raiding the tunnels any noise could get you found. Any noise could get you shipped off to The Wastelands or worse.

The wait was on. Although, to make it more interesting I did loudly sniffle every few minutes. That did her in.

"What is it?" She exploded, slamming her fists against her desk after about only four extra snotty, inhales. I cleared my throat like it was a banner of victory.

"The other Undermortals and I would like to take leftover food from the kitchen to our communities on the weekends. It's going to waste here and it could do good back home. We would need help to get it there, and seeing as you guys have all those shiny vans..."

She looked up, her head snapping to attention as she narrowed her eyes at me. Yeah, I knew this was a kamikaze mission, but no turning back now.

"Can you please do that for me, professor? I need your help," I said, putting on the glittering voice of a Golden again. Her hands tightened around the paper she was holding, singeing the edges.

"Why of course, anything for the Queen." She smiled, I smiled, adjusted the strap on my bag and ripped myself out of the cold, empty room and into the bare halls towards my next class. I was clearly already late, not that it mattered. The whole thing had been worthless.

Both of us knew she wasn't going to do a damn thing about getting that message to the Queen. I would have to get the prince to talk to me again. Or figure out how to get an audience with the headmaster.

It would have to be the headmaster if only because the look Rowan gave me as I walked into Professor Stones class made it clear he wanted nothing to do with me.

Don't worry, dude, the feeling was mutual.

Even though the feeling was starting to break up inside me.

10

ROWAN

'I SIGNED YOU UP FOR RUGBY. DON'T COMPLAIN OR I'LL TELL YOUR dad. - Uncle Ry'

The note was taped to my door when I stepped out to go to class this morning. There must have been a meeting last night, it was the only reason I could see Uncle Ryland coming to the school in the middle of the night on a Tuesday. I would have been pissed that he didn't stop by and say hello, seeing as my light was clearly on, but he was supporting my delusion that everything was okay and normal in my life. Even if my mom wasn't.

'Don't forget the mug' was scrawled on the back of the same note, the loopy handwriting one I would recognize anywhere.

I didn't know if I should send them menacing notes back, or just thank them. Well, thank Uncle Ryland. The mug was still tucked away at the bottom of my underwear drawer. It was staying there.

Ryland, however, seemed to be tapped into my long hours. Rugby was needed.

Between the purgatory of being dragged around by Sia, dodging her kisses and roaming hands, or being stuck in my room for endless nights and dodging the blood-filled dreams there hadn't been much for me at this school. I had always been a bit of a loner, but without my family I hadn't realized how much I had been fooling myself.

The last month at Imdalind Academy had been one long haze. It wasn't until that note that I realized how lonely I was.

Trekking down the long sloping grass to the rugby pitch, I took a deep breath and let my lungs burn in the crisp air, the moisture announcing that autumn wasn't that far off. Living in the caves of Imdalind my whole life meant that I didn't often see sunrises, I didn't often get to feel the crispness of the morning, when the air was filled with dew and the sweet tang of changing seasons. The air was buzzing with power, the deep energy of the earth lifting every hair on my arms, pushing its way into me.

The deep magic recognized me, just as I recognized the magic that gave me so much power. The power of a Drak. I shook my head, trying to dislodge all of the eager want that was trying to take hold and sprinted down the rest of the sloped lawn to the one thing that probably wouldn't bore me completely.

I knew Rugby. Rugby was Uncle Ryland's sport. He had taught everyone he could through the years. It was pretty much the only sport that was played anymore, the championship games and cups occurring nearly year-round. The game had mutated from what he had known, magic even being allowed in some clubs now.

A loud part of me hoped that the school club embraced the magic rules. I was desperate to do something other than cast basic skills and throw invisible bits of chalk at the blackboards when the teachers weren't looking. Judging by the way the players were jumping twenty or so feet in the air, I was in luck.

I had never played on an official team, but I had played with my family since I was old enough to hold a ball. This wouldn't be much different, except for softer when you get taken down. The stone pitch in the underground caves was rough on landings, I had broken my wrist more than a few times.

Unfamiliar faces turned to me as I grew closer. I hadn't seen any of the players in classes. They must all be third or fourth years. Even better. I wouldn't have to hold back. That lack of recognition didn't go the other way, unfortunately. With each step I took to them their eyes grew wider, the whispers starting as they gestured to those around them to look. Like I was some kind of circus sideshow. A tall kid with an absolute mop of blonde hair on his head fumbled the ball and went down, the guy next to him pushing him to the side as they both stared slack-jawed at me.

Great, it was like every other class and public appearance, thankfully this time I could actually say something to stop their gawking. They all looked like idiots.

"I guess it's not girls that turn into fly traps around a prince," I said the second I was within earshot. They all closed their mouths as though they had been remote controlled that way.

"Boys! Come on now! It's time to settle down, that's enough," A man who was rushing over to us yelled, clearly trying to call the silent boys to attention. Not that they needed it. No one was talking. They were all still staring.

The man who had yelled came closer. I recognized him at once. Thatcher Willems, a former Rugby player that used to front for Old Toomes South if I remembered correctly. He hadn't played for years. Looks like he had ended up at Imdalind Academy, as coach judging by the whistle around his neck.

"Ahhh!" He said, recognition dawning on his face. "I was hoping you would show up! I spoke to your Uncle last night; we are glad to have you here Rowan."

"Glad to be here," I said, taking his hand. "Glad to meet you, as well. I was a huge fan of yours and I'm excited to learn and play with you all."

A few snickers echoed from the back of the boys, bodies jostling as the whispers returned. I hadn't even realized I was putting on the formal prince voice. Thankfully none of it fazed Thatcher. He thanked me and turned back to the now whispering team.

The upside of meeting people who knew my family, or had been in a position of power in their own lives, was that they actually saw me as a real person.

"As I am sure most of you recognize our new player, but for the sake of formality, I would like to introduce you all to Rowan Krul, our new Fly Half." Thatcher clapped me on the back, jerking me forward as he beamed at the rest of the team with his own brand of pride.

The look was reflected in gaping stares and wide smiles as rippling arms pulled tight over equally as built chests. I would say they were all happy for my appointment, except that they all kept glancing between me and another player. A tall powerfully built guy who was covered in so much dirt that if it wasn't for the sweat I wouldn't be able to tell where the dirt ended and his dark skin began. He had clearly been there a while.

And I was taking the position he had been hoping for.

Except that no one was too fussed about it.

"All right," Thatcher said before anyone could protest, shoving me toward the boys who stepped aside and let me stumble into the middle of them. "Since Rowan is already dressed down, let's scrimmage!"

He blew his whistle once and everyone moved toward the pitch, more than a few shoulders and knees knocking into me as they made their way toward the center of the field. Let the hazing begin.

"I don't think they can help themselves," a deep voice said

from behind me. I threw my gear to the side of the pitch and turned to the last guy I expected to see. The massive dirt-covered man stood there, wiping the sweat and mud from his face with a rag that might as well be a permanent shade of brown with how much he was pulling off.

"Greer Darkly," he introduced himself, holding out a hand to me. It was only then that I saw the twists of a dragon tattoo over his arm.

An Undermortal.

The same images from my dreams pressed into me, but I pushed them away. He wasn't in them after all. He wasn't the one with his hands wrapped around my brother's neck.

"Rowan," I said, taking special care to pronounce my given name only, hoping that he wouldn't try to tack a 'Prince' on there for good measure.

He took my hand greedily, even squeezing rather than giving me the fish-shakes that most people did.

"Looks like I took your spot. Sorry about that."

"Don't worry about it," he said, batting the air away as we walked toward where everyone else was starting to link together. "I think I'll enjoy the next few days of not getting tackled every few minutes."

He smiled, trying to make his comment a joke but the joy on his lips was dead in his eyes. It pierced right through me, the breeze that was ruffling my hair feeling even colder than it had a minute ago.

"That rough?" I asked, ignoring the calls of the team behind me.

"Nah, they don't like anything different than them," Greer said, going back to wiping the mud off his neck. "But who does really? We are all here, fighting for what we love. Some of us are just trying to fight for something better."

"Get your ass over here, your highness. Leave the Drain

alone," one of the boys yelled over, everyone snickering and cutting off what I was about to say.

"You better get over there before talking to me gets you face-down in the mud," he smiled again, the emotion still trapped in the corners of his mouth, maybe it was dragged away by the suddenly icy breeze.

"That'll never happen," I knocked him with my elbow, the action inciting more yells and more catcalls from the already prepping team.

I made to run and join the scrimmage and start the game, but Greer didn't move. "Aren't you coming?"

"Nah, you only need one fly half," he said with a white-toothed grin, laughing as he wiped more mud off the back of his neck. "Besides, they got me pretty good last time."

"Next time, I'll switch you," I said, getting an actual smile from him. "Talk to you later, Greer."

I made sure to use his name, letting the word carry in the wind and drown out the derogatory comments I was running into.

My magic buzzed as I linked up with the boys, pressing my shoulders against the others as we prepared for coach to make the call.

"Finally, he stops asking the Drain to wipe his royal ass long enough to join us." Everyone laughed at the disembodied voice, the scrimmage shifting and moving right into me.

"Here I was thinking they were replacing the Drain with a real man, instead we get a Drain lover," someone to my left said, the mockery triggering more than a few snickers.

"He's no pussy! You've seen him with that Demarco, girl," another voice bellowed as we slowly began to shift, bodies pressing together as the scrimmage began. "Takes a man to control that whip."

They all laughed. I tried to join in, but the strong wisps of magic I had felt in the air earlier were growing stronger, triggering the sparks at the back of my neck. I pushed the magic away, shoving the wind and power and everything I didn't want as far away as I could get it. I was going to enjoy this.

Enjoy a regular game, with regular magic. Even it meant the lie about Sia Demarco was following me around like bad gas.

"That girl's gorgeous, have you seen her in spells? So strong. I heard she slept longer than anyone."

"Three weeks," I reluctantly provided when more than one head turned my way in question.

"Damn," a freckled kid right beside me said. "That's strength. Bet she matches you pretty well. Eternal blood and a strong Chosen soul. As it should be. None of those damn Drains, we showed them in the end. They can't tear us down, the Eternals won't let them. Isn't that right Rowan?"

They all laughed again, the riotous sound cutting deep. It physically hurt to force the smile that time, the reality of everything my father had said, and everything my father had forced me into beginning to settle in my heart. Healing ties. He had hoped for healing ties.

Except it only appeared to be creating a different sort of rift between them. The Goldens, the Drains, and me somehow lodged in the middle. I wasn't healing anything, especially with Sia on my arm. I was only empowering them more.

"That's enough, boys!" Thatcher's voice boomed over all of us. "Save the talk and show the prince what you're made of."

"Goldens forward!" They all yelled in unison, everyone moving the second the coach blew his whistle.

Shoulders, feet, and more than one elbow pressed together, everyone grunting as we moved back and forth until the ball moved into play and we broke apart. I didn't get more than two steps before I was slammed into the mud, face full of muck as they all trampled behind me.

I was more out of practice than I thought.

"Stay away from the Drain or you'll end up looking like them."

Or maybe not.

"Feet up!" Coach said, pulling me up and slapping me on the back, sending a spray of mud everywhere. "We finally have a full team, prince. Let's play like it!"

I ran after the others, my eyes drifting to the side of the pitch, and to Greer, who was bent over a bag, its contents spread over the dewy grass. He shoved everything back in before turning to cheer his teammates on, even though pain was clear in his eyes. Just like Gemma's in so many of the dreams I had had over the years.

Just like in my dream, as she facilitated Talon's last breath.

Pain. Suffering.

'We are all here, fighting for what we love. Some of us are just trying to fight for something better.'

My mother had told me once that nothing was certain. That everything could change, even sight, that sometimes the things I would see, that Draks would see, were more of warnings. Warnings of what could come if something didn't change.

After all I had seen of Gemma and her life, after all we had done to fix it, nothing had changed. If anything, it had all become a whole lot worse.

Something had to change. I was starting to understand what.

Maybe my mom was right, maybe I had to stop being scared.

But first, I had to stop blaming Gemma for things she has never done.

Things she may never do.

11

———

GEMMA

"I THINK I FINALLY CONVINCED THE GHOSTLANDERS TO GET THEIR act together and stop being so selfish," Kara said as she slid between me and Ed and we all began our customary meander through old stone hallways to the atrocious remedial classes we were all forced to take.

The Goldens were all retreating to the grounds, or their dorms, or the underground sparring halls that the older students were allowed to use. They were all too busy with their egos to care about what all of us little Undermortals were doing. We were all dragging our feet to avoid the classes that had quickly become one of the most abhorred parts of our days.

Yes, I said abhorred, although Professor Smythe would still have you believe we couldn't read or understand more than 'Meet Jack, Jack sat on a cat. Jack's cat clawed his ass.'

"Good," Ed said, Geo coming up on the other side of him, the two waving to a girl as she passed them, looking the pair up and down. I gave him a look. "What? I'm allowed to appreciate a figure or a person. Doesn't mean I have wavered from my true love."

Eddy threw his arm around Geo's shoulders, the two

laughing and walking as they waved to anyone who crossed their path. Including an especially irritated Golden who looked confused as to how they had ended up in the remedial hall in the first place.

"So, they are on board?" I asked Kara, ignoring the two men who were now loudly gloating about how excited they were to learn to count to twenty today. I would have hissed at them to shut the hell up, but they provided the perfect cover.

"Yes." Kara smiled and gave me a nod. "They were the last holdouts, so everyone is on board, we are just waiting on that last piece..."

Damn, Kara had some wicked good side-eye. She had always been a good fighter. When she was a kid she had even stood up to a Tarn soldier, back before they had started to kidnap and haul us off to The Wastelands. Guess I knew how she had won against the armored lackey; she had probably scared the guy off with a look.

"You sound like Eddy," I said, trying to force a laugh, but the sound was dead and laced with the foul aroma of frustration.

It had been more than a week since I had hoisted my panties and asked Anal-line to get the Queen a message. Seeing as I hadn't heard anything, I was sure that letter went into the dark sarcophagus that she housed her soul in every night and never came out.

"Yeah, well, maybe you need to give that guy a shot again..."

"If 'that guy' is referring to his royal highness of salty looks and jackassery, I'm going to stop you right there." I held my hand up, the boys still being loud and boisterous even though most of the hall had cleared out. "I still have a couple tricks up my sleeve."

I gave Kara what I had assumed to be a conspiratorial wink, but the girl stared at me blank-faced, confused.

"Don't forget, Kara," Eddy hissed, finally having disconnected himself from Geo, "she's besties with the Queen. They had girl time and everything."

"Threats, possible torture and a forced agreement to bind my magic." Yes, I was fully aware I was growling. "If that's girl time I have no interest in being her bestie."

Or being alone with her in general, ever again. The memory of those few moments was still like a bad dream that was gnawing at my spine.

"Well, whichever royal you want to get in bed with, I don't care. We are all waiting on you," Kara said, hands over her hips as she angled herself in front of me, stopping me in place and forcing the thinning crowd to move around us. Voices and stomping feet mumbled around us like a diverted river.

"Don't worry. I got this, even if I have to get in bed with one of them, I'll do it. Wouldn't be the first time," I shrugged, trying not to think of the shocked expression on the Prince's face when I had let slip about that particular escapade. Not my fault they treat that stuff like some kind of silken virtue.

"Poor meat-head Adrian," Eddy mused as though he was giving a speech at a funeral. "His sacrifices will not be forgotten. Ow!"

I slugged the poor guy in the arm so hard he winced. Yes, I had totally put a little bit of magic behind that. Hopefully, it would leave a bruise.

"You deserved it. Baby," I snapped, Eddy still rubbing his arm and scowling as the bell rang and the last of the Undermortals began shuffling into their remedials classes. Heavy oak doors groaned loudly as they snapped shut, leaving me and Ed standing in the middle of the musty stone hall.

"You coming?" Eddy asked, taking a few steps toward the still open door of Topher Smythe's classroom.

"Not yet," I gave him a smile and shifted my bag, the heavy

math books pulling at my shoulder. "I think Professor Smythe would miss my raucous arrivals. I can't be on time yet."

Our snickering laughs filled the now empty hallway as Eddy turned with a wave, vanishing into the overfilled classroom and I went about my usual time-killing hallway stalking, listening to the hum of voices and the buzz of magic that bled through the doors. Normally I would amuse myself with trying to identify which person each magic belonged to, but today I was having trouble focusing past the problem that didn't want to leave me alone.

Getting the food to the Undermortal communities and getting this whole mess started. Analine was a bust, Rowan was a bust, which basically left the headmaster himself. Difficult considering, I hadn't seen the guy since the first day when he gave that weird speech at breakfast.

Cail it was then, unless I wanted to call up the queen and ask for help. She had said to let her know if "I needed anything."

Call me crazy, but I would rather go through a third party than take advantage of that. Going right to her and asking for help was like admitting I was working for her. I was only playing at being her double agent and had no intention of giving in to that crazy woman. Play along, get my magic back, and continue toward the goal I had set years before. Asking her directly was directly against that.

No, thank you. Now, I just had to hope that she couldn't read minds, too.

I grabbed a piece of bread out of my bag, munching on it as I turned a corner on autopilot, brain occupied with disappearing headmasters and secret meetings. I nearly collided head first with a wall of plaid skirts and resting bitch faces.

Sia Demarco and her sheep standing still, arms over their waists as if they were waiting for me. They were standing in a line, like a plaid barricade. A plaid barricade of bitches.

The Bitchicade. I was so saving that.

"Oh god, did I walk into the bitch convention on accident? I am so sorry, let me back up, I'm sure there is a hallway that isn't full of shit around here," I sneered, knotting my face up in false disgust as I squished the bread in my fist. The softness hardened into a rock in one tiny flare of my magic.

"The only hallway that's full of shit is yours." So much for backing up, that froze me in place. It was clear she hadn't meant it that way, but bless her heart, Sia was loyal to her crappy comeback. Even if her crony's where all trying to stifle a laugh.

"Okay," the words stretched out as I tried to figure out something smart to respond with. "Sorry, I got nothing. I'll see you guys around."

I waved in what I assumed was goodbye, ready to turn and strut my way into class. I knew I was late now. I didn't get more than a step or two when a wild wind wrapped around me, tugging at my hair and blazer and trying to pull me back.

Ahhh. The Bitchicade had come for payback for me breaking Sia's nose and humiliating her in class and probably a few other things. Well, I couldn't say I hadn't seen this coming. Predictable bitches. I could handle this. I totally cracked my knuckles.

"Do you really want to do this?" I asked, letting my bookbag drop to the ground. "I mean, I'm three for zero, Sia. Do you really want to make it four?"

"No, your three for nothing." She smiled, her friends smiled I was left standing there, staring at them in confusion.

"Yeah... that's what I said." I mumbled under my breath. The more I was around her, the more I was starting to think she was as dumb as rocks. Either that or I was missing something about above-ground living that made every single bizarre thing about her make sense.

"I mean, you're nothing," she snarled, flipping her hair

before she took a few steps closer to me. "You don't belong here. You and your Drains keep strutting around here, thinking you belong. You don't. It's high time you realized that."

She took another step, her eyes darkening as her hand opened, sparks of what looked like yellow fire jumping between her fingers. That was more intense than a few days ago, good to know my resident bully hadn't been idle.

"It's time you pay for what you did to me. It's time you learn your place."

"As the best in class?" I took every ounce of strength to keep my face impassive, even as she growled like some kind of wild animal.

She flung her fiery yellow magic at me before I could really do much more than dodge and throw the nugget of stone bread at her face. Yellow fire ripped passed my head as the hard bread-stone hit her right between the eyes. She yelped and stumbled back, taking two wide steps before she regained herself.

"Dumb bitch," she snarled, patting at the dried blood that was oozing from the new cut in her forehead. Whoops. "I knew I should have thrown you off that cliff first."

"Why? So, it can be one and three?" Angry waves of magic rumbled underneath the surface of my skin, they pooled through my veins ready for use. Ready to pick them all up and throw them away from me again. Finally.

One smack on the head with a lightning bolt ought to shut her up. Except that nothing happened, no flare. No fire.

The waves of rage I had felt before had died completely down.

"Hell fucking sewer rats," I mumbled, dodging her next attack, using only a bit of wind to move it to the side as I took a lazy step back. Well, if I couldn't attack her, I could sure as hell play with her.

And dodge. And hope to hell she didn't burn my jacket. I had spent way too much time perfectly ripping the seams. I had a feeling she had been practicing to break through my shield.

Something that I couldn't even tap into seeing as my magic was locked away, again.

"You know, if you anticipate where your target is going and aim there you have a better chance," I yelled, watching her follow my instructions. I back stepped the second she sent an attack toward me, the thing missing again. Although, it did tug and burn a bit of my jacket before slamming harmlessly into the wall.

Shit. Figures.

Well, maybe not harmlessly. Some shattered stone fell to the ground, although it kinda looked like it had been attacked at some point in the past.

"Better, Sia! Try again!" Another attack, another step. Clearly, one week was not enough time for her to figure out how to do more than throw fire.

"You don't get to take my life away from me, away from any of us. You don't belong here, you belong underground. In any way I can manage it."

Well, that was darker than I expected.

I dodged one more attack, the sparks hitting against the back wall with little more than a sizzle.

"Shame. I thought you almost had me." I clicked my tongue at her, giving her a wink that only infuriated her more.

Rage was glowing her eyes, burrowing as she growled and heaved and took a quick step closer.

"All the glitters were never gold." I continued, letting my smile spread.

Okay, that time I might have gone too far.

Her hand raised as she screamed, bits of spit flying from her mouth, dripping over her nose and catching in the light of the magic that she was clearly hoping to kill me with.

"What are you doing, Sia?" The deep boom was unfamiliar, but the power behind it I had felt before. At the Gauntlet, in that little room after I had thrown a boulder on Sia's head.

But I had not felt the magic from him. Not from the guy with jet black hair and burning green eyes that seemed to be gleaming in the dim light of the hall. He looked as disheveled as I was. Hair a mess, jacket forgotten, tie pulled down. I swallowed and looked away, not liking the way my magic was heating. Not in a rage, either. Oh, hell no. I was not about to become a walking cliché.

"She attacked me, Rowy!" Sia shrieked, immediately beginning to cry.

Really? Did she not have any other card to play? Crying is her go to?

"I attacked you?" I shrieked, pushing myself back to standing now that whatever weight I had been hit with was gone and most of the older students had scattered. "I can't do anything but make a few sparks."

Of course, my supposed display at my weakened powers chose that minute to flare into a sparkling orb of swirling color, crackling and shining from the tips of my fingers.

"Really? Now you work?"

Was I imagining it, or did the corner of Rowan's mouth turn up?

"How did she attack you?" Rowan asked as I grabbed my bag and threw it over my shoulder, ready to high-tail it out of there. Leave Rowan to deal with his weasel of a girlfriend.

"She was waiting for me on the way to class, she and that guy, the fat one..."

"Fat?" I knew who she was talking about. Like hell if I was going to let her calling Ed fat slide. I was up and barreling through the hall, ready to break her nose again, but Rowan stopped me, one flat palm and a flare of magic freezing through me.

Okay, no. Prince or not, he doesn't get to come in and play puppeteer to my life.

"Let me go, pretty boy. I can fight my own battles."

"Get out of here, Sia." Rowan boomed, more dust falling from the ceiling. "When my family allowed you enrollment, we did so expecting you to uphold the values of the Chosen and to fit into the roll we have designed for you."

"You're dismissing me?"

"I expect better of you." Pretty sure the tone in his voice was rattling the rafters.

"My father will hear about this! You don't get to dismiss me," She snarled, little drops of spit flying in his face in her rage. He froze, eyes widening as she spun on her heels, taking two steps before he reached out and grabbed her, pulling her back.

"I'm not dismissing you, Sia. I'm telling you I'm disappointed. I will speak to you about this later."

"This is because you have a thing for--"

"This is because I am your Prince and value all life in my kingdom, those who I share my life with should have the same morals," He cut her off, every single word of that sentence stabbing and twisting in my gut, even he wasn't too pleased with it. Sia, however, lit up.

"Find me at dinner, Sia," Rowan said, that same commanding tone bleeding from him, bathing the stone and melting against Sia. The vile anger that I was so used to seeing on her face melting away and she smiled. She actually smiled.

He pulled her close to him, so close that from where I stood I could barely see her. It was just Rowan's torso, Sia's head, and four legs. Aww, they made such a cute two-headed monster when they kissed. Well, and all the time.

Sick. The two stared at each other like lovesick teenagers

before the beast who would be queen turned and left, leaving me alone with the Prince. The last place I wanted to be.

Stepping stone or not, I wasn't needing to bash his face in today. I was going to if I had to listen to one more second of his holy-man speech. I couldn't get out of that hallway fast enough.

"Aren't you going to say thank you?" He called after me, his voice echoing over the soot-covered stone, rattling the ash to the ground. I turned, but I didn't stop walking, keeping as much space between us as possible as he tried to catch up to me.

"Haha! No. I won't bow to you either. You don't get to be a rat's ass for more than a month and then come back in to a parade. You did nothing to deserve that." I couldn't even summon one of the shit-eating smiles I had been giving him. I was that pissed.

"I didn't ask you to do that." Was this guy for real? He clearly lived in another dimension. You know the one with white knights, and princesses, and parents, and food, and a perfect Utopia of bliss and ignorance.

"Yes, you did," I turned away from him, hitching the heavy bag onto my shoulder better. "The second you came in and saved the day you showed them all that you are better. Stronger. That you and your family control our life like puppets on a string. Everything in our life, right up to our death. I don't need any of that. I don't need any of you. I don't need a prince."

That last word burned on its way out.

"I saved you--"

"From what?" I was roaring now, my low voice sending him back a step. "Saved me from a punch in the gut and maybe a bit of singed hair? A broken bone? Oh! I know! The gunshots and stab wounds your armies have inflicted on us our whole lives." He looked as confused as his parents did, poor guy. "It's nothing I can't heal from. Nothing I haven't overcome before. I can fight my own battles. I will continue to rise above the shit of this world. You included. You can go back to not talking to me now."

He flinched and for a split-second, regret flooded my chest. It pulled me back and made my cheeks heat as I second-guessed everything. If I wanted a straight shot to the return of my magic, he was it.

This ego ridden, 'too handsome for his own good', bastard of an Eternal.

But just like his mom and her favor, I didn't care. Maybe I needed to go about this whole thing another way.

"I'm fighting for what's right. Standing up to one bitch with an ego and her mob doesn't make you a hero, Princey. It doesn't make you right, and it certainly doesn't deserve a thank you." I scoffed, curls bouncing over the shaved parts of my head as I turned on my heel, ready to leave him sputtering in the middle of the hallway.

Instead, I was stopped in place, his hand winding around my elbow. He pulled me back, his palm covering the torn jacket that usually hid my mark.

Everything stopped, the air shifted as though it was the one that was breathing.

His hand was hot, like the irons we use to cook the rats when they were left too long over the fire. That saturating heat was everywhere, it crackled over my skin, it ran through my veins and pooled in my chest with so much energy that I was afraid whatever Mira had put inside of me was going to break out. That my magic would shove it through my chest so that it could continue its race under my skin, continue to pull and press and drag me toward him.

Everything was magic. He was magic. I hated every bit of it.

"Don't touch me," I snapped, pulling away and staggering back as I tried to catch my breath. "I don't know what the hell you are playing at, or what that was. But don't do it ever again," I gestured to him wildly, I still wasn't able to get either breathing or heart rate under control right then. Even one step back was difficult, I was sure my knees wanted to buckle beneath me. My legs wanted to throw me back into him.

"It was..."

"Don't," I snapped. He was as breathless as I was and I really didn't want to hear the other side of that, of what the hell had happened. Or why he had tears dripping down his sexy face.

Ugh.

No. Not sexy. Nothing about this was sexy. Not tears. Not a prince. Certainly not the two of them together.

This was not in my wheelhouse.

I bolted down the hallway, toward my remedials class that at this point I had every intention of skipping.

"You're welcome," he called after me, but I kept running, not trusting myself to do anything right then.

I was either going to explode, or I was going to kiss him.

I hated myself for both of those options.

12

ROWAN

I HAD ORIGINALLY PLANNED TO SLEEP AFTER CLASSES LAST NIGHT. I had already told Sia that I wasn't feeling well and arranged with Greer to cover for me at Rugby practice. After last night, there was no way I was going to get to sleep. My mind was racing, magic buzzing in a furious rampage that by the time dawn crested the mountains I was finally able to gain control and the pressure at the back of my neck had dwindled down to a low hum.

Sleep was not happening, if only because I needed to make sure Gemma was alright. That she wasn't scared shitless after our magic had connected when I had grabbed her arm in the hall. Not that I was sure that's what had happened, or if she had even felt it. Either way, I needed to see her. To touch her again, to see if it would happen again. To make sure she was okay.

It was probably some kind of foolish 'white knight' bull shit that I had probably picked up from my dad, making sure the girl was safe, but even realizing that hadn't stopped me from getting to class a whole ten minutes early.

She clomped into our first class as she always did, although today, she was right on time. The bell hadn't even rung.

She was smiling, each step sending the streaming light from the windows glinting against a line of silver studs in her ear. The skull with sapphire eyes in her lobe was especially nice, it set off the purple in her eyes. I should have looked away, I knew I was staring, but I couldn't stop. Which is probably why instead of going to her desk, she came to mine.

"My liege thank you for saving me from the wicked bullies yesterday," she said as she bowed low, her near yells carrying over the class and pulling everyone's focus. The room went silent. "If you ever need any assistance, such as getting that stick out of your ass, or removing the parasite before she sucks the life out of your soul, I am at your beck and call."

Well, I guess she had recovered from yesterday.

The Undermortals at the back of the class roared in laughter, the Goldens gasped. I was left staring at her as she hopped over the aisle into her old desk, dirty boots propped up on the worn wood within seconds. Just like every morning. She gave me a wink as Analine entered, doing her best to silence the still laughing class.

"Thanks for that, Gemma," I said under my breath, grateful that my voice didn't catch on her name.

"Anytime, Prince Rowan." It was hard to ignore the way my stomach flip-flopped at that. "Of course, you might regret that now that you seem to think I'm not worth avoiding anymore."

Even I couldn't ignore the pang in her voice, the hostility that was breeding under the surface as she looked away, giving someone at the back a wink before turning forward again.

"Does this mean I'm still a half-douche?" I leaned over my desk, my lanky body blocking the aisle as I whispered to her, aware that all of the hopeful Goldens around us were listening in.

"Oh no, after the last month you will always be a full douche. You gotta like save the world or some shit to get back to half-douche." She gave me that bright smile that I realized I had missed, my stomach flip-flopping as she winked and turned to Analine who was already announcing today's task before even turning to the class.

My cousin was confused as I was that Gemma was back to her old seat, but thankfully said nothing about it. Good. How she treated the Undermortals sometimes grated on me, I doubted with how active my magic was I would be able to avoid standing up to her and not pulling rank if she was to try something.

Thinking about it was making me agitated and I started doodling monsters in the margins of my books as she began class.

"Today we will begin working on the recreation of the timeline of the first thousand years," Analine said, shuffling papers and handing stacks out to the first person in each row, who grabbed one before passing them back. "You will be working in pairs for this project so I suggest you choose your partner carefully as they will be responsible for half your grade."

She had barely finished speaking when the class broke into a buzzing, everyone partnering up, and every girl directly around me turning expectantly. They batted their eyelashes and flipped their hair in a wave of enchanted sparkles that I was sure was meant to ensnare me. I, however, had turned to the one person who was doing neither of those things and was instead staring at the questions on the paper with a curled lip.

"Who was Filare? Rat crap on a stick. Guess I should have been paying attention."

"Gemma," I hissed, the girls around me leaned in closer, like I had hissed their name. The girl in question, however, turned slowly, eyebrow tweaked as she gave me one of those smug grins.

"Yes, your majesty?" Damn it she even bowed a little bit, her hands waving to the side in what I was sure she thought was a flourish and not a bird trying to take off.

"Will you pair up with me?" I choked on the word, my voice cracking like I was going through puberty again. Of course, she didn't miss it.

"Pair up?" she repeated slowly. I could feel the color grow over my cheeks, turning me into a furnace and pricking at the back of my neck. "What do you mean by 'pair up' Rowan? Because I can do all the pairing. Name your price."

She was leaning over the wooden L of her desk now, her purple eyes glinting mischievously as my stomach swooped at the sound of my name. I was going to have to get her to go back to calling me Princey if this kept happening.

"I mean do you want to work with me on the program, Gemma," I tried to put as much seductive teasing into my voice as she had. Honestly, I was glad that I had kept my voice in a normal octave that time.

"I dunno," she said with feigned innocence, looking at all the blondes who hadn't given up hope on me yet. "Isn't there an application process or something?"

"Oh, be quiet and get over here," I groaned, letting my magic shift and wrap around the desk, pulling hers closer to mine with a groan that matched that of all the others doing the same thing. It was only then that all of the hopefuls retreated to their desks with a moan.

"Testy, testy. You know, you sound like an old lady," Gemma said, scooting her desk away a tad, the grind of metal against stone loud now that most everyone had paired up.

"No, I don't. Now get back over here," I said, trying to pull her back over to me, but she slapped my hand away. I jerked; I don't think anyone had reacted to me like that before. Correction: I don't think anyone had the guts to.

"I'm giving us a respectable distance, partially because I don't like to be seen too close to jerks or people who think girls are weak and need saving. But mostly because the wicked glare Professor Analine is giving me has me scared for the loss of my fingers." She gave me a smile, angling herself away from my cousin who was, sure enough, sending daggers right into the back of the girl's head. I could have sworn that even her curls were quaking in fear.

"Analine's harmless," I sighed, knowing it was only half true. "She's kind of always been a bitch."

"Always?" Gemma said, looking from Analine, to me, to the paper where her eyes went wide. "You know, I kinda forgot she was your cousin. Mostly because after getting escorted by Wynifred for a day I can't imagine how Analine came into existence. Well, unless they summoned her from hell."

"It's been a topic of debate for decades," I chuckled, even my mom at one point had theorized that she was just resentful that she wasn't that cool. "Kinda makes you rethink your whole douche ranking system doesn't it?"

"You know," Gemma said under her breath, tapping the eraser of her pencil against the corner of her mouth. "If Analine is the standard of ultimate douchiness. I think I can knock you down to a solid eighty percent douche. It fits you."

"Hey!" I jerked in my seat, speaking loud enough that a few people turned around.

"Accept it, Princey. You haven't worked your way back into my good graces yet."

"Yet, you paired up with me." I moved her closer to me, metal and stone grinding loudly. This time she didn't fight me, but she did throw her head back in a loud laugh that buzzed in the air. The sound of her laugh was almost as bad as my name on her lips. My stomach was swimming in eager nerves, the back of my neck swimming.

"Well, duh," she waved the paper between us. "This isn't

some psychological evaluation like in defense class. This is your family history. I just so happened to be doing the assignment with the answer key."

"Are you kidding me?" I hadn't really looked at the sheet before I had asked her. If I had, I might have opted out of this class in its entirety. For me, this class was more of a lesson as to what of our family history was shared in the public eye. I would be lying if I said I had paid even a slivers worth of attention. I suddenly had a feeling that Analine's glare hadn't been meant for Gemma, but for me. "Great, so we are essentially cheating."

"Hey, you're the one who asked me. It's all part of the path to saving the world and regaining your half-douche status." she smiled, tapping the first question on the paper that was between us. "Now, who is Filare?"

"My grandmother," I said absentmindedly, looking over the questions and the associated directions. *"Pick one of the above questions and create a presentation for the historical event. You can do a skit, a speech, a diorama, or a slideshow.'* A diorama? What the hell is a diorama?"

"This is amazing," Gemma giggled from beside me, hanging over her desk to look at the paper. I could feel her magic radiating from her, the power bleeding closer as if it wanted to press against mine and she wouldn't let it. I swallowed and pressed my power against my heart, very much aware that this was not the time or place for us to recreate what had happened last night. "I say we do a skit, and we do this one..."

She tapped the paper again and my heart fell to my toes as I read *'Detail how Ilyan and Joclyn's choice to be bonded changed the outcome of the war.'*

"Oh god."

"Oh yes," Gemma was still snickering, although her boots were up again, this time on my desk. "Straight A's here I come."

13

SIA

'Father.'

I could count the amount of times my father had called me on the phone on one hand. He had always preferred to send one sentence messages demanding different things, or setting expectations, or informing me of ways I could have accomplished tasks with better grace. But to call, and within the hour of school letting out for the day, this could mean nothing good.

Even so, my chest tightened in excitement, my magic flying into overdrive as I clenched my phone.

"I'll be right back," I mumbled to Miko and Tasha, the two only giving me a nod before they went back to their conversation. Although, I didn't miss Tasha's quizzical stare-down as I darted into an empty classroom on the left.

The girl had no patience. I sent her a crude gesture before closing the door behind me. But she only laughed.

Bitch.

Orange rays broke through grimy windows as the sun dipped under the wooded mountains. It would have been a lovely little escape if not for the frustration that was settling into the floorboards. The cramped room was piled with desks and covered with dust, I doubted anyone would be busting in, but I wasn't taking any chances. I locked and shielded the door, knowing my skill wasn't formed enough to block out sight or sound. Still, it would have to do.

"Hello?" I asked with an irritated sigh, holding the phone to my ear and scowling into the sunset.

"Hello, Sia," My father's voice rumbled through the speaker, the emotionless tone straightening my spine. "How is school?"

The guy was not fooling anyone.

I laughed, the harsh sound echoing off the empty desks, "Save the formalities father. I'm alone."

"Good. We need a status update for your task," he quipped, the line clicking as the shoddy service in this area gave way. I was actually amazed the call didn't drop. I slid into one of the dusty desks, my skirt riding up a bit.

"Which task?" I asked innocently, checking the room for open doors or listening ears.

"The one concerning your next-door neighbor." My heart picked up to a painful ratchet.

So, he knew that Gemma had been roomed right next door to me. No surprises there. He knew everything, although this time he was more meddling than informed.

I couldn't even be upset, the placement of the two of us together had been serendipitous. Especially last week, when I had realized that her late-night parties weren't parties at all.

"I take it that was your doing," I said with a malicious smile, the glee breaking into my voice. Leave it to my father to show his love for me by giving me easy access to the girl he wants me to kill.

"Of course. We need you to succeed, Sia. We cannot accept failure in this. Now, where are you in this task? I had expected to have the Drains to be sobbing in mourning by now."

That irritating tension that had been wrapping its way up my spine flowered into something like worry.

"There have been some roadblocks," I spoke quietly, my ear pressed to the phone as I strained to hear any sigh, any gasp of air that could warn me to his response. There was nothing but the spine wrenching sound of his teeth grinding together. Just the sound was ripping my spine apart from the tension.

"Roadblocks?" he hissed through his teeth, the speaker crackling. "Sia, we have trained you better than this. Do you really think you will be welcomed home if you fail us a second time?"

No.

I already knew the answer to that, they had been clear in that matter when I had lain in the caves of Imdalind, before the king had arrived to welcome me to magic. I wasn't dumb enough to think that his displeasure would end with my disowning.

He would rather see me dead than carry on his name in shame.

I would rather be dead than live with that. I had no interest in living a life if it wasn't one to pride my parents and carry on all that they have done for this world.

"I will not fail you." My promise bounced off the stone walls as I stood, the heels of my red strappy shoes clicking loudly in the dust as I paced.

"Then why isn't it done?" I was frozen in place, anger bristling at the snap. It was as if he had already decided the task was a failure.

That I was a failure.

The bastard. It wasn't as if I hadn't tried. I had, three times. Each time she had found a way to block me.

To beat me.

To humiliate me.

I wasn't about to tell him that. Instead, I let his

disappointment act like gasoline against my resolve, everything fanning into a rage.

"They didn't exactly teach us skills for killing on the first day, father." I was no longer attempting to calm the fury. I could feel it mixing with my magic, rippling over my skin as though it was its own flame. A living breathing rage that sparks from my fingers, rippled over my skin.

If only he could see, then he wouldn't be second-guessing me.

Professor Stone had said she had never seen such control in a first-year.

Perhaps I would pay him a visit and show him how strong his daughter was. Why he should trust in my abilities.

"Then don't rely on magic." His dead voice sunk through me, extinguishing both fury and magic as my hand dropped to my side.

"You wanted it to look like an accident, father. I can't exactly gouge her eyes out and expect people to think that I tripped." I extinguished my flame with a snap, snarling into the phone in my agitation. He laughed again, but the sound was heartless, he clearly didn't think the scenario was funny.

"If you want to prove yourself worthy of the power you have, daughter, perhaps you should consider learning the skills you need on your own."

Daughter.

I froze, hand to my ear, facing the large windows that were in desperate need of being cleaned, staring at the last sliver of ember sky outlining the mountains before the dark of night took them. One last memory of light, I had a feeling that my father's patience was as thin as that gossamer line.

I didn't want to know what darkness waiting for me after his light was gone.

"Understood."

"Glad to hear it," his tone was clipped, the silence that followed so deep that I almost hung up. I nearly jumped when his harsh tone crackled in the speaker. "We are waiting for your tasks to be completed before we move to the next phase of our plan. Notify me when your roommate has left for home. I hear Christmas at home is nice."

"I think she will enjoy it."

Bands of eager worry were winding over my chest, my mind already buzzing at the task before me.

If he wanted her dead by Christmas than I had been moving much slower than he had expected. I supposed the warnings of failure were warranted. No wonder he was upset.

If I wanted to regain any of his acceptance in this I would have to orchestrate her end before the snows fell. I was out of time. Seeing as my magic was not strong enough to end her on my own, I was going to need more than Miko and Tasha to accomplish this.

I needed people I could trust.

That would do anything for me.

Finding people in the school that were loyal to my cause and the CCC should be easy. I already knew the perfect person to point me toward the right students. She saw enough of them every day...

"What of your prince?"

I flinched at the sudden question. If he had expected my task with Gemma to have been completed by now, I did not want to know what his expectations were with Rowan. I had put all of my work into the prince and had not been able to accomplish much more than getting the useless lump to sit with me at lunch.

The guy wouldn't even kiss me of his own accord. I still couldn't figure out why, I had plenty of hungry eyes following me, plenty of offers for secret flings. I had even entertained a few. It wasn't as if I was undesirable. I was starting to think there was something wrong with the guy.

"Wonderful," I lied, pushing a grin into my voice lest he picked up on my worry.

"Have you felt his magic spark against yours yet?" My father asked and I shifted my weight, pressing my back against the cold stone wall, away from the now black sky. "All it should take is a bit of prodding, or his hand against your mark to create the spark--"

"I am sure it would have if the guy had any magic," I cut him off, twisting my free wrist enough to stare at the raised brand the Vilỳ had given me. The brand I had tricked him into touching more than a dozen times. Still, nothing. "I can't feel anything from him. I've tried. I haven't even seen him do more than a few tricks. The guy is as powerless and pathetic as a Tarn."

"He has magic, I assure you." There was something like hunger in my father's voice, but before I could ask, he plowed on. "There are rumors circulating that suggests Rowan may be more powerful than even his mother."

"What rumors?"

"I am not going to disclose that over the phone, Sia." My father snapped. I flinched, slamming my back against the wall as though I had been slapped. I had been on the other end of his hand enough that I could fairly feel the stinging heat against my jaw and cheek. "We would like to move this up to a priority."

"A priority?" That knot in my chest was returning, winding over my muscles and I straightened, pushing off the wall to pace through the dark room, my mind buzzing.

Capturing Rowan was a priority. Gemma needed to lose her head by the end of the year. The task before me was mounting.

"Yes, do whatever it takes, Sia, link your magic to his. Even if the connection is forced, it must happen."

I had no idea how to even accomplish that, but I kept my mouth shut and said, "Of course."

"We need to have this done in the next few weeks. Can you have your magic connected to his by then?"

Weeks? He wanted my magic connected to the prince, and therefore the prince in our palm.

Something wasn't feeling right.

"What will connecting my magic to Rowan's do? Will it bond me to him?" I don't know why, after years of wanting exactly that, the idea felt ominous. Wrong. "Will it be able to help our cause if he does not agree to it? From what I am seeing, he is a Drain loving rat kisser. He may not be willing to help."

"Willing or not, he has skills we need and once your magic is tied to his we believe you will be able to extract them. Use them. Everything is riding on this, Sia. It's riding on you."

"Understood." I sank back into the wall, glancing out the window and onto the darkening grounds of the academy. Four dark shapes that were streaking toward that ugly silver tree by the wall.

Even in the dark I could make out the electric pink of her hair. My magic was instantly crackling, heart clenching as I tried to see who she was with. That fat kid, obviously. I couldn't make out the other two.

"Should I be concerned that you cannot complete this task?"

"No!" I spoke too loud, jumping up from the wall to pace again, the loud clack of my shoes feeling like some kind of countdown. "I'll do it."

"Good, prove it to me. I need to see some progress on both tasks by this weekend."

This weekend. My heart had become a stone in my chest.

"Yes, father." I didn't hesitate, refusing to let my sudden panic bleed through my voice. Short of attacking the bitch from the window I wasn't going to accomplish anything by this weekend.

"Wonderful." For the first time, he actually sounded pleased. It didn't last. "We will be in touch."

He hung up before I could respond, leaving me in the darkness, in a school that was suddenly devoid of sound.

Weeks ago, I had assumed these tasks to be easy. I had assumed that Gemma would be bleeding in her room howling for mercy. Assumed that Rowan's magic would be connected to mine. How could they not? I had never failed. Never wavered. Not until Gemma with her saggy ass and vile hair waltzed in and burned everything to the ground.

If I wanted to succeed in both tasks, one thing was obviously clear; Gemma had to go first.

I stood in the middle of the dark room, staring at the four figures as they vanished into the darkening grounds, pieces of a plan falling into place.

A way to use Rowan and get him to accomplish everything I needed.

14

———

ROWAN

"So, Rowan." The sour-faced woman across the table from me was attempting to strike up a conversation for the third time, the smile she was trying to force onto her face not reaching her eyes. "How is the listy?"

I plastered my own falsified grin onto my face, waving the still full fork in Samantha Demarco's direction.

"Better than my father's." It wasn't exactly a lie. It was mildly better than my father's. But it was also listy. The leaf stew always twisted my stomach. Unfortunately, it was widely known that it was the king's favorite meal, which is why I was being force-fed the stuff in a dining room that was probably double the size of ours back home.

"Oh! That's so good to hear!" Samantha Demarco gushed with a little bit too much bravado, giving both her husband and daughter that same simpering smile. "Chef has been perfecting her recipe for years. Perhaps she could write up her recipe and you could give it to your chef."

"That would be lovely," I lifted my glass to her before taking a drink, the weird tangerine water they had served me almost as foul as the listy.

Tangerine water. listy filled with what looked like truffles. A table big enough for twenty in a dining room edged with gold and what I was sure was ivory, the expensive additive twisting my stomach.

No one had seen an elephant in decades. Although there were rumors that there were still some in the American tundra, but the continent was too bombed out for anyone to know for sure.

Their entire house and everything they had rolled out to impress me was nothing more than a gaudy reminder of the things that I hated most about this world. Like school. Like this ridiculous arrangement. We didn't even live like this at home. We didn't have a chef I could skip home and take the recipe to. We took turns making meals and were even responsible for cleaning our own rooms. The lines of maids that lined the walls behind Samantha and Giovani made it clear that that was not the case.

I didn't belong there.

Foolishly, I had left my room on the weekend to give Cail a letter for my mother. Instead, I ran right into Sia who practically dragged me to her home for 'weekend dinner'. She hadn't even given me time to change, which turned out to be an amazing oversight on her part. Sitting in my torn jeans and a faded 'Fraggles' shirt was the only thing that was making all of this palatable.

"We will have to have your parents over soon," Giovanni said, the deep bass of his voice rattling their massive chandelier. He didn't even look at me. "Especially if this keeps going the way it seems to be going. We would love to celebrate the process of joining our two families with a dinner."

I had chosen the wrong time to put food in my mouth. I choked on the damn leaves. Food clogged my airwaves and sent me hacking, jerking so violently that I sent both my dish and my glass over the table. Right into Sia's lap.

The girl shrieked, jumping to her feet and she shook her hands before her. As if that would get the leaves and liquid off her. The stuff was so damp that it had attached itself to her glistening white dress like boils, the dark green broth dripping down the fabric and staining it tears of sewage.

"Oh my!" Samantha said, jumping to her feet, although neither she nor Giovanni actually made a move to help. Giovanni was still sipping on his tangerine water. At least I was trying to dab at her dress with the white napkin.

"I'm so sorry." It was so hard to keep my face straight, not laugh and enrage the squealing Sia more, but I managed it. I was trying to grab at the bits of food now, but with how she was prancing around I was having a hard time even getting close to her.

"Sorry? You're sorry? Look what you did to my dress!" Her shrieking had turned to a deep boom of rage, her magic shaking out of control as the massive chandelier shook. "We were supposed to get our engagement pictures in this dress! Now look at it!"

"Engagement pictures?" Good thing there was no food or drink in my mouth that time because that would have gone all over her too. Instead, I stumbled away, gross napkin in my hand as a maid moved to take my place.

"Let me do that, Your Majesty," she said, her fingers shaking as she took the napkin from my hand.

Her fingers were burned and scarred; her arm covered in tattoos. It was clear she had tried to cover the heavy black drawings with makeup, the beige layer was a shade off from her skin tone and not nearly heavy enough to hide the lines. I could easily make out what almost looked to be a bird, flying through a sun. If I hadn't been so used to the faint lines of my aunts' tattoos I may not have seen them at all.

I grabbed her hand before she could fully move away, leaving Sia to wail behind us.

"Where did you get these?" I asked, my fingers hovering not over the tattoos, but the painful red marks that twisted over her fingers and wrists. I was sure I had seen marks like these before, on different fingers... I couldn't place them, I was too horrified by the melted flesh.

"They are burns," she stumbled over the words, diverting her eyes to Giovanni who had stopped drinking the foul yellow water to stare at us. I think that was the first time he had looked at me all night.

"From where?" I asked, narrowing my eyes at the now smiling Chosen bastard.

"She works in the kitchen," Giovanni responded, his dead eyes blinking once before he looked away again. "Burns are common in our servants when they first begin their employment. They don't have kitchens in those tunnels after all. We do our best to help heal them, to teach them of our ways. But they are stubborn."

"Stubborn?" I asked,

"Yes, I am sure you know as your family has so foolishly allowed so many to enroll in that once great school." He wasn't smiling, everything about him dead, that same hollow feeling filling me as the words echoed in my head. 'Foolishly'. 'Once great'.

I blinked, clenching my teeth, not trusting myself to say anything right then.

"Now, will you please allow her to clean my daughter's dress, seeing as you have ruined it. And on such a special day too."

"How unfortunate." Nothing in Samantha Demarco's voice

made it sound unfortunate. "The engagement pictures will be ruined."

'There is no engagement, I snarled the words in my head, jaw still clamped shut as I locked my hatred for this entire situation away as I tried to keep my feet on the floor and not charging toward the other maids, all of which stood with the same poorly covered tattoos, the same burns on their hands. On their arms. On their necks.

Two maids were now furiously trying to scrub the listy from the white fabric, scrubbing with the already stained napkins as Sia cursed and blamed and threatened.

"Clean this up now," she snarled with a low growl that I was sure she hadn't intended me to hear. "Clean this up or I'll bring the CCC in here again. You know I can."

I had no idea what she was talking about, but watching how she treated them was revolting. It would take little for me to scrub the thing clean, but I wasn't going to blast any kind of magic into a room that was already filled with the reaching, prodding, powers of not one, but two women.

Sia was bad enough, but her mother's magic was like a monster tapping against the wall of my shield as it tried to find holes.

Did they really not realize that I could feel every movement of their magic in the air? Probably not, considering that Sia thought my magic had been 'turned on' or some shit.

It was making me feel violated. Like hands were rubbing over me, over my chest, my legs, my arms, my... I shivered.

"I don't understand why you did this," Sia said, turning her vitriol from the maid to me. "You knew this was a special occasion."

"No, Sia, I didn't," I spat before I could stop myself. The words were shaking with the anger that was now pumping through me, I clenched my fists around my jeans, desperate to keep my hands still and my magic locked away. "You asked me to dinner, and I came to dinner because..." I paused, what I wanted to say clearly not going to work in this situation.

Because I was forced.

Because I was trying to stop a war.

Because it was my royal duty.

Each reason, each excuse, twisted in my gut, the lies lifting like bile in my throat.

I didn't want to be there, just as I didn't want to be at school. But seeing those maids, their skin branded, their eyes downcast. It was clear that nothing I could ever do would stop this. No amount of fake kisses and handholding was going to tip the scales toward the unity my parents hoped for.

They wanted marriage; they weren't going to get it. I needed to get home, call my father, and end this pathetic game.

I was done.

I needed to get through this disaster that I had wandered into, and away from the danger that was buzzing behind each of their eyes. While I was sure I could battle myself out from any disaster, I didn't need to give them any further access to me. Or any tips as to what was hiding inside of me.

"I'm here because you asked me." It was the best I could do, smooth things over to get out of this mess. I would figure everything else out later. "You. But this game is not one I am interested in playing. A fight for the crown? A battle for a prince? This is not how magic is meant to find its match," my voice caught, my magic buzzing, but not for the girl that was staring at me with wide eyes. For the other, whose magic had sparked through me with one touch from her elbow. I swallowed, trying to keep my voice regulated as I continued. "This is not how I wish to find my mate. I'm sorry Sia, I had hoped that this would turn out differently."

"Are you... are you breaking up with me?" Her voice caught

as she tried to force those tears to the surface again. Although this time they didn't look like they were going to do the job. Her rage was boiling off of her, even the maids had stopped trying to clean her dress, stepping back in fear.

She wasn't the only one that looked ready to commit murder. Giovanni was staring at us in furious hatred, the man going red as a vein in his neck pulsed. Samantha looked like she could care less. She was sitting in her chair, tapping on a phone as her jaw pulsed.

"You can't break up with me!" Sia exclaimed, the tears finally breaking through her anger, the false things sliding down her face as she wailed, fists still balled up at her sides.

I sighed, running my hand through my hair. I wanted to tell her that we were never together, that we were never a couple. But that was a lie, we were. She had thought so, because I had led her on.

It was my fault. I had let that happen.

Gemma was right, I was a full douche at this point.

I should have stood up to my father. This was my problem and I needed to fix it as eloquently as possible. Having never been in a relationship before, or broken one up, I wasn't quite sure what to do, but I gave it my best shot.

"I need a break, Sia," I said meekly, not sure of how else to extinguish that rage that was sucking the oxygen from the room. The level of magic in this massive room was becoming dangerous.

"I need to think," I ended lamely, kissing her hand and bowing to her parents before I swept from the room, not giving them a chance to respond. Although I could have sworn I heard Giovanni say "send them all" right before the sound of breaking glass echoed through the halls.

It was then I started to run, streaming past more maids as I ran through the halls; not through the front door and to the private jet that had flown us there. Instead, I plummeted out of the first open window I found and into the open air.

Into the crisp night air that felt more weightless than it ever had before, if only because it knew right where I was going.

I grabbed my phone the second the door to my dorm had snapped shut, the full reality of everything slamming against my chest. It had been a long, somewhat chilly, flight back to school, a long time to think. I listened to the phone ring as I kicked off my shoes, the connection clicking alive as I sat on the side of my bed.

"I've ended this charade with the Demarco's. I can't do it anymore. They are wretched people and we never should have agreed to this."

"Hello to you too, Rowan," Angela said, giggling the second I finished talking.

"Shit," I swore under my breath, causing Angie to giggle further. "Ang, why do you have moms phone?"

"I was playing a game." She was still giggling.

"Ang, go get mom." I pinched the bridge of my nose, trying to stave off the swirling ache that was occupying my frontal lobe. Angie laughed, her little voice echoing off the old speaker of my phone before it faded altogether.

"Hello? Rowan?" This time I actually listened, making sure it was my mom before I launched into my tirade.

"Mom. I've ended this thing with the Demarco's. It's been three months, far too long for this kind of bullshit. I just got back from dinner at their house--"

"Why were you at their house?" She interrupted her voice harsh.

"Because dad told me to befriend her and date her or

something so that the Chosen don't go all bat shit crazy. So, I went to her house for dinner, which was listy mind you, and vile." I knew one person who shared my dislike for the stuff, although she didn't even laugh. I was pacing the floor now, bare feet dragging over the soft carpet that was feeling like sandpaper in my agitation. "But I'm here to tell you that is bull. They are already batshit crazy and nothing I can do, or anyone I can date, is going to help with that."

"What did you see?"

I froze. No fight. No telling me I was emotional. A stern voice, a question loaded with far too much accusation. Maybe I should ask the same question of her.

"I didn't *see* anything. I was just there. I'm fairly certain they are keeping Undermortals as slaves. Slaves that they are burning and torturing." The word shouldn't even exist in our vocabulary, yet it was burning the air and poking holes in my memory.

"'*Get your hands off of me, Drain, or I'll make sure that the next time the CCC liberates a sewer they track you down as a special favor. My mother would see to it. We could use a new toiletry maid'.*" I mumbled it to myself, the words the same from that dream before the explosion in The Gauntlet when the Sia who wasn't trying to kiss my butt had stood before Gemma. Before Gemma had brought the roof down on top of her.

"What did you say, Rowan?" Mom asked, thankfully she hadn't heard that.

"Mom, do you know what the CCC is?" There was only silence on the other line.

Silence that dragged on until the sound of my breath was like a cyclone.

"Rowan," Her voice was soft and I tensed, falling back on my bed. "I need you to tell me what you have seen."

I lay still, staring at the tiles on the ceiling as the last of the sunlight reflected over them. There was no way I could wiggle my way out of this, I either answered or she would show up at the foot of my bed.

"I told you, I haven't seen anything. I'm still blocking them. You know I need to, I will continue to do so." I tried to keep my voice firm, to drive the point home for what was the hundredth time. Hard considering my head was spinning, my vision drifting in an out of focus. I snapped my eyes shut.

"Rowan--"

"Aren't moms supposed to protect you from danger?" I interrupted, rolling over on my bed to scowl at the drawer that concealed that damn mug.

"This mom has been through enough to know it doesn't always work that way." I could barely hear her through the static crackle of the phone.

"It should. Because this power is dangerous."

"I know what you saw when you drank the water scared you, Rowan, but you can't spend your life running away from it," she continued, her calm voice cutting through the silence.

"That's not exactly helpful, Mom."

"I know, but it's the truth?" She hesitated the air going dead for a minute as I tried to control my breathing. "What happened at dinner?"

"Besides the slaves?" I snapped, sitting up again, the motion twisting through my head painfully. "I was forced to eat listy with hateful bastards that you arranged for me to marry."

"We didn't arrange--" she began, but I was no longer in the mood to have this conversation.

"Well, they were all ready for engagement photos."

"They are doing what?" My headache was now wrapped around my head in a spiral that was making it hard to think through. "Well, trust me, we won't let anything like that happen. You won't let anything like that happen." She laughed like it was some kind of great joke. I resisted the urge to throw my phone. "Hold on a little longer, Row--"

"Hold on?" I had meant to yell, it came out more like a gasp.

"Yes. I know it sucks but there are things happening that we need to get cleared up first. We are working on it, I promise."

"Mom, I already broke up with her. I'm done, I have to be. Whatever you are working on will have to be without me kissing the Demarco's ass. Fix it okay. I'm done. I need to pee," I tacked on the excuse so she wouldn't stutter her way in uninvited and ended the call, adding an 'I love you' before I did so.

Then I threw the phone against the wall.

15

GEMMA

"READ IT TO ME AGAIN," I SAID FROM WHERE I LAY ON MY BED, pillows and blankets piled behind me as I popped another grape in my mouth. Eddy gave me a look from where he was sipping coffee, scrawling all over the one white piece of paper that I hadn't already covered with monsters.

"'Your most kind and humble highness of the world'," Eddy began, unable to get through the whole sentence without laughing. "Are you really sure you want to start it that way?"

"Really sure. Stop second guessing me, Ed. She seems like the kind of person who likes people telling her how awesome she is."

"Either that or you are kissing ass," Eddy said, taking another sip of coffee before scribbling something else on the page.

"Exactly," I said through a mouth full of grapes. "Continue."

"'Your most kind and humble highness of the world. I would once again like to thank you for the magnanimous opportunity to attend your wonderful institution. I have been learning so much about magic, power, and the war of good and evil. I was very pleased to find out you were fighting against the trash of evil'. I really don't think we should phrase it that way. How about 'fighting for the side of good.'?" Eddy asked, gnawing at the end of his pencil.

"Yeah, sure, I like that better anyway." I popped another grape in my mouth while he scribbled away.

"Fighting for good..." He mumbled before continuing on. "'As you recall, when we met after the Gauntlet, as well as in previous correspondence, you asked me to tell you if there was anything I needed. Well, it has come to my attention that there is a lot of extra food at Imdalind Academy. We would like your assistance to deliver the leftovers to the Undermortal communities and feed those of your people who are starving and in need of your assistance. With your gracious help, we could begin delivering food as early as next week. Your humble servant,' blah blah blah... What do you think?" Eddy looked up from the letter we had been slaving over for the past few hours, his eyes somewhat glazed over.

It was the weekend. We should be practicing that weird expansion trick that he was still struggling with, but we had bigger problems. It had been six weeks since school started, six weeks since my communities sole source of food and supplies were taken from them. I didn't want to think of what state they were in. Even without the added benefit of passing information and starting our rebellion I needed to get this food train going.

"I think it has enough ass-kissing that she won't be able to say no," I popped another grape and jumped up from the bed, digging through the piles of clothes and food that were littered over my floor in search of my boots.

"Let's do this!" I held out my hands, slipping into my oversized shoes.

"Let me copy it down clean and pretty first," Eddy said, batting away my grabby hands. "How are you going to get it to her anyway? Walk to Imdalind?"

"I was thinking about that," I mused, tapping my chin. "I

could always try that stuttering thing we learned in class. Pop from one place to another."

"You know only Drak's can do that, and you are certainly not a Drak." Eddy laughed at me and I stuck my tongue out at him. "If anyone's gonna try that it's me. I have a bite from a supercharged first of his kind Vilỳ, after all. I'm a special edition. I should be able to do all the things."

"So am I! You heard what she said, the longer they sleep..." I wagged my eyebrows at him teasingly, but his face fell.

"How long did you sleep for anyway?" He asked, his face deadly serious. It was not a good look for him. "I didn't know you then."

"A while," I said with a shrug, locking the information down as deep as it could go, even though it had been pounding against my head since Mira had let that bit of info slip.

I had slept for six months. Months. Not weeks. Not days. Months.

I was actually questioning if I was a freak. I would have to see the Vilỳ that bit me to know for sure as to what had bitten me, but there was no way I was going back there.

We had locked that part of the world away for good reason.

"Probably still don't have magic as strong as yours though." I teased, mussing his hair and getting the conversation back on stable ground. "And I don't see you stuttering anywhere."

"Okay fine, so stuttering, or using our super-powered Vilỳ magic is out. So, what's left?" I could see Eddy physically scratching items off a list in his mind. "The prince seems to be talking to you again."

"Correction, the prince is allowing me to pester him again. I don't think we are in favor territory yet. Besides, Rowan and Analine aren't the only ones here. I've already decided. I'm going to walk right to headmaster Cail's office, bat my eyelashes a few times and demand an audience." I put my hands on my hip, tapping my toe impatiently as he scratched the last few words onto the clean sheet.

"You're going to flirt and a demand an audience of an Eternal?" Eddy asked, chuckling at me as he folded the paper up into fourths and wrote "Queen Joclyn" on the front. Or I think he did, I couldn't read those swirly letters that he preferred. Which is why I had also volunteered him for this job.

"Exactly. He won't be able to say no," I said, snapping the letter from the table before he could add more swirlies. "This has to work. If it doesn't, I have every intention of breaking my way out of here next weekend."

"You've already tried that, Gem," Eddy said, leaning back in the chair and holding the coffee up. "You know it's not going to work."

"I'll make it work. You read Adrian's letter. We can't leave them to rot." I nodded to the folded scrap of old newspaper that was leaving a dirt smudge on the top of the table. It might as well have been burning a hole in it.

"'Twenty missing. Knives from the roof. Twice this week. Hungry.'" Eddy repeated from memory, the words buzzing in my head.

It had taken us an hour to translate the mess of circled letters, words, and doodles that had come in during mail call that morning. Every phrase that we pulled through was a grim picture. I would figure out how to solve the rest of that, right now all I could do anything about was the food.

"I won't let them starve," I hissed to myself, shoving the letter in my pocket and taking off toward Cail's office.

"Make sure you come back in one piece," Eddy called behind me as I left, waving a hand as he sipped his coffee. Something he was always doing lately.

I shot him a look he didn't see and shut the door behind me as quietly as possible, lest I summon the Bitchicade next door. I could hear her crying about some dress and a spoiled plan on the other side. Shattering glass accented each shout, the sound so loud that even I jumped.

Yeah, there was no way I wanted to deal with that today.

"Drama. Drama. Drama." I took off down the hall, making a beeline for the cafeteria and the line of offices in the hallway behind.

I had no clue which belonged to headmaster Cail, but I would knock doors and beg for information if I had to. This was getting done. I would even poke myself in the eyes and bring on a few fake tears.

I had no interest in turning into a mini Sia, but this was an emergency so I might as well take a page out of her book.

Rumbles of noise filtered from the cafeteria, all the older students studying, practicing and nibbling on the piles of food that covered every single table. Even the empty ones.

Fucking wasteful Eternals.

Rage was not going to help me get my point across, no matter how much I wanted to tell them how big of dipshits they all were. I took off past the cafeteria before my fury took hold, stumbling into the hall of doors that was twice as long as I expected.

"How many teachers does this place have?" I mumbled to myself, thanking everything in the world that was good and not smothered in death that these things had placards.

L. Stone

M. Hayward

G. Gregario

Some of the names I recognized, some I didn't, it was when I got to the end of the hall that I stopped short.

A. Krul

C. Krul

R. Krul

"Rowan Krul. Well, well, well," I mean, if I ever wanted to be a stalker, this would certainly be helpful information. Right now, I felt like one of those bleary-eyed girls that follow him around, especially when I heard yelling from beyond the door.

"Trouble in paradise?" I chuckled to myself. At least Rowan could control himself enough during a lovers spat to not throw shit around his room like a toddler.

He was a total douche, even more so since he missed our skit extraordinaire in Analine's class, but maybe the fact that he wasn't throwing a full-on temper tantrum evened it out.

"They were all ready for engagement photos!"

Ouch. I'd be screaming too if I was one step away from permanent attachment to the leech.

I turned from the yelling that was starting to sound too much like tears to the door on the other side of the hall, the one labeled 'C. Krul' and knocked twice. 'C. Krul', it sounded like the ridiculous children's book they were forcing us to read in our remedials class.

"See Krul. See Krul run. See Krul fall on his face in a pile of shit. See Krul sad." I said that last part right as the door opened and Headmaster Cail peered through the crack in his door, brows furrowing as he looked me up and down.

"Yes? Gemma. This is my private quarters. What are you doing here?" He got angrier and more frustrated with each word.

"Oh!" I said, looking up and down the hall. Rowans, presence was suddenly making sense. "I didn't realize."

I really needed to get out of there. If only because I was sure those were sobs I heard coming from Rowan's door. As I had already mentioned before, I don't do tears of any kind, Prince tears included.

Cail noticed the sound too, his eyes narrowing toward the door as a bit of warm wind soared by me, drowning the sound. A shield I realized, putting two and two together. Good to know I was actually listening during most of my classes.

"Well?" Cail snapped, pulling my focus from the door. "What can I help you with?"

"Oh! Right!" I pulled the haphazard and very wrinkled paper from my pocket, jutting it toward him with what I hoped was a humble expression. "I have this letter for the Queen. When I met her before, she told me to tell her if I needed help with anything. And I do. I wrote it down."

I tried beaming at him, still holding out the letter. He still didn't move.

Damn, I really sucked at this being nice stuff.

"You can read it if you want. Or I can. It's a letter. We used the word magnanimous and my friend Ed did the spiral writing. See." I pointed it out, trying to force a bigger smile, it slid off my face with the dark narrow glare that he was giving me.

Ugh. I didn't know what was worse, Analine throwing insults, or Cail throwing scowls.

"Can you get it to her, please? I know she would really want to help if she knew. Please?" I was officially snapping, my hand shaking from holding out the letter so long, the paper starting to flap around like it was caught in a breeze.

Thankfully Headmaster Cail took the paper, staring at the writing for a second before he shoved it in his pocket. Mission success!

Well, half success. I was still going to celebrate.

"I will make sure this gets to her." He whispered, he sounded much more earnest about it than his sister did, even with the scowl.

Who knows, maybe he always looks that way.

"Thank you so much," I tried to smile again, giving him a nice toothy smile as he shut his door. "I'll never bug you here again, I promise!" We will just have to hope he heard that last part.

His door was already closed, leaving me alone in the hall with Rowan's hissing anger and a throb in the mark the Vilỳ's bite left behind, electricity rumbling from the bite on my elbow. Like it wanted me to help the prince or something. Stupid magic, it was all going haywire after he played himself the white knight last week.

I turned, ready to barge through the door and hug him or some shit, but instead took off down the hall, hand over my elbow.

God, all this playing nice was exhausting, I hated having to think about what it would be like every second of the day. Worrying about who liked me, who didn't, if I was smiling enough, if I was smiling too much, if my hair looked right... No one had time for that. Let me be me. Sod all the bitches that don't like it.

I shook my hands, my shoulders, and cracked my neck in an attempt to shake off the sludge of trying to be good. As if it were as easy as that. I had a feeling that all this nice guy bullshit was starting to stick.

Shit.

To be sure, as I was about to turn the corner and head back to my room, I sent some magic to Rowan's door, accidentally on purpose setting it on fire.

Yep, still got it.

16

ROWAN

"IF YOU DROP YOUR LOWER FINGER THE POWER STRINGS differently," I whispered, leaning toward Gemma as she worked on sending an attack toward an apple. She was supposed to be cracking it straight down the middle, but so far had only been able to explode the sucker.

"Drop your lower finger?" Gemma scoffed, her laugh echoing over the stone. "You do realize that doesn't make any sense, right?"

I shook my head and grabbed two more apples from the crate. Quickly severing mine in two, while she exploded yet another.

"Damn it!"

The usual stair that we claimed as our own was covered in a slick coating of liquified apples.

Still, it was better than the rest of the class. Most of them hadn't been able to do anything except knock the apple over.

Well, except Sia who had been able to cut the apple into two pieces, that while not equal had earned her the praise of Etma Diarius and me several smug looks. She had been trying to weasel her way back in my life for the past few days. I had made it very clear on several occasions that it wasn't going to happen, I still had to peel her off me more than once.

"Why can't exploding the damn thing be good enough? I mean it's the same thing, right?" She was now drawing squiggles and lines through the apple smear with her magic.

She had excellent control of her power and her manipulations of the elements, but only in some things. In so many ways she reminded me of Angie when she was three and would explode things in lieu of throwing a toddler temper tantrum. It's a good thing my parents were patient, I think we went through four-bathroom remodels that year.

"I think you've spent too many years blowing up shit to know what to do," I said, setting out two more apples. "You gotta slow down and focus on each cell of the apple."

"Dropping lower fingers and focusing on the cells of an apple?" she said, clearly mocking me as the corner of her mouth quirked. "That's not what Diarius said. Wait. Is this some kind of super-secret royal training you are giving me? Do I need to sign a waiver, or be threatened by your dad again?"

I shook my head, "You did not get threatened by my father."

"Oh yes, I did. Ultimate life threat. I could tell he was serious too because he gave me the look." She screwed her face up, her eyes narrowing as her lips pulled into the slightest of frowns. I almost lost it. She looked like him, well, if he had purple eyes and a pink curl-hawk.

"That's a little freaky how uncanny that is."

"Could be worse," she shrugged, "I mean, does your mom do that staring into your soul thing, often?"

"More often than she should." I looked down, suddenly hyper-focused on the apples.

We were officially heading into treacherous ground. I had felt the pull of sight when my mother had been with her, I knew she had seen sight. True sight. I wasn't interested in talking about it.

"Sounds like it scares you as much as it does me." I didn't miss that her voice had taken on a lower quality. Hesitant. Afraid.

I glanced up, she wasn't even looking at me, she was staring at the window, her eyes flaring like a sunset against the sun as it dipped closer to the mountains.

"Give me your hand," I spoke in little more than a whisper, but she jumped as though I had yelled.

"Why? So you can zap me again?" Her voice was harsh, the fear from before swallowed by her teasing. I could still see it in her eyes. Her worry dug into me, even as my magic went into overdrive.

She had felt it. She had felt the flare as our magic connected. As the power recognized...

I swallowed, not ready to acknowledge what that meant and held out my hand, desperate for her to grab it, to feel that power swirl again.

"No." It was taking everything in me to keep my voice level. "So, I can help you to cleave an apple rather than destroy it."

"No thanks, your girlfriend has been giving me some serious side-eye and I think I like my head in one piece."

"Not my girlfriend," I said between clamped teeth. Gemma didn't care, she smiled broadly and leaned in. Her eyes were so close that I couldn't pull myself away from them.

"Tell her that, Princey." We turned as one, Gemma waving enthusiastically at a stone-faced Sia, who was looking right at us. Judging by the depth of her scowl she had been staring at us for a long time.

"Hi!" Gemma said loudly, still waving. "Good job on the apple! I'm glad to see your doing better."

I had no idea what she was talking about, but of course, she chose right then to attempt to split the apple in half again.

It exploded again, Gemma laughing raucously at herself.

"Drop your lower finger," I tried to prompt, she wasn't having it.

"Naw. Besides, I think I like it better this way." She gave me a broad smile as the bell rang and another apple exploded, showering the side of my head with liquid fruit.

Judging by the grin, by the laugh that rattled over the room, she had done it on purpose.

"Thanks Gemma," I whispered, waving my hand and cleaning the apple away.

"No prob," she gave me a wink and my heart gave a little stutter, the hairs on the back of my neck lifting as my magic reacted. "I can't let you move out of your douche status that quickly."

With that she was gone, leaving me in the massive room to gather my books and head down to the Rugby pitch, ready to douse some of my raging emotions with a few good tackles.

It took some skill to dodge around Sia, who was already yelling after me before I had stepped more than half a hall out of the classroom. I picked up my pace, darted into a lesser used hallway, down an empty flight of stairs, around two more corners and she was gone. There was no way I had gotten rid of her that easily, though. I kept moving, nearly running through a shortcut into a lower hall. I expected the place to be empty thanks to school letting out for the day. Instead, I came face to face with dozens of tattooed and pierced faces. One familiar grin standing out of the crowd.

"Greer?" I asked, causing his bulky figure to turn, a teetering stack of books in his arms almost falling at the movement.

"Row? Damn, what the hell are you doing here?" The bulky

man shuffled, two books heading to the ground. I caught them easily, a little tug of my magic causing them to soar in my arms.

"Would you believe I took a wrong turn?" I asked, grabbing a few other books from his pile and adding them to mine.

Greer didn't even flinch, though he did roll his eyes. He was the only person in this school that knew me, even then his knowledge was limited. I wasn't ready to tell him about exactly why I disappeared for days. Or the dreams of blood-soaked tunnels that I had been having since I arrived there.

But it was nice to have someone to talk to, even a little bit. Besides, with his big laugh, calm demeanor, or quiet caring he reminded me of my family. It would figure that the only people that had even remotely accepted me were those that had been the most ostracized. Looks like I did fit in.

"Avoiding Sia again?" Greer gave me a wink and turned down the hall, guiding us through the waves of Undermortals that were now openly staring at me.

"She's still trying to adhere herself to me," I whispered, smiling at a few of the gaping students. I had only been in this hall once before. Then it had been empty besides Sia and her cronies when they cornered Gemma. I would have to remember to avoid this at all costs.

"You thought the remedial hall would be the best place to avoid her suction cup fingers? Or the lips that will suck out your soul?" He sounded like Gemma, but I wasn't about to tell him that. I calmly placed another book back onto his pile.

"You can't deny it's not true, Row."

"You're right, which is why I'm not saying anything. I'm just going to keep walking down this hall, carrying your books."

"Rowan Krul, the benevolent prince," Greer said with that booming voice of his. I almost punched him.

"No, thank you. I'd sooner punch you than let that nickname stick." I gave him a look, I had told him enough about that. He should know better, but the guy was giving me that wide grin that was stereotypical of him. I winced.

Damn. I braced for it, but never could have guessed what was coming.

"Go ahead, prince, punch me!" Greer was in full-on bellow now, pulling the focus of everyone around us including a guy about my age with a tattoo around his eye, the jagged spikes almost the same as my Aunt Wyn's.

"Nice tats," I said, gesturing to his eye. The guy was giving me a look, but with one smile he faltered and almost walked into a door.

"You know, if you keep doing that you are going to get a reputation."

"As long as it's not as the King's perfect son, or 'that sickly prince with that bitch for a girlfriend'. Anything is better than that." Greer laughed so hard he nearly sent his teetering pile of books to the ground.

I barely caught them, but this time I put them all on his pile.

"What are all these for anyway?" I asked when I caught sight of the topmost book, the old tattered volume looking about a hundred years old, 'Math for a New Age' printed in faded letters.

"There's a reason it's called the remedial hall, Row." Greer sighed, shifting as we walked past dorm after dorm. I could tell by the space between the dorms that there were much smaller than what I had been given.

I was going to have to talk to my cousin about preferential treatment.

"We don't have school back home, so they 'catch us up' but it's more like four years of belittling us over knowing nothing. These are for the classes I miss because of Rugby practice." He jostled the books as his magic flared, the lock to his door clicking open before he kicked it wider and darted inside.

"Dude," I said, reluctantly following him inside. It felt like a weird invasion of privacy, which was odd considering that my brother would literally blow my door off its hinges when he felt the need to pester me.

But no one had been allowed in my room at the academy, I had assumed everyone else was the same. But everyone else also wasn't locked away in the teachers' hallway. With prying eyes and critical teachers.

Which was probably another reason I had been placed there. What better way to make sure my father's poster child doesn't sleep around? After Talon I was sure it was a necessity.

Despite its size, his room looked about the same as mine. The sitting area with a small kitchen, an attached bedroom and I assumed a bathroom. It was like my dorm except shrunken down and with thankfully less gold.

I really needed to talk to Cail about this. Downsizing seemed like a nice idea; I would even sign some kind of chastity clause if it would get me out of there.

"Don't worry," Greer said, grabbing the books from my arms and setting them on the very clean counter of the mini-kitchen. I paced in the sitting room, trying to decide if I should sit or not. It's times like these when I realized how awkward I really was. "I read through most of these in my first year. At this point it's all busywork. I'd rather be playing or sparing, but the powers that be would rather torture us all."

"Was that directed at me?" I gave him a smile, but his returning grin was less than enthusiastic, missing some of his usual joy.

"Depends. Are you the powers that be?"

"No," I tried to smile but it ended up being a smirk, "but I am related to them."

I ran my hand through my hair nervously, hating the reminder.

"Well, let them know that some sparring wouldn't go amiss, if you can." He was trying to play it off like a joke, but his eyes were still dark. Hooded. It was clear there was more truth there than he was trying to play off.

"Aren't you a third year, Greer? You guys are lucky. You get to use the underground, right? I've been thinking of crashing that party. One can only take so much of basic cleaving spells and shields."

"Well, if you go, make sure to take me with you." He didn't even laugh, he leaned against the counter, his shoulders sagging. "We can't get past Professor Krul half the time. The wicked sister is a bane in my side."

I raised an eyebrow at him, "Wicked sister?"

"Yeah, sorry. I know she's your cousin and the headmaster's sister, but it's not like she tries to hide her hatred of us. Calls us 'Drains' to our face, gives us extra homework. All the older students are supposed to use the old kitchens to spar, but if she is there, forget getting in. And seeing as we can't practice on the grounds or in the halls..."

He shrugged, grabbing two apples off the counter and throwing one at me. I had about enough of apples for today but I didn't throw it back. I just held it, scowling at the shiny surface.

"If you can't practice, you can't advance."

"You can't succeed," Greer tacked on, taking a bite of his apple. "Come on, your royal highness, we're going to be late. Not like Coach will care about you, but I'd rather not have to do five extra laps."

Greer was back to grinning as we walked out of the school and onto the grass that led down to the pitch.

Greer was already talking about some poor Golden who failed at creating an inverted flame in his class today. I listened to his story about the fireball, entertaining him with how I had accidentally balded my Aunt Mira with my first attempt.

It was nice to talk, to laugh, to have Greer clap me on my back and tell me how bad-ass I was and not ask for more information about my family.

With every step over the grounds, every step we came closer to the pitch was beating a weird painful truth into me. I couldn't stop thinking about what I had seen of Analine's treatment of the Undermortals, and how much worse it might be when no one was there to stop her.

But she wasn't the only one. She wasn't the only one who had uttered that vile word, who my father had scolded on more than one occasion.

Talon had warned me about loyalties and promises and threats of death. But more than that, he had threatened my brother Dramin's wife, Patrice.

I think it was time to find out exactly what Dramin had been about to tell me in the council hall, and just how much the feelings of superiority and prejudice had bled into my family.

The thought made my heart ache.

"Any bets on how many laps I'll get?" Greer asked with a smile and a wink, breaking through my thoughts.

"Even if it's twenty I'll still run them with you." I gave him a wink and slapped him on the back. Earning us a glare from the players that were already on the pitch.

"Oh, my benevolent prince, what would I do without you?"

I didn't want to answer that.

17

SIA

He was laughing.

Laughing.

A wide smile was spreading over his face, those emerald eyes sparkling as though they caught fire. I saw the light in them from where I sat on the other side of the sparring amphitheater of our defense class. I heard that laugh as it bounced over the noise of the class. It was pissing me off.

Rowan and I had dated for more than two months and he had never looked at me like that. He had never blushed. I wasn't even sure he had ever smiled. I nearly threw the apple at the bright pink head of the bitch he was smiling at, it was in my fist, my long nails already digging into the flesh. But then the bell rang, the two of them already parting ways, his eyes still following her.

Fecking bitch didn't know what she was doing.

It would be perfect timing to take off after her and teach her a lesson for trying to move in on my man, but I wasn't ready yet. Next time I faced her would be the last time. Everything needed to be perfect for that to succeed. We weren't ready yet.

It didn't matter, I had bigger issues.

I had been trying to talk to Rowan for the last week. Hard considering he had vanished for a few days after the dinner that hadn't gone anywhere near according to plan.

I still wasn't sure what had happened, the plan was foolproof. Get him drunk and bond my magic to his.

His magic and health were weak enough that it should have been nothing. Even after spiking both the listy and the water with old Ukrainian Vodka he hadn't submitted to my magic. He was a sloppy drunk, no better than the Tarns as he spilled listy all over me, insisted that we were broken up, and then stormed out of the house by way of a window. The prince had lost control of his senses.

I needed to help him see that, see that we were supposed to be together. If only because my father's warning in his outburst following Rowan's screaming exit had been crystal clear.

'If you don't complete your task with Rowan by the end of the month, I don't see how you will be able to complete your first year of school, let alone the first semester.'

The words followed me as I was escorted out of our estate, it raged through my veins on the jet back to Imdalind Academy. It had turned into a mantra as I waited for Rowan to emerge from yet another of his sickly vanishing acts. He had finally reappeared three days ago, but I hadn't been able to get him alone since, not that I hadn't tried.

Rowan stepped down the massive stairs toward the door with giant strides. If I didn't move fast, I was going to miss him. I shoved everything in my bag, ignoring Professor Diarius' praise about my apple splitting skill and raced over the spell stained tiles of the amphitheater and after the swaggering dark-haired prince.

"Rowan!" I yelled, trying to push all the sweet and pleading into my voice that I could. The word was still more like a shriek, but I didn't care. "Row!"

He moved faster, weaving through the hoard of students with a weird grace. Of course, now he doesn't look like the derpy, incapable royal. I picked up my pace, yelling and waving with a wide grin, even though I kind of wanted to rage and pull him into one of the classrooms. Force him to listen.

"Rowy! Wait!" There was no way he didn't hear me, but he didn't slow or turn.

"Rowan!" I tried again, turning the heads of the students that were heading to their dorms after the end of class, none of them parting to let me pass.

"Fecking Drains, get out of the way," I snarled, pushing a blond with a big ring in her lip out of the way as I tried to catch up with Rowan, the guy now disappearing around a corner.

Shit. I was going to lose him again. This couldn't be happening to me.

I moved into run, the prince was only steps away now, but instead of moving forward, I fell back, slamming to the ground as someone grabbed my backpack and pulled.

"Who the hell do you think you are talking to?" the girl with the lip ring snarled at me, hovering over me from where I lay on the floor, people snickering and gathering around for some sort of epic showdown.

Fine. If they wanted a show I could surely deliver.

Seeing as I wasn't going to be able to reach Rowan I might as well vent some frustrations. I needed to practice for what I had planned for Gemma, anyway.

Why kill one Drain when I can get away with killing two?

"You. Fecking Drain," I snarled, narrowing my eyes and lifting my legs to kick her in the nose before I flipped myself to my feet.

The heels of my red shoes had almost made contact when the girl narrowed her eyes and flicked her fingers in my direction, sending my legs and arms flat against the floor.

Shit.

An older student. Third year judging by the way she was smiling.

Well, I needed a challenge.

"Geeze. Will you listen to the mouth on this one? She seems to think she's better than us for some reason." The girl smiled, more than a dozen low chuckles following behind. I let the sound wash over me, fueling the crackle that was buzzing under my skin, waiting for the time to strike.

"I *am* better than you," I snarled, shifting my weight enough that I could tell if her magic gave way.

"Oh yeah? Then why are you lying on the ground?" The laughs duplicated; her smile spread as she turned to everyone around her. The girl's pride took hold and her magic slipped enough that before she could turn back to me she was soaring straight up to the ceiling, arms and legs flailing as she screeched.

Laughs turned to gasps as I jumped to my feet in one quick movement, flipping my hair and smoothing my skirt as the girl slammed against the ornate plaster, sending the lighting fixtures up and down the hall into a flicker.

Anyone who wasn't watching before was sure as hell watching now.

I gave them a sweet smile, catching the girl on her fall back to the ground and slamming her against the opposite wall, arms and legs spread awkwardly.

It was a beautiful image, a Drain on display.

God, it felt good to actually attack one of these vermin. I could only imagine how jealous all the Goldens behind me were, the twinkling laughs were near enough to a confirmation.

I would have turned, told them all it would be their turn soon enough, but I didn't dare look away from the frightened animal before me.

"I will never be below you." I stretched my hand out to her, holding her in place as I sent one bright red streak right into her gut. The trick one that Miko and I had been practicing on roaches and birds for the last few weeks.

It had been entertaining watching the bug twitch and scream with sounds I hadn't known they could make. Watching the same in this Drain was glorious.

The red magic darted into her, every muscle and bone twisting under the spell. I could see her twitch, see her jaw lock against the scream that she was trying to keep in. But she couldn't hide the pain, she couldn't hide the fear that was shining through those eyes. The same fear echoed in gasps and shrieks that rattled around me.

"I could never be below your filthy scourge. I would never want to be." I should be nervous. Nothing good could come from this display, I had to be breaking about a dozen rules. Yet, I couldn't help the grin that spread over my face as I stepped closer to her and sent another attack directly into her heart.

That time she screamed as the magic tried to rip her apart, the unearthly pain a beautiful song that sent a few others gasping, and more than a few sets of panicked feet running in the opposite direction.

Wimps.

"You and your kind are rodents. I will do my part to exterminate you. All of you."

My fingers flexed, one more beam of red shooting from my fingertips. The red triggered more screams from the echoing hall, the sounds duplicating as my attack hit an invisible barrier. Instead of crippling the Drain I had plastered to the wall, it ricocheted back to me.

I was knocked back for a second time, but instead of being pinned to the floor I was writhing against it, fighting against it as I locked my own scream inside fighting against my own attack.

My veins were filled with a twisting, dangerous fire. Every part of me was trying to move in an unnatural way, to break apart and burn and writhe and scream. Gritting my teeth, I fought against the pain, heaving as I rolled and pushed myself to my knees, forcing my magic to fight against the attack, to prepare to end the girl who was now heaving and gasping in a position similar to my own.

Except that she was not alone. Four Drains had run in to help her, the tattooed monsters lifting her up and carting her away. Or trying to, she was as interested in continuing this fight as I was. I lifted my hand, ready to send one last attack after her, one more trick that I was ready to try, armed and ready.

"No more, Ruby. You can continue this fight another time. Geo, get her to her room. I'll be there in a minute." A familiar voice commanded from above me, a pair of old, ugly combat boots stepping between me and my prey. I hissed as I turned my head to face Gemma, who stood with a glare darker than I had ever seen from her, that damn fat kid hovering over her shoulder as always.

"Get out of the way, Drain. She wants to fight. Let her fight." I kept my voice as stable as I could, forcing myself to stand before her. I wasn't going to take her down now, but I wasn't going to cower beneath her either.

"She's had enough of you, Sia." Gemma stepped to the left, keeping herself in my vision and blocking the still snarling 'Ruby' from view.

"Are you the Queen of the rats, Gemma? The rat queen?" I snarled at her, my body finally starting to relax and I took a shaky step forward, letting my magic pump in preparation. "You know what they say about vermin. If you want to knock them out, start at the head."

She didn't even flinch at the warning, at the magic that I was letting spark from my fingers, the perfect little lines darting from finger to finger.

"Is that why you are heaving in a hallway? You started at the head?" She didn't smile, though a few of the still lingering Drains snickered, the sound louder than what I had heard from my Goldens. The sound everywhere. I stepped back, head turning at the dozen Drains that were surrounding me.

"You don't want to fight me, Sia," Gemma said, waving off a few of the Drains who stepped back as though they were going to leave, but all they did was block the exits.

What the fecking hell was this idiot playing at, thinking that she could gang up on me? Exhaustion was wracking my body, but I had fought through worse. I had been trained to fight through worse. I would not let her get away with this.

This was exactly what I had been waiting for, a perfect moment handed to me.

I couldn't help but smile.

"Yes, I do." I stepped forward, flinging my hair behind my shoulder with a tiny bit of wind. "I was going to come find you, anyway. Remind you to stay away from my boyfriend."

She blinked, a tiny laugh peeking on the corner of her lips. Damn, I was going to punch her smug face in before all this was over.

"Your boyfriend?" I could have sworn she was laughing at me, that kid Edward wasn't even trying to hide his laughter.

"The prince." I pulled myself to standing, everything still aching as I faced her, my magic had mostly healed. "He's mine and you need to back off."

"You think I was trying to get in 'your boyfriends' pants?" She wasn't even trying to hide her laugh now. "You're cute. You're also delusional."

"Don't deny it. I saw you--"

"Seriously Sia. I'm getting tired of beating you and putting your gleaming Golden ass through the rat's nest. To be honest, it would be nice if you actually won one."

"I would have if you hadn't butt in."

"Sorry. Still lost. Don't touch my people, Sia. Got a problem? Come after me."

"That's been the plan all along." Miko and Tasha were going to be pissed that they weren't there for this, but I didn't care, I sent my magic right to her. Not the red fire that had gnawed at my bones, but the black smoke that danced through the air, ready to end her.

It would have too, if the deadly attack hadn't banged against her shield, what little had made it through scurried away with a bat of her hand.

"So, we are going for, what is it now? Five losses?" She laughed, she didn't even raise her hand when the plaster over my head cracked and rained down over us, whatever she had meant to hit me with coming from all directions.

I attacked while she laughed, her eyes trained on her friend, her defenses down. Instead of the smoke that would stop her heart, or the red that would twist her nerves. I sent a good old blast of pain and wind her way, the yellow sparks hitting right into her heart and shooting her back into the wall that was already crumbling from its previous occupant.

"You don't have my boyfriend to save you this time. You don't have anyone to save you."

I stepped forward, ready to send the death blow as she peeled herself from the wall and

"Stay back, Eddy," she snarled, hurling herself like a rugby player toward me.

I attacked again, the black smoke whipping through the air as she watched it, horrified.

It was almost there.

This was almost done.

Then it was gone. The smoke was gone. The rattling hall was gone. Everything was silent and still and clean. As if someone had pressed pause on the world.

"Holy hell," Gemma gasped, pulling to a stop, her sass replaced by something I could have sworn was fear. "Not again."

"What in the world is going on here?" A loud irritated shout cut through any question, the door behind us banging open as Analine Krul came sprinting into the hallway.

I could have sang her praises as Gemma and Edward's face blanching to a pale white. The Eternal, even though she wasn't much taller than me, was a giant as she swept passed me, bee-lining for Gemma and her side-kick while all the other Drain's ran down the hall and into adjoining classrooms like the rats they were.

Rats running from the light.

"What in the world do you think you are doing," Analine snarled, leaning over Gemma. The girl didn't even flinch, the two of them stood, chins up, staring right at her. "Why are you ganging up on a single student?"

"I'm not ganging--"

"Stop!" Analine snapped, pressing her hands up in exasperation as Gemma was thrown back into the wall. She didn't even fight, she just glared, her jaw tight as she stared down the beautiful Eternal who was quickly taking over Mira's spot as my favorite.

"Hey! You can't do that!" Eddy said, running up behind Analine grabbing at her as his own magic sparked with something white and weird that I had never seen before.

"Child, you don't want to mess with me," Analine said with a wave of her hand, sending Eddy into the wall besides Gemma.

I couldn't help it, I laughed and clapped my hands, looking around in hopes that someone else was there to witness this magic moment. It was just me, Analine, and the two Drains.

I didn't even try to push tears into my eyes, it wasn't needed with what Analine was doing right in front of me.

God, it was beautiful.

"You have broken more than a dozen rules, you and your vile vermin have ganged up on one of the most respected students in the school--"

"Oh, give me a break," Gemma started rolling her eyes before Analine flexed her fingers and they both flinched. Ed even whimpered, his chubby cheeks sucking in.

"You have attacked a respected member of our school," Analine paused, stepping closer and placing her hand beneath the still sputtering magic of Eddy. She winced as his magic hit her skin. "As well as a teacher."

"What the fuck?" Gemma screeched as Analine released her hold on the two and they tumbled to the ground. "You want us to attack you? I have no problem smearing your Eternal shit stain all over the walls."

Gemma lifted her hand, ready to fight, but I sprinted forward pushing myself between the two like some kind of bodyguard.

"Why don't you like us, Gemma?" Now I pushed the tears, letting my voice warble and whimper. "What have we ever done to you?"

"What? You are fucking crazy." Gemma blanched, stepping back as she ground her teeth. God, she was little more than an animal.

"Don't worry about the Drain, Miss Demarco," Analine said, patting me on the shoulder. I could feel the warmth of her magic through my shirt. "She doesn't--"

Analine froze as Gemma smiled, her eyes a haunting red as they reflected the light, her magic starting to pulse.

"Professor?" I asked, heart pounding in fear that Gemma had done something, but Analine was staring at the end of the hall now, her eyes narrowed as if she saw something.

As if something was talking to her.

"What is it with all you pompous assholes?" Gemma asked, magic still buzzing. "You keep breaking down like old toilets."

"Smell like it, too," Ed added on, the two stepping closer. Prepping.

I flinched, Analine was still staring down the hall.

"Professor?" I asked again, lightly tapping my foot against her own. That time she jumped, her eyes wide as she looked from me to the two rats before us.

"Get out of here, Gemma," Analine snarled in little more than a hiss. "Get out of here before I take you to the headmaster."

Gemma and Eddy looked at each other, clearly as confused as I was, before they took off down the hall. Analine grabbed my arm, dragging me in the opposite direction.

I tried to fight her, but she kept pulling, even when I tripped and landed hard on my knee.

"What are you doing?" Analine snarled after we had turned the corner, and she had dragged me into a weird little alcove that was dripping with ancient magic. "What the hell do you think you are playing at?"

"I'm--" I started to say, but Analine smashed her hand over my mouth and pressed me against the wall. Her voice was little more than a whisper as she snarled at me, inches away.

"You keep attacking that girl and I won't be able to keep stepping in. It is vital that I retain my position at this school. You are threatening that."

She gave me one look before she stepped back, dropping her hand and letting me breathe better.

"Stepping in?" I was trying to wrap my head around this. I had always known she hated the Drains, it's not like she had been quiet about it. But this was different. Active. "What are you saying?"

"You and I agree on one very important point, Sia. Our world should have more class and a lot more order. However, my family does not agree with me. I wish to stay at Imdalind Academy and make sure that your spoiled little asses keep rising to greatness, but to do that I can't keep rushing in to stop you from getting expelled."

"She's just a nasty Drain, Professor Krul. Trust me, no one will miss her when she's gone." I was firm, confident, and I had hit a nerve.

"You are a fool, Sia Demarco. That girl is being watched. She has all the Drains in the school bowing to her like she's a queen. You don't touch her, Sia. I won't save you another time. Do you hear me?" Analine jabbed her finger into my chest, a sharp jerk of magic moving into me.

Warning understood.

I cringed, nodded and cowered against the pain that was now blossoming. Analine only narrowed her eyes at me before she turned away, ready to bolt down the hall.

"Wait," I gasped, still wincing from her warning. "What if I can't leave her alone. What if I--" I hesitated. Clearly, Analine longed for a world without the filth. That was clear even without her admission. I had already planned to go to her to find older Goldens who might be willing to help me finish my job. Even knowing of her desire, I had no way of knowing how far she would go.

She was an Eternal. I can't imagine her rising to an extermination order.

Saying anything more was a risk. But if I couldn't attack Gemma, if she was being watched. I had no other choice than to risk it.

"Explain." Analine stood at the edge of the shadowed alcove, watching me, her eyes flashing with something close to fire.

"My parents are working on something," I paused, watching

how she reacted. Trying to feel her magic for some sign of excitement or fear. There was nothing from her, nothing but a slight twitch in the corner of her mouth.

It was enough.

"I have a job to do. With your cousin. With her." I nodded my head in the direction we came from. "If I don't succeed then all of my parent's hard work will go to waste."

"And if you do?" She leaned in, I could nearly taste the eagerness in her tone.

"Then both of us will get what we want." I hoped I had said enough. That she understood.

That I hadn't said too much.

The silence lingered behind us, a heavy weight filling the alcove as she measured me, and I, her. I suddenly questioned if I had made the right choice at all.

"Come with me," Analine whispered, wrapping her arm over my shoulder as she led me down the hall. "I think we need to have a little chat."

I would be worried, but there was a smile on her face, a matching one blossoming on mine as she led me to her office.

It was a different path, a different Eternal, but I had a feeling that I was about to work myself back into my father's good graces.

18

GEMMA

"Go ahead, try it, see how big you can make it," I nudged Eddy forward, closer to the slug that I had already swelled to the size of the widow's dog back in Last Pyre, the poor withered thing always tucked underneath the trolley seats to stop the others from eating him.

I wouldn't eat this slug though. That would be foul. I was already considering a firm 'no mucous' policy.

"I think it's already big enough, Gem." He was whining, pushing against my hand as I prodded him forward.

He may not like it, but he was going to do it. After having to save Ruby from that bitch, Sia, it was clear we needed to work harder on the basics. Something that was only validated when he was reamed for an hour by Professor Gregario and his mustache about his inability to 'grow a tomato', something that about only half of us could do anyway, we were growing things. This slug just so happened to be what I found first.

I'm amazed I did. The light dusting of early autumn frost from the morning had melted, regrettably before any of us could play in it, but there was still a bite in the air. Normally when it got this cold the little bugs and things would disappear.

This guy would wish he had by the time we were done with him.

"He can always be bigger," I strained, still pushing my shoulder against Eddy's shoulder blade. "If you don't move I'm going to throw you into him. Trust me when I say it will not end well."

He hustled so fast that I fell down, flat on my face on the grass that lay in massive stretches around the campus. This particular lawn had quickly become my favorite. Not only was it always empty, the Goldens preferring to sit on the benches of the interior courtyard and stretch out around the fire pits now that it was getting colder, but the massive tree that towered over us was the most amazing thing I had ever seen. Even before autumn had started to change the world, bright red leaves painted it like a crimson stain against a blue sky. Now that it was colder, and most of the leaves had begun to change, it was even more amazing, the red specks dangling like ornaments from silver branches. The beautiful thing towered over everything, taller than any other tree around. It hardly looked real, but sitting below it felt safe. Both from the sun and everything else in the world.

After so long living underground and hunting in the cities at night, too much sun was painful. But I didn't want to be away from it. I didn't think I could ever get enough of the feel of the heat against my skin, the way everything was warm and the air felt alive. I remembered little of my life before magic, but there was more magic in the sun than I had ever felt run through my veins.

"Fine, walk me through this again," Eddy said, scowling at the slug as it was scowling at him, beady eyes waving through the air like micro-flags. We probably should hurry this up, I had a feeling the monster was contemplating how to eat him.

"Okay, now focus your magic on the slug," I instructed as I

scooted into the shade, folding my legs underneath me and pulled at the strands of grass. "You gotta let it flow through the air to the thing, think about swelling it up."

"Swelling? Why in the world would I want to swell it?" He asked, his voice stuttering as he stood with his hand forward, little wisps of brightly colored smoke dancing around his fingertips, but growing no closer to the slug.

"Fine. Make it get bigger then if it doesn't make you queasy. Just make it bigger." I said, leaning back on my arms and kicking my boots off. I was really regretting wearing my tights today. There was something about the tickle of grass against my bare legs that was like magic.

This would have to do, for now. I threw my hands behind my head and shut my eyes, letting the sun fall over my face, seep into me and turn me into some kind of magical battery.

I didn't even flinch at the cold breeze that moved over my skin, I had grown up in freezing underground cement tubes. This was amazing.

"It's all making me queasy." His voice was closer, he had obviously given up on the slug. But if he thought I was making the thing smaller he had another thing coming.

"If you want, we can work on making him explode instead. Goo, everywhere."

"Gross." Ed was full-on whining now, his massive shape hulking over me and blocking out my light, and therefore my battery-powered cynicism.

"Don't be a baby, Eddy. Focus on making him get bigger and he will." I poked him in what I assumed was his thigh, but was a bit too firm and wet to be Ed's thigh. That better not be the damn slug.

"It's actually more complicated than that." The sun turned to ice with the sound of that voice, the hoity-toity sneer drifting down from the heavens like some irritating angel. What the hell was he doing here?

"Aren't you supposed to be scowling at me from a distance?" I snapped. "Or did you master that square on douchebag prince bingo and are moving on to scowling from nearby?"

"I haven't been scowling at you from a distance," Prince Rowan said, I could nearly hear his brow furrowing.

"Could have fooled me. Especially with the way your girlfriend went all psycho on me and my friends." I smiled at him, eyes still closed in firm defiance of his existence.

"Sia's not my girlfriend, Gemma." He sighed, the sun popping back into existence as he stepped away before thinking better of it and rushed back.

I groaned. "Go tell her that. I think I actually enjoyed the scowling more than whatever this is."

"I want to talk to you." His husky whisper ran over me in a tickle of energy that pricked in the base of my spine. I stiffened. I didn't know what that was, but it was sure as hell not welcome.

"Well, do it from over there. You're blocking my sun," I said, opening one eye to glare at Rowan.

I should have never done that. The firm wet thing I had poked made more sense. Rowan stood over me, wearing tight black shorts and a white shirt that might as well have been painted on with how it was clinging to his skin. Sweaty, sweaty skin. It dripped from his hair and beaded on his arms and shoulders like little droplets of starlight that reflected the sun in all directions.

Mini sweat rainbows.

It wasn't the sweat that was causing me to lose eighty percent of my mental capacity, because sweat is gross. Muscles, however...

In his baggy school uniform and messy black hair, I never would have guessed he was hiding all of this. I swallowed, slowly, as I tried to find some snappy comeback to hit him with. But all thought had left, the smile he was now giving me was not helping with that.

"What are you wearing?" I gasped, choking on the words and glad something else didn't come out.

"Clothes," he said, looking down at himself as if this was normal for him.

"And sweat, apparently. You sure you weren't wrestling giant slugs somewhere around here?"

"I was playing rugby." He puffed out his chest like that meant something.

"Is that something I should know? Or lick off you?" He rolled his eyes at me.

"Don't lick me. Ever."

"Fine by me," I said, laying back in the prickly grass again. "You don't know what you are missing."

"Can we get back to the slug," Eddy said, his voice shaking. The showdown between him and the slimy dog was reaching an apex.

"Let me help. Engorgement isn't about thinking about making things bigger. It's expanding the cells within a thing." Rowan explained, back to ignoring me, thankfully giving me back my sun.

Instead of basking in it, I rolled over, opening my eyes as his hand extended to the slug that was now growing and shrinking in size as simply as if it was breathing itself in and out of existence.

"Woah. Cool." I whispered, a bit too loud seeing as Rowan turned, giving me what I am sure he thought was a shy smile.

I was absolutely mesmerized. There wasn't a drop of magic coming from his hand, I couldn't even feel the buzz of his magic in the air, even though he was clearly using it. The movement of the slug was a perfect motion; smooth, simple, beautiful. Well, as beautiful as an expanding slug could be. Eddy had now turned a fine shade of green.

"Is the slug too much?" Rowan asked, shrinking the thing back down to a normal size and letting it disappear between the blades of grass. "Ummm... let's see."

He jogged away, toward the bushes, the muscles in his back pulling with the smooth motion of...

"What the hell is going on, Gem?" Eddy hissed when Rowan was out of earshot. "Did you put him under a spell or something?"

"A spell?" I didn't even think we could do that. Or maybe we could. Why couldn't I stop staring at him? He was leaning down now, his shorts bent over...

"Damn it Gem, snap out of it and stop staring at his ass." Eddy hit me upside the head as he hissed at me, something which I thoroughly deserved. "What is going on?"

"Like I know? He's barely talked to me for two months and his girlfriend is on a murderous rampage. I'm pretty sure I didn't invite him to our slug swelling party."

"Well, don't mess it up. He came over here. That's a good sign," Eddy said, still watching him as he hiss-whispered at me. "We need him."

"Yeah, like I'm the one who messed it up before." I rolled my eyes at him, trying not to look at the way Rowan's back was flexing as he continued to scour through the bushes.

"Well if he tries to save you again don't tell him he's full of himself." Eddy was serious. What? Did he forget everything about me in the last ten seconds? That was not going to happen.

"He *is* full of himself. He's a fucking prince who has scowled at me for over a month. Surprise-surprise, I can't read his mind," I hissed that last part, sitting up and snarling before he turned around, both of us snapping to attention and smiling like we were all innocent and shit.

"Here, let's try these," Rowan said as he jogged back, three long sticks in his hand, which he promptly handed out to me and Eddy.

"Ummm," I began looking at my stick like it was a snake. "I don't need this."

"Seeing as you thought engorgement was thinking about making things bigger, you clearly do." He gave me a wink and I about hit him with the stick. Up until two seconds ago it was my job to prod him. He was stealing my thing.

Fine. It's on.

"Okay fine, prince. Teach me how to expand a stick." I used the stick like a baton, twirling it through the air as I bowed to him from where I sat in the grass. Rowan shook his head, Eddy giving me a warning stare from right behind him, which I ignored.

"Close your eyes and focus on your magic." I gave him a look, the single raised brow hopefully telling him how stupid he sounded.

"That's the same damn thing every teacher tells us when they are trying to teach us something, Princey." I still didn't know what it meant.

"Well, then try it. Focus on your heart, on the way your magic moves. The way everything around you has energy, you can feel it. Your magic, the magic of those around you." His eyes were closed now, his voice breathy and far away as everything grew silent. The birds, the wind rustling through the leaves, I could have sworn they were whisked away.

I swallowed. Had it gotten a few degrees warmer, or maybe I had been transferred to the edge of the sun. Rowan wasn't the only one sweating. I mean, Eddy was too, but that was mostly because he was grunting and gasping trying to get the thing to double in size.

"Well, they say it's not something you learn until next year,"

Rowan suddenly said, his eyes snapping open, flitting right to me, making my breath catch. "But it's worth a shot anyway. Once you master that, you can push your magic into the stick and see it from the inside. Each cell, each fiber, each ridge, then you can prompt it to grow."

He was still looking at me, his green eyes dark and smoky as the broken tree branch in his hand doubled in size. A nice big stick in the palm of his hand. I nearly choked.

"Your wood got bigger," I said with as straight of a face I could manage, Rowan growing as red as a watermelon as the stick fell to the ground. Eddy was reduced to gasping laughs behind him.

Rowan looked ready to melt into the grass, but I gave him my biggest grin.

"Please, Princey. Tell us what happens after the wood grows nice and big."

He kicked the stick away, every scrap of exposed skin turning a nice red color, like my feet after I had left them in the sun too long. Eddy was still standing behind him, although he took a noticeable step back, his eyes bugging out of his head as he watched us, still desperately trying to motion for me to stop.

"Is that really where you are going to put that?" I asked, nodding toward the shrinking branch. My grin was stretching so wide it hurt. "I think you missed."

I sat there, purposefully spreading my legs an inch just to watch the guy's blush deepen. Instead, he exploded.

"Can you grow up?" He said it so loud that a bunch of other sweaty guys who were passing by turned and snickered before shuffling away with one stony glare from the prince.

"Excuse me?" I was up before I could stop myself, moving dangerously close to the guy who was now growing darker rather than a brighter shade of watermelon.

"Grow up, Gemma. Stop playing whatever it is you are

playing. Stop being so selfish, before you kill someone." He grew louder with each word. The tree behind us was shaking dangerously, at though the massive thing was trembling in fear.

Okay, so maybe I should have listened to Eddy's warning.

"Is that what you wanted to talk to me about? That I need to stop being selfish?" I roared, stepping even closer to him. "Me? Selfish. Says the prince who disappears for days at a time to hide in his estate rooms and eat candies. The prince whose mommy pampers him and keeps his precious constitution safe from all the mean Drains so he can date a girl who tried to murder more than one Undermortal in your masochistic race. The prince whose family shits on my people and locks me up so I have no chance to help them. Tell me, Rowan. When was the last time you did something for someone other than yourself? When was the last time you tried to help anyone?"

"Gemma, stop," Eddy mumbled, still backing up, we both ignored him.

"I tried to help you!" He roared, the tree continuing to shake overhead. Blood red leaves fluttered around us like angry rain. "I tried to stop you from killing her! From hurting everyone!"

His voice vibrated the air, my magic bubbling with anger as I opened my mouth, ready to unleash hell on the bastard prince. Instead, my throat closed up.

"What? Killing who?"

"I tried to help," he continued on, like that somehow answered my question, or clarified anything of what he had said. "I've always tried to help."

"Stop fucking trying and do something, then," I hissed, my confusion in what the hell he was talking about thankfully drowning my anger enough that I wasn't yelling anymore. "Tell your cousin to stop shitting on my people. Tell Cail to help me get the food out. People are starving. Not like you even notice anything beyond your glistening walls to care."

I snarled, looking up to him as I let my magic flare. I knew I was playing on dangerous ground but I didn't care. I would fight him. Part of me wanted to see what he was capable of, if he was capable of anything at all.

"You don't care, do you?" I said, letting my magic flare around me until I was sure he could feel it. "Or is it that the rumors are true and you're too weak to do anything."

Black fire flames in his green eyes, the ebony anger pooling over his face as he roared, the air filling with fire as a crack echoed through my ears, the sound rattling my skull. I flinched at the sound that was too close to a gun, the sound made worse as a thousand bright red leaves rained over us as he leaned closer and hissed in my face.

"Never call me weak."

I could only stand there, leaves falling over me as I watched him go, Eddy looking behind me in horror.

I didn't dare turn; I didn't dare turn from the retreating back of the prince. His words echoing in my head. Long after he had gone, long after the leaves had settled around me like a blanket, did I turn around to find the tree cleaved in two. The trunk was split right down the middle, sending the two halves to the ground, bows snapping under the weight.

"I told you not to piss him off."

19

ROWAN

I HAD OVERREACTED.

Then I had overreacted further when I had returned to my dorm and thrown one of the overstuffed chairs through the window. Glass and stuffing were easily repaired, but it didn't stop my father's disappointed scowl from filling my mind, his eyes flashing dangerously blue as he reminded me to 'watch my temper'.

Maybe this time all of those reminders and disappointed looks had a point. After nearly three months in this school, sleeping longer than before, and dealing with Sia and everything else, I was clearly walking a fine line.

Suppressing my magic was making everything more volatile. I needed to keep it under control if I was going to regain control of the dreams and my magic.

I was about as far away from that as I could be, considering that one buzz from my phone sent me jumping and the lamp on my bedside table shattering to the ground.

"Shit!" I yelled, barely catching the phone that I had thrown above me, Angela's picture twisting through the air as the screen flashed.

Thankfully, I had shattered the lamp and not the phone.

"Hello? Angela?" I said, the second the call connected, my heart in my throat. "Is everything okay?"

"Yeah." Her little voice was swallowed by static, the connection buzzing. "Did I wake you up?"

Wake me? I glanced at the thankfully unbroken alarm clock on my nightstand. Two a.m.

"No, no. I was up."

She was the only one, besides our parents, who really understood what was going on. In a way, it was nice to have at least one person who knew. My throat closed up, the hairs on the back of my neck pricking up as I sat upright on the bed, the blankets I had been laying on shifting underneath me.

"Wait. Angie? Why are you awake?" The tension didn't leave as I waited for her answer, listening to her breathing and all the 'ums' and 'ehs' that usually came before she found her words.

"I had a bad dream." That could mean so many things, especially for her, it did nothing to ease the tension.

"Did you tell mom about it?" I asked, pinching the bridge of my nose in an attempt to banish the headache pounding at the base of my neck. I didn't know if I was in a place I could help her.

"Mom's not here." Her voice was nothing more than a whisper, but it slammed against my head like a bass drum.

"Dad?" She exhaled, she knew what I was doing.

"They are both gone, some emergency thing. But I don't want to talk to them, Row. I wanted to talk to you." Nine years old and she could already put me in my place. She clearly inherited that from mom.

I leaned back against the headboard, pressing my spine against the carved wood as if it could brace me for what was coming.

"What is it, Angie?"

"Dramin said you were my age when your sight first came, when Mom had you drink from the mug. Can you tell me what that was like?"

The wood I leaned against cracked in two places, whether it be by magic or by pressure, the sturdy support would have never been enough to prepare me for that.

"Why did he...? What did...?" Nothing was forming, words were falling through the cracks as I was. Everything sped past me as that night and the memories that I had spent years locking away sucked all the oxygen out of the room.

"He told me because I had another one of those dreams, like when I was little. He said you had one like it." Normally, I would tease her that she was still little, that Drak powers didn't set in. Tell her that a bad dream was a bad dream. But my jaw was still working on its own, my heart migrating into my throat now. Words weren't coming anytime soon.

Luckily, she plowed on, every word she spoke adding to the pressure on my chest, pushing me through the abyss that had opened up behind me.

"I saw Talon and Analine with you, they were yelling. Then some glass broke and there were swords, and blood, and a little girl was screaming. She looked like me, Rowan. Can you... can you see yourself in sight?" There was a pause, the tense air filled with breathing, filled with my tears as those damn images from my very first sight pushed their way back into existence. "Rowan?"

She couldn't make me say it. I wouldn't say it. I couldn't stomach it. It all hurt too much.

"I wouldn't know, Angie. I don't have sight." My voice caught with every word, her little gasping breath pulling through the static of the phone and making it clear she was crying.

I wanted to hold her. I wanted to run home and hold her and take all of this away from her. She shouldn't have this. No one should have this. But I couldn't move, I was trapped in a dorm room hundreds of miles away, staring at the remains of a broken lamp on my floor.

"I know you do, Row."

"I don't," I snapped, my hand shaking against my ear.

"Please tell me, Rowan," she whispered, her words broken by her sobs now. "I'm scared. I need to know. Is everything I see going to happen? Are you going to kill me?"

I forgot to breathe, I forgot to cry. I was free-falling through the abyss now, frozen in a bed that was as hard as steel, tumbling past a life that I had tried so hard to force into reality, into one that I didn't want. Into a moment I first saw ten years ago, the one and only time I had drank from the mug and felt the black water hit my tongue.

My mother had been pregnant, the baby coming soon. We knew it was a girl based on her magic and so my mother decided to have my first sight be of the baby. My little sister. She wanted my first moment as a Drak to be full of all the joy. The laughter. Her first steps. I saw every wonderful moment, right until the last one when I stood over her, her blood on my hands as I laughed. My malicious chuckle echoed over everything, my eyes smothered in the charcoal light of sight as her tiny frame slunk lifelessly to the ground.

As I ended her.

I didn't want that. I had done everything to stop it. But it was still there, everything I had done to save her was for nothing. Angie had seen the exact same thing.

I wanted to scream, to run away from the memory, from the moment. But I was trapped inside of it. It was everywhere, like a toxin pulsing through my veins.

"Rowan. We can change it, right? Please tell me we can change it."

"We can change it," I answered her sobs, although my voice

sounded hollow and dead in my own ears. A reflection of my soul.

"Everything you see is pliable. Sights are echoes of what may come, warnings of things that could be. We can always change them." I echoed exactly what my mom had told me years ago. The words ones I still did not believe. No matter how much I wanted to. "Mom saw dad's death. She even saw her death in the war. But none of that happened. They are both still alive. You are still alive."

"But for how long--"

"I won't let that happen, Angie," I cut her off with a snap, the phone cracking as I clenched it. "I won't let anyone hurt you."

"Have you seen what to do?" she asked after a moment, the sobs in her voice lessened somewhat.

"Ya," I lied, staring at my dresser, at the drawer that held the mug my mother had sent me with. The one I hadn't held since that first day, the ugly thing looking like nothing more than something a child would make.

Everything was pulling me toward it, a breeze moving over my neck as something powerful prodded me closer.

Begging me to hold it. To drink. To see the images that had been twisting through my mind.

"I told you, I'm going to fix it."

"Okay, I believe you. I trust you," she paused, "I love you, Row."

"I love you too, Angela," I whispered, watching the specks of salt water accumulate on my bedspread as I cried.

"Come visit me this weekend, kay? And bring that girl I saw you with, the one you were kissing."

"Kissing?" My head snapped up, staring into those vile moments with Sia that I was suddenly scared that Angie had seen.

"Yeah, your girlfriend." Her giggle seemed out of place

against what we had talked about. Against the tears that were still falling down my cheeks. "I like her hair. I wish I had pink hair."

I was back to clicking and gasping instead of actually forming words.

"Ang... what--?"

"Bye, Row!" The phone clicked off before I could even catch my breath, the room twisting together in a swirl of color. Color and magic and power that would give nothing more than to drag me down.

I might just let it.

20

—————

SIA

THERE WAS FAR TOO MUCH CHATTER FOR THIS EARLY IN THE morning. The sun hadn't even fully risen, but the grounds and expansive halls of my home were full of light and energy. Eager preparations and commands echoed through the closed door and whispered through the window that had been cracked in hopes of defusing the rancid smell of my father's preferred cigars. It hadn't helped.

I had helped the CCC prep for a raid many times before. I had even gone on a few, shuffled to the back to watch the aftermath rather than be at the head where the carnage was. This time, however, I had been taken away by my mother's personal assistant, Kay. The stern-faced woman said nothing more than to 'wait here' before she locked me in to a room I had been in only a handful of times before.

My father's office had always been one of those forbidden rooms growing up. Much like my mother's dressing room, or the servants quarters. As a child, I had heard Father yell, scream and rage from the other side of these walls. But now, I was locked on the inside with the cluttered hard wood desk, and the drawers of trinkets and tokens from his adventures around the world and all the communities he had conquered.

There was a painting given to him from a king in Japan, photographs of graffiti and rotted out trains. Piles of what looked to be rocks sat atop papers of reports from The Wastelands and the new camp they were trying to open up deeper into the nuclear dead zone, where the concentration of valuable fallout debris was deeper. We needed bodies to mine it, and the Drains provided the perfect source.

It was to only thing they were good for.

"Get the north company ready to move," my father boomed, his voice echoing as loud as his shoes against the wood floor, every beat bringing him closer to his office. Exhilaration thrummed with each step. I straightened, smoothing skirt and hair and gripped my phone harder, staring at the number on the screen.

"I want them to come in from the south side, intelligence says there is a tunnel there that they don't know of."

The door squeaked open, my father and the CCC captain, Jer, strutted in with the sound of two full-grown bull elephants. It wasn't far off from the truth. The two were massive men. Their demeanors were as large as they were and made even more ominous by the black-armored uniform that had replaced their usual suits. The skull masks that were set atop their heads only added to the oppressive display.

Seeing them in their raid gear made my heart sing. Soon, I would lead my own raid, father had given me my own skull mask when I was only ten.

I had almost grown into it.

"The one on the left, near the old station?" Jer asked, grabbing two papers from my father.

"Yes."

I sat still, watching my father shuffle papers as Jer stood at attention. Neither of them looked at me, my father's silent dismissal of me was screaming in my failure, but I ignored it. I sat still, silent, maniacally straightening my hem with one hand as I clutched my phone with the other. The damn thing was turning into a lifeline. Especially with how the old man was acting.

"Once we secure this one and redistribute those Drains we will have all the entrances to the river surrounded. We will be two away from taking the city," my father said, his eyes scanning over a map of Prague pinned on the far wall.

That same map was in millions of classrooms and books, I had even seen it painted on to buildings. Looking at it now, was like looking at a child's drawing. It was colored with prisms and squiggles that I didn't understand.

"We will be ready in an hour, Giovanni. We should arrive just as they begin to wake up for the day. Too tired to do anything, not that they could in the first place."

"Wonderful. Tell Samantha about the change in plans and have her prepare the new Drains for the water." It was only then that he turned to me, his narrowed hatred the first acknowledgment of my presence. "I have something to deal with, first."

"Yes, commander." Jer's response was firm and booming, but it might as well have been a grumble with the tunnel of my father's stare that I had been sucked into. It was only when the door snapped shut that the gunshot of our conversation fired. My father slammed his fists into his table, sending a pile of what looked like lude photographs drifting to the floor.

"What are you doing here?" He didn't look away, neither did I.

"I have news." I straightened my back, my fingers still tight around the phone.

"I hope it is that the princes magic has sparked against your own, or perhaps that the Drain has been eliminated." I tried not to flinch at his snarl, his lip curling.

"No, but this is even better, I can--"

"You mean to tell me you have been successful in neither of your tasks?" he cut me off, turning away from me to the cabinet that was tucked into the corner. The massive carved wood closet stored multiple mortal guns, most ones he had procured from neighboring countries that were ruled by other magic users than the Eternals, not that there were many left.

"I have a plan," I spoke up, scooting to the edge of the leather chair to get his attention. He didn't turn. "There is still time to accomplish both, but I have learned--"

"Your time expired the moment you arrived here with no success," he said, equipping one gun after another, tucking them into the straps and pockets that lined his black armored uniform. "We have waited patiently for months and you have failed us again and again. I suggest you look at your future carefully, because it no longer lies with us."

Shit.

Shit. Shit. Shit.

I had never felt tightness in my chest like this, felt this bitter taste of failure.

He might as well have dismissed me with how fast he was moving to the door. He gripped two guns in his hands when I jumped up, the chair tumbling to the ground behind me.

"I know how to defeat the Eternals." I was firm. Thankfully he turned, although it did not miss my notice that he cocked the larger of the guns, the electronic core in the massive weapon whirring to life.

Even with the pressure in my chest and the powerful man that was glaring at me. I was calm, standing tall before my father as he waited, eyes narrowed enough that I knew I had permission to continue.

"I had the Drains life in my hands, I was moments away from completing the task, but I was stopped."

"You came all the way here to tell me of your defeat, you are no daughter--"

"I was stopped by a Krul," I interrupted, taking a step forward. His nostrils flared and I quickly moved back. Now was not the time to push my luck. "A Krul who calls the rats by their true name."

"Analine." The curl in his lip was not a good sign, but I plowed on.

"Yes."

The tension in my chest was reaching a breaking point, but I waited in place as he exhaled. His eyes softened, although the look was more in pity than in triumph.

What the fecking hell was going on?

I had handed him an Eternal on a fucking silver platter.

I was suddenly nervous about how he would handle the other, much more important part of my news.

"Father, Analine has given me--"

"Analine is a dead end, child." My father's jaw was tight, even though the guns dropped to his side. He was looking at me. He had called me child. "Analine thrives on the love and power the Goldens give her. She abhors the Drains only because they do not respect her, because they do not feed her ego. She has no interest in causes unless it ends in parades in her name. She would rather belittle children than actually act on anything. Her self-righteous efforts do not align with our cause."

"That may have been, but it is not anymore." I let the smile creep out.

"Your love of the Eternals has blinded you to rational thinking. She has no interest in you--"

"I don't believe that to be true anymore," I cut him off, my hand jutting out to stop him as he turned to leave. His dark scowl dug into me but I wasn't about to shrink away like a wilted flower. Not that cowering in fear would do any good with those guns. "Her alignment has changed, she gave me the number of someone who might be exactly what you are looking for."

I spoke slowly, determined to drive every point home as I held the phone out to him, the white screen displaying a name and a number.

His eyes darted to the number and back to me, the shock carefully masked as he shouldered the smaller gun and took the phone from me, still staring at the screen.

"You can't be serious, Sia."

"I am. Analine was quite clear of their interest." I refused to look away from him, my magic pressing against air and skin in its excitement. He clearly didn't reciprocate.

"What if this is a trap? What if your poor attempt to redeem a failure ends in my death? Or perhaps it would be better if it ended in yours?" He jutted the phone back to me, forcing me to take it. The screen was still illuminated with the number. His message clear.

I swallowed and squared my jaw. Fine. If he needed proof that I wasn't a pussy, so be it. Perhaps he expected me to die within minutes of making the call. Less blood on his hands and a solution to his problems, I supposed.

My jaw tightened, a humorless chuckle escaping as I pressed my thumb against the number and the echoing sound of dialing filled the office.

Once.

Twice.

My father's grin stretched with each buzz of the phone, his victory growing as my dread swelled into a nauseating balloon.

Then the screen changed, everything going white as a voice echoed through the speaker.

"Hello. I've secured the line." The deep male tone rattled

through my spine. He sounded different than I expected. More mysterious. More powerful.

"Hello?" I said, unsure of what else to say. My father stepped closer, his victory fading into skeptical shock, his face as pale as the blinding light of the phone. I had never seen the screen go so bright before. Must be some weird kind of magic.

"Is this Demarco?" He spoke again, more of the tension in my muscles leaving to be replaced by sparks of excitement.

"Yes, the youngest. And the oldest," I added with a look to my father, who still hadn't regained any color.

God, what I would have given to smile at the old man, to laugh at his once smug grin and slap him with one of my own.

The voice on the other side of the line was doing that well enough.

"Good. I've been waiting for your call since Analine told me. I've been trying to make contact with you since that fucking Drain got put in that school. I have to say, that Cathedral was quite the show. Sent everyone into a fit over here," he chuckled, the sound a darkness that I hadn't even heard in my father before. It flared through me like a drug. God, I wanted more of it. Of him.

"So, tell me," he continued after a moment. "What can I do for you?"

21

ROWAN

"Check." Cail gave me a grin, his toothy smile stretched wide as he dragged his knight over the board to my king. He was two moves away from winning now, if it wasn't for my last surviving pawn it would have been checkmate, although if I knew Cail...

I didn't look away from my cousin, his smug grin stretching as I monitored the board with my magic, the power pulling a perfect replica of the board into my mind. We had been playing this game for the last half hour and up until a minute ago, I had assumed that I had been winning.

But Cail would never make a move so bold unless there was still a guarantee he would win. There. The Rook. Once my pawn was moved, presumably to take out the Knight, the Rook could sweep in and knock my King on his ass. Ending the game. I did another sweep, still not looking away from my cousin. He had said check, not checkmate so moving my King had to be the only option. I didn't see anything that would get me in trouble.

Slowly, I reached my hand forward, dramatic flare supercharged. I tapped my pawn before moving my King back one square, just as slow and loud as he had moved the Knight.

The sound of stone scraping against stone echoed off the crowded bookshelves and wood-paneled walls of his office, mixing with the crackling fire that was becoming needed as the temperature continued to drop.

"That was close," Cail said, not so much as hesitating to reach forward and grab the rook. Moving the piece in the opposite direction, he took out my Queen and perfectly aligned himself with my King. "Perhaps one of these days you will actually defeat me."

"Shit," I swore, knocking down my king for him. Once again, I had only looked ahead one move, not the two or three that was really needed in this game. It was why I never won, not against Cail. Not against anyone. I always forgot to look ahead.

"Language," Cail said with a smile, beginning to clear the pieces away, placing them gently in the stone and wood box that he treated as carefully as one would a baby.

"What the hell, Cail? Like you're one to talk," I snapped, handing him five of my pawns before leaning back in the overstuffed chair and throwing my feet up on the now empty coffee table. I checked my watch, I had fifteen minutes of bliss left. I was going to enjoy every minute of it.

"Well, I am supposed to be ruling over you or some shit, I might as well make it seem like it from time to time." Cail's smile twisted playfully as he sat back in his own chair, producing a pipe which he quickly flared to life. "You know, just as you are supposed to make it seem like you are an everyday student."

I audibly groaned, closed my eyes and laid my head back against the seat. So much for enjoying my last fifteen minutes.

"How did I know these Royal Dispatch lessons weren't just going to be getting my ass beat in chess and breathing in your second-hand smoke? Although, three months before a lecture is a record I suppose."

Cail chuckled at that, just as the air filled with the aroma of cinnamon, or whatever he had put in his pipe. From day one I had known what this 'class' was: the one place I could be myself. Uncle Ryland had tried to duplicate that with Rugby. It might have worked too, if it wasn't full of slathering elitist Goldens.

Greer was the only decent person on that team.

Cail and I had never been close, mostly because for my entire life he had spent the majority of his time at the school. Now that I was at the Academy, he had provided an escape, even if it was filled with cinnamon scented air.

"It's all about proprietary, cousin." He blew out a wave of smoke, the colors twisting in the air before shattering towards the ceiling. "Appearing the way you want them to see you. We want them to remember you are a member of the royal family, so you get to come here every day for me to clobber your ass in chess." He chuckled at his own joke, but I wasn't about to join him.

That was the last thing I wanted, and the main reason I had not wanted to come to this school. So much for being able to avoid any of that.

"Is that why you are always locked in here?" I asked, gesturing to the room that I had only seen him out of maybe once or twice before. "Smoking, reading, and scaring the first years about their upcoming exam?"

"Occasionally, I lecture a student or two about how using magic in the hallways is dangerous," he said through the pipe in his mouth, the smoke still lazily drifting up to the ceiling.

"How thrilling." I threw my head back again, looking at the pressed iron plates that lined the ceiling.

It was inlaid with a pretty design, the leaves and swirls almost like something out of another world. Elegant, but marred by magic stains that made me wonder how old they were. If the swirls of black smoke were remnants of the war, or were where

Cail blew off some steam after all his treacherous hallway decorum lectures.

"How are you getting along, Rowan?" Cail said after a few minutes of silence, the question tightening up my spine. I didn't shift, however, I kept looking at the ceiling. Perhaps if I stayed still for fifteen minutes I could avoid this conversation altogether.

"It's been months and I have heard nothing more from the teachers other than that you seem displeased and have missed quite a bit of school." He took another inhale as I lifted my head, arching an eyebrow at him. "Don't worry, I haven't said anything. So far everyone thinks you are weak, sick, and dying...."

I forced a cough and collapsed deeper into the chair, leaning against the arm as Cail continued to exhale plumes of purple smoke around us.

"I suppose there are worse things. Like being in a fake relationship." I was trying to keep my voice as steady and as diplomatic as possible. It wasn't working and the corners of Cail's lip twitched, holding back a smile.

"Yes, you ended that in glorious fashion, didn't you? Although we all would have appreciated a warning."

I didn't want to get into it. Thinking about Sia was not what I needed right then. Not when my dreams had shifted, when I had someone else I couldn't get out of my head...

"Have you ever felt your magic spark against another?" I refused to look at him as I asked the question, still scowling at the ceiling.

"You mean like the beginnings of a bonding. Of finding your mate?"

"Yes." I pressed my lips together.

"Did your magic spark to Sia's--"

Cail's question was cut off by a loud pop and a gasp. I didn't even jump at the sounds that had been a regular in my life. I expected the smell of sulfur and the wave of magic after one of my parents stuttered into Cail's office. What I hadn't expected was the overwhelming aroma of blood to flood the air, the metallic aroma drowning out the burnt cinnamon smoke from Cail's pipe.

"Ilyan!" Cail yelled, jumping his feet as I turned in my chair, heart falling to my toes at the towering king behind me.

"Dad?" I barely recognized him. His hair was unbound, flowing halfway down his back, the ends drenched in blood. The golden ribbon that was usually bound in his hair was tied around his wrist, barely visible beneath the blood-streaked jean jacket he wore. Jacket and jeans.

I had never seen my father wear jeans; I have never seen the ribbon out of his hair. Those images alone should have been shocking, but it was the amount of blood that was dripping from him that scared me the most. It was everywhere. It absolutely covered him.

"Are you injured?" Cail asked, placing his hand against my father's, checking him for injuries. The king didn't move, his blue eyes digging into me, his lips pressed into a hard line. He clearly hadn't expected me there.

That's okay. I hadn't expected this either.

"Dad! Is everything okay?"

"No." I wasn't sure if the gruff snap was in response to me or Cail as he looked away from us, already pulling a phone from his pocket. "Get Mira. Ry and Wyn should be here any minute. Jos is bringing Dramin."

Cail said nothing before he sprinted away, a shield snapping around him and smothering him from view right as the door opened and closed as though it was being pulled by a phantom. It was an old trick, but I still jumped, mostly because of the way my blood-covered father was now searching through the low cabinets of Cail's bookcases, slamming doors and throwing piles of books to the floor.

"Dad?" I asked, my voice shaking as much as my hands. I tried to reach him, to help him, to do something, but the world was shifting too fast, everything spinning.

"I'm sorry, Rowan," Ilyan said, opening up cabinet after cabinet, slamming door after door. "I didn't know you would be here. Cail usually warns us, it must have slipped his mind."

"Warns you?" I asked, still trying to process what I was seeing. "How often do you come here? How often do you come here covered in blood?"

My panic snapped into logic as I stepped behind him, his search escalating before he finally found what he was looking for. An old cracked mug. One of the brown earthen things that you could summon Black Water in.

"Why do you need that?"

I took a bigger step back, fear on top of fear compacting against my spine.

"More lately," he said, turning to look at me. "This is not for you."

He stood on the other side of Cail's desk, the mug teetering on top of the mess of papers that usually covered the surface, pulling me into it. I took another step back, forcing myself to look from the mug, but I only found my father's blood-streaked face.

"What's going on?" I tried to keep my voice strong and steady, even though I knew that if it came down to a battle of wills, there was no way I could win against him.

He hesitated, chest heaving as he looked from the mug, to the door, to me, the pressure in the room growing with each of his ragged breaths.

"Dad? Please. You're covered in blood..."

"There has been an increase in attacks lately."

"An increase...? I didn't even know we were having attacks." Before I was able to riddle him with the million other questions that were racking my brain, the door burst open on its own, a flood of magic following the air in.

The door slammed shut, four bodies appearing out of nowhere as their shields dropped with a pop.

Mira, Cail, Wyn, and Ryland. The last two as covered in red as my dad.

"Ry!" Mira shrieked, jumping into his arms. Ryland's hands left marks against the bright white of her shirt, streaks of crimson smearing everywhere.

"I'm fine, lecture later," Wyn said to her son, rushing past the three of them and giving me a side glance as she bolted across the room.

"We bringing him in already?" she asked, jutting a thumb in my direction. "I thought you wanted to give it a year?"

"I didn't know he would be here," My father said, now clearing the desk of papers, the harsh tone so unfamiliar that I was starting to question if I knew the man at all. "If I had we would have brought Mira to Imdalind, not the other way around."

"Hence the mug?" Wyn asked, arms folded over her chest as she stared at the thing with as much disdain as I felt.

"Hence the mug." My father said, giving me another intense stare. As if his glare alone could scare me away.

"I need someone to tell me what's going on. Because I'm about to lose it," I snapped, wishing there was a way to dig my heels in, or whatever the mortals would do against their parents.

"Ever since the Gauntlet there have been outbreaks in some of the tunnels--" Wyn began, turning to face me, although my father's stern face still towered from behind her, glaring into both of us.

"Not yet," Ilyan said, snapping his fingers toward Wyn who instantly closed her mouth. The glare made it clear it was not an action of choice. "He's not ready."

"Ready for what, Dad? I don't know if I can be ready if I don't know what's going on!"

"Not yet." My father's blue eyes shimmered with damp emotion before he returned to the table, furiously stacking and moving the clutter off the desk. It was only then that I realized his hands were shaking. "You're not ready for this, Rowan. I'm sorry. I need you to go back to your rooms. I will find you later."

"Ilyan, none of us were ready when the world came knocking. None of us." Ryland said, peeling himself away from Mira "You think Jos was ready for my damn house to implode around her, or Cail to throw her out of a window?"

I looked at my cousin Cail in confusion, but he waved me off, like he hadn't thrown my mom out of a window.

"Or me to be used as a bomb and kill my own brother," Mira piped up, striding past me to stand next to Ryland, both of them facing the king like some kind of wall. The bravest and dumbest wall I had ever seen.

"He's not ready!" Ilyan yelled, his voice cracking as his hands shook, at the bookcase behind him cracked in two. Books and papers poured over the floor in a literary waterfall. It was as I had done with the tree, the family temper peaked through. "I will protect my children, Wynifred. No matter what. You understand that better than anyone. Now, get him out of here."

"But Ilyan--" Wyn started, any counter cut off by yet another pop, the room erupted with smoke and a single scream as my mother burst into being, Dramin draped over her shoulder. Blood was pouring from a large gash in his chest. He wasn't moving.

"Take him!" my mother yelled, Ryland and Mira grabbed Dramin right before he hit the ground. So much for clearing the table, my father pushed all the papers to the floor, only the mug surviving the onslaught.

Not that it mattered, I couldn't look away from my brother. I couldn't hear anything past the thump that was rattling my bones as my heart tried to remember how to beat. Blood dripped from him like rain, it covered my mother. It covered the floor.

I tasted it in my mouth, I was sure I could feel it against my skin, like every dream. Every night. Every sight.

The attacks. They slammed into my side, taking the last of my breath as the world spun away and pulled me into it. I didn't want to know what had caused this. But I already knew.

Dramin grunted as they laid him on the table, the blood free-flowing over his chest and dripping to the floor.

The whole world was dyed red.

"Rowan," mom whispered, pulling my focus as she grabbed my hands. The blood that covered her streaked against my skin as she held my hands against her chest. "I need to pull my magic to save your brother. I know you don't want this..."

"It's not that... It's..." I couldn't find the words, and seeing all that blood. I had seen that blood other places. I couldn't do this.

Everything locked up as I stepped away, even as I needed to move forward.

I needed to help him.

"I know. Which is why you need to leave," she said as my father handed her the mug. She placed her hand over the rim, filling it right to the top as I had seen her do a million times before. This time, instead of drinking the black water, she handed it right back to dad who took it over to where Dramin was laid over Cail's desk, blood pooling over the sides of the wood.

"We will come see you later, I promise." I didn't miss my

notice that she hadn't said anything about telling me what was going on.

"Don't bother," I hissed, pulling my hands away from hers. "I'm not ready. Go heal Dramin."

I was pissed, I had meant to snap, to shame, to do anything to vent my frustration. But saying his name, seeing him laid on the table, I couldn't. My voice caught in my throat and it wasn't until Cail was pulling the door open behind us that I even realized he was dragging me away.

It was like I was watching a horror movie, my mom's hair moving in slow motion as she raced to Dramin.

Mira, Wyn and Ryland held him down as my father moved mother's hair back from her neck, revealing the dragon shape brand behind her ear, the mark of a chosen glistening as she drank from the water, as she poured it over Dramin's wounds, as my father pressed his finger to her mark, as they all began to scream.

I had no idea what I had just seen. But it didn't matter. I couldn't even turn to Cail to ask before my magic surged, everything spinning as I was sent to my knees, my own scream ripping through the air.

I didn't even have time to push the sight away.

The Drak magic had connected me right to her.

22

GEMMA

"It's five fucking o'clock. In the morning. I am going to murder whoever is knocking on my door!" I stomped across the floor of my dorm, making as much noise as I could without my boots, simply not caring who I disturbed, or how much beauty sleep of Sia's I was disrupting.

You know what, screw it. I stomped around more, flinging the door open and half expecting her ugly scowl to be laughing at me. It wasn't her.

"Who the hell are you?" I asked the smiling woman on the other side of the door. I suddenly felt out of my place in the underwear I had fallen asleep in, seeing as she was dressed in some kind of candy-striped business suit and bright red heels. No one looked this nice at five in the morning. Well, except her. Whoever she was.

"My name is Patrice." Her wide smile and perky nature made me even more sure she was a figment of my imagination. Happy business women should not exist at this god damned hour of the day. Ain't no one got time for a smile that big and painted on.

"I'm sorry?" I was being kind of snappy, because five in the morning, but her smile didn't falter.

"May I come in Gemma?" Still didn't know who 'Patrice' was, but I doubted someone would send a smiling assassin my way, and even if they did, I could use the workout.

"Sure, come in," I held the door open wide as she shuffled by me, her heels not so much as making a noise on either the stone floor or the heavy carpet in my room.

Shit. Maybe she was an assassin, or a hallucination, or a ghost. Either way, I could take her. My magic was still all alive and supercharged from having been woken up so abruptly. In fact, it felt completely normal. Like I could do anything, almost like when we held our midnight meetings. Maybe the Štít was sleeping.

I lifted my hand to check, but caught her staring at me and dropped the hand behind my back.

"So, who exactly are you?" I asked, leaving her in my living room to grab my robe. Not that I needed to cover up, but she was looking at my tattoos funny and it was weirding me out.

I had inked a whole ocean scene over about forty percent of my body when I was fourteen. It covered much of my back, my stomach, my left arm, and leg. It was full of bubbles and seaweed and fish that we had copied from a book I had found. In the center of my back, a mermaid, dreaming of a world she could never have. Maybe only two people had seen the whole thing, make that three with this lady and her slack-jawed stare.

"What are you doing here?" I demanded, very aware that all of Ed's leftover coffee cups on the little table were starting to rattle. It had been so long since I had felt more than a trickle of my magic. It was very quickly getting out of control. Weirdly, she didn't look scared.

"I was sent by the royal family to help you," she began, stepping around the chairs and looking around as though she had never seen a dorm before.

"Help me? I'm really going to need more context than that."

She smiled again, pulling a folded paper out of a hidden pocket in her suit thing and handed it to me. I didn't need to open it to know what it was, I had seen that curly writing before. Our letter had worked. Thank God Cail wasn't as big of a douche as his sister and had delivered the thing.

"We have all of the vans pulling in now," Patrice said, stepping around my dorm like I had invited her in for an inspection and not a casual chat. "We will have time to load the food and send anyone you choose to their respective communities with as much as they can load. I will escort you to your community, if you agree of course."

She paused, turning to face me from where she stood by the bathroom, eyes narrowing into me. She clearly wanted an answer, all I could do was nod. I was still too shocked to really compute that this was real and not some twisted hallucination. Just to be sure, I walked over to the little kitchen thing and slammed a drawer on my hand.

"Holy mother!" I screeched, jumping back and waving my hand through the air, shaking off both the pain and my momentary lapse in judgment.

"Good lord, are you alright?"

"Yeah," I grumbled, still shaking, still jumping around, still clenching my jaw so as to keep the scream in. "Just making sure I'm not dreaming."

"I can assure you that you are not." Strangely, that time she didn't smile. "Now, another condition for this arrangement is your help. The Queen and King would like you to investigate the recent attacks that have been waged against the Undermortal communities. Who led them? What the goal was? Find out if any counter-attack against us or the Chosen is being planned. Can you do that while we are there?"

I swallowed, I knew that royal bastards were going to put me to work sooner or later, it was part of her deal for letting me keep my magic. I hadn't expected it to be quite so full of espionage. I was suddenly faced with the reality of being their spy. I had no other option but to grit my teeth and give her a solitary nod. Which I did.

"Wonderful," Patrice said, clapping her hands together. "If we want to deliver the food to as many of the Undermortal communities as possible we need to hurry. I believe it would be best if we get on the road before the other students begin to wake up?"

I gave her a nod. Yeah, very good. I hadn't been the only Undermortal that had been attacked by the golden spawn in this place. The less of a reason we gave them to target us the better.

"Perfect." she clapped her hands together, bouncing the toes of her shoes, her heels clacking against the floor that time. At least I knew she wasn't a ghost. "Now, go rouse your friends and have them meet in the cafeteria. My husband will be arriving to help us next week, but this week--"

"Next week?" Interrupted her, my heart pounding excitedly against my rib cage while her smile returned. "We are going to do this more than once?"

"Yes. Every week. We are excited to help. Unfortunately, my husband Dramin is preoccupied this week. Under the weather, we shall say. He should be tip-top in no time."

"Dramin?" I asked, searching the worry the was burrowing in her eyes. Something about her husband was worrying her. The name clicking into a place a second later. "The prince. Meaning you are..."

"Able to kick your ass if you get out of line." I stepped back. I hadn't expected those words to come out of her mouth. She gave me a sweet smile that didn't quite match her appearance, no wonder she was worried about her husband. She probably expected to have to kick my ass then and there.

"Yes. Now go."

She scooted me out of the room, closing and locking the door behind us with a snap of her magic. I didn't even have time to argue over the fact that I was still in a robe, I took off down the hall racing toward Eddy's room and hoping to every Eternal in existence that he knew where to find everyone else.

"I can't believe they let you out," Ed said, bouncing excitedly on the plush bench seat in the middle of the van before he popped another of the fried carrot straws in his mouth. I would be worried that he would eat them all before we got to Last Pyre, but we had bins and bins of them at our feet.

More than enough for Aria, the kids, and even Ed. He could eat all he wants; we were almost there and I was about to see how everyone had been faring since I left them.

That was the part that had me fidgeting in my chair.

"I'm sure the queen is just having a momentary lapse in judgment," I said, stealing a carrot fry of my own.

A scoff echoed from the empty backseat where Patrice sat, legs crossed, staring out the window as if she was caught in a daydream. The sound was the first sign she had given that she was still there, still shadowing my every move. She hadn't said much since we left, which was probably for the better.

I would rather Ed or anyone else that was currently streaming to their communities not know the darker side of what had gotten us this privilege. I had warned them I was a double agent; I don't think any of them knew exactly what that meant.

I cringed and sat back against my seat, watching the city I had never actually seen stream by the window. My entire life had been underground, watching the sun and the clouds dance over the blue sky from behind the bars of a grate. A prison.

When I finally did emerge, it was under the guise of night, just like the creatures we shared the tunnels with.

But this sprawling city of iron and glass was impossible in the kaleidoscope colors of the sun. Massive buildings stretched to the sky, their reflective glass side making them look like crystal tears from the sun. They exploded from a ground of square brick buildings and rows and rows of houses that gleamed of white stone. Some of the houses that we streamed by were as big as the school. As big as that massive room in Last Pyre where we all slept.

Seeing the wealth as we rushed through the streets to the poverty made some of that slowly building trust evaporate. How could any leader look at this for so long and let it happen?

It made my heart ache.

"Remember," Patrice said as the van exited the long motorway, making a beeline for the darker, older buildings that were more familiar. "I will be with you the entire time. So please watch your behavior, I won't make myself known unless something is needed from me. Or if you step out of line, Gemma."

"Yeah, yeah, I got it." I ignored the look Ed was giving me and sat back in my chair. I folded my arms over my chest but not before I shamelessly lifted a few carrots from the bag. Popping one in my mouth, I threw the other at Patrice who promptly disappeared from sight, pulling that same shielding trick I had seen in Gregario's class on the first day. I barely flinched, Eddy however shrieked and plastered himself against the tinted window of the van, the driver jerking at the noise and sending us veering to the other side of the road.

A car honked, the driver swore, and Eddy shrieked again as the same car sped within inches of the window. Even my heart was pounding in my chest, sure that I might have died or worse.

"What the hell?" he sputtered, still looking between me and

the open-air that Patrice had both appeared and vanished in. "What. The. Hell."

That time I very clearly heard the Eternal laugh.

The rest of the trip was spent discussing how the more advanced shields work, Eddy begging the empty back seat to demonstrate again, which she obliged to a few times.

"Eternals suck. They can do all the cool things," he moaned as the van turned, the road growing uneven.

I gave him a look, I was sure he could do the same with his super cool ancient Vilỳ bite, but I would have to remind him of that later. Our grumpy looking Chosen driver grumbling as we drove into the old MidCity stop that led to Last Pyre.

The large lobby had been where the vans had picked us up to take us to the Gauntlet what felt like a lifetime ago. It had been where we had sorted the food and supplies from months of raids. It was where we slept when the summer flood got too high. It was where I had first dreamed of the world I could create with the magic that buzzed in my veins.

It was in ruin.

The tiles that had once been set into the floor were pulled up in rows, as if a monster had dug its claws in. The mural of flowers that covered the left wall had a massive crater in the middle, colored tiles showered over the ruin in specks of haunting color. With all the lines of smoke and a still burning stack of wood near the entrance to our home, I was amazed the place was still standing at all.

"Oh my god," I gasped, gripping on of the front seats, needing to see better, but needed to see anywhere else. "What happened?"

"That's what we need to know," Patrice whispered from the empty air behind us. "There was a string of attacks two days ago, four communities fell. But not this one."

"This is as far as I can get." The driver's voice cut in with a dead drawl, his fingers clicking nervously against the steering wheel as he peered at the doors at the end of the once grand entry. His magic was drifting from his skin, sitting heavy in the air as he fidgeted. He clearly didn't want to be there. I was suddenly worried that he was going to take off the second we unloaded the supplies.

Muscles coiled over my shoulders as I reached for the sliding handle of the door, my fingers weren't shaking, thank God, but they felt like they should be. The air felt heavy, like it was made of water, as I wrapped my hand around the handle.

"Wait." Patrice suddenly said, causing all three of us to turn, although she did not appear this time. "Do you two feel confident to attack should something go wrong?"

"Attack our people?" Eddy asked his voice cracking. I dropped the handle as though it was made of a hot iron.

"No, I doubt your people would attack you, especially with Gemma here." The disembodied voice was not aiding with my inability to swallow, or breath, that I was currently experiencing. "But I can sense quite a few bodies and their placements are worrisome. There's a large man, hovering over ten others, maybe more. I think they are sleeping."

I couldn't even register the fact that she was sensing and seeing people from the back of a van a half mile away. My fear had built up too far, the emotion quickly replaced by the anger that had fueled me for so long. The need to protect my people. To save them. I had been away for so long, and now they were right there. I could actually do something.

My magic wasn't illegal anymore. I wouldn't pass out after a few fireworks.

"I can fight if I need to. I want to fight if I need to." I said, looking in the general direction of the Eternal.

"Perfect. Then you take the lead. I'll stay hidden. Alexander," she addressed the driver, the man jerking at his name. "You start unloading. Once we've established that everyone here is safe and why whoever attacked them retreated, we will leave."

"What if they are not safe?" I asked, Eddy's shoulders falling.

"We will do what we can," Patrice said before she popped back behind her super-powered Eternal shield, leaving me and Eddy to exit the van with a look we hadn't shared in months.

Raw, eager, battle-worn fear.

"You ready to set the world on fire?" he asked in a whisper as our feet splashed through puddles, the red hue ominous against the light that bled through the open grates high above us.

"I'm always ready," I grinned, pushing my hand before me and sending the door on its hinges, the massive slab opening without so much of the creak it had always had.

Ice dripped down my spine as we burst through the door, down the stairs and into the massive sea of blankets and huts and smiling faces and the people that were my people. That were my family.

Except, there was nothing there. Nothing but a few forgotten wads of blankets and belongings that used to be someone's home.

"What the hell?" I sputtered as my heart did. "Where is everyone?"

"Through here," Patrice whispered from behind us, a bit of a breeze tugging at my hair before the door that led to one of the tunnels opened, the big red X painted on the door.

No.

Oh god, no.

My father and I had put that X on the door years ago, only days before the CCC had carted him away. The X was the usual sign for a cave-in or dangerous walkways, your basic every day stay the fuck away warning. Except that one was a lie.

"What are they doing in there?" Eddy asked, rushing to the

door, oblivious to what was going on. "That's caved in. They must be in trouble if they went that way."

"Let's hope that's all it is," I mumbled to myself as I chased after him, the door opening further before we could get there, Adrian and about twenty others filing through the door, only to freeze at the sight of me.

"Gem," Adrian gasped, his expression fluttering between shock, fear, awe and everything in between.

He was already rushing me, his arms open, the awe settled in his eyes. Adrian swept me up in his arms, crushing me against him. He was mumbling about how long it had been, how he missed me. Every other pleasantry that I had no interest in.

I couldn't fight him. I kept watching the door, waiting for everyone else to appear. To burst through in waves of the people I loved and surround us.

No one else came through.

"Where is everyone?" I asked, wiggling out of his arms to race to the door and peek through, that same breeze rustling by me as Patrice whispered 'I'm going to go check'. The breeze rippled over the standing water in the long-forgotten tunnel as Patrice raced down it, away from us.

Away from everything I needed to say. I closed the door behind her. Not enough to lock her out, but enough I would know when she got back.

"Where is everyone, Adrian?" I asked again, turning back to them all.

"They are all gone," Adrian whispered, his big brown eyes wide, although there wasn't a hint of a tear there. "You were gone for so long, and the CCC kept coming and coming. We couldn't fight back."

His voice cracked, his eyes growing red as his hands pounded against his thighs, everyone around him just as tense, just as forlorn. I could see the pain, the loss, the horrors looking back at me. I had seen them enough. I had lived through them enough that they didn't need to tell me anymore.

"They wouldn't let me come back, Adrian. You knew they were going to lock me in that school--"

"You left us all to die, Gemma." He snapped, all of the emotion evaporating into the anger that had fueled me for so long. The anger that was trying to boil its way to the surface now. To ignite the fire that had extinguished without me knowing.

"I'm here now," I said, as powerfully as I could, straightening my back as I faced him, his lip twitching.

"Yes, you are here now." His voice was kind, soft; nothing near the guy that I knew. He was so fake he might as well have been molded from all the rat shit that was shoved in the corners of this place.

He closed the gap between us again, holding me close to him, his nose buried in my hair as he whispered, "Too late to do any good."

"No," I snapped, pulling myself away from him, he didn't even fight me. "It's not too late. We brought supplies, but more than that, we brought news." I paused, glancing at Eddy who gave me a nod of confidence, and then at the partially opened door. It hadn't moved.

"Is it news of the death of the king?" Adrian asked, looking to the few men who were around him, all of the arms folded over their chests as they shook their heads. This was even worse than the Bitchicade. I had a feeling that one wrong move and they would try to pummel me to death. "Or have you found a way into the caves of Imdalind? I would gladly take that, you've been locked up there so long I had given up on you."

"No, but we are getting closer to an attack, the food is the start. The Undermortal Chosen are delivering food to all of the communities. Once we organize, we can fight."

He raised an eyebrow, "You are sending people to empty tunnels. The CCC has done nothing but attack. You are too late."

"We will never be too late to take on the Eternals--"

"You expect us to take out the entire royal family?" He interrupted a wave of laughter moving from him to the guys around him.

"It will be all of us, together," Eddy said, raising his voice until it rattled against the broken CandleEars that hung from the ceiling. Or what was left of them. Most of them had been burned and pulled to the ground. "We are ready for this, Adrian. They won't be able to stop us."

"What? A hundred or so baby chosen, bowing to the king to rise up against him?" Adrian laughed a few of the men behind him chuckling as well. Men. They were all men. Where was everyone else? "You are too late. The Eternals have already made their move. I've heard the whispers about them in the tunnels. Right alongside the CCC, that black-eyed bitch telling them where to attack."

"What are you saying?" I asked, my chest tight, checking to see if the door had moved. If Patrice had returned.

"Are they killing our people?" Eddy asked with a snarl, stepping between me and the door as though he was expecting a fight.

"No," Adrian shook his head, a wicked smile spreading over his lips, "they are the ones taking them away. We are going to fight back in other ways."

"What are you suggesting?" It didn't miss my notice that Eddy was moving closer to me. So many years protecting me after a fight that he had clearly forgotten he had magic himself.

"You got bit, Gem," Adrian said with a glance to the door. "There was one Vilỳ left behind. There might be others."

"We killed the one that bit me," I snapped, a rock forming at the base of my spine and quickly migrating to my throat, bouncing against my bones the whole way up. "My dad smashed his head with a rock."

"Did he? I'm not so sure," Adrian said, shrugging and glancing toward the door, the heavy metal open more than it was before.

Shit.

She was stealthy.

"You won't find anything," I lied, working to keep my face still. "You're wasting your time."

"Better than sitting at school doing nothing."

I flinched as if I had been punched. It felt like it, but I still stepped forward, more aware than ever how small I was against him.

"Adrian, don't be like that," he didn't even respond, I guess those days were gone. Fine by me. "We brought food, we don't have much time, but we have plenty of food. Some new blankets too."

I gave Eddy a look as I passed him, trying to wag my eyebrows or something in an attempt to tell him that Patrice was right there. I'm not sure it worked, but he didn't say anything more as we walked to the van, Adrian and his posse whispering behind us.

"We need to get out of here," I whispered when I thought we were far enough ahead of them. I wasn't even sure any of them heard me. Eddy was still looking behind him and gesturing to them to hurry up.

Thankfully Alexander hadn't been idle. The entire van was unpacked, piles of boxes and bags littered around the tailgate. Without a word, they all grabbed their fair share and turned back toward the main room.

Toward the door with the bright red X.

"We will be back next week," I whispered to Adrian as I pulled him to a stop, tightening my hand around his forearm.

He looked at my olive hand against his dark arm before attempting to pull away, but was pulled closer until all I could see was his, the chocolate orbs bloodshot and angry.

"Don't bother. We don't need you anymore. Your prince, however..." He smiled and my jaw dropped, pulling his arm away with a jerk as I stood.

I didn't even know how to fight him. How could I? I didn't even know how he knew.

"Adrian, what-?"

"Bye Gem. Thanks for the fuck." He waved behind him, everyone laughing as they carried the boxes away, no one looking back as they stomped through the door and away from us. I stood, stomach-churning as I watched them go, listening to Alexander pack the van back up, Patrice whispering to someone from inside the darkened interior.

"Do you really think that Vilÿ's alive?" Eddy whispered, looking from me to Patrice.

I didn't answer. I watched Adrian dip through the door, shutting it behind him, knowing that it was. Knowing that he had already found it.

We drove home in silence, even Patrice was quiet, although visible, in the back seat. By the time we returned the sun was already setting, the biting cold of early winter already moving over the ground and making everything sparkle with frost.

"Every community is reporting the same. Fast Fire, New Hearth, even the Ghostlanders came back with the same report. They say that the Eternals are there, carting people away while the Tarn armies lay waste to our homes." I whispered to Patrice, the two of us standing on the front steps of the school, the icy air moving up my arms as I recited what I had learned after arriving back, the whispered reports following me through the halls.

Each one feeling like a dead weight against my heart. Even

my magic felt sluggish again, like being back in the school had closed that Štít back up.

"What are they saying of us?" She asked in nearly a whisper, although the line of muscle in her shoulders exposed her fear.

"It's no secret that the plan has always been to rise up against you," I said, hating the way my stomach was knotting together. "But it seems the communities have another plan. There are whispers of an uprising, but we are no longer involved."

I hesitated, looking into the last line of light as the silver moon replaced the sun. The air was heavy as she waited, as if she knew what I was going to ask next. As though she knew all the answers and was waiting for me to continue on.

"What did you find in the tunnel?"

"I think you know, Gemma."

The rock in my heart had moved into my throat, I could barely form words.

"My father had kept it to do the same thing Adrian is doing now. But when he was taken, I couldn't pull myself back into that cave. Their deaths were my fault. Because I had been bitten, because they were trying to protect me. I didn't want anyone to have this curse, to feel the pain of loss. I thought I could fix it on my own. Plus, I might have liked the attention." I rubbed my nose, trying to smooth the guilty wrinkles there.

What was wrong with me? Spilling my heart out to this woman, an Eternal. The bastard had been my sworn enemy my whole life. Now they were everywhere, acting like normal people.

I pulled my face into a scowl, "It was fun blowing up your shit."

"Indeed." I could have slugged her with the laugh in the single word, but I had a feeling I would end up plastered to the wall. "Unfortunately, those days are over."

"You say that like we've already won. That this world isn't going to keep shitting on us. It will."

"Not if we can help it. There is one thing about the King and Queen that I always respected. They learn from their mistakes. They know of what is to come, and that this is how it always should have been," Patrice said turning back toward the now brightly lit school behind us. "I am beginning to think that boy was right from the beginning."

"Who was right?" I asked, boots slamming against the frozen asphalt as I ran after her, nearly sprinting into the building and the radiant heat it offered.

"Next week, same time," she said simply, purposefully avoiding my question. I would have pestered her more, but I had a feeling she wasn't going to answer me either way.

"I'll have my husband with me, remember," she continued, heading through the sleepy students that were starting to moving through the halls toward their dorms, every head turning after us in awe. Crap, guys, it was an Eternal, not a woman with twenty boobs sticking out. "Clothes would be preferable when we arrive, although I do really like your tattoos."

She turned right as we reached the door, holding her hand out to me in what I had assumed was an offer to shake. But the second I reached for her she turned her arm, rolling up her sleeve and displaying her bare wrist, the skin that was usually branded with the mark of a Vilỳ void of the mark. Her forearms were another story, the tattoo of a flaming rabbit was clearly visible near the crook of her elbow.

Although the design had changed since she had been inked, I recognized the brand immediately.

"Fast Fire?" I gasped, recognizing the tattoo at once. "But no mark?"

"A story for another time, perhaps," she smiled, true joy

peering out at me. "Thank you for helping me to remember my people, Gemma. For helping all of us to remember our people."

There was no smile on her face because her eyes had devoured the emotion, it beamed from her like the fire was inside of her, the tenacious determination of an Undermortal pushing through.

She leaned forward, pressing her lips against my forehead before she was gone, out the front door and into a waiting car. Leaving me standing, staring, and in complete awe.

23

ROWAN

A LAUGHING MAN CLOGGED MY SIGHT. I COULD SEE HIS HEAD thrown back, his shoulders heaving. But I couldn't make him out beyond the dark hair that swayed in his cackle, I couldn't look at him long enough to see. My sight kept pulling me past him, the thousands of people who screamed, who ran away from the man. Away from the hundreds that chased them. The tunnel swelled with blood as children cried, tattooed masses flowing down the darkened tunnel like waves. Haunted eyes stared at me from people who were little more than skin and bones. And through it all, burned fingers. Burned fingers pressing against glass, against skin, against the tears of a child. Against Gemma's lips as she whispered something I couldn't hear.

The sight kept twisting, kept changing, kept torturing me with image after image of things I never wanted to see.

I woke with a start, blankets falling away as I sat upright, heaving in minty air as the dark room twisted in and out of focus. Mint, pine, and a heady aroma of the Drego, a bark from a tree long since extinct that buzzes with old magic. That combination was usually only used for life-threatening injuries. Unless I had fallen into a metal spear when I collapsed, the

Drego being burned in my room was not a good sign. Nor was the magic that was pulling through the darkness toward me.

"How long was I out?" I asked, to the darkness, not even flinching when the bright screen of a cell phone burst into view, the screen illuminating the face of a woman who had been covered by a shield until a second ago.

Wyn sat in a chair, legs folded, foot tapping to some music she was listening to in her lone earbud as she clicked her pink polka dot nails against the screen of her phone.

"Figures you would wake up on my shift," she signed dramatically, pausing briefly from tapping on her phone to smile at me. "Now I've gotta be the one to ask you the tough questions."

"You can start by answering mine," I mumbled throwing my hands over my head to block the light of the phone, the dim was pounding over my skull like a broken drum. I could feel every electrical current as though it was a live wire.

"About five days." She finally answered, clicking the phone off and shoving it back in her pocket, plunging us back into thankful darkness. "Your parents will be here as soon as they can."

I half expected the room to ignite in the snap and smell of a stutter, but everything remained quiet and dark, Wyn's breathing and the slow chirp of a cricket outside my window the only sign that time hadn't completely frozen.

"I take it they are busy."

"Yes."

I sighed, the memory of Dramin on that desk rattling my breath, the reality freezing me to the bed as images from my dream mixed with it.

No. Not a dream. A sight. A sight so strong that I hadn't been able to stop it. It didn't feel like the dreams that pushed their way into my unconscious, the magic that had taken me was power, filled with the magic that was always rumbling under the surface.

It felt the same as it had the first time. I hated it just the same.

"Did I say anything?" My voice was deadpanned, the tension that was holding me in place as I waited for the answer. To know how much my magic had reacted. How much of the Drak came to life inside of me and if there was any chance of pushing it back down to the dark pit that I kept hoping it would die in.

"Yes." She inhaled, as I ground my teeth together with an audible hiss as the truth slammed into my gut. As much as I had tried. As much as I had worked, the power was still there. Stronger than ever.

"Is Dramin okay?" I asked before she could expand on that answer, twisting in my bed to look at her, or rather her outline as she leaned closer to me.

"Your brother is fine. He is already healed and back on the front lines."

"The front lines. That makes it sound like we are at war." The prickles in my neck were stronger than before, I could already tell that pushing the Drak magic away was going to be impossible from now on. "Will you tell me what is going on?"

"I can't do that, Rowan." She said, leaning back in her seat and pulling her vibrating phone toward her, tapping on the screen again. It was only then I noticed the bloodstains on the top of her fingers, the dried bits still stuck to her wrists.

I swallowed.

"You can't, or you won't." The snarl in my voice flared all on its own, the temper that I always had such a hard time controlling rising up in a boiling rage. It had never felt so strong before, so all-consuming.

It was as though my magic had been sleeping all this time and just woke up. Just like before. With my first sight. I didn't want this. I had worked for years against this. No matter how hard I pushed against the power this time, it wasn't going anywhere.

"Can't," Wyn said, putting the phone back in her pocket. "Your father bound the truth from you. None of us will be able to tell you what's happening."

"Well, isn't he a peach." I wanted to use a much more colorful word, but with the possibility that they would show up any second, it wasn't worth the risk.

"He's trying to protect you, Rowan. He's trying to protect everyone. It's what he's best at actually." She laughed at something I didn't understand, nor did I care to. They were all acting like idiots and I had no interest in dealing with it.

"I don't need to be protected. I need to know what's going on. My brother was lying on a desk, his chest cut open. Every single one of you were covered in blood--"

"Well, to be fair you weren't supposed to see that," she interrupted me. I ignored her.

"And now I am having sights of tunnels flowing with blood and bodies, and laughing men leading armies through the rivers like they are conquering countries," my chest tightened, power spreading through the muscles in my back like wings, everything tensing as I tried to banish the damn stuff.

"That's what you said," Wyn gasped, speaking slower as she scooted from couch to bed. As if being close to me would buffer what she was about to say. Even with no light I could see the trepidation on her face. I could taste it in the air. "You said 'the man who drips with blood will conquer the world, smear it with ash and paint the future that was once the past.' or something. Hold on, let me check my phone."

"Stop!" I bellowed, causing her to jump and the phone to fall to the floor as I jerked to sitting, everything spinning. That one outburst reversing any success I had in banishing the powerful flood of magic. It was everywhere, dripping from my pores like poison.

"I don't want to know what I said," I heaved, trying to control my temper and my magic. "I don't want to see what could happen. I want to know what is happening now."

"It doesn't work that way, Rowan. Not anymore." My rampage was drenched in the ice water as my parents stepped into the room, my outburst so loud that I hadn't even heard them come in through the door like normal people.

They even looked like normal people, well as normal as they did for us. The only exception was that my father's hair was falling out of his braid, the golden ribbon still wrapped around his wrist. It didn't take much to figure out why. Must be hard to fight with long golden strings flowing from you like a tail from a kite.

"I need to know what's going on." It wasn't a question. I did my best to push the demand home by throwing the blanket off me and jumping to my feet. But the world spun as magic and gravity worked together to take my feet out from under me and send me to the ground.

I was barely able to catch myself, falling into the bed instead of Wyn who was instantly on her feet. I grabbed the bedspread, pressing my forehead into the cool cotton as I tried to find my balance and tried to release the pressure that was fighting to explode out of me.

"You've been pushing the magic away too long, Rowan. It's going to take some time for it to adjust--" My mother rushed over to me, hands stretched out to help me to my feet or push me back in bed - she didn't get more than a few steps toward me. I held out my hand, pushing her back as I heaved, everything aching as I forced the magic away.

Forced everything away.

"I have to push it away!" I ground out, turning toward my

mother, her silver eyes flashing with black as my head spun and my vision flashed to red as her magic tried to join with me.

Red like blood.

Like Dramin's.

Like Talon's.

Like Angie's.

Like Gemma's.

Like mine.

I roared in agony, my heart bursting from the images, from the pain, from the tears that were dripping from my cheeks.

"I don't want this, Mother. Nothing good comes from seeing the future. Nothing but pain comes from knowing someone's past. Not when you can't change it. Not when those images, that pain. It's real. It's real. It's everywhere. Take it away." I tried to push the emotion down with the agonizing power, but everything kept bubbling and tensing against my spine until I was starting to lose control of my body.

"Rowan, we can't. I can't" My mother whispered, moving closer, her hands reaching again.

"Take it away," I sobbed, my back arching as the magic flared again, connecting to something I didn't understand. "Take it out, please."

"Rowan. You know we can't do that. Let us help you," my father whispered, leaning over the bed towards me. His hands were warm as he wrapped them around mine. His magic was already plunging into mine to help me calm, to help me control the overwhelming power of my magic, of the Drak as he used to do when I was little.

I didn't have another choice. I let him in, his hands holding mine, my mother's wrapping over my bare shoulders. Everything slowly began to ebb, and for a brief second I felt human.

Normal.

"I can't watch this destroy you. How much longer are you going to do this, Rowan?" my mother whispered the moment my breathing returned to normal, her warm cheek pressed against my slick one.

"Just a little longer. Please." It was the only answer I could give her. I wanted to say forever, I wanted to have been right and to be able to push it away, to never see, to never feel that overwhelming power of a Drak again.

I was starting to think that wasn't possible anymore.

I knew that wasn't possible anymore. This was my new reality. This was the hell I was born into.

"When you see..." I asked my mother, still heaving. "Do you see good too?"

"So much good," she said, her hand rubbing up and down my spine as she tried to calm me. "Yes, there is bad. But there is also good."

I nodded into the bed. "I know."

I did. Because as much as I had seen and pushed away, I had still seen Gemma. I had still been able to help her, even if it hadn't gone perfectly. Even if she didn't know.

"Well, when you can no longer hold it in. Let us know." My father whispered, his hands tightening around mine as he pulled himself over the bed to be closer to me. "Me, your mom. All of your family. We will all be here for you when that time comes."

"When the end comes," I whispered, able to finally take one breath without my magic feeling like it's about to devour me.

I didn't know if it was dramatic or not, but at that moment, it certainly felt closer to the truth.

"You don't have to hold the world, Rowan," my mother whispered, pressing her lips against my cheek for a fraction of a second. "Not on your own."

All I could do was cry.

24

SIA

I hated that I still looked for him.

Everything had shifted, the world had changed and opened up in a whole new realm of possibilities. I didn't need that spoiled prince anymore, but my eyes still scanned the halls. I still lingered at the edge of his hallway, waiting for him to emerge. The hall remained empty all weekend and into the school week.

He had been missing for nearly a week, six days, starting on the day my father had raided the tunnels and cleared the scourge from two cities. Six days from when my phone had burned white-hot and the deep voice had burned a new place in my soul. The two had to be connected.

Not that I cared.

I shouldn't care.

I shouldn't be concerned with the sickly, pathetic, royal. I had bigger things to worry about, especially since tonight was to be the first meeting with the owner of that voice. Every muscle in my back was tightly coiled, my stomach dancing as the hours clicked closer to the end of school. To the weekend, when it would be appropriate for me to leave the school.

When no one would know or care where I was going or why. My nerves had clearly gotten the best of me. I hadn't felt excitement like this since the Gauntlet, which was possibly why I had chosen to sit in a different seat than my usual for this class.

Why I had placed myself right beside the pink-haired anarchist who had made my life a living hell the last few months.

She had almost lost me my birthright. Lost me the respect of the only people who mattered in this world. Thanks to Analine's gift, she was no longer part of my task but I sure as hell wasn't going to let her get away with all her shit. Besides, this was the best way to pass these last few anxious minutes.

"You know," I sneered, leaning over the side of my desk towards her. "Just because you can't write and read doesn't exempt you from the work."

She froze, the pen she had been using to carve some grotesque shape into the surface of her desk stilling as she turned, her ugly purple eyes narrowing at me.

"Just because your head is full of air, doesn't give you an excuse to fail." Her smile spread as my jaw dropped, my breath catching as my magic sparked in my chest and pulled my muscles tighter.

The smart-mouthed bitch! She had gotten away with that stuff long enough. I heaved, nostrils flaring as I forced through a cleansing breath. I knew exactly what I wanted to say. Knew all of the nasty torments that had been brewing in me for months. I was better than her pathetic, childish games.

I was winning. It was time she knew that.

"You won't be singing the same song tomorrow, trust me," I let the warning drip from my smile, my eyes flashing as I let slip the threat that should have sent her running. Instead, the corner of her mouth pulled up in a smile.

"Why? Am I scheduled to kick your ass again?" she whispered, still not looking at me. Like her ugly doodle was more interesting than what I had to tell her. "I didn't have anything in my calendar. Or did you only tell your boyfriend, so he knew where to save--"

"Can I help you two with anything?" Professor Gregario boomed from right above us, sending both of us jerking, Gemma's pen breaking in two and spreading ink all over the place. "Cheating is not tolerated in my class."

"Shit!" she screeched, attempting to clean up her mess and instead staining her hands with ink the same shade as the foul tattoos that lined her arms.

"Oh! I wasn't cheating professor." I turned to professor Gregario, giving him an innocent smile as I waved the still empty page of the pop quiz we were supposed to be working on. "Gemma here was asking me about question one. I told her I don't give out answers to people who don't do the work."

My voice lowered as I turned to the now ink-smudged Drain, her eyes narrowing as I threw her to the wolves. This had worked out better than I had planned. I had simply meant to taunt her. Instead, I was going to do my best to send her cowering to the corner.

Take that bitch.

I waited for her shock as Gregario turned, ready to punish the bitch. Too bad we weren't in Analine's class, the backlash would have been even more glorious, this would have to do.

Instead of cowering beneath the stone-faced teacher, she rolled her eyes and grabbed the crumpled piece of paper from the corner of the desk and handed it to the old man.

"Question One. Describe the bite of a Vilỳ. The bite of a Vilỳ is often denoted by a raised brand-like scar on the skin," she rambled, already going back to cleaning up the ink as Professor Gregario unraveled the paper. "Often, they can take shapes that reflect the power of the giver, or of the receiver. Would you like Question two as well?"

My teeth ground together as I stared at her, as Gregario chuckled and walked away saying, "Quiet please, while others complete their work."

I ignored him and leaned closer to her. I had enough of her. This weekend couldn't come fast enough.

"Nice try, Sia," Gemma whispered before I could say anything, having finished cleaning the ink up and going back to her drawing. "Shall we add this to your list of losses."

"I can lose all I want, I'll still win." My lip curled as I leaned closer, thinking back to all I had helped create last weekend. All the deaths, all the slaves, knowing that this week, after tonight's meeting, was going to be even better.

"Seriously?" Gemma said, not even a drop of fear on her face as she chuckled. "Is there something wrong with you, or are you just incapable of making a logical comeback."

I jerked against the desk, the feet squeaking against the stone floor as I controlled my raging temper. I needed to fight, to hurt, to maim. I wondered how bad the punishment would be to end her now. Not worth it.

Not anymore.

"I can never lose," I hissed low enough that no one around us could hear. "Even when you think you have won, you still are below me. Ten feet under like the Drain you are, watching as I send a thousand loaded guns towards your people. Marching them toward certain death, filling your pathetic shit-filled drain with blood."

Gemma shot to her feet, the desk overturning behind her at the aggressive movement. Everyone turned as she roared, her hand wrapping around my neck as she pulled me up. My own desk clattered to the ground as she gripped me, blocking off my breath as she tightened her fingers. Murder painted her eyes, the color darkening as her magic raged under her skin. It felt like poison. Festering, vile poison. Fitting. I tried to laugh, but all that came out was a muffled gasp and a choking noise.

"Miss Gemma!" Professor Gregario yelled in alarm, everyone else gasping and moving away in a panic. I stayed still, letting her magic curl through me, feeling the vile heat of her hatred.

"You will never be above me," Gemma snarled, not even turning to the teacher or the students who were now screaming. I tried to grab her, to claw her eyes from her head, but she had wrapped something around me, her magic pressing against me from all directions. I couldn't move. I was frozen, choking, as the bitch snarled and spit in my face. "I know what you are. You will not live to face your own sins, of that I promise you."

"Gemma!" Gregario was screaming now, more and more students pressing against the side walls with wide eyes, like they were looking at a demon.

Maybe they were, I could see it peer through the near black of her eyes.

"Gemma! Stop this!" Someone yelled as I pushed my magic out with all my power, snapping her binds and sending her stumbling, although she didn't let go of my throat.

"Wait, bitch, tomorrow you will cry like the rest of them," I said with the last of my air, pushing at her hands to get a bit more. "Tomorrow you will remember how pathetic and useless you are."

She didn't get a chance to respond before a white slice of magic slammed into her side. Gregario's magic sent Gemma soaring through the air and against the back wall, and me to the floor to gasp and sputter. Everything burned and ached as oxygen flooded me, Golden's running to my side as Professor Gregario rushed her.

"Are you okay?" Miko asked, the first to reach me. I gave him a deep glare and focused on my breathing. What use was he in this game if he just stood against a wall and watched.

"They told me you were controlled," Gregario said from the other side of the room, his massive frame towering over Gemma as she untangled herself.

"I am controlled," she hissed between clenched teeth. Her entire body was shaking as she stood. He must have hit her with something hard, good. I gasped a few times and pushed tears to the surface, my wails pulling back the focus of everyone who had turned to them. They shouldn't forget the victim so easy? Forget the victim, forget the crime, forget how dangerous and out of control the Drains are.

"Go visit the headmaster," Gregario snarled, the guy still clenching his fists. "Have him check your magic and find your keeper."

I pushed out another cry to mask my smile, leaning against Miko as Gemma stomped back to her overturned desk, and her bag that was lying innocently on the floor. Even through the burning in my chest, it only took a flick to upturn the bag and empty the contents all over the floor. Goldens giggled as Gemma snarled knowingly. I cried louder.

"You deserve what's coming to you," I said between heaving breaths, watching her stuff her things back in the bag.

"Likewise," she said, throwing her bag over her shoulder and bolting out the door. Everyone around me cheered as she left, her ugly pink hair flashing through the door as she walked out the door, nose in the air.

"Perfect," Miko said from beside me, his hand running up and down my arm in a way that was starting to feel more than comforting. I muscled him away and pushed myself to my feet, bee-ling toward Gregario who was still snarling in the corner as he repaired the broken plaster in his wall.

"Professor?" I breathed out with a sigh, forcing my voice to shake. His irritation melted to worry the second he turned, his eyes dropping to my neck and flesh that I was sure was marked by both the hands and magic of the Drain. Lifting my chin so he could see better, I let out another shaky breath.

"Would it be alright if I left for the day? I had plans to go home this weekend and I feel that I need to leave to be safe. The king..." I purposely let my voice catch. "The king promised me I would be safe. I don't feel that right now."

"Yes, yes, of course," Gregario said, panic sliding across his features for a moment. "I'll make sure to inform Cail of what happened today."

"And the king?" I forced another sniffle.

"Yes, my dear, yes." He turned back to the wall then and I bolted away, tears gone as I grabbed my bag and strutted out the door, ignoring Miko's curious glance as I went.

The hallway was empty, everyone was still in class. It would have been so easy to follow Gemma, to send a bit of magic into her back and force her to pay for what she had done. I would have, if I hadn't been handed a much larger prize.

My legs couldn't move fast enough as I bolted out the front door of the school, heading towards the large hanger that stood on the other side of the grounds and the jet that had been waiting all day to take me home. I didn't even stop to drop off my bag, I couldn't get there fast enough.

It was with a relief-filled sigh and a smile that I walked into the hanger, notifying the pilot in the lounge to prepare to leave with a flip of my finger before I made my way to the sleek white jet that stood out amongst the hokey hand-me-downs so many other Golden's relied on. The staff was already lowering the stairs by the time I arrived.

"Miss Demarco," one of Drain workers mumbled, bowing her head as I arrived. Mary? Martha? They were never here long enough for me to remember their names anyway. "We didn't expect you for a few hours, ma'am."

"Well, I'm here now," I said, shoving my bookbag against her chest. "So, get to work."

Ignoring her extended hand and offer of assistance I ascended the stairs, taking them two at a time in my eagerness to get inside and sink into the squishy chair beside the window that was my favorite. Turning into the cabin, however, I found the chair to already be occupied, a mop of dark hair peeking over the top of the chair, expensive trousers and shoes crossed over the side.

"What the hell?" I snapped, bolting my way over to the chair. Fucking new help, they couldn't do one thing right. "What are you--"

I stopped short, words failing as I faced the man who had stolen my chair, faced the grin and the bright blue eyes that I had seen only once before: on the dais before the Gauntlet. Where he had stood with the rest of his family.

"Come now, youngest of the Demarco's. I thought you were expecting me," Talon said, rising to his feet, his massive frame both wider and taller than mine. I felt like a child beside him. A pathetic, useless child. All I could do was stare, my mouth open slightly.

"I am." I squeaked out, he smiled with a grin that I could have sworn stopped my heart.

"Good. Now, let's have some fun before our meeting, shall we?" He smiled again and my knees buckled, but not from the grin. I sagged against him as his hand slid around my back, his arm lifting me to press against him, his lips crashing against mine, tongue desperate as they parted them.

My magic as it went absolutely crazy.

Fire and lightning shuttered through my veins, every bit of

magical energy that I worked to restrain pressing against my skin as it tried to flock to him. To connect with him.

"Fucking hell," he murmured, pulling away from the intensity of the kiss to look at me. I was still trying to catch my breath, but the guy was looking at me with a powerful glare that made all the energy between us multiply.

"I guess my days of women and madness are over. Sia Demarco, you are mine now."

25

ROWAN

They never told me what was happening. Although I had heard enough, and seen enough that I could put it together.

The Chosen have been revolting against us since the explosion at the Gauntlet, more than the explosion of the cathedral on that first weekend, more than the picket lines from when the school first opened. Pickets don't cause stab wounds, well unless you plunge them through the hearts of the people you are protesting against.

Flashes of past and present invaded my mind, they throbbed against my skull in a painful rhythm and I pressed my palm to my head, doing my best to calm the magic that I still hadn't been able to regain control of. Sparks of frightening Drak magic came in waves that twisted my bones, pressing against my flesh until I started to shake. The last few days had been better after my father bound the power, but it hadn't been able to stop the sights. Not completely, so I had remained locked in my room. Being around anyone, especially Gemma and any risk of her magic flaring against mine, was not going to end well.

But that meant if I wanted answers to what was going on, I needed to be tricky about it. Wandering the hallways at five in the morning on a Saturday was not usually my forte. I was sure Cail would be pissed when I barged my way in, but seeing as my parents and aunts and uncles had made themselves scarce, he was my only option. A little booze, a game of charades and hopefully some shuffling through his desk and I would be in business.

I shifted the heavy bottle of liquor I had stolen from Wyn and turned the corner, immediately slamming into a massive pile of pots and boxes that I could have sworn was hovering all on its own.

"Shit!" Someone yelled as everything scattered, pots clanking, boxes bursting open, glass breaking and covering us with fruits vegetables and what I was sure was leftover listy, judging by the smell.

"What in the world," I snarled, trying to get the food and listy off me, turning to the girl who was trying to do the same.

Oh shit. Oh shit. Oh shit.

This was a mistake.

She wasn't supposed to be here.

"What the hell, Rowan?" Gemma snarled, peeling some of the foul leaves off her shirt and sending them hurling my way. "Can't you watch where you are going?"

"It's five in the morning. Why would I watch where I was going?" I hissed, throwing my own wad of food at her, looking at the doors around me and waiting for someone to pop out and yell as us. Surely someone had to have heard that. "I didn't expect anyone else to be up."

"Well, surprise, you're not the only insane person pretending to be a vampire." She gave me a grin and threw more of the foul stuff at me, this time hitting me square between the eyes.

The smell of the stuff was nearly as bad as the wet sticky texture. My stomach twisted in threat of turning out. I had about enough of this stuff to last a lifetime. Now it was stuck to my face like spackle.

"Vampire's aren't real." I scraped the listy off my face, ready to throw it right back at her. She was already prepared, armed, and chucking more of the green clods my way.

"Shows what you know, Princey. You're the one disappearing for days, walking the hallways at night, and allowing a blood sucker of a different sort to hang off your arm. Rowy!" She shrieked that last part in a near-perfect Sia impression. I jumped turning on my heel in expectation of the steam engine to be boiling her way around the corner, steam flowing from her ears.

"No one's there, loser," Gemma prodded, throwing another bit of listy at me, which I artfully dodged as I jumped closer, my hand covering her mouth as I silenced her.

"Shut up!" I snarled, looking at the door again, but nothing moved, not even a light beamed from under the doors. What was this? The hall of the deepest sleepers known to man?

Nothing else in the hallway was awake except me and Gemma, who cackled as she shot magic through my hand in an effort to get me off her. I hissed and jumped away, shaking my hand as if it would banish the pain, but the skin was already swelling up and turning red.

"You afraid I'm going to call her to your side like some kind of obedient dog?" Gemma laughed, throwing more listy against the side of my head before she turned to clean up. "Because I am sure she would. She might even wear a little bell if you asked her, wag her little tail while her ears perk up and she chases her tail."

"Oh god, I think I might pay money to see that," I laughed, loud and joyful. It felt so good to laugh, after the last few days it was much needed. Besides, the image Sia prancing around like a derpy dog was near perfection. Although I already knew she would be some overbred spoiled thing that expected to be carried everywhere.

"I thought she was your girlfriend?" Gemma gave me a look as she continued to pile boxes one on top of each other. "It's not nice to laugh at your girlfriend."

"How many times do I have to tell you, she's not my girlfriend, Gemma." I folded my arms over my chest as if that somehow settled it.

"God, you royals. You collect women, you are born with a permanent scowl, and you don't know how to clean up after yourselves," she sighed exasperatingly, nodding her head toward the broken bottles and spilled contents that were making the hallways smell like a burning farm.

"Not true, we just don't waste time doing things the hard way," I gave her a smile, waved my hand once and let the tiniest bit of my magic run free. I couldn't risk too much, but even the little bit of release was sending prickles of excitement over my skin. Trying to pull me closer to her.

I focused on the bottles, trying to push Gemma and her smile from my mind.

Waves of smoke flowed from my fingers, a breeze and a snap of wind moving over everything, pushing the listy back into bottles and bottles back into boxes and everything repaired and stacked itself. I even gave an extra gust of wind to clear the foul odor away.

"You trying to prove you're not weak?" Gemma said, not giving me so much as a smile and she moved to pick up her boxes again. "Because I already got that message when you destroyed my favorite tree."

"Destroyed? What are you talking about?"

"You ripped apart the only wonderful part about this place. Turned that massive silver tree to splinters all because I called you weak." She narrowed her eyes at me.

It took me a second to figure out what she was talking about. That moment outside by the tree felt like it was a million years ago. I pressed my palms against the back of my neck, flattening the hair and pricks of magic that were trying to congregate there in my shame.

"I'm sorry, Gemma. I didn't realize."

She froze in her work, glancing at me with an expression so soft someone might have had to knit it there. It was gone before I could get a second look.

"You're sorry for destroying such a beautiful old thing. Or sorry for being the world's biggest douche. It's official, your Prince Douche, you can't take it back now. That's what I'm going to call you from now on." She was beaming with that same smug grin again, her eyes lighting up as she laughed at her own joke. Her laugh, her eyes, it was such a beautiful image that I didn't even care that she had called me Prince Douche.

"Both," I whispered, my magic starting to prick up as hers flared, as I felt her power in the air. Mingling with mine. Dancing with mine. Wanting mine.

I tried to push it away, ignore its existence and convince myself that all the blissfully ignorant stories my parents, my aunts and uncles, and Dramin had told me were true. I had Talon for a brother, after all. He didn't seem to be bound by the same rules.

I did.

My mouth went dry as the heavy dark waves of the Drak pressed against me, fighting with the binds to reach her. To feel her.

Her laugh died as she turned to me, eyes wide in shock. As if she felt it too.

What I wouldn't give to touch her. My fingers ached, my heart thundered as I reached for her, for that tiny piece of hair that had fallen over her eyes. It would be so easy to just move it back. To touch her.

"Stop staring at me, Rowan." Her usual mocking tone was shaking. She was shaking. We both were. "You don't want your girlfriend to catch you looking at me."

I don't know if she had tried to push a joke into her voice, but it was lost in the wispy sigh, in the way she was looking at me, as the step I took closer to her.

"I told you she's not my girlfriend." My fingers twitched, wanting to grab her fingers, to trace the tattoos on her arms, to nip at the piercings in her ears.

She shivered. I nearly stepped back.

"I can't figure you out. You avoid me all the time, your girlfriend stalks me like a serial killer, you glare at me like I've killed your family," I flinched. I couldn't help it, the image came in a flash and I stepped back, leaving her gasping.

"Do you hate me, or just my kind Rowan?" she asked with a snarl, swallowing once before she continued, not even giving me the chance to answer her question.

"Help me clean this up, Princey." Her voice cracked as she turned away from me, away from my touch, taking her magic with her as she started busing herself with the already repaired food, before deciding to pick it up and run away.

"What is all this food for anyway?" I asked, grabbing the top two boxes from the massive pile she was trying to maneuver.

"My people are starving, Rowan. Your parents are helping me get food to them," she smiled like there was a secret hidden in there, but plowed on before I could ask. "The CCC has been raiding them nearly non-stop--"

I dropped the boxes I had been holding, sending pans, listy and more broken glass over the stone floor. So much for cleaning up.

"What the fuck, Rowan? Do you need to go plug yourself into

a wall or something, recharge your batteries? Did they let you out of your box too early this time?"

"The CCC," I gasped, cutting her torment off with a single questioning quirk of her eyebrow. "You know what that is?"

"Of course I know what that is. It's The Chosen Council for Community." I tensed. I had heard of that before. I had heard of that many times. It was the brainchild of Samantha Demarco. A council for the betterment and equalization of our communities.

By the harsh tone in Gemma's voice, I was thinking that might not be all true.

I still remembered when she had gotten the votes to start the thing.

"You mean that group that cleans up neighborhoods, feeds the poor, stuff like that?" Judging by the hatred that was flaring in her eyes, that wasn't what it was.

"It sounds so pretty when you use their wording, but the only cleaning up they are doing is burning our homes, killing my people, and carting children off to a life of eternal servitude. Thousands of Tarns, raiding people with no way to fight back. The fucking CCC, they deserve to die. All of them." She was snarling, her lavender eyes flashing as she stared at me, pushing her hair back behind her ear.

Her fingers fluttered against her hair and my heart stopped, the air stopped.

"Where did you get that?" I asked, grabbing her hand and holding it between us. My magic flared with the contact, her breath catching so quick that I was sure she felt the electric spark. I pushed it away, staring at her hand, my thumb fluttering above the burn on her finger, not daring to touch it.

"Where did you get that burn?" I asked again, shaking her hand again to get her attention.

"I... ummm..." she stuttered, clearly still trying to catch her breath. "Your mother, that water stuff."

"Black Water," I sighed, everything aching as I mumbled the words that had been filthy and vile for most of my life.

The burn was the same, same as all of the maids at the Demarco's. I knew I had seen it before, on Gemma's finger. My dad had a similar burn that covered his entire right hand, but it had been there so long that it had mostly healed, now looked like his skin had melted. But Gemma's was fresh.

All of the maids were fresh.

The Demarco's, the CCC, they had Black Water. They were burning the Undermortals with it.

I said nothing to her as I bolted away, leaving her alone in the dark hallway.

26

GEMMA

WHAT WAS I DOING HERE?

I had no idea what I was doing here.

Being a stupid ass bitch is what I was doing here.

I shouldn't be here.

Something was clearly wrong with the guy. Last time I saw him he was taking off down a hallway, rambling about the CCC like a crazy person and leaving me to carry all those boxes alone. Nothing like a dapper prince at all. Yes, I wouldn't have accepted his help, but it was the principle of the thing.

That's it, I was getting out of there before someone caught me and shit really had to go down.

God, I was a fool.

I turned around so fast that I nearly fell over. In fact, I thought I had with how hard I impacted against the stone wall chest of a man who had apparently stepped right behind me as I had paced. It was that chest that sent me to the ground.

"Holy hell!" The boulder of a chest said, I shook my head, looking up at the face I recognized at once. He had been to a few late-night meetings and had even helped deliver food to his community the last few weekends.

"Greer?" I asked with a gasp, taking his hand and allowing him to pull me up. "What are *you* doing here?"

"I could ask the same about you," he chuckled, peering around me to the door I had been pacing in front of for the last few minutes. "I have a date."

"A date?" Yes, I might have squeaked a bit.

"Yes, of the best kind." He lifted a book, the old leather cover similar to the one we used in basic spells, but clearly more advanced. "Get your head out of the gutter, Gem. I happen to know he has no interest in guys. He's got his sights set on someone else." I rolled my eyes; it wasn't like it was a secret who had spent months sucking Rowan's face off.

"This is a study date," Greer finished and I think my jaw dropped.

"God, I think that's worse," I mumbled, attempting to step around the bulking man and high-tail it back to my room. He quickly countered, his wide smile flicking wider as he chuckled.

"Why don't you join us, Gem, seeing as you are already here." How in the world could one man make me feel so trapped?

"I have better things to be doing that reading books with two losers." The barb completely missed. Greer chuckled, he had clearly been around me too much.

"Well, I'm going to tell him you were here either way. So, you can't escape, he will know that you were stalking around his door." Greer continued to chuckle, weaving his arm around mine and practically dragging me to the door.

"You're not giving me a choice, are you?" I dropped my feet, letting him drag me.

"No, you have no choice boss lady." He was laughing so loud now that I was sure everyone inside the rooms could hear him.

"Fine, but I already know this is pointless, he hasn't been seen in over a week. He might be dead in there." I was sure, well,

I tried to sound like I was. My heart was pounding so fast my chest was starting to ache.

"He's not dead, I promise you." Greer knocked on the door with a firm fist, three hollow beats thundering through the hallway. A second later the door was thrown open, loud music hitting me full in the face.

"I was starting to think you weren't going to--" Rowan began, the prince's wide smile staggering when he saw me. "Gemma?"

"Look who I found in the hall!" Greer roared, shoving us past Rowan and into a room that I wasn't completely sure I was supposed to be in.

"Are we saying 'found'? Because it feels more like a full kidnapping situation." I spoke loud enough that both of them could hear, Rowan was mumbling and shifting his feet as he stood plastered to the door.

"We could also say stalking. I mean, you were the one peering under the door frame," Greer continued. I pulled myself away from him, jumping to my feet and instantly sinking into the carpet that was far too plush.

"I was not!"

"Tell his benevolent majesty that," Greer waved at the now smiling Prince and sunk into one of the large chairs, clearly sinking a few inches into the thing.

What was this? A room made out of marshmallow?

I thought my room was nice, the furniture in this place was actually inset with gold. Judging by the sparkle it had diamond inlays or some shit. I could strip this place and make a pretty penny if I wanted. Next time, maybe.

"You kidnapped me, Greer. I was only here to smear this on your door." I gave him a smile and pulled out a glass jar from my pocket, the gurgled green gunk I had swiped from lunch congealed against the side of the glass.

"Of course, you were." Rowan smiled with a crooked grin

that somehow made him look more rugged, the emeralds in his eyes pulling all the light from the room.

"You left so fast the other night, I didn't want you to miss out." I placed the glass in his hand, careful not to touch his skin and stepping away the second I knew he wasn't going to drop it. I didn't want to risk that shit again.

"So kind, as always," Rowan said, that smile still plastered on his face. "Won't you join us, Gemma?"

He gestured to the couches and the chair that Greer wasn't laid over, eating food that was laid out on the table with unearned zeal.

"Uh, no thanks," I was already trying to sidestep him, but the guy wouldn't move, he was still flat-backed against the door. "I delivered my gift, but thank you for your magnanimous hospitality Prince Douche."

I was really starting to like the word. Magnanimous. Not douche.

"Ha! She really does call you that, doesn't she?" Greer erupted from behind me, his mouth full of fruit. "The benevolent majesty."

Rowan ran his hands through his hair, the dark shag pulling over his eyes, I forced myself to look away and breathe. Definitely breathe.

"I'm going to regret you two meeting each other, aren't I?"

"Meeting?" I nearly scoffed. "Greer and I are cut from the same cloth. He's part of my resistance and attempts to overthrow the royal family. You know, you."

Greer choked on a grape, the loud hacking cough not even breaking the stare down Rowan and I had going on.

"Going for full honesty are we, Gemma?" There was a tad bit of warning in his voice, but I ignored it and shrugged.

"It's not like it was ever a secret. We are both royal bastards remember."

"Nice, Gem!" Greer boomed, having recovered from his shock. "I like it!"

Shit.

Rowan's eyes narrowed, his smile stretching. "Gem?"

"Douche," I responded without hesitation. He only smiled more. What in the holy fuck was going on?

"Come on, Gem, you'll like this," Rowan said, finally leaving the door. "We've been working on some fourth-year stuff, break up the monotony of this place."

"More like, I've been getting secret, possibly cheating, lessons from the master," Greer added, still laughing, still eating more grapes, clearly Rowan had put out the platter with him in mind.

"Whatever, Greer. Don't be handing out awards to royal bastards just because they're pretty," I said it without thinking. Rowan smirked, that playful light I had seen in his eyes a few times gleaming.

Teasing.

Hot damn, my stomach was inventing its own carnival.

"You think I'm pretty?"

"Pretty douchey," I rolled my eyes, taking a step back as the two guys chuckled. Greer was looking between us with too much of a knowing glare. I did what any girl would do, I flipped him off. They laughed harder.

"Tonight is 'stationary explosions'," Rowan said sinking into the wide couch and throwing his legs over the armrest. A second later the grape in Greer's fingers exploded. The guy shrieked and jumped off the couch, looking between his singed fingers and the Prince who was laid back and smiling. I don't think he had even moved. "Any interest?"

I stood still, blinking at them both as Greer perched himself on the coffee table, the two already chattering about the why's and how's of what he had done.

The door was unblocked, my escape was ready and waiting. Damn it all, I couldn't move. Everything about being there was wrong, but they were doing magic. Really cool, harder than dumb shields and floating feathers type of magic.

"Shitting rats on a storm grate," I snarled under my breath and earned myself a side look from Rowan. "Fine. Show me what you are doing."

I stomped my boots and made my way over to the two, sitting on the coffee table and crossing my legs beneath me. The hole in my lace tights that I had been poking at for the last few days spread over my knee.

"The idea is to send tiny whips of your magic into the object, while still keeping it connected to the source. Think of it like a fishing line. With a tiny tug..." He was looking right at me, his eyes wide and deep as they looked right through me. So intense--

The lamp on the end table exploded.

I jumped so high that the table I had been sitting on cracked. I jumped even further.

"Sorry," Rowan whispered, shoving his smile down. "I should have warned you."

"Is this what you have been doing for the last week?" I asked, my boots stomping on the broken pieces of glass as I inspected the remains of the lamp. It didn't escape my notice that Greer sat up, looking between me and Rowan.

Weird.

I pressed my lips together, leaning against the table that had once held a lamp and now was only home to Rowan's feet.

"Wait. You didn't tell him you are exercising your royal privileges of ditching class for the last week?" I clicked my tongue and shook my head, picking up one of the pieces of broken porcelain and pinching it between my fingers. "Some friend you are, Prince Douche. I mean, if you are gonna ditch you might as well share the wealth. What's your secret, anyway, because you miss a lot of school. I mean, it's *a lot* of school."

"Letter from home?" Greer asked, popping a grape in his mouth before immediately spitting it back out looking at it as if it was about to explode.

"He does have Royal Dispatch classes," I said, pocketing the porcelain and folding my arms. "Are they sending you on secret missions?"

He had been smiling up to that point, but I must have said something very wrong, because his features darkened, his brow pulling into a scowl.

"No," the word was more of a snarl when pushed through clenched teeth.

"Touchy, touchy," I was suddenly regretting coming at all. Not that I couldn't take the spoiled brat, but I didn't want to go the way of the lamp.

Greer was equally nervous with the narrowed side-eye he was giving me.

"I have to be here," Rowan said after a minute, no longer looking at either of us. "I've been trained my whole life. Coming here is like a formality. I'm bored."

I gave Greer a look, both of our brows furrowed, I don't think either of us had expected that. Expected him to be... not a royal douchebag.

"I'm going to be honest," I said with a bright grin, working to break the tension. "I thought your reason was going to be so much cooler than that."

Rowan sat up, the worry on his face falling.

"Agreed," Greer tacked on before Rowan could respond. "I mean, everyone says how sickly and broken you are. No magic what-so-ever."

"Just a rickety baby royal with no control except to explode things," I said as sarcastically as I could, before fixing him with a smile. "Oh wait. That's me."

Greer laughed while Rowan smiled and shook his head, his eyes darting back to me with that same bright light I had seen in his eyes when I first got there. Light and joy. It almost swallowed me whole. I had to look away, pushing my hair behind my ear nervously.

It was only then that I realized that Greer was staring between the two of us, a wide ugly grin on his face.

"So, show us how to explode this, Princey. Starting with Greer's nose ring." That wiped the smile off his face, and mine.

It was only then that I realized I had been smiling. Actually smiling.

Damn it. I should have never gone in there.

27

———

SIA

I blushed so hard I was sure the roots of my hair went red.
Even one glance at the text message was sending my heart into a
flutter of activity, my magic reacting as though Talon was
standing right there, his hand running up and down my spine.

I shivered and tucked the phone away; it wasn't worth it to
risk anyone finding out about this. Not until all of this was over.

"Okay, girl, you need to spill right now or I am going to lose
it," Tasha said from beside me, looking from the phone shaped
lump in my pocket and back again. All of that giddy joy instantly
deflated.

"I don't know what you are talking about." I tucked my bag
close to my side, suddenly questioning how much Tasha had
seen. Questioning what lengths she would go through to get her
answer. "Even if I did know I'm not about to tell you in the
middle of the hall."

"Uh-huh." She gave me a wink and eyed my pocket again. I
quickly shielded the thing, not like I could do more than make it

bulletproof. "Trust me, Miko and I have noticed you checking your phone and walking around with a smile on your face."

"What does it matter if I smile?" I snapped, a little too loud, causing a few people to turn.

"Easy. You only smile before you are about to severely injure multiple people," Tasha waved her hand to the side flippantly as we turned the corner toward her dorm, thankfully there were fewer people there. "So, either you have become a serial killer, which I wouldn't be against provided the targets are Drains. Or, you got Rowan back."

I smiled again, knowing the answer was so much better than they assumed. Luckily, Tasha misunderstood my meaning.

"Rowan. Knew it." She nodded, proud of herself, pulling me around the last corner and toward Miko who was leaning against the door.

"Took you guys long enough, I was about ready to bail," he said, pushing himself off the door so Tasha could open it. The door swung open to a room cluttered with everything from clothes, to food, to failed experiments. Everything coated with the pungent smell of rot and smoke.

"Remind me why we are meeting here," Miko said, closing the door behind us and locking us in with the stink. "Because unless we fumigate, I can't stay here long."

He flung his hand forward, the window sliding open as I pulled a wind through the main room, getting as much of the trash and the smell away from us. Unfortunately, the whole place turned into a trash tornado. Tasha shrieked some profanity as my wind knocked her off the couch and replaced the balled-up blanket on the couch with one that was hopefully less covered in crumbs.

"We are meeting here because I don't need my neighbor seeing who is visiting me. I don't want to risk her overhearing." I pushed another wind through the room, sending more papers and half-eaten bits of food into a trash can. "I had hoped that Tasha would have cleaned up."

"You should know me better than that," Tasha said, throwing her legs over the side of the couch and kicking off her shoes. Thankfully it didn't add another layer of stink to the putrid room.

"Well, if we are to endure this you better have good news. Like, you spiked Gemma's drink and we are expecting a notice of her death any minute." Miko was carefully cleaning off the few remaining crumbs off one of the green side chairs. He fell into it with what I had to say next.

"Gemma is no longer our target."

"Excuse me?" Tasha sat up as though she had been shocked, the partially eaten apple still clutched in her hand. "That's what you are walking around smiling about? That you *don't* have to kill the Drain anymore? Here I was thinking that your magic had connected to Rowan's finally and we could start to move forward with the takeover you had planned."

It took far too much effort to keep the smile from creeping over my lips. The giddy joy that was becoming a new normal twisted into something beautifully nefarious.

"Will you two shut the hell up and listen?" I snarled, sinking into the chair opposite Miko's and leaning forward. "We found another way around our tasks. Gemma can live, for now. With the new addition to our group we should be able to bypass the issues she presents and move forward."

"So, you have bonded your magic to Rowan's?" Tasha asked with too much shriek.

"No. Better."

The two stared at me. Yes, I knew I was being cryptic, but it was hard to know what to say when I was in this school, the window opened to one of the many courtyards below. With a regretful sigh, my magic snapped the thing shut.

"What is this, Sia, torture?" Miko grumbled, throwing his head back into a pile of what looked like old newspapers. "We need air."

"Get over it," I snapped, he didn't even deserve a glare for how much of a whiny baby he was being. I was too busy digging in my bag for the phone that was vibrating again.

"According to my father, we needed Gemma gone to eliminate the threat of uprising within the school. Knock out the head take out the snake sort of thing." I waved my hand to the idea and went back to digging through my bookbag, fully aware that the two were talking to me. "We needed Rowan because his magic, while weak, has something that we needed. He was our easiest chance to infiltrate the royals which was the last piece we needed to take over Imdalind."

I grabbed the phone, letting the bag drop to the floor as I looked up to the two of them, their focus undivided, even though Miko was noticeably breathing funny. They stared, they knew me well enough to know that I wasn't going to give them the news easily, no matter how many times Tasha tried to guess.

"I found someone even better." I had expected some kind of awe or surprise, instead, they looked confused.

"But not Rowan?" Tasha asked after a minute, still stuck on the pathetic prince. Figures. She had been the one to point out Talon originally. Now it's all Rowan this, and Rowan that.

That fecking bitch.

I bet that's why she's so focused on Rowan; she wants Talon all to herself. Well, she can wait and get bitched slapped with my news.

"I bet it's Analine," Miko said with a smug grin. I always knew she would be a great ally.

"You're both wrong." I smiled and leaned back, nodding my

head toward my phone and letting my magic ignite within it. The screen flaring to life. "My magic connected to someone."

The screen glowed as they both leaned in, staring at the background picture of two intertwined hands that hadn't been there last week, and the message alert that was burning a hole into the ceiling.

'*Talon: After the raid this weekend I am taking you out to celebrate. I know of a great island...*'

"What the fuck?"

"Well there goes my chance to ask you out," Miko said with a laugh at the same time that Tasha mumbled, picking up the phone to stare at it.

"Are those your hands? What did it feel like when your magic connected? O.M.G. Did you kiss him?" Tasha's questions were coming in at rapid fire, still staring and tapping at the phone as she tried to figure out the password. I held out my hand and brought the thing right back to me, she knew me well enough to be able to guess the code and I didn't need her snooping around.

"Stop prying, you whore," I snapped, Tasha giggling as she sunk down into the chair. "I don't kiss and tell."

"Sure you don't," Miko said, giving me a wink, although I didn't miss that the regret in his eyes was very real. Poor boy, he really did have a crush on me.

He wasn't the only one. If I had known I would have had some fun with him while I was still trying to coax Rowan out of his shell. Now, he would have to get over it like the rest of us. I flipped my hair behind my back, giving him a smile as I turned back to Tasha.

"Miko's right, all we hear for weeks is Rowan, Rowan, Rowan. Now you are quiet and smiling like a loon. What's the deal, Sia? Don't lie."

"Nothing's wrong," I sighed, stretching a shield around us,

trying to spread my magic the way that Talon had taught me last weekend and block out all sounds. "This is real and I don't plan on losing it. Besides, Talon is *much* better than Rowan, in many ways."

"Knew it," Tasha giggled, Miko was looking like he was going to be sick.

"But with an Eternal playing for our side, we are one step closer to enacting our plan. I'm one step closer to being the new Queen." They both froze.

"I'm sorry," Miko asked, looking between me and Tasha. "Did you say Queen?"

"Yes. Everything is beginning this weekend. The last community of Drains is being taken, Last Pyre, home to our very own bubblegum brat. It will cripple her efforts as well as I could have. With her neutered, and the tunnels clear, it opens us up to the dark line."

The dark line, an area on the map that divided the country in two. It had been overprotected for as long as anybody knew, which could only mean one thing. An underground well of power.

We had found out what it really was just a few years ago.

"The dark line? That's a rumor." Tasha was scoffing, but Miko's jaw was set, his eyes hard.

"I assure you it's not," I said, sitting back in the chair, my thumb running over the clasped hands on the screen of my phone.

"We gained access to it a few years go. A pool of Black Water." Both of their eyes went wide. "My parents harvest the water to use on the recruits. We were hoping to trigger Drak magic in them, create an army of visionaries to tell us how to overtake the Drains, and anyone else in our way. According to Talon, it's been disrupting the Queen's visions. With the Queen out of commission and the dark line opened..."

"We have a straight path into the heart of Imdalind. Into the royal families underground castle." Tasha finished with wide eyes that I wasn't one hundred percent sure were actually seeing anything.

"So, who wants to join us on a raid this weekend?"

All they did was smile.

28

ROWAN

My heart was trying to pound its way through bone and flesh long before the heavy knocks on the door sounded.

We had invited Gemma to join our make-shift study group tonight. I say we because it was mostly Greer who had done the asking; done the conniving and planning. It was also Greer who had bowed out at the last minute and decided instead that he 'needed to wash his hair.'

Yes, the short shorn black man with that wide grin had used the excuse that he needed to wash his hair. He had sold me to the wolves. He didn't know what fire he was playing with.

My magic had mostly settled after last week's connection, my father's bind settling enough that I could easily control my magic again without the Drak power taking over. Although, I could still feel the magic. Feel the heavy power as it tried to take its rightful place. There was no stopping it now, no matter how much I hated it, I let it out, little by little, as I tried to find another way to control the power.

I would figure it out.

I had to figure it out.

Pushing as much of the magic down as I could, I walked

toward the door, straightening the dark grey V-neck I had chosen that morning, subconsciously knowing it was my best shirt, and who was coming by.

My hand was still on the knob as I stood there, taking one steadying breath as I felt her magic through the door, felt the waves of her power try to move against mine as they had since that day they had sparked.

"Hello, Gemma," I said, before the door had even opened all the way, my heart tensed, hoping to see that glimpse of a stunning smile again, instead she stood, hip popped, hair in curls, scowling as she popped her hip.

"Hey, Princey," she crooned, giving me the shit-eating grin she usually did and muscling her way into my room. "Where's Greer? I expected him to be at the end of the hall ready to drag me in again."

I shut the door, lingering with my palm against the wood before I turned, dragging my hand nervously through my hair.

"He's not coming," I sighed, shifting as even her teasing grin twitched out of place.

"That rat bastard," she snarled, jumping up from the couch she was about to sit down on. "No offense, but it's probably not the best idea for me to be here. I mean, I've wanted to kill you at some point in the last thirty days."

I knew she was right, having her alone was dangerous. Even with what I knew was brewing between us, it's not like she's even been quiet about her end goal. Scarier still, I knew she was telling the truth.

"Are you going to kill me now?" I asked quietly, sitting down on the couch opposite the chair she was still standing in front of, safely placing the coffee table between us. Like it would do anything to have a splinter of wood in a magic battle.

"The jury is still out on that," she mumbled, tugging at the frayed edge of the shorts she wore so often I was sure she had more than one pair.

"Well, don't worry. If you decide to try your hand, I'm sure I can take you," I said, throwing one of the grapes I was holding at her. She didn't even dodge, just scowled. "We are sparring partners after all. At some point I am going to have to kick your ass."

"If that's how you think it's going to go down, then you are sorely mistaken." She laughed with a mocking groan, her eyes flashing with a spark as I felt her magic flare in the air.

The sensation was so powerful. I had felt it the first time when I had seen her the other night. Having the majority of my magic flooding through my veins was making all of these sensations more intense. More greedy. I sighed and pushed the feeling away, now was not the time to explore that. She was still pacing before her chair, eyes continually darting back to the door. I was sure infiltrating magic would send her running for it.

"Oh, I know that's how it's going to go down. I'm used to getting my ass kicked by the King and his stubborn brother. I'm excited to win for once." She had no idea how true the statement was. Yes, I was sure Gemma would give me a run for my money, but I surely wasn't going to go down that easy.

"If you always lose, how do you know you'll win? Maybe they've been going easy on you your whole life and you suck so bad you think you are losing with them at full power." She was smug, her prod meant to hit some tinge of regret or truth. There was none there. If I was ever able to do what Angie asked and bring her home, she would know just how much those two 'go easy' on anyone.

"Could be," I shrugged, "I'm sickly remember." I gave her a fake cough and she rolled her eyes, glancing back at the unlocked door before she finally sunk into the overstuffed green chair.

My heart released a bit. The blood pumping again. She was staying. I really wasn't sure if this was a good thing or not, but I couldn't ignore the way everything loosened, magic included. It was already trying to make a bee-line for her. I pulled that sucker back. She was still freaking out about our magic sparking. Like hell if I was going to let her catch wind of what was really going on.

"If your sickly than I'm destined to be the new queen. Oh, wait..." She tapped her index finger against her lips, a whisper of that beautiful genuine smile from the other day peeking through, it was almost enough to stop my heart again.

"You gotta get through me first--"

"Not a problem," she interrupted, throwing her legs over the side of the chair and stealing a grape from the bowl on the table. "Latest rumor is that you are as dead as a doornail and have been sent home because you were so sick you couldn't even walk. I guess your magic ate you alive."

I couldn't help but laugh, my belly shaking as the ridiculousness of the whole thing bled through me. It wasn't the first time I had heard that. Unbeknownst to me, that rumor had been going around for years. Somehow, it got funnier every time. Probably because this time my magic had actually eaten me alive.

"My poor parents, they will only be down to one perfect son," I chuckled, pressing my magic against my heart as she turned, her perfectly red lips pulling up. "I hope it was a good death."

"Oh, the best, very bloody. Someone was trying to say you were lost in an epic battle in the old Americas," she ate another grape, taking one bite before she froze and turned, speaking through a mouth full of grapes. "Wait. I thought you had two brothers?"

"One is as far from perfect as you can get. Clearly, my loss would be devastating." It was hard not to let out frustration in those few words. Talon had only grown more agitated over the years and the last few days before I came to Imdalind Academy still stung in the worst possible ways. I had never known so much hatred to live in him.

"Ah yes, how could I forget, Talon," She rubbed her jaw and sat up abruptly. "You know. The fact that Talon exists and is related to you, has got to remove at least ten points of your douchebaggery scale."

"Gee thanks."

"I've met Dramin, he's pretty cool. So, another ten points off." She waved her hand to the side, but I had frozen, the couch suddenly seeming hard and cold beneath me.

"You've met Dramin?" Dramin and Patrice were essentially the black sheep of the family. They were there, I saw them all the time. But they were more likely to be fundraising and touring kingdoms halfway across the world than cavaliering around Imdalind Academy. They were at The Gauntlet because we all had to be at The Gauntlet, yet Gemma had met them.

"Yeah, he and his wife help us with the food. He's cool. Acts like he swallowed one of those old-timey novels with a chesty man on it sometimes. But still cool."

The description was accurate, but I still choked on the water I had chosen that moment to swallow, the fluid burning as it went down the wrong pipe.

"Is there anyone in my family you haven't met?" I asked, she leaned back in the chair folding her ankle over knee as she contemplated, counting on her fingers like she had them all memorized or something. She probably did.

"Are we talking immediate or extended, because I think at this point all I'm missing is that little one from the Gauntlet. The kid."

"My baby sister," I hadn't meant the words to sound harsh, but hearing her talk about Angela, seeing her smile, it sent my

Drak magic boiling, the little bits I had released bubbling at the base of my neck as they tried to pull me into sight.

That sight. I had no interest in seeing it.

I closed my eyes, pushing the magic away and forcing myself back to the conversation.

"How is that you have met all of my family and no one is dead?" I asked, pinching my nose as I continued to press the magic away. "Wasn't your entire goal to end us all or something."

"Well, yeah, but that Mira girl restrained my magic," she sighed, looking up at the ceiling, avoiding my stare as her brow furrowed together. "That and some sickly douchebag prince taught me a few things."

"Oh yeah, was it remorse?" I asked, remembering that very first conversation.

"Fuck no." She made a face like she had eaten something sour. "It was that everyone needs to learn to control their temper."

"Gee thanks. Now you really sound like my dad." I sighed and fell back against the couch, suddenly wishing I could help her destroy an apple rather than continue this conversation.

She put on the same face she had before, dropping her voice as she tried to match my father's deep accent, "Now son, don't go blowing up trees and food."

"You're really stuck on that tree, aren't you?" I cut in, turning my head to glare at her from where I lounged on the couch, but she plowed on.

"Be nice to snotty rabbits--"

"Rabbits?" I said between laughs, the look she was giving me making the chuckles come deeper.

"Don't let Sia Demarco suck out your soul." She finished with a gasping breath, her face returning to normal as she joined in laughing.

"I'm glad I could teach you remorse," I said, earning myself a look, but I plowed on. "You taught me something too, you know."

"Was it how to peel off Sia Demarco's lizard skin and reveal the monster trapped beneath, I mean I gave you enough hints." That smug smile was back, her usual teasing making a grand return as she deflected, her shields up high as I dug into something that scared her.

Something told me to back off, but I continued forward, fighting the need to grab her hand as I leaned forward.

"No, it was that I am in fact a selfish prick and that maybe I need to think of others sometimes, even if it scares me."

"Damn you, Rowan," she sighed leaning back in the chair and giving me a bright grin, the real true smile that spread over her face stopping my heart. "I can't call you a douche anymore."

We sat there, smiling like loons, every bit of my strength focused on keeping my magic restrained in my chest, restrained away from her, even though I could very clearly feel her power prod against me. Feel the warm need as it tried to connect with mine.

As we understood something about each other.

Something deeper.

Something I don't think anyone could break.

29

GEMMA

"Do you guys have some weird blinking language you created without me, or are you speaking directly into each other's minds? Cuz you look insane."

"Shut up, Ed" I snapped, flicking my fingers at his far too close face as I once again tried to pull my focus from Rowan. Something that was proving hard to do, it was like something about him was pulling me into him. Toward him.

I had felt it first the first time he grabbed my arm after he tried to save me from his girlfriend, but after last night it was nearly impossible.

Of course, he would choose today to make his grand reappearance at school.

At least he hadn't tried to come sit with me or something. But he wasn't sitting with Sia either, even though the girl kept shooting him dirty looks. He was sitting with Greer and his friends, mostly Undermortals who looked bewildered about what he was doing there. Except there were two girls who kept giggling and waving. It was driving me crazy.

It shouldn't be driving me crazy.

The whole thing was wrong in a million different ways.

"Gemma," Eddy was whispering in my ear now, leaning so close that he might as well have been my Sia equivalent. Sick. "Gemma, take off your top."

I laughed so loud that more than a few heads in the cafeteria turned, including Sia, who had been so busy staring at Rowan that she had missed the stare down I was in with her boyfriend. Or not boyfriend, I couldn't keep track.

She saw it now, however. In one flash of red in her eyes, I got my just desserts.

Or rather a bowl of cauliflower soup exploding in my face.

Everyone around me burst into laughter, Eddy and myself included as I scraped the mushy bits of vegetables off my face. Thank god it wasn't that gross leaf stuff, I had a feeling the Undermortals would use the green goop as spackle rather than food.

"Keep your eyes on your own kind!" Sia yelled from across the cafeteria, her mouth open and ready to dish out some more elitist nonsense when Rowan snapped her name with a sound that was pure threat. The girl sat back down with a scowl.

The laughter died into confusion, as everyone looked between Rowan and I in whispers and ping-pong eyes that made it clear that everyone had figured out what had happened. Great. This was going to make the rest of my day more interesting. To be honest, I had kind of been dreading it since he strutted into Professor Analine's lecture about types of magic a full half-hour late; wearing his full uniform none-the-less. I don't think I had seen the guy actually wear the tie and jacket since school started.

The image of him looking all dapper and shit was seriously making everything worse.

"Rats on a platter, what is wrong with me?" I hissed under my breath, scrubbing away the last of the soup with the napkin, careful to keep my head down even though I knew he was looking at me again.

"You mean beyond the fact that the prince seems to have an obsessive crush on you," Eddy was giggling again, his shoulders bouncing up and down.

"He's looking at me again isn't he?"

"Yep." Eddy was laughing again. "So is Sia. You're getting it from two directions."

"Perfect," I said, leaving enough of the soup on my face to make it obvious that I didn't care and sat up straighter. "Wave to your new best friend, Ed."

We laughed, leaning in as we waved enthusiastically at Sia, the bitch going a gnarly shade of pink as Rowan laughed at us.

"Oh, you are so going to pay for that," Eddy said through his smile, still waving enthusiastically at her as more and more people noticed, waves of giggles creeping over the crowded cafeteria.

"Yeah, well, maybe she'll knock some sense into me," I mumbled, picking at what was left of my food. I was glad she had exploded the stuff, if only because it gave me an excuse not to eat it. My stomach hadn't stopped spinning.

"I've been trying to do that for weeks," Ed mused through a mouthful of soup. "It clearly hasn't worked?"

"Weeks?" I wasn't following.

"Yeah, Gem, I saw you checking out his ass the day he destroyed your tree." I whipped to him, hair tickling over the freshly shaved sides of my head. He wasn't looking at me. "I don't think you were breathing."

"Oh whatever," I snapped, nearly snarling as I punched him in the arm.

He didn't flinch, but he did drop his spoon, giving me a bit of side-eye.

"That's how I know I'm right, by the way, that you like him a little more than you want to admit, and a lot more than you know you should."

"You are so not right," I was fully focused on my food now, scooping up as much as I could so as to fling it in Eddy's smug face. Maybe I'll put it on his neck. It'll be a nice addition to his tattoos.

"Oh yes, I am. You can ignore it all you want, Gem. I promise you I'll keep it a secret, but your walls go up every time you get too close. Those snappy powerful walls that you led with for years, they protect you know when the one person you know you *shouldn't* like is shattering everything that you worked for."

Ice coated my soul as I sat, my fingers clenched so tight around my spoon that the knuckles were turning white. I wasn't even sure my heart was beating anymore. I sure as hell wasn't breathing.

"What is it, Ed? You get magic and you turn into some wise old man?" I didn't turn, and I sure wasn't going to look up to Rowan. Even though I was sure he was still staring at me, even though the cafeteria had begun to clear out.

"No, Gem, I've known you for almost ten years. I've seen those walls for just as long, for all sorts of reasons. I saw them with Adrian too, even if you don't want to admit it."

It was then that I turned to him, a spoonful of cauliflower soup armed a ready, he didn't even flinch he just smiled.

"Don't worry, I think in the end you realized that Adrian wasn't worth it," he said, fingers slowly lowering my spoon back to the bowl. I didn't even fight him, I didn't think I had the energy to. The entire room was going hazy, my body numb as everything Eddy said hit hard and true.

So, fucking true.

"He wasn't. He was a liability from the beginning." I was snarling now.

"You know I'm your best friend, Gem, and you're mine. It's why I'm here with you. I see your walls, they just don't bug me." he shrugged.

"Are you sure?" I asked, trying not to use any of the teasing banter I usually did, it came out anyway. "Because they seem to be bugging you now."

"No, they don't." He was looking right into me, whatever life was in the cafeteria dying away as he grabbed my hand. "I want you in my life, Gem. I'd try to date you if I liked boobs, but I don't. I like you the way you are."

"Even with the boobs?" I smiled, so did he. He clearly knew what I was doing.

"I see you let those walls down more often now, mostly because of him." He gave a nod toward Rowan, I stubbornly sat still. "They come right back up, sure, but the cracks are showing, and they are beautiful."

I opened my mouth, trying to swear or curse or something at him. He deserved a good 'fuck you' right about then. I couldn't speak, let alone move.

"I don't want you to miss out on a good thing, Gem," Eddy whispered, his hand soft on my shoulder as he leaned in. "It's okay to let people in. Don't worry, if he hurts you, I'll be the first to punch him in the jaw."

"I'll punch you in the jaw," I snapped, shoving his hand away and throwing soup in his face.

He dodged.

"Love you too, Gem."

I turned away, sitting still and silent as Eddy gathered his bags and left with only a slight ruffle of my hair. I only looked up when I thought the cafeteria was empty, only to see Rowan, the guy slowly making his way to the exit, the flirting girl from before trying to keep up. He didn't look at her, though, he looked at me. He smiled at me, he waved at me.

I sat and stared, feeling some of those cracks in my perfectly defined defenses grow.

"Damn you, Eddy."

30

ROWAN

"Are you fucking mad?" I yelled, the snap echoing over stone and causing my mother to jump.

I had left the lunchroom in good spirits, but the second I walked into Cail's office I was met by my parents, rather than my cousin.

They weren't covered in blood, thank god, but what they had to say wiped the smile off my face as fast as if they were.

They were going into the caves, to track and cage the CCC, end the Chosen's uprising for good. They weren't there to invite me to go with them, no. They wanted me to come home for the weekend and keep an eye on Angela, because the plan was for the whole royal family to go with them.

All of them, heading into a war. Not that I doubted they could win, but good god could they handle this a different way.

"I know it may seem crazy, but it is needed. The attacks that we've been facing for the last few months have suddenly stopped," my mother said, dropping my father's hand as she stepped closer to me. "We need to know what's going on. We need to put a stop to this. No more games."

"You're insane, both of you," I snapped, fists clenched at my side as I tried to keep my magic in check. Harder now that so much more of it was available, but at least things hadn't exploded. "They are beating the shit out of each other; you're already stretched too thin with whatever it is you are doing and now you guys are going to feed yourself to them."

"Unless you have seen something--" my mother began, her voice so quiet against my yelling that it was almost swallowed by it.

I tensed, a flash from my dream from a month ago filling my head. The screaming children, the wall of knives that cut them down. The mines.

But I had told them that before. Besides, you didn't need sight to know how bad of an idea this was.

"I'm trying to regulate the power, mom. I'm not ready to start chugging black water."

"I know, Row. But, perhaps you have heard something."

I exhaled with a bit of a groan, I knew what she was talking about. It wasn't making this any easier. I wasn't about to go ask Gemma if her revolution knew anything. We had found out about the CCC's role in this, and their apparent supply of black water, because of her. Even I knew she didn't know anything more than that.

"Mom, this isn't smart," I said, trying to keep my voice stable. "Going after the CCC, it's too dangerous."

"From what we have learned about the black water, we can tell what their attack patterns are doing. They are trying to clean paths to the underground wells." My father's voice was strained as he looked at me, suddenly looking like he was paper thin. "We need to stop them before they take control of one, assuming that's where they've been getting the water, of course."

"This just... it doesn't seem wise. Can't you look into the future and see if this plan has a positive outcome?"

"I can't look into the future at all. Not now, not until your power stops blocking me. Not until you accept--"

"What?" I snarled, stopped her as my fists clenched at my sides. That time one of Cail's books flew off the shelf. It was only the one, but my parents still exchanged a look. "Me. I'm the one blocking your sights?" The way her lips pressed into a tight line was answer enough.

"Mom, why didn't you say anything?" I could barely speak, the words were a gasp as I pushed the shock away. They felt like knife slashes against my chest.

"I promised you I would never push you, Rowan."

"So, you sacrificed the safety of our people. You--" I paused the word getting stuck in my throat as a million dreams, a million flashes, a million moments hit inside my mind like they were making their own orchestra.

"I did this." I fell into the large leather chair with a crash, the air in the room as heavy as my guilt.

The room was silent for a moment, I was left sitting in my pain until the hollow step of my parents came closer, my father sitting on the large table we usually used for chess.

"Rowan," he began in a tone softer than I was used to from him. "We wanted to do what's best for you. All parents do, but we also make mistakes. We haven't been parents for very long--"

"Talon is over fifty years old," I interrupted him, the tension in my chest loosening with the ridiculousness of it.

"And look at all the mistakes we made," Father grumbled, his elbows on his knees as he leaned closer to me. "We are going to continue to work to repair this, but that does not mean we will push you."

Part of me wanted to yell at him to push me, to rage, and force, and not be quite so damned understanding all the time. We needed to fix it, but I wasn't even sure if me chugging a gallon of black water could do it. I couldn't turn back time, at least I didn't think I could. But I couldn't make the words come, I sat in the pain of my guilt.

"Even if you and I were to look into the future, Rowan, we wouldn't be guaranteed to know the future," my mother said, sitting on the arm of the chair. "We wouldn't know the outcome, or the battle, but we know where they are. We knew how to end them."

"Don't do this, please. I'll keep up this shit with Sia if I have to. I'll make her think I'll marry her if that's what it takes. But don't do this."

"It's already done." Ilyan's voice was firm, "we leave Saturday morning. We need you to watch your baby sister. Can you be home Friday night?"

I knew that I didn't really have a choice in the matter from the very beginning, but now it was final. No fighting them. No fighting *with* them. Just babysitting.

I had barely nodded before my mother rushed me, kissing my brow and giving me another smile, my father giving me a tight-lipped nod.

"We love you, Rowan," my father said, his eyes shining. "Thank you for doing this."

With that they were gone, leaving me alone to rage and scream and curse to the heavens. Instead, I sat still, the silence ringing in my ears until the bell rang and I made my way to class. My magic pushing me forward, as I fought the need to run after them.

When I reached the Defense classroom, Gemma was lounging beside the window where we always sat, legs up, head back, looking as serene as she had beneath the tree.

I still had to find a way to make that up to her.

Seeing her like that was like seeing a different side of her, like a peek into the girl that was hiding behind all those piercings and tattoos. Little moments that peeked through, they were becoming more frequent. Each time they arrived I think I lost a little bit more of myself to her.

Last night had been beautiful, each moment keeping me company through the long night as I replayed them. I had chosen to return to school this morning because of last night, knowing if I could keep myself controlled with Gemma, alone in my room, that school could be a breeze.

Now, my blood was boiling, everything angry and frightening. That beautiful woman lying in the corner of the classroom felt like a minefield.

I had been gone so long, I had no clue what we were working on. Maybe I would get lucky and it would be shielded. Less chance of accidental magic mingling when everything was lit by fire.

"Hi, Rowan." She gave me a bright smile, that snap igniting in her eyes as she looked from me to Sia, who was already glaring at her like the two were arch enemies. "You're looking particularly clean this morning. Fresh."

"Thank you?" Yes, it was a question, I wasn't really sure how else to respond to that. "You look nice as well. Beautiful."

That last word kind of leaked out. She jerked up, narrowing her eyes as though I had uttered the most offensive word known to man.

"Excuse me?"

"Cauliflower soup." I stuttered, digging myself into a hole, her eyebrows raised a good inch, the silver in her piercing catching in the light.

"Cauliflower soup is beautiful?"

"No! You are! I mean you're clean! Beautiful and clean! Ha!" I spread my fingers out as I tried to force out a laugh, looking like one of those clowns that pop out of boxes.

She was looking at me like I was crazy.

What the hell was that?

Forget digging, I was burrowing underground. With how much my cheeks were heating and my magic flaring I could melt myself six feet under with little issue.

"Are you sure Sia didn't suck your brain out through your mouth? I know you say she's not your girlfriend, but it looks like the damage has already been done. I would be totally willing to take care of her for you if that's the case." She smiled wickedly, her snark emanating around her like it was its own separate being.

"Yeah, maybe," I mumbled my foolish answer still gnawing at my nerve endings. "I mean, no! I don't want to know what taking care of something means to you."

"Your loss," she shrugged her shoulders, going back to basking in the hidden rays of sun that were sneaking through the window, a whisper of her grin peeking through.

"Beautiful." Why did I say it again! Her eyes popping open in a uni-scowl that could melt flesh. Luckily the teacher saved me before that happened.

"Good afternoon, class!" Professor Diarius yelled the moment she entered, her usual perky voice drowned in intense dread that cut through the chatter and sent ice down my spine. There was only one reason to be nervous in a class like this. "Today we will begin sparring with our partners."

"Havno," I swore in Czech and earned myself a look from Gemma even though everyone else had broken out into bursts of fear and excitement, there was even a whoop from an Undermortal near the front. I was frozen in place, my heart thundering, my magic shivering against the panic that was making me want to throw myself out the window.

This could not be happening. I knew my father's binds would hold, but I had let too much magic out the last few days. I wasn't really interested in testing the limits of that. Especially with the girl who was looking at me like she had massive plans to kick my ass.

"Settle down, everyone. I know you are excited, but this will be the start of what's to come. Do not expect anything special, do not try anything other than the basics. No fireworks." The excited faces fell to nothing as she recited the rules, although the disappointment was short-lived. "We will be attempting the attacks we learned from last month first, you will be expected to keep your shields up throughout the duration of class in a test of both stamina and skill."

Everyone was nodding and shifting, excitement and nerves coating the classroom like grease. At least I didn't have to worry about the shield, I had pretty much kept a shield around me since day one in this place.

"Now, pair up with your assigned partner. Shields up, and let's see how long you last. First person to zap their partner five times will win the round. The student with the most rounds won at the end of class will win a free class this Friday. Good luck."

Everyone shifted, faces eager as they moved to stand into what they had assumed was fighting position. Ten feet away from their partner, hands up like they were going to get in a long-distance punching match. They wouldn't last two minutes against my uncle Ryland. I wonder how long Gemma would hold up against him. Against me.

Maybe that was why, under her ass-kicking scowl, she looked nervous.

"I say we skip this crap. Lay in the sun and casts shields around the flies," she said, her voice shaking enough that you could tell she was trying hard to sound normal. "Or maybe we can zap your girlfriend a few times and watch her jump."

She gave me a sidelong look before turning, toward Sia who had squared her jaw in preparation for battle. The bubbly facade was gone, she looked like the girl from my dream. Like the girl who snarled down to her maids as they desperately tried to clean her dress. The real Sia. I shook my head. I really was desperate if I was going to agree to go back to fake-dating her.

"Naw, I want to see what you got, Gemma. Besides, I seem to recall you saying you were going to beat my ass." I gave her a wink and earned myself a scowl.

"You looking for another opportunity to show off that temper of yours?" She scooted closer, the twisted grin I had seen so often in my dreams taking over her features.

Exhilaration. Excitement. Hunger.

"Well, aren't you?" I couldn't tell if she was taunting me, or flirting with me, but it didn't matter I reacted as if it was both everything super heating as I moved closer, the smell of her skin dripping over me.

"Not a bit," I said each word slowly, breathing her in, my already agitated magic jumping into a flood. This was a bad idea, didn't matter, the thought was gone in one flash of her lavender eyes.

"Prove it." She smiled, jumped up and assumed the same position everyone else was. Ten feet away, hands raised, ready to fight.

"What are you doing?" I asked, running my hands through my hair.

"Fighting?" It was a question, her eyes narrowed from me to those around us as she checked her position, moving one step closer when she was content that she was doing it right.

"You have never fought before, have you?"

"Not unless you count dodging your leach girlfriend and her Bitchicade."

"What?" I couldn't stop the snicker, I had no idea what she had said, but I loved every second of it.

"I told you, Princey, I've only ever blown up things." She gave me her usual grin, she clearly wasn't being one hundred percent honest. Knowing her she was checking those around her to make she looked just as innocent.

Innocent and ready to blow things up.

No wonder the attack in the Gauntlet had gone the way it had. She literally didn't know how to do anything else. As much as I wanted to send her packing in defeat, I would have to do so gently. She wasn't as trained as I was. This could go bad very quickly.

"Hit me with your best shot, Gemma," I taunted, snapping a shield around both of us, instead of just around me. I could dodge or destroy whatever she sent my way. It was everyone else I was worried about, who knew what she was about to blow up.

Her magic went flying, a massive orb of orange and green ripping through the air, grey smoke trailing behind it in deathly ribbons as it made its way right to me. I batted it away with one swipe of my hand, the fire fading to nothing.

"What the...?" Gemma snarled, already preparing her next attack.

"Care to try that again?" I was smiling now, the look on her face wiping a bit of the tension and anger away.

She fumed, nostrils flaring, lip twisting as she took two steps back, both of us looking to make sure Professor Diarius was occupied. I was sure what we were doing wasn't in her 'no fireworks' rule. I shouldn't have looked, the fire she sent toward me slammed me right in the shoulder, electricity firing through the coils of muscle, flaring over my back as my nerves were ripped to shreds. I clamped my teeth together, locking the scream inside and letting only a groan escape as I fell to my knees.

"What is going on over there?" Diarius's shriek was drowned by my grunts as I fought off her attack, my spine still trying to detach itself from my nervous system.

Gasps rippled around us as everyone realized exactly what

was going on. Everything hurt, but I slammed my hand forward, forcing a mostly useless attack at her in a line of grey smoke that she easily dodged. Probably for the best. It was the pure form of what she had accidentally hit me with, I didn't know if she could withstand the pain.

Or if I wanted her to.

"You were supposed to shield yourself!" She shrieked, pure horror on her face as I continued to stagger and jerk around like a broken puppet. I laughed at her, straightening my neck as my magic put the last of my nerve endings in place.

"I've had worse." My voice was so strained that I wasn't sure if she believed me.

"Shield and light attack, you two!" Professor Darius continued to yell, clearly thinking this was all a mistake. Neither of us turned, I instead sent another attack her way, the ribbons meant to bind around her legs and knock her off her feet, she dodged them stealthily.

"Yeah, except now I've attacked a prince. That's going to look great on my criminal offenses list." She sighed, rubbing her neck as she waved sheepishly to Professor Diarius, before trying to attack me again, sending the weak sparks we were supposed to be doing my way like some twisted show of faith.

Didn't matter, the furious woman was still heading our way, she looked like a bull.

"You collecting titles?" I taunted letting my magic build behind me. "At least you're no longer planning on making Prince Killer one of them."

"I can still change my mind." She winked at me and flipped another attack my way. The speedy thing buzzed and cracked its way to me. I barely dodged it, sending it in the opposite direction, toward the crowd who screamed and ducked before it hit against my shield, sending their panic into awe, a collective gasp buzzing through the barrier.

"Well, now is your chance. You only get one shot," I nodded my head to Diarius, who while trapped on the other side of my shield, was already fighting against it. It wouldn't take her long to get past it though.

"Stop this right this instant!" Poor Diarius. I kind of felt bad for her.

"Don't tell your mom," Gemma said as she sent a ribbon of red my way, the weird attack heading right for me. It never made it.

"It's my dad you have to worry about, trust me." I slammed my hands forward, my magic prickling and warming on the back of my neck as the orb of light I had created slammed through me. It blazed in a blast of light, soaring towards her, devouring her attack on the way. She barely dodged out of the way, flinging herself onto the floor, before the orb slammed into the shield, the floors of the massive amphitheater rattling from the impact.

"Who's weak now?" I taunted, taking two wide steps to where she lay flat-back on the floor, attempting to push herself to stand. She was half sitting up before I stepped over her, holding her in place. Pressing my hands toward her, the air around them growing dark.

Dark.

My father's binds were still in place but the powerful Drak magic was desperate to get out, to reach her.

I quickly dialed down the intensity before it got out of control.

I stood with the class behind me, the shield still keeping them from us as Gemma laid on the floor below me, glowering in wicked defeat. It if wasn't for Professor Diarius still yelling at us to stop, I would have forgotten they were there.

Neither of us moved, she was trapped and I just stared at Gemma, waiting.

"You are going to make me say it aren't you?" She laughed, throwing her head back and ignoring my impending attack altogether.

Normally I would expect my opponents to throw a sneak attack and send me tumbling through the air, but I didn't care if she did, I was frozen over her, her magic wrapping around me. Filling me.

"Prince Rowan," she began nefarious snark twisting her laugh as she reached toward me, toward my hands that were still buzzing with threatening magic. "You're not weak."

She spoke calmly, every drop of snark gone as she whispered the words, as her hand wrapped around mine.

The heat of her touch, of her magic, tickled over my skin, the warmth pricking at the back of my neck as everything began to spin, as the binds snapped, as everything went red and black and foreign.

"Shit," I said, fear tightening up my spine. Her laugh ended as she lifted her head to look at me.

All the joy in her face faded away. She saw.

"Row--?"

She didn't even get to finish my name. She didn't get to say anything more before I reacted, panic and fear taking control as liquid energy flew right at her unprotected, unprepared face. I was barely able to change the attack in time, the powerful force slamming into the stone behind her head and showering us with bits of stone and wood.

Everyone screamed in shock, the screams growing as I directed another attack toward the ceiling, popping the shield and burrowing into the ancient mosaic that my father had commissioned for the ceilings. Tile, plaster, and paint fell over everything, the screams duplicating as I looked at Gemma, as I saw my own black eyes reflected in hers.

I said nothing before I ran, not even bothering to grab my

bag before I hurled myself through the window, my magic pulling at the wind and catching me before I hit the ground, supporting me as I took off.

Desperate to get myself as far away from her, as far away from Gemma's knowing stare as I could.

31

GEMMA

EYES AS DARK AS THE HOLLOW END OF A TUNNEL SWALLOWED THE light, they swallowed my breath as they sucked me into them. As he stared into me, the smile of victory nefarious underneath the ebony gaze.

I had seen those eyes before. I knew exactly what they were and why the joy of this little match had evaporated.

"Rowan?"

His smile faded to shock, to fear, then to a panic as the stone beside my head shattered in a stone rain that beat against my face, tugging at my arms and shoulders as he took off, hands over his face as he threw himself out the window.

"Rowan!"

Everyone was still screaming. Still yelling. He had barely thrown himself out the window when I was up and running.

I don't know why I went after him; I don't know why I cared if some dumb prince had thrown himself out the window. But I did.

I didn't get more than a few steps towards that window before the ceiling came down, before the walls around us crumbled and everything fell apart in the sound of screams.

Throwing both his and my bag over my shoulder I threw myself out of the window after him before I could think better of it.

It was only after my feet had left the windowsill that I remembered I hadn't mastered that flying with wind thing. I didn't even know where to start to be able to accomplish that. I was sure the freefall out of the window wasn't the best time to figure it out.

Too late.

Luckily, the exploding and collapsing building behind me had garnered the attention of a few students on the grass, one of them seeing my leg-breaking fall and sending a cushion of wind my way. The pillow of nothing caught me before my feet had collided against the grass and sent my femurs through my knee caps.

That would have put a damper on this whole thing.

"Thanks," I heaved, readjusting the bags. He mumbled some question about me being okay before everything was drowned out by the groaning, crumbling stone of the amphitheater. We turned as the twists of metal and breaking glass cracked through the breeze like ice and the side of the building came down.

"Oh my god! What is happening?" Someone else yelled in alarm, but I ignored them, running off in the direction of the dorms, leaving them all to stare in horror at whatever was happening. The earth shook as I bolted, the groan so loud now that I was sure the earth was opening up rather than a building imploding on itself.

And he said he didn't explode buildings.

Everything settled as I reached the door to the south side of the school, taking one look back at the dust and smoke that was concealing what was once a training hall.

"Shit." I snapped, catching the eye of four tall Skřítek guards that were taking off after me. Where had they even come from?

"Good job, Gemma, the one time you aren't responsible for blowing up the building and you take off. Because I need to look more guilty. Hit a prince. Blow up a building..."

I prattled on to myself as I weaved my way through the halls, bags bouncing against each individual ass cheek in a painful rhythm as I turned one corner then another before darting into the teacher's wing where I had spent way too much time lately.

Always know everything about your enemy, that way you can make an easy escape.

Or be aware that the guy you pretend not to like had inherited his mother's freaking Drak ability. Although with the horror on his face. With the way he had run, leaving rubble behind him, I had a feeling that that bit of information wasn't exactly supposed to be common knowledge.

His door was two steps ahead, the thunder of footsteps and yelling behind me growing closer. I wrapped my hand around the knob, pushing my magic into the metal and sliding the lock open as I had slid manhole covers back into place in every other escape.

"Oh god, oh god, oh god," I hissed to myself, relocking the door and turning on the spot. Heart in my throat, I stared at the door, waiting for the voices to pass, waiting for the door to open and me to... what? Attack? I was so used to running and fighting that I honestly had no clue what to do in a situation in which you were actually innocent.

Well, except for stealing the prince's book bag and breaking into his dorm room. Which made it even more asinine that I had gone there. Or why I was chasing after him, well, other than the look on his face, the fear in those black eyes. I didn't know black eyes could be so expressive, so consuming. His were.

The voices faded away and I dropped the bags to the floor, books and fabric hitting against that ridiculously thick rug.

"Rowan!" I hissed into the dark room, peeking around the

room with the couches, and the room with the sinks, and the room with the bed. Far more rooms than I had in my place, which I was suddenly grateful for. Too many places to hide, especially after I discovered a door that led to a bathroom the size of my entire dorm, and four more that held clothes. So many clothes.

The only other place I had seen so many clothes was in a store we had knocked over after we realized we could get shoes for everyone in one shot. He probably had just as many pairs. Clothes, bathrooms, a door that hid food. But no Rowan.

"Prince Douche," I snarled through a bite of the apple I had found on the counter. There was no answer. He wasn't there.

Putting the apple on the little foot table, I grabbed a piece of paper and a pen there, ready to leave him a note, when I saw that someone else had already done so.

'Row-

Accidents happen. Good is in everyone and everything, Rowan. Even you. Cail gave me the letter at your insistence, I'll take care of it. We are getting closer on the Demarco's so you need to hold out a little longer. Call me if you need help.

- Mom'

I only understood about half of it, but it didn't matter. The part that I did understand set me on my ass, sinking into a chair that must have been partially made of a cloud.

He was right. Sia wasn't his girlfriend. The entire thing had been a total farce. But even more shocking, he was the one who asked about the food stuff. He was the one who had worked that out.

Prince Douche.

Damn it. Now I really can't call him that.

I swallowed. He may have destroyed my tree, but he had still been listening. He had learned something.

I sat, stupidly staring at the paper that had been folded and unfolded so many times that the seams had started to fray. The twirling ink on the word mom worn over so that it was barely legible. Like the drawing from my mother that I used to keep in my pocket. She couldn't read or write, but when I had woken up and she was gone, a drawing was in my pocket. I missed her so much I wore it through.

"Rowan!" I jumped at the screech that echoed through the window in the bedroom, the familiar agonizing howl trying to claw the nerve endings out of my eyeballs.

Sia.

Well, in the sake of running, I better get on that. Stuffing the letter in my pocket, I grabbed my book bag and took off. Not out the window, but through the front door, which I had the misfortune of not checking before I darted into the hallway and into an already shrieking face.

"Row-- You!"

"Oh! Hi, Sia," I tried to be nonchalant, choosing instead to get the hell out of there instead of prod the bitch like I usually did. But then I turned and saw the chalky ghost that Sia had become.

She was covered with so much dust and rubble that she could have sprouted up from it. Building troll.

"You know, if your rash is that bad you should probably stay inside."

Sia was fuming so much that the dust was shaking off of her, making it look like steam shooting from her ears. She looked like the toilets on a summer day, when all the stank was drifting up. Okay, maybe it was actually the perfect look for her.

"Sia the toilet," I said under my breath, which only made her fume more.

"Where is he?" She finally roared, more ash shimmying off her as the same Skřítek guards from before plowed through the hallway behind her. "Where did you put the prince!"

"Where did I..?" Yep. I was right, running had been a mistake. "I didn't put him anywhere; He ripped a hole in the roof and flew out the window."

"No! You killed him! I saw your magic go right through him before the roof came down on top of everyone." And she was crying. Again.

"Okay, dipshit. If I killed him why would I come back to drop off his bag and not fly back home and celebrate the start of the fall of the royals?" My chest burned with each word, the plans I didn't want any more feeling like acid in my mouth.

I shook my head, completely missing Sia's flinging of sparking acidic ribbons flying right to me.

Well, shit. This was going to hurt.

"That's enough of that!" The magic attack vanished with a pop, the guards that had been pursuing me, finally catching up. Not just guards, Mira was right at the head. It was Mira who had spoken, her brow furrowed in condescending agitation as she glared at Sia. I hadn't seen her there a second before, not that it meant anything.

She was an Eternal, she could probably do that stutter thing, and that shield thing.

God. I had really underestimated Rowan, for all I know he was in his room the entire time.

Mira and the guards raced down the hall, all of them dressed in black from head to toe, as if they had been stalking us like shadow ninjas. Creepy. Especially given that Mira looked like she was ready to kill one of us. Her long blonde hair was pulled up in a knot on top of her head, her eyes narrowed as they darted from me to the window to the door and back again.

"Gemma, we have been looking for you." Mira began, flipping her fingers in a tiny flick that I don't think she expected me to see. The guards did, however, a few of them vanishing from sight as the others shifted, stepping around us. Or, I guess me.

I jumped. People vanishing was not really something anyone expected, or got used to.

"You blow up a couple of buildings and no one trusts you." I sighed, stepping back from one guard, then the other. I must have looked like a ping pong ball.

"So, you did blow up the building?" Sia shrieked, pointing her finger wildly in my direction.

"No. I've blown up others. This one as all--." I froze, looking from Sia to the pocket that held the letter, something nagging at me.

"I know you did it. Confess!" Sia said, forgetting to fake cry so she could glare at me.

"We were sparing. He was winning. And then..." I paused, looking between Sia who was shaking so hard dust was falling from her shoulders and Mira who stood calm as could be considering there was a chance I had killed their prince. Then, I did something I never thought I would do.

"I said something nasty about his freaky ass mom," I said with as much venom as I could force into my voice, Sia's jaw sagging as though she had been poisoned. I could have sworn Mira was suppressing a smile. "He was so pissed, but I wasn't about to let him win. I don't lose. I attacked him, but he dodged it. He hit the floor, then the ceiling and then he was out the window, calling me a crazy bitch."

"Well, one part of your story is true. You are a crazy bitch," Sia spat, lip curling until Mira turned to her, the fake tears sprouting up like the shower drains when the floods came through every spring.

"So, you don't know where he is?" Mira asked, still looking at Sia who was now cranking it up a notch and trying to produce actual tears.

"Nope. Hence why I came here. To apologize for being a bitch." I said, folding my arms over my chest as I glared at Sia, her tears slipping as she stifled a laugh. "That and not end up a ghost from a collapsed building."

The tears were once again replaced by a scowl.

"Don't worry. I know my nephew, everything will be okay," Mira said, waving away the others who had been trailing behind her, the last of them vanishing without so much as a pop.

I totally jumped again.

"Wait. You are going to let her go?" Sia's tears were forgotten now, more dust falling off her as she pounded her fists against her thighs.

"No, I am going to let *you* go, Miss Demarco, we have no use for you at this moment and I am sure there is another hallway nearby that you can haunt. Gemma and I are going to visit the headmaster, so off you go." I don't think I had ever seen anyone put Sia in her place so fast.

Mira might be my new favorite, would have told her so too if Sia's expressions wasn't flipping from crying, to furious, to pouting so fast that I was starting to wonder if her brain was broken.

"Come with me Gemma," Mira said, pulling me from Sia who jumped nearly to the ceiling as a disembodied voice yelled "Boo!" right beside her.

She screamed, three booming males voices laughed and I squealed with a sound I didn't know I could make.

Sia was staring furiously at me from the middle of the hall as we walked away. My squealing laugh continued as Mira pulled me around the corner and toward who knows what.

"I can die happy now." I sighed, stuffing my hands in my pockets and following after Mira with my nose in the air.

"Excuse me?"

"Nothing, just embedding her expression in my mind while

you lead me to my untimely end." I was trying to be totally nonchalant about this thing, but I couldn't, my voice still caught, my heart twisting itself around my throat like it was trying to tango with the thing.

"I'm not leading you to your end. Cail is not going to kill you. It's a building, not a dynasty." Mira's response did little to calm my dread.

"That would make sense, I mean, Headmaster Cail probably doesn't carry out his own murders."

"Oh, he does all his own killing," Mira said, her face so deadpan that I wasn't about to question her. "But he also doesn't kill innocents."

"You think I'm innocent?" I stopped in place; my mouth dry as I tried to swallow away my shock. There were dramatic pauses in the hallway from this girl, I had to run to catch up. "Or do you believe that mumbo jumbo that the queen's been throwing around?"

"I believe *you*."

"Why?" I gasped, earning myself a sigh. "I mean, yay!" I threw my hands in the air with exaggerated glee. "But why?"

This might have to go down in history as a first.

"Because it's my job."

"It's your job to believe me?" My voice echoed as we turned another corner. I could have sworn I heard the shuffle of feet, like we were being followed. But even with one quick turn, no one was there.

Mira kept walking forward, like I wasn't spinning around like a human top.

"No, it's my job to guard the royal family."

All thought of additional guards swarming around me was forgotten, "Aren't you part of the royal family?"

"Yes." There was that tiny hint of a smile again.

"So, you guard yourself?"

"I guard my family."

"So, does that mean you have been watching Rowan the entire time?" Man, really sucks to be him if that's true.

"And you."

"But I haven't seen…" I paused and looked around again, instead of looking with my eyes, I felt with my magic. The added pressure of other people and their power so faint I barely found it. "Damn, you're good."

"I was trained by an evil king who was trying to end the word," she said, stuffing her hands in her pockets as she smiled at me. As if smiling would make what she said normal somehow.

"End the world, like the guy who Ilyan and Joclyn stopped?" At least I had paid some attention in history class.

"One in the same." She sighed, slowing as we grew closer to the office where more than a few people were gathered, the king and queen in the middle of them all. "I killed more than I let live those first years."

"Ummm. So, are you the one who is going to kill me then? Because I promise you I didn't blow up that hall." I was suddenly back to evaluating escape plans. I hadn't fully eliminated jumping out the window.

"No, no death. Not here. I know you didn't blow up that hall. I follow you, remember?"

"Still creepy."

"Plus, I control your magic."

"You control…?"

She stopped, turning to me and smiling so broadly I had to question how much the wicked king had taught her. How much she still retained.

"Seriously Gemma, what did you think the Štít was for? The bits of stone will turn your magic off without some sort of barrier. I get to control it, like a remote." Her grin stretched, the light in her eyes gleaming as that deadweight I had felt on my chest since day one lightened. My magic buzzed through my veins, same as it used to. Same as it did every night when she was probably sleeping.

"Holy shit," I hiss-whispered, staring at my fingers as they hummed.

"Pretty cool, huh?" I really didn't know what to say to that, cool was not the word I would go for.

I was leaning more towards a solid 'total bullshit'.

My magic snapped back to a low roar as we turned another corner, toward the open door and a buzz of voices at the end of the hall.

"So, no blowing up buildings for you anymore." She gave me a wink, like she still thought this whole thing was cool. "I know of only one other person with the strength to do that and he is MIA, so you have nothing to worry about. Even without all that, I would have known. Working for Ilyan and Ryland for all these years has taught me one very important thing."

"What's that?" The queen was looking at me now. Her silver eyes were devoid of any black as she peered through the hall, her brow furrowing

I almost went back to the whole running away thing, but I was sure any of them would catch me before I got too far.

"How to spot a tyrant," she said as the queen walked our way.

I laughed, but she was dead serious.

"Any around here I should know about?"

"A few. But don't worry, you're not one of them." I twisted to her, waiting for her to finish, to give me the names, but she smiled. "You lied for the prince, Gemma. Tyrants don't do that."

I was stuck in place, her words pounding against my skull.

She was right, I had lied and covered for a prince. For a damn Eternal. What was wrong with me? What was I anymore?

"Hello again, Gemma," The queen said as she reached us,

her smile wide before she spread her arms. I cringed, expecting an attack, a slap. It could go either way.

Instead, she wrapped her arms around me and pulled me into her.

"Thank you for caring for my son."

What. The. Fuck.

32

ROWAN

I flew home to Imdalind.

Home to the underground circuit of caves that had been my entire world up to a few months ago. I had hidden in there, ignoring truth and fate and pretending the dreams I had were nothing more than that.

Coming back, I realized how small and dark the once safe tunnels were, how much I had coated the stone with lies while I let the world around me burn.

I had blocked my mother's sights. I was as responsible as the rest of them.

The fact that I had also collapsed an entire wing of my father's precious Abbey was inconsequential at this point. Right now, I needed to talk to my mother.

Finding her may be nearly impossible, seeing as they had stuttered out of Cail's office less than an hour before, but this was as good as a place to start as any.

The only question now was where to start. Their massive suite, or the dark tunnels that led to the underground pool of black water that was kind of like a temple to her.

To me.

Standing in the middle of the massive stone courtyard, I could feel the floor hum with the power. The rock pulsing like a heartbeat, pulling like a deep current that was pulling me toward it.

It had always been there, but now, with so much of the Drak magic flowing through me, it was so much more pronounced.

Before I could stop myself, I turned on my heel. My heart moved in time with the heat of the stone as I walked down the darkened tunnel that I had avoided for the last ten years, when I had sat beside the pool and filled the mug for the first time. When I drank for the last time.

The energy in the stone drifted into the air, it vibrated against my skin as everything hummed.

Hum in the silence, as though the energy was singing inside of me, accented only by the pound of my feet against the stone as I moved faster. Faster.

I needed to move faster.

"If they are telling the truth... if they found a raw one? What do you think that means for us?" I froze, not because of the voice. But because of who it belonged to.

It wasn't my mother. I didn't know of one other person who was allowed to be down there. Who *should* be down there.

All that thrumming magic twisted itself into a panic in my gut as the high-pitched voice of the woman moved closer. Not one, but two pairs of footsteps coming right behind.

"I'm assuming good," Analine said with foreign glee in her voice, I pressed myself against the wall, knowing she and whoever she was with were close.

"It all depends on how it's used." If Analine was bad, the answering voice was worse.

Talon.

The steps grew closer. I remained in place, magic boiling in time with the pulsing stone as two figures turned the corner and came face to face with me. They both jerked as though they had been punched, Talon's features quickly rearranging into something closer to fury as he shifted something behind his back.

"What are you doing here?" He was clearly trying to keep his voice even, trying to push a bit of surprise into his features. Nothing could mask the shock in his eyes, even if Analine hadn't been such a huge giveaway. Her usual smug snarl was missing, her eyes darting around me, looking for who I was with.

"Odd. I was wondering that about you as well." I said, folding my arms, if only because it was the only way to control my magic right then. The power was growing closer to boiling rage. "I mean, it's been a while since I've been down here, but I'm pretty sure there is nothing that would interest you..."

I shifted, trying to get a look at whatever he had shifted behind his back, but he countered me, stepping closer so as to block my line of sight.

"Aren't you supposed to be at school?"

"Yeah, school's canceled, someone blew up a building," the two looked at each other, eyes not even trying to hide their alarm now.

"I wonder who that could have been, come to turn in the little Drain this time." I chose to ignore my brother's jab, even though he was smiling so broadly it was clear he thought he had been handed a win.

"Where is mother?" I asked, looking between them and down the long dark hallway. I half expected her to be standing passed it, looking in on us. But I couldn't feel her magic anywhere, no matter how far I stretched my magic to look.

Now that I was actually looking with my mind and not

letting my magic drag me away, I wasn't sure she was there at all.

"The King and Queen were called away. There was an emergency on the outer edge of our kingdom," Talon's voice rumbled over the stone, pulling my spine as though his tone was some kind of trigger.

We rarely spoke to each other that way, if only because it was irritating enough when we had to do it to others. But Talon looked right at me, his proud voice loud, the air prickling around me as the skin on my neck lifted.

I swallowed, "What emergency?"

They hadn't been planning on going after the Demarco's and their army until the weekend, I had seen them less than an hour ago. Surely if something had happened so soon they would have told me.

"None of your concern, Atty," Talon snapped over any answer Analine had been about to give, her mouth snapping shut as Talon stepped closer to me, his frame so close now that I could feel the heat of his magic, of his shield buzzing above his skin. "Leave the tough question to the adults."

He was expecting a fight. With the intensity of the layer of magic that was smothering him, he was ready to put up quite a fight.

"Okay, so here's an easy one. Why were you down by the water?" I could visibly see Talon's shoulders straighten, Analine stepping back as her own magic flared. "Why were you in the Temple. You're not a Drak."

"Neither are you, Atty." God, every time Talon used that nickname I wanted to slug him. He knew it too with how he was smiling.

"Actually, I've been having second thoughts about that."

"Why?" Talon said with a laugh, turning to Analine who gave a half-hearted laugh. She hadn't taken her eyes off me, off my hands. "You gonna go save some more Drains? Pull them out of the tunnels and set them free like the vermin they are. Or, if what Analine says is true. *She* is." He clicked his tongue and shook his head. "That fucking Drain you make eyes at every morning."

"She's not a Drain." I cut him off with a snarl, taking two quick steps forward as the rock in the stone next to me cracked like lightning. I didn't have to turn to know I had done that. Talon's smug smile was enough.

"Control yourself, Atty, or you're going to drop the world."

I totally tried to slug him. My fist only got about halfway to his jaw when his magic slammed against me, throwing me into the wall. Stone cracked around me in jagged broken lines.

"I warned you when all of this first happened that she wanted to kill us, Rowan. That she wanted to hurt us, me, you, Angie. Instead of keeping your distance you have buddied up to her. Now you are crawling into bed with her."

"Excuse me?" I snapped, pushing myself off the wall, resisting the urge to fight back. I may be boiling, but I wasn't stupid. "I traipsed around that hellhole for months with that bitch Sia Demarco. If I had been crawling into bed with anyone it's her, and I ended that bullshit."

Saying the words, the reminder of what I had done, was churning my stomach. I didn't need that thought in my head, especially when I could still remember how my magic had reacted to one touch from her. Vile Disgusting. Unwanted. So much different than Gemma's.

"Sia Demarco is not part of this," Talon snarled, more anger in his voice than I had expected. In fact, he looked about ready to explode.

"Not anymore, thank god." Saying it aloud calmed my brother enough that his magic wasn't crackling in the air anymore.

"Well, if we are going to win this, you need to stay away from both of them. Sia is no longer your concern. And the girl..." Talon said, taking a step closer to me. "Her part in this has nothing to do with you."

"Win?" I interrupted, my voice nearly a whisper as I sat up. "What do you mean win? What battle are you playing, Talon?"

"There is no battle. There is no winning," Analine said, finally stepping forward and back into the conversation. I wasn't sure I believed her. "We are trying to unite everyone, Rowan. You know this. You know you have a part to play in this."

"A part that does not involve the Undermortals." Talon clearly had to concentrate in order to use that word. "Any of them."

He was clearly trying to drive some point home, both of their expressions heavy as they peered into me. My magic buzzed against my neck, the same images from before blending with another flaring in my memory with that haunting moment of Gemma's hands wrapped around Talon's neck.

"What are you saying, Talon?" I said, forcing calm through me as my magic boiled again, the power pushing me forward, down the long tunnel.

"We don't want anyone to get hurt, Rowan. You especially." Talon tried to put his hand on my shoulder, I dodged him. "I know you want everyone to live in peace, and they can. Perhaps you can come with us. Perhaps you can help."

Analine shook her head, eyes wide as she stared at Talon, trying to get his attention, but the guy was only looking at me, his hand still reaching toward me.

"Help with what?" I glanced between the two, both sets of suddenly eager eyes, staring into me like I was some kind of prize. The intensity, the glee. I had been met with the hopeful glare of dozens of women for weeks, watched their eyes graze over me with some hungry lust that always left me feeling unclean.

Now, I felt like I was swimming in shit.

The look these two were giving me now was more predatory, a hungry stare that dug into my nerve endings, every muscle in me screaming, begging, me to run.

Talon smiled, "If you are embracing that power. Embracing that magic, I know you can help. Help me. Help the cause. Perhaps even help our parents."

Everything ached as I stared at him. His words sunk in as he shifted, dropping his hand and shifting his weight, giving me a glimpse of what he had held. A canteen.

A canteen filled with water.

Black water.

My eyes snapped to his, jaw dropping. What in the world would he have need of Black Water for? Mom could summon it from anywhere, and I highly doubted she would use it in battle. Anytime the water touched non-Drak flesh a sight was triggered. I had seen in happen once before, when Angie knocked over moms mug as a toddler.

"I don't know what you are playing at, but I think you need to go. I think you need to leave that bag with me. I need to find our parents. I think I need to talk to our father before I make any decision about what I am going to fight for, and who I am going to avoid."

I didn't move beyond swinging my hand forward, palm up as I waited for him to deposit the water pouch. Thankfully he did without complaint, although Analine said something so low and fast that I couldn't make it out, even if Talon hadn't cut her off with nothing more than a glare.

"I'll see you in class tomorrow, cousin. Goodbye, brother." I made sure not to use their names, to keep my voice impassive as

I watched them go. Felt their magic retreat back to the main hall of Imdalind and then vanish from sight as they left the caves.

I still didn't move. I just stood in the middle of the cave, the water sloshing in the canteen I held as my magic picked up, pulling me down to the end of the cave, to the water that part of me knew had all the answers.

Instead, I ran knowing right where my mother was.

33
———

GEMMA

THE HUG WAS NOT THE WEIRDEST THING TO HAPPEN.

I had been shuffled into a room with every Eternal I had met so far, the royal family all clogged inside of Cail's office, Mira rushing in and out as she oversaw the issues that arose due to Rowan having blown up a building. Rowan, not me.

None of them questioned it. Mira explained what happened, the King looked at me with a smile and commended me for holding my own against his son, and that was it.

Well, not it-it, but they hadn't said anything more about what happened in Defense class... or the fact that Rowan's eyes had gone black. "Thank you for caring for my son," the Queen had said, and then nothing else.

It had taken me a few minutes of listening to them ramble about reconstruction plans to realize why. They didn't know.

Either they didn't know he was a Drak, which I highly doubted, or they actually believed my story about me insulting the Queen and Rowan flipping his shit. Damn, the kid must really have a temper then if they didn't even question it.

I wasn't about to bring the Temper Tantrum Prince and his black eyes up again though, because after they had discussed

297

the plans to have the students rebuild the amphitheater as a lesson in magic the queen turned to me and spoke a truth so plainly that if I had been able to eat anything at lunch would have had me throwing up all over her.

"So, I am being told that the Vilỳ who bit you is alive."

I shouldn't be surprised she knew; Patrice had come along on that little mission after all. But still, hearing her say it felt like a betrayal somehow. Especially knowing where Patrice came from. She should be on my side. I had clearly lifted her up on some pedestal she didn't deserve, she wasn't an Undermortal anymore.

"Yes." I nodded, it really wasn't worth it to lie at that point. "But the guy, Adrian--"

"A real peach," Wynifred cut in with a wicked grin, probably replaying her last interaction with him, the one where she had thrown him into a wall and made him smell his own junk. "Seems to think that being made of pure muscle is enough to take me on."

She and Thomas chuckled. I would have joined in if the Queen wasn't giving me her mumbo jumbo scowl. I shifted, maybe if I didn't look at her she couldn't see straight into my soul like she did last time.

"Yeah, well, he has the Vilỳ. He's biting everyone in my community with it, at least that's what Patrice said," I looked to the lady and she gave me a nod.

"Yes, we went there last week to retrieve it, but it seems that everyone in Last Pyre has gone."

"Gone?"

"Yes, as far as we could tell. We were hoping that you might know where they are?" The king stood behind his wife, his hand on her shoulder as they both stared down at me, both of their looks together someone magnifying the eternal x-ray of the queen, I shifted again.

"I don't." I couldn't force myself to look at them.

"I expected as much. In fact, it seems that many other communities have vanished, with the raids and attacks that have been taking place lately it's understandable, but it makes it hard for us to protect them."

I nodded, not knowing what kind of response to give her. We had heard from the others that the Eternals had been intersecting with the raids and saving many of the Undermortals from the CCC, but it was still kind of hard to believe. I still wasn't quite ready to go spewing information to her about it. Even if I knew where they were.

"We need to know where they have gone, Gemma." The king began, the deep booming of his accented voice pulling my focus right to him. "Especially if they have a Vilỳ--"

"Why would it be so bad if they have a Vilỳ?" I interrupted him, Ryland stepping forward like he was going to throw himself before Ilyan like he was some kind of shield. "They would be like everyone else."

"Yes, but untrained, uncentered magic can be dangerous," Queen Joclyn said, leaning forward and resting her hands on her knees. Screw this, I looked right at her, furrowing my brow as I popped a shield around myself. Like hell if I was letting her get in. "The bite from a poisoned Vilỳ on its own can be dangerous. I'm actually surprised you survived it. So many of those bitten by a poisoned Vilỳ exploded in those early days."

"I'm sorry, did you say exploded?" I jerked back, all thought of some epic stare off gone. All of them gave me a nod, expressions from disgust to worry to even awe in the case of Mira looking back at me.

"Yes, which is why it's important that we find them. I need you to ask everyone you work with for food and in those late-night meetings," I jerked back in my seat, damn the freaky queen really did know everything. Damn Draks. Just like her son. Fuck, what had he seen? Before I could go down that inevitably scarring Rabbit hole, the Queen continued. "Ask them if they know anything of any of the communities. We need to know what happened and where they have gone."

Eternals spy school take two was officially in session. At least this one was as easy as the last one, I could get the information and pass it on without anyone knowing I was collecting information for the royals.

"We also need to know the leader's names of each community and would like your help setting up meetings with them," The kings blue eyes flashed, they didn't look away, they sunk in as ice settled in my veins. "We would like to start working alongside your people. I need your help to make the connection."

Shit.

The room was filling up.

The low squeak of my door as it opened and closed was less of a steady rhythm now, the low hum of voices increasing as more and more people came in filling every chair and couch and piece of floor as they always did.

I was still in my room. I hadn't been able to force myself to leave.

I wasn't scared, I didn't have time for that shit. But perhaps I was apprehensive about what was about to happen. This could go one of two ways. Considering I had snapped my shield to myself and not the room I was clearly expecting it to go the worse way possible.

"Are you going to come in any time soon or do I need to shave my head put on a skirt and lead this shit myself," Eddy peered around the side of the open doorway that led to the sitting area, wagging his eyebrows in practice for his epic drag appearance.

"It'll never work," I said, harsher than I expected, as I jumped to my feet. "You don't have boobs."

"I dunno. If they keep giving us such delicious food I might," he winked at me and puffed out his chest in a beautiful display of male boobage.

I couldn't help but laugh, the sound turning to shrieks as he continued his pursuit, tits out as it were.

"What do you say, baby, wanna hook up sometimes?" He was putting on some weird voice that was only making the whole thing worse. I pushed him away, desperate for air.

"I have sat here on my ass, waiting for this--”

“You’ve been waiting for me to come on to you?” Eddy smirked, still puffing out his chest.

“No. Stop trying to get in my pants, Ed.”

"Wait. Does that mean you want me in your pants? I thought we were going for something more regal..." I pressed my hand against his mouth before he could say anything else and fixed him with a mighty glare. He shut up, was still smirking though.

"You don't even like my pants."

"True," he said, slowly lowering my hand. "But there are some pants out there I like."

He wagged his eyebrows at me and licked his lips. I ignored him and strutted into my room, freezing in place. The room was packed, more so than it had been two weeks ago when we had held out last middle-of-the-night mixer.

"If they try to kill me, promise you'll jump in front of the bullets," I whispered to Eddy, who stepped around the wall with me.

"Aw, hell no. You're on your own babe." Ed gave me a look and slid onto the clogged couch, right next to Greer who gave him one of his wide smiles. I wasn't sure if that smile was a flirting one, but wasn't going to step in. Besides I had bigger problems than where Eddy was swinging his bat.

"Seems we are the popular hangout tonight," I teased, gaining a few laughs as I perched myself on the arm of the couch like I usually did. Everyone instantly moved in, people in the front sitting on the carpet so that the people behind them could hear.

I was actually amazed my room could fit this many people. Of course, it would be the worst popular time to have this happen. More people meant a high chance of inciting a mob.

I glanced at Ed, who gave me a thumbs up that I almost shoved up his nose. He was too positive, and apparently a shit bodyguard considering that he immediately turned to start chatting up Greer. He was more interested in the guy than to how this was going to end up.

Whatever.

"As usual," I began, trying to ignore the nagging voice as to why they were all there, or that this meeting was going to turn into a disaster. "Let's start with updates from Saturday's food run. How are the communities faring, who is ready to fight--"

"I think we are all ready to fight after that display yesterday," someone said from the back, although no one turned toward him. If anything, they leaned closer, eyes wide and looking right at me. I could have sworn Ed groaned from beside me. It might have been me, though.

"You not only knocked down part of the building, but you tried to kill the prince, too," Ruby said, her face thankfully bruise-less after her run in from Sia.

"she almost succeeded too," someone else said, "I was there. The guy took off screaming out of the window."

I sunk down onto the lamp table, sending the porcelain thing rattling as I plopped down. Damn it. They all sounded like Sia, except for them it wasn't flabbergasted anger. It was awe. Fucking, awe. Because we were clearly one step closer to what I had promised them on that very first day.

What I had spent my life working towards.

What I had changed my mind about, or was being ordered to change my mind about. I sighed, Rowan was causing far too many problems for me. I would have to unpack that later.

"Damn. If we can get that close to killing that idiotic prince, then ending them all should be easy," a voice piped up, battling over the eager buzz that had finally made an appearance and stilling everyone.

Not that I knew what it felt like, but I could have sworn a metal spike was plunged straight down my spine. Everything had gone rigid and cold as I looked at both Eddy and Greer, the only other two in this room who had met Rowan, who knew the truth. Well, part of it. They both looked ready to explode.

Well, I still had a few bodyguards on hand.

"I'm not sure that's the best course of action anymore," I began, making sure to lift my voice enough to pull everyone's focus. Considering what I had said, I could have whispered and still gotten the same effect.

Every eye turned to me, every gaze narrowed as a wave of whispered moved through the Undermortals, a powerful ripple of angry magic following right behind.

"You tried to kill the prince," a Ghostlander piped up, the guy muscling forward from where he and his companion had been standing at the back of the room. "You *almost* killed him, and now you have second thoughts."

I paused, debating how much to correct them, how much of the truth I should divulge. I had a key to disaster on my palm, burning a hole through my palm. Waiting.

I balled my fist and shoved my hands in my pocket as I stood, stepping atop the coffee table as I usually did. yeah, it totally made me a target, the fuming guys behind me would have to deal with it.

"My intent wasn't to kill him." Everyone immediately started to whisper, the magic boiling in the room. Instinctively, I moved my shield from around the room, to around me. Chances were everyone was asleep anyway. I was having a good hair day, didn't want someone to mess that up by trying to take off my head or some shit.

"If it wasn't to kill him, then what were you doing?"

"We were sparring. It was Defense class." I narrowed my eyes dangerously, but no one recoiled, they met the glare head-on. Stupid, stubborn, Undermortals.

"So, you wasted an opportunity to kill him--"

"I won't kill him," I quickly interrupted, my heart thumping painfully at the truth in the words, fear tightening around it like ribbons. Fear and joy mingling in a dangerous concoction. "Rowan is not our enemy. None of the Eternals are out enemy. They wish to--"

"You said you were a double agent." The Ghostlander nearly yelled, too loud. Hopefully, no one was wandering around at five am because I was sure they would have heard that two doors over. "Turns out they have you in their pocket."

"They do not have me in their pocket," I was snarling, the Ghostlander just smiled.

"How much did they pay you, you traitor?"

"They didn't pay her anything!" Greer roared, jumping to his feet as Eddy did. "I play rugby with the Prince. He is a genuinely good guy. You have seen his family Dramin and Patrice work with us every weekend to deliver food. What more do you wish to see to know that they are on our side?"

"A little bit of food does not repay a lifetime of repression."

"Our people still died at the hands of the CCC because they did nothing."

"They cannot be nice for a month and expect us to forgive centuries of arrogance!"

The voice plowed over one another. They rumbled and grew

and buzzed so loud that I was sure the walls were vibrating. If not from the noise, but from the angry waves of magic that were washing over everything.

"Stop!" I roared, throwing any spec of caution to the wind. "That's enough! We have been wronged, we have been used, but they are trying to make amends." I lowered my voice, knowing whose wall my dorm shared a room with and not wanting to take any chances. "They are fighting against the CCC, you have heard that from your own communities. You have seen their attempts to give our people homes and a better life. I have heard whisperings that soon they will face them head to head."

I paused, looking to the wall as though I would see Sia on the other side with her ear plastered against the wall. Knowing her she was probably fast asleep, wrapped in the skin of the undead that will grant her eternal youth and couldn't hear a thing.

"Ilyan has asked me to work with you all to arrange--"

"Ilyan?" Kira cut in, my once loyal supporter looking affronted. Everyone around her mumbling and whispering. "You on a first name basis, now?"

"No, I mean--"

"Save it!" One of the Ghostlanders interrupted. "We don't want to hear it. I ate your lies about being a double agent. I believed that you could actually pull this off. I thought she almost killed the prince. I was sure I put my faith in the right person. But you've been lying to us all along."

"Let's go."

The door swung open then, taking away any chance to explain. One by one, everyone filtered out. More than one person spat towards me as they left, every single one scowling as Ed, Greer, and I continued to try to pull their attention.

In seconds, the room was empty, leaving the three of us

standing alone in the dripping anger of the near mob that had left.

"Well, no one tried to take you down," Greer said at full voice, his booming laugh followed right behind.

"They might have if they let me finish. If they knew why Ilyan wanted to speak to them," the two boys turned to me, but I still stared at the door, the solid wood having slammed shut seconds before.

"Adrian, the leader of Last Pyre, has found a Vilỳ," I said, Greer gasped, Eddy nodding once in confirmation. "The royals are too trusting, too confident to think much of it. But I know better. I think he's building an army."

34

SIA

"ADRIAN, THE LEADER OF LAST PYRE, HAS FOUND A VILẎ." I repeated what I had heard verbatim, my father's eyes widening. Talon's brow furrowed. "From what she said, she thinks he's building an army. If I had to guess, he's used the thing already. They might have more than a few magic wielders."

"A Vilẏ? Where did they get one of those? The ones at Imdalind are so locked up even I can't get to them." Talon scoffed, the harsh sound bristling against my spine and I gave him a look. The guy smiled with that heart-stopping grin that always sent my knees shaking. Not today, this was too important.

"I doubt it's one of the ones that you guys have," I said, giving him smug grin. "Since it's from her rat hole I bet it's the one that bit her. They kept it alive, now they are going to use it."

"A wild Vilẏ," Talon said, his hands rubbing together with the same eagerness that was smothering his features. He wasn't looking at me anymore, he was focused on something far away. "The magic those grant in their bite is second only to one. If we could get that we could build an army of our own. A real army, not just the Tarns with guns."

"We could bite the Tarns." My father's eyes were hungry, the two men now looking at each other as though they were fighting over scraps of meat. "Thousands with powerful magic, under my control."

"Our control," Talon corrected. I expected my father to scowl, to rage, but the two laughed, clapping each other on the back with the weird camaraderie that had formed over the last week.

It would figure that I would find my magic's mate and he would be the perfect match for the world we were building. Seeing that hungry violence in his eyes was begging me to drag him back down to my old bedroom again. The guy looked at me like he could read my mind, blowing me a kiss as his magic caressed the base of my spine.

Damn him. He knew he was driving me crazy, and he knew I loved it.

"Do we know where Last Pyre is?" Talon turned from me, giving my father a dark look before the two men strode over to the map on the wall. The old thing was marred with chicken-scratch writing and colorful stickers for the communities that had been emptied or attacked. Most of the red dots lined the main tunnel that circled the old city of Prague, the dark line. The Drains had been cleared out over the last few months in an effort to clear a path to the dark line, and the to the underground palace the royals occupied.

After Talon had joined our cause, those plans had shifted. The tunnels were cleared, but instead of clearing the caverns, Talon had suggested we move south, clearing the communities closer to the Academy buildings and an old tunnel system the royals still used. The thought was that if we took control of the tunnels, we could control their movements better. Especially valuable seeing as only Joclyn and Ilyan could stutter.

"It's here," my father said as I walked around the desk to join them. Talon instantly moved to hold me against him, magic flaring as skin pressed against skin. "We had been saving it for the end, waiting for Sia to end the bitch before we sacked her home. The idea had been to make her watch as we ransacked the place, but Sia was never able to get her hands on the Drain."

I lifted my chin, meeting his glare head-on. I shouldn't be surprised that he still hadn't gotten over my failure. I had literally handed him a prince and once the bonding was completed, an Eternal daughter. It still wasn't good enough.

Fine. I would be the one to retrieve the Vilỳ myself, show him exactly what good his daughter can do.

"What are these?" I asked, pointing to the two yellow dots that stood between our estate and Last Pyre, the names Safe Home and Fire Fate barely legible.

"Sister communities," My father said the words as though they were poison. "Or so the intel says. They are being monitored, we believe Last Pyre may have moved there in the last few weeks. If we were to take them out before Last Pyre, chances were high that Last Pyre would come to the rescue, and vice-versa. We would need to take them out all at once to assure our success. So we left them alone while we waited--"

"What do you think the chances are that those communities are part of the army this Adrian guy is building?" I cut my father off, not really wanting to hear him drawl about pathetic girls that are about as useless to us as the rats that work in the kitchens.

"High," Talon answered before my father had a chance. He didn't fight back as he normally would, but his jaw tightened, his eyes narrowing at the map. "If you are right, and Last Pyre has moved south to Fire Fate, he may already be building an army. If he's been doing it since Gemma was carted off to Imdalind Academy some of those bitten by that deranged little creature are already awake, and already have magic running through their veins."

"They are already ready to fight," my father finished for him, turning away from the map to where Talon held me against him. Eager malice swelled with the magic as the two smiled, my father giving a low laugh before he turned back to the map, slowly peeling away the two yellow specks. "The fool has already built an army for us. An army with the same goal, to end Ilyan and Joclyn's reign."

"So, we get the bastards to fight for us?" I asked, twisting in Talon's grip to look at him, but he held me fast, resting his head on top of mine instead.

"Better. If one man is willing to raise up an army of Drains after Gemma left, my guess is that Gemma wouldn't let them. Gemma squandered that gift but this man is ready to take control of the situation. Take control of their world." Talon chuckled, his eyes focused on the map on the wall, his magic burning away at the tiny speck marked Last Pyre, burning a line right to the Academy, right to the underground palace in Prague.

"If there is one thing I know, it's how to work with power hungry men," Talon said, still staring at the map. "Giovanni, I believe we have found that scapegoat we talked about. I think I know just the piece of flesh to bring him over to our side. There is only one beautiful and cunning enough to convince a Drain to fight for our side."

They were both looking at me now, a different sort of eagerness trilling between me and Talon, the guys tongue darting out to lick his lower lip the lustful hunger pulling between the two of us, I pressed myself against him.

"Can you do it?" My father asked, but I didn't look away from Talon, from the blue in his eyes as he pulled closer, peppering kisses over my collarbone, up my neck, in the hollow under my ear.

"Never doubt me, father. The Drain is ours, the Vilỳ too. This

Adrian already wants what we do, all it takes is the right motivation."

"The right promise," Talon cut in, his hand tiptoeing down my spine.

"Even if I break it," I moaned as I stretched back, Talon leaning around to kiss me, the last word swallowed by his lips as my father laughed.

"Then prepare, I expect it done by Saturday night. We have a few royals to take after all. I'm sure that's a battle they won't want to miss."

GEMMA

I HAD NEVER EXPERIENCED A TRUE AUTUMN, WITH ITS CRISP BITING air that smelled of rain and nature. With leaves that twisted into a million bright colors, until they faded into lines of brown that cut into the pale blue sky. Everything dripped with grey, but it wasn't the grey of stone walls and the early winter chill of sleeping against cement far underground.

It was the grey of clouds and silver sunsets and crispy mornings with frost and spider webs.

That all was magic in its own right. I wasn't the only one who was gob-smacked over it. There were so many Undermortals wandering over the grounds that I had considered moving our meetings from the cramped confines of my bedroom to crisp air and chilled breezes of a world I had never known existed.

Yes, I knew that was dramatic. But after living an entire life away from actual seasons, and sun, and even beds, everything felt dramatic.

Meeting in the outdoors, during the day was a pipe dream, especially now that I knew Mira was following me around like a stealth helicopter. The weight in my chest was turned on, so she had to be close. On top of the school roof, peeking out from behind the bushes, standing directly over me as she stared down with the most intense expression known to man.

I was sure with just a glance she could scare more than a few Undermortals away. Hell, I couldn't even see her and I was already wanting to engage in a stank-eye match. Even though I knew she would win.

She wasn't about to let up either now that Rowan blew up a whole wing of the school four days ago. You could still see some lazy smoke drifting up from the rubble, dust choking the air as the older students learned how to put it all back together.

The boy hadn't been seen since.

I didn't know if that was a good thing or a bad thing. Those dark eyes were still following me everywhere, the stare as intense as the secret I carried. I hadn't said a word about it, not even to Eddy. I was needing to have a conversation with my sanity.

But those eyes...

"Gem!" Eddy shrieked from where he lay beside me, belly down, staring at the grass as he worked to grow a tiny seed he had placed there. "Gem, look at this."

I groaned and rolled over, body aching after having laid in the shivering sun for so long. I loved this weather, but I wanted to try spring and summer too. Some of the older Undermortals said that it gets so hot you want to walk around naked. I didn't believe them.

"What is it?" I grumbled, chin on my hands as I looked at the grass he was staring at so intently, expecting a rose or tulip, or something to be sprouting up, but all that was there was the faded green of the grass.

"Look!" He said again, his face still contorted as he stared at the grass.

"Do you have bad gas or are you trying to light the dirt on fire?" It could go either way with him. But I didn't get an answer besides a quick smack upside the head, he didn't even look away from the ground. The ground that was now full of tiny little blades of grass, lime green baby spikes that were pushing their way toward the icy sun.

"Woah," I gasped, shimmying forward to get a better look.

This magic was similar to the whole expansion stuff we had learned a month or so ago. But instead of making things bigger, you were making them grow. It should be easy; except I had spent so long blowing things up that giving things life was proving to be a whole different set of issues.

For once, Eddy was ahead of me on something. I couldn't be more proud. Maybe he would become a master and I could convince him to repair that poor tree above us, the silver trunk and branches finally matching the other barren death around us. Not that I expected it to come back to life after what Rowan had done to it. The poor thing was still cleaved in two.

"That's amazing, Ed," I said, the surprise in my voice catching me off guard. I didn't dare talk too loud, like I would scare the baby grass away if I yelled too loud.

"I know," he whispered, scooting closer to the baby grass, his hands flat on the ground. "I had put a sunflower seed in there, so clearly I am still doing this all wrong, but I'll take it."

He chuckled, I laughed and rolled back over to let the sun splash over me again. "You're still doing better than me."

"Does this mean I can rub your nose in that then? Here I was thinking I was going to be super powerful and instead..." He trailed off, grunting as he focused on his magic again.

"You're growing grass." I turned my head back to him, giving him the biggest cheesiest grin ever. He didn't see it, but mostly because the grin had fallen right off my face, my heart giving a shuddering start as everything from neck to navel turned to lead.

"Shit," I gasped before my senses came about it and my eyes

focused on the pair that was walking across the grass a few hundred yards away from where Ed and I laid under our skeleton tree.

"What?" Ed asked, hands flying from the ground as if he was going to protect me and instead, breaking contact with the soil and the plants that immediately stopped their growing process.

"Shit," he echoed me as his poor grass wilted, before following my focus and the two buzzards clinging to each other on the other side of the sloping lawns outside the school.

I could practically hear her high-pitched shrieking laugh.

Sia, and who, for a split second, I had thought was Rowan, laughing, talking, and... kissing?

"Is that Sia and the Prince?" Eddy asked in a hush, clearly having seen the same thing. Both of us pushing ourselves a little closer to the grass, as if they wouldn't notice two long uninformed people laying there. Maybe we would just look like logs.

"It better not be him," I said to myself, a leaden weight pushing itself tighter against my chest. Everything felt like it was closing up, seeing him with her causing some kind of physical pain.

Screw that shit. I pushed it away, well, as well as I could. I couldn't quite alleviate all of the pressure.

"I don't think it's Rowan, but it's definitely Sia," I said a little firmer, as if I was willing to make it true.

"No, not that prince. The other one. Not the nice one who thinks he's funnier than he is. But the other, other one." I looked at him like he was crazy before twisting back to the couple who went back to laughing, although they were plastered close enough together that they might as well have been doing other stuff.

"Ryland?" I asked, expecting a shriek and a snarling wife to abandon her stalker duties and take off down the pitch, there wasn't so much as a whisper hidden in the wind.

"No, doesn't that guy and his wife follow around the king and queen like lap dogs. They wouldn't be here." I couldn't give him more than a smile, he had no idea how right and very wrong that statement was. "I think it looks like Talon."

Eddy pushed himself up on his elbows as the two walked away, her irritating laugh fading away as the corset of nerves unwound.

"Although they do look quite a bit alike don't they?"

"They do," I don't think I had noticed before, but especially from a distance they all kind of blurred into one mass. Dark curly hair, tall, broad shouldered muscles. I'm sure they both had blue eyes too, not like Rowan's green ones.

His black ones.

I sighed and rolled over, throwing my arms over my face as if that would help banish the memory. It made it worse.

"What are they doing together, isn't she with Rowan?" Eddy asked, lacing that corset back over my chest with a renewed force.

"No, he finally got his senses together and dumped the bitch," I said with too much snarl.

"Careful there, Gem. You are starting to sound like you care for the guy." Okay, maybe I needed more snarl. I really didn't need him thinking I had gone soft on the guy. Except it was Ed, and the look he was giving me made it clear that he already knew.

"The guy got too excited while sparring, almost used too powerful magic on me that would have killed me and no one has seen him yet," I said, reciting the story that the Queen had concocted and everyone had been sticking too.

"Uh-huh," he said before going back to the grass. He didn't

believe that either. "It's okay to like the guy you know. I won't call you a traitor," he paused, "to your face."

I growled and smacked him upside the head. "Go back to your sunflower seed you loser."

It was the best comeback I could give him. It barely stuck. Mostly because my guilt was gnawing at me, digging into my soul like last week's bread. Moldy, soggy, lumps of betrayal.

He was right.

I was a traitor.

A traitor to my people that I promised to fight for. I lied for a prince, I conspired with a queen, I buddied up their guard. I was pretty sure I was falling for the same despicable prince I had lied for.

Black eyes and all.

"Shit," I mumbled, the sound more of a groan as I pressed my hands into my eyes and tried to focus on the way the sun was beating against my skull, the cool breeze running over us. Focus on the things that were real. Not some fanciful delusion that if I kept following was going to get people hurt.

Eddy chuckled at my dramatic outburst, before returning to mumble to the grass, his grumbles sounding like an incantation. The deep bass mixing with the bird song that was twittering over us, filling the quiet afternoon with a normalcy that for a moment felt okay. Like maybe I could be okay with my crush, okay with the choices I made.

Although I had the very real feeling that the second I left and walked back into my school and towards my people that I would have to leave that all behind. Leave it to rot like the shattered fragments of the tree we laid under.

I had loved that tree, too.

"Hello, Gemma."

Bars of iron jutted through my spine, that metal corset locking against my chest and heart as they forgot to breathe, to pump. I lay frozen beneath that voice that I would recognize anywhere.

I didn't even need to peek behind my arms that I had thrown over my eyes. I could feel his magic in the air, feel it twist around me. I don't think I could ever forget what that felt like.

"Hello Rowan," I whispered, trying to figure out what to say and how to react to the shy voice that was right above me. To the boy, I had pestered for months, who had more secrets and more depth than I ever would have guessed.

I could only do one thing, pretend that it had never happened.

Except, when I finally did shift toward the handsome prince who squatted beside me, arms on his knees as he played with a few shards of grass; I remembered that it did happen. All that pain, and fear, and panic I had seen in his ebony eyes was real. I couldn't ignore it.

Any of it.

I didn't want to.

"You're okay?" I asked, my voice cracking.

"I'm okay," he said with a nod, and I did probably the dumbest thing I had ever done in my life.

I threw myself into his arms and gave him a hug.

36

ROWAN

There she was, blissfully laying under the remains of her tree, arms thrown over her face. She looked so vulnerable. Innocent.

It had taken a lot of guts to come back from Imdalind after what happened. Even more to tear myself out of my room. But as she had told me on more than one occasion, I needed to stop being quite so selfish.

Seeing her there, so calm, the pink in her hair reflecting the sun, the curls spread over the grass. It made the trauma of leaving my hiding place feel a little bit safer.

Eddy looked up as I came closer, his jaw-dropping before it broke into a wide smile. Pressing my finger to my lips in a plea for silence, he gave me a wink and went back to mumbling at the grass.

"Hello Gemma," I said, voice wavering as I knelt beside her, pulling a few strands of grass from the ground as if fiddling with the things would help my stomach to stay in place and not fall through the center of the world.

She tensed, my back straightening as I felt her magic flare, nervous energy pricking against my spine as the powerful stuff drifted unseen toward me. Reaching for me, as I wanted to reach for her.

I swallowed, the knots in my swimming stomach tightening. I wanted it, but I didn't know if I would get it. If she would ever trust me. Not after what she saw. Mira had said that she hadn't told anyone what had really happened, but that didn't mean she was going to welcome the freak into her life.

I had almost attacked her. She had seen what I really was.

"Hello Rowan," she said, her voice as shaky as the knots in my belly. She didn't move from where she lay in the breeze, hair twisting in the wind, her magic pressing against mine. Eddy's head twisted between us like it was on a string.

Finally, she moved her arms. Those lavender eyes stared at me, shaking as she saw me, as her magic swelled.

"You're okay?" Her voice was stronger, not a touch of fear in it. I couldn't stop my lips from turning up at the sound and the light that was in her eyes, barely a scrap of fear bleeding through her gaze.

"I'm okay," I whispered, my fingers aching to reach out, to hold her. To promise her it would never happen again, to thank her for covering for me. To plead with her to understand.

I didn't get one word out before she lept from the grass, her arms wide as she wrapped herself around me, both of us tumbling back into the grass. For a split second my fear, panic, and years of Uncle Rylands slightly paranoid training kicked in and I could have sworn she was attacking me. But then her skin made contact with mine and her magic flooded into me.

Electricity sparked through my veins, her power winding through me unchecked as it mingled. As it danced. As everything became fire. I knew I should shield against it, that I should push her away lest I risk the already shredded binds of my fathers to break and the Drak to break free again.

But I didn't care.

I didn't fucking care. I held her against me, my hand pressing against her back, against her neck as I buried myself against her, smelling that tangle wood aroma of her hair. The one that always followed her around. The one I had dreamed of. The one that I was losing myself in.

"I'm sorry," I whispered against her hair, hoping she could hear. "I'm so sorry."

The words were like a trigger and she was up, jumping off me and to her feet, leaving me lying in the grass and staring up at her. I could practically see the snarky rage drip back into her features. Her eyes sparking mischievously as she put her hands on her hips.

"You better be sorry. You almost killed me and left me to clean up your mess," she snapped, eyes blazing. It would have been frightening if the wind wasn't picking up the loose curls from her mohawk in just the right way. "I have a reputation for destroying buildings, you know. Now, thanks to you, prince killing."

I would have smiled, I could see a tiny bit of a grin trying to pull its way through her teasing scowl, but her words resonated a bit too deep. I had already heard a few shocked whispers as I made my way through the school to find her. It was ridiculous that they would believe that.

"Did they really think you killed me?"

"Your girlfriend does. She loves telling everyone about it," she snapped with a look behind her, as if Sia was going to appear there and knock her on her ass.

"Not my girlfriend."

"Yeah, we know," Eddy said with a chuckle, the kid still staring at the grass.

"Don't want to hear it," she said, sinking back down to the grass and leaning against the shards of the tree. "I'm glad you didn't blow yourself to Timbuktu, your majesty."

I may have been imagining things, but my title didn't seem to have nearly as much vitriol in it as it usually did. She didn't seem quite so flippant. So angry. That same bit of caring was peeking out again.

"Nope. All in one piece." She didn't respond, although Eddy was still looking between us like we had turned into one of the prince hookup movies.

Amazed. Shocked. Angry.

She really hadn't told anyone what happened.

"Eddy, right?" I asked, holding out my hand. He took it reluctantly. I put a shield over my palm in case he tried anything stupid. He squeezed, which actually hurt. Dude was strong. "Nice grip. I thought my douchebag brother would be the first one to break my knuckles."

"Woops!" he said, dropping my hand, although I wasn't one hundred percent sure the response was genuine. He was now shifting his weight, looking between me and her like we were a bomb about to go off.

"Don't worry about it, I'll have to show you some old grip games we have back in Imdalind," I said, still looking at Eddy, ignoring the pull to turn. "That is if you will join me when I go back home for the weekend tomorrow."

Eddy paled, Gemma turned, both of them looking at me with wide eyes.

"Did you just invite us to the palace," Eddy asked with a deep chuckle, the guys' eyes still wide and staring.

"Yeah. You two, and Greer. I have to watch my baby sister, so I think it would be fun to take some..." I paused, weighing every single word I could put there. Wanting so much to say one, but saying another instead. "Friends."

They looked at each other, some hidden language passing between them before Eddy laughed.

"You are inviting the girl who tried to murder your family in your home?" she asked, raising one of her brows and sending the piercing there glittering.

"Yes, it is quite possible I have gone mad." When she phrased it that way it did, anyway. "I seem to recall you saying you have never met Angela and as chance would have it, she would like to meet you."

"She said--" Her voice trailed off, her eyes unwavering as she stared at me, chewing her lip.

There was something there, in her eyes. Something I wanted to calm and soothe and chase away. But, I wasn't sure how. Knowing her, if I tried she'd bat me away.

I knew she could do it herself. I still wanted to be beside her.

I stepped closer.

"Well, we better get going!" Eddy said loudly, cutting the silence like a butcher. "Gemma and I have a castle takeover to plan--"

"You can go, Ed. I'll catch up later." Gemma cut him off, she didn't even move, she stayed there, leaning against the broken trunk, eyes closed to the sun. "I gotta talk to Prince Douche anyway."

Nice to know my nickname lived on.

"Ha! Douche." Eddy chuckled with a weird sound, grabbing his jacket and laughing his way down the hill without another word.

Leaving us to drown in our own awkwardness.

She laid calmly beneath the broken branches of the silver tree, I writhed my hands behind my back as I tried to figure out what to say.

"Is there a reason you are keeping it a secret?" She asked, dragging me into the pit of nerves that was twisting around my feet, holding me in place. "Or am I sacrificing everything I believe in for some stubborn royal."

"There is a reason," I whispered, my heart beating so loud it thundered along with each word, shaking my vision.

"Which is?" She opened one eye and then the other when it became clear I wasn't going to answer her.

"Fine," she sighed, leaning forward and grabbing a handful of grass, throwing it at me although it didn't get anywhere close. "You can leave then. I'm busy."

"Throwing grass?"

"Yes."

She drifted to silence, her magic still pressing against me, wanting me. I shifted closer.

"Draks are super powerful. I mean, you saw my mom..." I let the words drift off, knowing it was only part of the truth. I only knew part of what had happened in that interrogation room so many months ago. But the way her lips had pulled into a tight line made it clear she had not forgotten. "I've always pushed the power away. When I was little," *and now*, I added to myself, "my dad had to bind my magic to keep me from hurting myself or others."

I paused, watching as her face contorted in a shock that I didn't quite understand.

"It's a danger having me here at this school, to be honest."

"Well, sounds like we have a few things in common." She forced a smile and as she scooted closer, closing the cavern between us, although still not close enough that I could reach out and grab her. "We are both super-powerful mega beings that have our magic bound."

She gave me a wink. I couldn't help but laugh, so much of the weight that had been sitting on my chest pulling away. As though I wasn't holding as much of the world anymore.

Stupid Atlas.

"Well, you did blow up quite a few buildings..." Her smile had faded that straight lipped smile making a return. I exhaled, scooting myself closer to her this time. "Thank you for covering for me. Thank you for keeping my secret."

"You owe me is all," she teased, knocking her feet against my knee and sending a twist of power through me. Even without skin contact I could feel her. Weird.

"Well, I think I have that covered," I jumped to my feet, heart tight as I held my hand out to her, waiting, terrified she wouldn't take it.

She stared at my hand, at the tiny hopeful smile I was giving her and reached her hand forward, sending that live wire of energy through me. So magnetic. I would never tire of that.

Pushing down the sigh, I pulled her to her feet, pulled her closer, until she stood inches from me. Her smug grin was gone, she looked up to me, curls falling over her face as she stared. As she waited. It took me a second to realize that neither of us were breathing. I couldn't move, I just stared at her, lost in her eyes as I did the stupidest most cliché thing ever.

I pushed the hair that had fallen over her eyes back. My fingertips grazed her skin, hungry to run over her ear, down her neck, and towards the warmth that was drifting between us. To touch her. Hold her.

"Make it up to me, Rowan," she said, her voice a little more than a gasp, pulling me back to my senses and I dropped my hand.

I needed to pull it together. This was going to be hard enough with the way our magic was trying to lock us together like magnets.

"Come here," I said as loudly as I dared, trying to sound like I was in control of myself, not that it mattered, the second I turned her around in my arms, her back inches from my chest, my hands against her thankfully covered shoulders, I was back to having trouble breathing.

"What are you--"

"You are learning to make things grow, yes?" I interrupted her before I lost my nerve, or control of my magic. The second seemed like the much larger threat.

She only nodded.

"Let me teach you the way my mother taught me. The way my father taught her. None of this staring at seeds stuff. Power. Real power. Is that okay?"

Again, a nod.

"Are you sure? I have never heard you so quiet before." I leaned closer to her, looking around where I had placed her in front of me. God, I was sure the air around us was nothing but electricity.

"Do what you are going to do Princey, before I lose my nerve and throw you across this field just for giving me that wicked eyebrow quirk you think is so damn sexy."

"There you are," I said with a laugh, moving back behind her, letting my hands run down her arms, my fingers fluttering above her skin until I reached her hands. Stealing my breath, I intertwined my fingers with hers and pulled her closer to me.

She didn't pull away. Although her heart was a thunderous beat against my chest, her body was calm, her fingers tight around mine. Warmth radiated from her, her magic dancing through me and I leaned over, letting her hair tickle my nose as I whispered in her ear, doing my best to keep my voice regulated and my magic mostly contained.

"Close your eyes, Gemma." I smiled when she shivered at the touch of my breath against her ear. "Focus on the power that's flowing between us. On the way, your magic is moving with mine. On the way, my magic is dancing with yours. Can you feel it?" She was back to nodding. "Perfect. Now follow my magic. Move with me through the dirt, through the soil, into the tree..."

"The tree is dead," she gasped with a bit of hostility, her magic shivering as she tried to move away, I held her hands tighter, wrapping our arms around her, holding her in place against me.

"So is a seed. So is a rock. There is life in everything, Gemma. You need to learn how to tap it, how to bring it back to life. It's there just waiting for it. Can you feel it?" I didn't dare move, I held her, basking in her warmth as I guided her magic to the parts of the tree that were still struggling to live, refusing to give up.

Just like her. Just like me, in so many ways.

"I can."

"Push your magic into those parts, into the life. Prod it to grow, press into the tree, fill it with your power and whisper for it to grow. To heal."

"But I--"

"I'm going to help you, Gemma," I whispered, holding her tighter against me, my thumb running over a bit of exposed tattoo on her wrist. She didn't shy away. She didn't pull back, she just melted into me, her magic traveling right alongside mine.

"Follow my magic. You can expand a slug, I know you can heal a tree."

She chuckled, her face screwing up as she stood with her eyes closed, focusing on the power, mumbling the word 'grow' over and over. Her power was everywhere, mine right alongside hers as they twisted, as they sparked and lit up inside the tree. The tree that was glowing, the bark twisting and breathing as life moved back into it. The trunk pieced itself back together, as bright red leaves burst from its bows once more.

"Look, Gemma," I whispered as the last of the branches snapped back together, as the large red leaves burst into life, the autumn sun catching against the bark and sending the silver into a glistening beauty.

It wasn't just the tree. Everything around us was glistening, as though the air itself had caught fire.

"It's beautiful." she gasped, her hands tightening against mine, as she pulled herself into me. As she leaned her head back.

"It is." I knew I wasn't talking about the tree.

I think she knew too.

"Rowan?" She asked, her voice a gasp against my neck. "I lied." I tensed when she hesitated, my brain running through every single terrible possibility. "That eyebrow quirk is damn sexy. You're damn sexy."

I couldn't help it. I couldn't stop myself. I leaned down to her, brushing my lips against her cheek as for the first time I kissed a girl that I wanted to kiss. As I felt the heat of her blush under my lips, as my magic went crazy.

I barely contained it, I barely held it at bay under my father's binds.

That was until she turned her head, until she pressed her lips against mine.

Until she kissed me.

And all those powerful binds were turned to ribbons.

37

SIA

THE SMELL REMINDED ME OF THE GAUNTLET, OF THE SLIMY FILTH that dripped from the walls. The way the train station before the tasks stunk, clogged with Drains and worse.

It was the same smell of liquid rot and death, the fecal drifts even more assaulting. It had grown worse with every step we had taken to this place, the air glistening with it as we walked from the field the car had dropped us off in and toward the gaping hole in the earth and the dilapidated wasteland. Tile was everywhere, smoke-stained walls and gaping holes making it clear that the space had been used for target practice lately. You could barely make out that tile mosaic on the wall, the words 'MidCity' the only thing that remained.

"This place is filled with magic," Talon whispered, spreading his hand forward as his own heavy power joined the dripping magic that clung to the walls, invisible lines of his ability stretching everywhere.

"Well, we know we were right. The guy has an army waiting for us," I whispered, carefully stepping around a puddle of who knew what. I had specifically worn a pair of one-month-old sneakers I had been planning to throw out, but I wasn't quite ready to fill the soles with rot quite yet.

"Don't be cocky, darling," Talon warned, dropping his hand and leading us toward a crumpled slab of metal in the corner. The doorway led to halls and stairs, and eventually other caves. Each step taking us further into a disaster zone, the walls growing more pockmarked and burned.

Actually, more so. Now that I was looking, the explosion wounds in the main hall had been more strategic, made to look as though they had been attacked, as though this place wasn't safe. But these, these were everywhere. As though someone couldn't control their magic, as though it was exploding out of them. Just like Gemma at the Gauntlet.

I shuddered and pushed myself forward. I knew what I was walking into. I wasn't unarmed anymore. I wouldn't let the rats get away with that twice.

"How many Vilỳ does this guy have exactly?" I mused, no longer watching for puddles, but for giant craters that would swallow me whole.

"All it takes is one. There is no limit to their poison. Or their bite." Talon had lifted himself up, his magic shimmering around him as air carried him toward yet another door, this one marked with a bright red X. He didn't even offer to help, or to help save my shoes from the muck. I would have to remind him exactly what I was supposed to be to him. Lost puppy wasn't it.

"My grandfather, may he rest in peace, used to collect the poison and inject himself with it. He forced my Uncle Ryland to receive a bite as well, all in hopes of strengthening their power."

I hopped over a smaller pothole and froze, "Wasn't Prince Ryland born with magic?"

Talon turned to me slowly, his face already spread into a wide grin.

"He was. He was bitten to make him stronger." Desire was

clear in his eyes, that hunger I had seen the other day suddenly making sense. Power. He wanted it as badly as I did. Fecking hell, even without our magic connecting I think I would have fallen for this one. Tasha was right, I should have chosen this sex-god from the beginning.

I would have thrown myself into his arms, but he was already moving away, hand out as his magic stretched to see who was behind the door.

"So, if an Eternal can be bitten to strengthen their magic, does that mean that anyone can do the same?" I asked, leaping over the last of the holes to join him. This time he reached for me. "Even a Chosen?"

"Are you saying you want more power, darling?" His voice was low as he grabbed me, pulling me against him with such force that I lost my breath.

"I've always wanted more power. Why do you think I was willing to settle for your pathetic," I kissed him, "weak," another kiss, "and dare I say significantly less attractive brother?"

Talon laughed, his lips smashing into mine with a moan. His hands fanned against my back as he kissed me, as his tongue gently parted my lips and tasted me. He pulled away far too soon.

"Wait until I bond you to me, darling," he crooned, his breath hot against my lips as he snuck another kiss. "You'll have more power than you can handle."

I was already begging for that, pressed myself against the other power that was between us, but right then, the door with the red 'X' opened and Talon nearly dropped me to the ground, stepping toward the hulking man that stepped out with fire in his eyes. Little golden flames peered out at us like burning fires in the middle of his blackened skin, the unphased smile a nefarious cut of lightning amidst the flames.

"Talon Krul." The man spoke with more familiarity than I

expected. I looked to Talon, but even if he recognized or knew the man, he showed no sign of it.

"You must be Adrian," he said, the guy laughed with a booming sound that rattled my bones.

"I had hoped I would see one of you soon, which one shall I kill first?" Adrian's smile spread, his hand lifted as the same drippy illegal magic I had seen on Gemma on that first day sparked to life. Whether I wanted to or not, I stepped back, bringing my magic right to the surface.

"Well, if we had our way, you would kill Gemma first, followed directly with the King and Queen," I said, letting my own magic flare like we were caught in some measure of strength. Neither guy laughed. Talon smiled with that smug crooked grin of his as Adrian stared, the last of his magic falling to the ground as he stared at me. I didn't even blink, you didn't blink when you wished to control feral dogs after all. This guy was as good as that.

"We would like to work with you in this task," Talon cut in, pulling Adrian's focus. "And pay you handsomely when you return with my parent's heads on a plate."

With that, we both turned to Talon, to his wide grin and eyes that were dancing in a fire that I don't think I had ever seen before. It was a beautiful thing, seeing so much power pump through him. So much joy.

He had spoken of me being Queen before, of being his queen, of being Queen of everything. I didn't think he had meant that.

The idea of it made me smile, his hungry light reflecting through me. He wrapped an arm around me, both of us facing the dark-skinned Drain who smiled with a grin that was like a lamp in the dark.

Greed, hunger, power.

They bathed the air and Adrian stepped back, holding the door open for us.

"Sounds like you and I have plenty to talk about, why don't you come in?"

38

ROWAN

"I BLEW UP A BATHROOM ONCE," ANGIE SAID WITH A GIANT GRIN ON her face as she placed one of the playing cards on the table. The green six smothering the blue card and making Greer screw up his face. The guy had been losing since Angie had roped us all in to playing this game this afternoon.

I'm actually surprised it took so long to bring it out. It was her favorite game. She hadn't brought it out until after lunch on our last day. I guessed it made sense, she had spent most of the rest of the time dragging Gemma, Greer, and Eddy around the massive system of caves in what could be easily interpreted as a grand tour of your enemies lair. But Gemma didn't seem to care anymore.

Every minute was spent comparing her home to ours, all of us declared moles thanks to our underground habitats and tendencies. Angela found it far more entertaining than anyone else did.

But, to be completely fair, I wasn't fully paying attention.

I had been watching Gemma.

I hadn't been able to see her alone since that kiss. Since that moment when our magic truly connected for the first time. I had been the one to be kissed, but I didn't mind it. Because it didn't matter who had kissed who, just that I had gotten to kiss her, to hold her, to run my hands over her skin. The literal girl of my dreams.

That kiss had turned into a bit of what my parents called a 'make-out session; with both of us laying in the grass and kissing and holding. It took everything to keep my magic from exploding. Feeling her magic mingle with mine had been like some kind of balm to the powerful Drak in my blood. Her power calmed mine enough that I could control it. In the end, she laid in my arms as we watched the sunset, as the air began to chill. I kept us warm with my magic as we laid together, fingers dancing, hearts beating...

"Rowan!" I jumped straight out of my seat, my cards flying into the air as I turned toward the door in a panic. Everyone laughed. Ed and Greer giving each other a high five while Angie nearly fell off her own chair. Gemma, however, laughed smugly as she folded her arms over her chest.

"Care to return from whatever you were smiling at and join us," Gemma asked, giving me a wink and making it completely clear that she knew exactly what I was smiling at. The gentle tug of her magic against mine was even more of a promise, her widening smile an admittance that she was doing it on purpose.

Damn this woman.

I needed to get her alone. Damn Angie insisting that she needed to sleep in her room for some girl time. But Angie's insistence hadn't stopped Gemma from trailing her fingers over my arms, or tugging at my magic, or biting her bottom lip when she was sure no one was watching.

My magic sparked, the world shifting a bit as my neck began to heat. With none of my father's binds and all of Gemma's teasing my Drak magic was becoming uncontrollable again.

Damn it all.

"I'll be right back," I mumbled, my magic pulling all my cards back on the table as I made my way to the door, practically running for the bathroom as everyone laughed louder behind me.

"What?" Angie shrieked as I turned the corner, and then another, not for the bathroom but for some silence. Some calm to settle my magic. All this teasing was sending me into a boiling mess. I needed to breathe. Two minutes.

That's all I needed.

"You are going to make it very hard to control myself," I whispered, the second I felt her magic tiptoe closer, Gemma's smiling face peeking around the corner a second later.

She leaned against the wall, folding her arms and smiling with that mischievous grin that was so inevitably her. I would say she looked wicked, if she wasn't biting that lip again.

"Control yourself how?" I wasn't sure if she was teasing or not.

"My magic is not currently bound, Gemma," I whispered. "It's dangerous."

"You don't scare me, Rowan. No part of you scares me."

"You say that now." I tried to push a laugh into my voice.

"I already told you I'm not going to kill you," she teased, resting her head against the stone wall. "I don't kill people I like."

"Like?" I knew she was teasing, but my voice caught anyway, the high-pitched worry pulling through. Her smile spread, the weight of her magic against my skin growing, even though she didn't step closer.

"Yes. Like. Don't be greedy."

"But I am greedy." It was me who stepped forward, she didn't even move. Even when I lifted my finger and ran it down the length of her arm, pausing above the mark of her elbow, the raised brand of her Vilỳ kiss. "Perhaps that's why I've been trying to get you alone. Greed."

"Greed for what?" Oh, this wicked little beasty, she truly was going to drive me mad.

"For you," I whispered, my fingers spreading to run over her hand, to curl around her fingers, her fingers lifted, granting them access. "For more of you."

"You know," she said, watching our fingers tangle as she pushed herself off the wall, taking the smallest of steps forward. "I was starting to wonder if I was ever going to get you alone."

I didn't let her make the first move that time, I pulled her closer, my fingers tightening around hers. Her chest hit against mine, her eyes looking up to mine as I towered over her, my free hand winding around her back as I pressed her against me, heat and magic mingling as my hand trailed up her spine, fingers soft against her neck, against her chin.

Her lips parted, a desperate shaky breath fluttering over my lips, pulling me in like I was under her control. Tenderly, I brushed my lips against hers, the faintest touch shivering through her as the fireworks of our magic glittered over arms and backs and sparked in the air.

"Are you sure you only like me?" I murmured, teasing her with another faint kiss, with my hands as they tickled over her neck and she shivered.

"Yes, now shut up and kiss me, Rowan."

I did just that, holding her against me as I devoured her, my tongue running over her lip as I gently parted them, as I tasted her, pressing against her, her leg lifting over my hip in a desperate need to get closer. To feel everything.

With a groan, I gripped her hips, lifting her off the floor. Her legs wrapped around my waist as I pulled her to my level. I twisted, placing her back against the wall, pressing her between me and the cold stone, the thin layers of cotton shirts an unwanted barrier.

Twisting my fingers around the hem of her white cotton

tank, I moved to lift it, to press my fingers to her bare abdomen. I didn't get above her navel before her wrist captured my hand and she pulled away with a mischievous smile.

"You greedy prince," she said with nearly a snarl. "I'm going to make you wait for that."

"Wait?" I gasped, letting my thumb run across the taut flesh of her abdomen and making her shiver.

"Yes," she captured my hand, holding it between us. "At least until we are not in a hallway and your baby sister can walk in on us."

"Point taken," I said, allowing her to slide back down to the floor, although I kept her hand in mine, our palms pressing together as our magic continued its tango.

"I wish I knew what this means," she whispered, her hand flat against mine before she intertwined our fingers, the magic sparking between us in little stars. She jerked at their appearance, but I held her still against me, my hand flat against her back.

I knew why she was afraid, I would have been too if I hadn't seen those same fireworks when I was a child, when I walked in on my parents...

"It's our magic," I whispered, watching her for any sign of fear, any chance that she would pull away. I wasn't sure she was ready to hear this. Telling someone they are destined to be with you, was not easy. Add into what we had been to each other mere months ago and those few words felt like an impossibility.

"Yeah. I figured that much out, you psycho," she snapped, trying to pull away again, I leaned closer, pressing my lips against her forehead. She stilled. "What is it Rowan?"

"Our magic..." I faltered, pulling back so I could see her. "It's fated. It means we were meant to be together."

"Meant to--" she stuttered, the fear I had been worried about flaring in her eyes, tightening in her jaw. She tried to move away again, but this time I let her. I wasn't about to force her into this. Into anything.

"Yes," I nodded, my heart aching as air flooded the space between us, my magic searching for hers even as she began to withdraw. "Don't worry. I'm not going to go off and order a wedding cake--"

"Wedding! What the hell is wrong with you?" she shrieked, okay that joke didn't hit correctly. Best to stick with facts.

"Not every one of my kind finds their true mate," I said, still watching as the horror in her expression deepened. I couldn't back down now. I was in too deep. "Not everyone with magic has one. That's what it is, that's why our magic sparks together. It's why I avoided you after I felt it the first time--" I paused, her eyes widening.

"In the hallway after Sia attacked me." It wasn't a question. She knew as well as I did.

I nodded yes, "I was scared. I know you're scared. I'm not going to force you into anything, Gemma." My heart caught at saying her name aloud. "I don't exactly come without some oddities."

I gestured to my eyes, closing them to avoid seeing her expression, the truth. We hadn't exactly talked about it yet.

"You're right," she said, less hostile than I expected. "You're a freak. Join the club."

I opened my eyes, she had stepped closer, although still not close enough to touch. I didn't move, I didn't dare.

"I can't marry you, Rowan. I'm not even sure I can date you. But if this is all we can do..." she faded off, her lips pressed into a tight line as she stood there, staring at me from behind her curls. Waiting.

I stepped forward slowly, moving her hair back before I grabbed her hand, before I pulled her closer.

"It's enough--" I didn't get a chance to finish before feet

thundered through the halls, a door slammed and Angie, Greer, and Ed yelled my name, another voice mixed in with it.

"Gemma!"

"Rowan!"

"Find him!"

The joy in our magic evaporated, the world evaporated, everything falling to dread as four people blazed around the corner, Greer carrying Angie as the two guys trailed behind my blood-covered Aunt.

"Wyn?" The scream froze my throat and the sound was more of a choke.

"We need to go," she snapped, pushing past us as more voices started to echo through the caves behind us, these ones angry. Violent.

"Go?" I asked, grabbing Gemma's hand and stowing her with me as we chased my Aunt. Luckily, she didn't pull away.

"Yes. To the safe house, if it's still safe. I don't know. Just get your asses in gear and follow me," she was mumbling, leading us at a near run as we took off deeper into the caves, towards the living quarters and the back door entrances that I had been told were sealed long ago.

"What is going on?" I demanded, pulling alongside Wyn, who only gave me a snarling look before turning another corner and leading us all into my room. I didn't even care that it was messy and gross and smelled of sweat. I stared at Wyn, waiting as she barred the door.

"That attack your parents had planned. Turned out your fucking brother has betrayed us all." She didn't even need to say which fucking brother. I knew. It was clear on everyone's faces that they knew. "They were waiting for us. A few of us got out but..."

She paused, listening at the door. But there was only silence, the cold dead unwanted silence.

"Who?"

"I don't know, Rowan," she snapped, going through my drawers now and pulling clothes out like they were streamers. "I came here to get you two out of here, before Adrian and his fucking army reached the caves."

"Adrian?" Gemma asked from behind me, her shock as dead as I felt. But I didn't turn. I didn't ask. I watched my aunt as she kept searching my room. I didn't have to ask for what.

"Where is she?" I asked. Wyn froze and turned, her dark eyes swollen with that dangerous fire magic that she alone carried.

"That's what I need you to tell me, Row. I need you to help me stop this war before it has a chance to start."

"War?" Greer asked, but I didn't move. Wyn didn't move. We stared at each other, every minute ticking closer to a finality that I had fought against for so long. That I was still fighting against.

Until Gemma stepped beside me, her hand wrapped around my own, as she said, loud enough for the guys in the room to hear, "If anyone says one thing out of line, Row, I'll be the first to punch their faces in. I've got you."

"Knew I liked you," Wyn said, finally breaking the spell and letting me breathe, letting everything settle as Gemma's magic flowed through me, as she gave me another one of the beautifully rare, genuine smiles.

"Consider me your ass-kicking bodyguard," she whispered, before reaching up on her tiptoes and planting a kiss on my jaw.

I exhaled, everything feeling numb as I walked away from the warmth of her hand, from an easy life that never would have been mine.

Two steps to the dresser, my magic pulled the drawer open, the underwear already pushed aside as if it was waiting for me.

Waiting for this moment.

My fingers shook as I reached for the thing, the hardened mud warm under my fingers, buzzing through me.

Begging.

Needing.

I held it for only a second, wondering if there could be any good in the power before I covered it with my palm, filling it to the brim.

ALSO BY REBECCA ETHINGTON

For the always up to date list of super awesome books I've written, visit here:

www.rebeccaethington.com/complete-works/

THE WORLD OF IMDALIND

The Imdalind Series (complete)

Kiss of Fire, Imdalind #1

Eyes of Ember, Imdalind #2

Scorched Treachery, Imdalind #3

Soul of Flame, Imdalind #4

Burnt Devotion, Imdalind #5

Brand of Betrayal, Imdalind #6

Dawn of Ash, Imdalind #7

Crown of Cinders, Imdalind #8

Spark of Vengeance, Imdalind #9

Flare of Villainy, Imdalind #10

Imdalind Academy

The Gauntlet, Book One

Rogue Royalty, Book Two

Broken Renegade, Book Three (Oct 2021)

Reluctant Seer, Book Four (Jan 2022)

Imdalind Ruby Collection

Demon Lost, Semester Five

Misfit Shifters (RH)(Complete)
Zero Fox To Give, Book One
For Fox Sake, Book Two
Fox Chance in Hell, Book Three

THE WORLD OF THE OKIVAN

Of River and Raynn

Catalyst

Requisite

Sypher

THE OTHER WORLDS

The Through Glass Series (Complete)
Book One: The Dark

Book Two: The Blue

Book Three: The Rose

Book Four: The Cut

Book Five: The Light

The Through Glass Box Set

ABOUT THE AUTHOR

Rebecca Ethington is an internationally bestselling author with over a million books sold. Her breakout debut, The Imdalind Series, has been featured on bestseller lists since its debut in 2012.

Born and raised under the lights of a stage, Rebecca has written stories by the ghost light, told them in whispers in dark corridors, and never stopped creating within the pages of a notebook.

Find me online
www.rebeccaethington.com
contact@rebeccaethington.com

THE COMPLETE IMDALIND SERIES

BOOK ONE: *Kiss of Fire*
BOOK TWO: *Eyes of Ember*
BOOK THREE: *Scorched Treachery*
BOOK FOUR: *Soul of Flame*
BOOK FIVE: *Burnt Devotion*
BOOK SIX: *Brand of Betrayal*
BOOK SEVEN: *Dawn of Ash*
BOOK EIGHT: *Crown of Cinders*
BOOK NINE: *Spark of Vengeance*
BOOK TEN: *Flare of Villainy*

THE ACADEMY BOOKS
The Gauntlet
Rogue Royalty
Broken Renegade
Reluctant Seer

Find me online in my Facebook street team! We have monthly giveaways, sneak peeks, competitions and more!

Introducing The Imdalind Ruby Collection

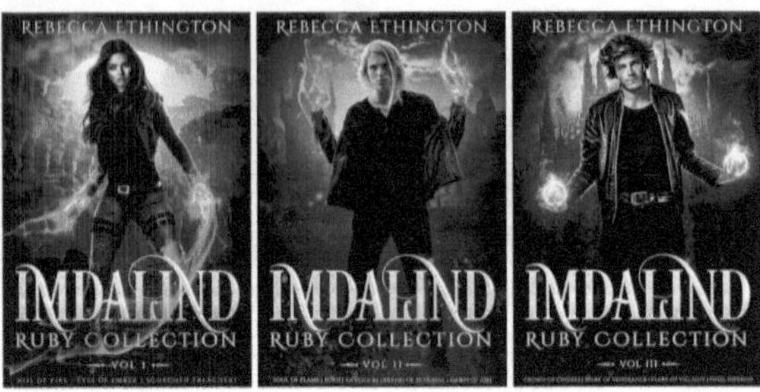

The entire Imdalind Series, in chronological order, with over 100k in new content and point of views. Extended Editions aren't just for Hobbits. <3

Grab your copies now.

9 781949 725346